MW01110414

LOST GODS BOOK I
SUN AND SHADOW

To Creston,
Thank you!

A. Muraro

ADRIAN MURARO

STORY MERCHANT BOOKS
LOS ANGELES • 2018

Lost Gods Book I: Sun and Shadow

Copyright © 2018 by Adrian Muraro. All rights reserved.

No part of this book may be reproduced or transmitted in any form or by any means, electronic or mechanical, including photocopying, recording, or by any information storage and retrieval system, without the express written permission of the author.

This is a work of fiction. Names, characters, businesses, places, events, locales, and incidents are either the products of the author's imagination or used in a fictitious manner. Any resemblance to actual persons, living or dead, or actual events is purely coincidental.

ISBN-13: 978-1-7323411-3-5

Story Merchant Books
400 S. Burnside Avenue, #11B
Los Angeles, CA 90036
www.storymerchantbooks.com

www.529Books.com
Editor: Lisa Cerasoli
Interior Design: Lauren Michelle
Cover: Claire Moore
Illustrations: Rosabel Rosalind Kurth

To family, in all its incarnations—the one we're born into and the ones we find.

Contents

SUN AND SHADOW

ADRIAN MURARO

Author's Note

This book is divided into several sections. The first is, as the cover suggests, *Sun and Shadow*. After that are three somewhat self-contained short stories. When I first wrote them, I had planned on anthologizing them along with many others yet to come. But, it turned out, the story had other plans. Threads came together, and I found myself intrigued by the thought of putting the characters in the same room, so to speak. I started writing a novel.

I rewrote a fourth story I had been working on and wove it into the beginning of what became *Sun and Shadow*. The rest, I decided—"A Song, Love," "Seeing Only Shades," and "Breakwall"—would stand better on their own. Chronologically, each takes place before the events starting on page one. If you wish to skip to these stories and read a sort of extended prelude to the novel, feel free to do so. That's what I consider them—my own introduction to Miranda, Des, Luc, and others.

If you just want to dive into the novel, don't worry—the short stories will be waiting for you when you get there.

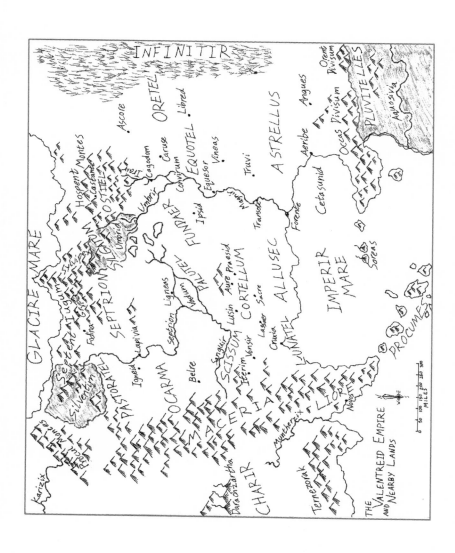

LOST GODS BOOK I

Sun and Shadow

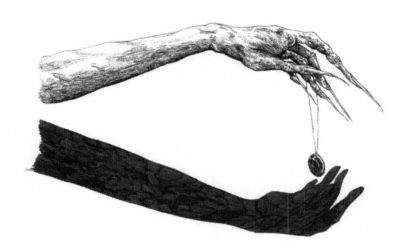

1

Aure was quiet. The silence screamed to the chosen initiates who knew why the streets were skeletons, barren of living flesh, bone white under harsh lamps. Cut off from the hush beneath the city lights, Francesca walked with a straight back. Perhaps her fencer's posture was why the Lady Ciusa hated her more than she did the other servants. Francesca knew her brother, Amadore, would disapprove of her standing out.

Fuck him.

Her time as an informant ended tonight. No more would she avert her eyes and bow and acquiesce to Ciusa's every fancy. She'd had other, more demeaning jobs, but held onto some pride.

Passing a polished bronze mirror, she once more smoothed her hair and dark, cheaply elegant smock. Francesca allowed nothing of her appearance to stray from place. She carried a platter balanced on one hand. The bottle of Oratas wine was open, tested by the guard of this wing before filling the crystalline vessel next to it. The guard was not poisoned, because the poison laced the glass.

Quite a glaring hole in security—one she had passed along early in her employment. For six months, Francesca had spied on this woman at her brother's behest. Amadore called it the will of the Noblest, those ancient, enigmatic victors of undemocratic elections who led the vampires of Filvié Noctirin. But she was sure her brother's agenda, overlap though it may, was his own. It always was, when it wasn't their parents'.

Francesca had reported diligently on every aspect of Lady Ciusa's private life she could access. The spying was a favor for the sociopolitical clan, payment for the aid it had given upon her vampiric awakening, and subsequently, Azran's. But assassination? That would be an investment.

War was coming to the streets of Aure—perhaps not tomorrow night, nor the next. Perhaps not for months. But every incremental restriction the bureaucrats forced on the vampires, petty or crippling, brought it closer. There was talk now of decriminalizing the murder of her kind—"slaying," they called it. This would not be a grand war, like the one looming in the west. No, this was a fight for independence from the chains slowly choking the rogues of the empire, the so-called "deviants." A melodramatic summary, taken from the collective consciousness of Filvié Noctirin. Almost certainly not the whole story.

Francesca turned a corner, heading for Ciusa's bedchamber. To her right, a narrow window overlooked the city, dark squares of rooftop marring the sea of light below.

Azran, her husband in all but ceremony, did not want a war. He held hope that the clash would come and go with a scuffle or two. Back-alley skirmishes. Maybe a short-lived riot. Then, everyone would compromise and move on. He was an adventurer, but no fighter. It had taken no small effort to convince him to carry a blade in his boot. Francesca knew how to handle necessity—one of many ways they complemented each other. In most things, they found a balance. Maybe there was a balance to be found in this clandestine conflict. Was neutrality an option?

Amadore had insisted otherwise by giving her the poison. The target was chosen carefully, and not just because of Ciusa's influence and allegiance. She was one of a handful of nobles who pulled the Senate's strings, yes. But to those who knew what to look for, this murder would be like raising a bright banner over Francesca and Azran. Amadore knew that—wanted that, offered his aid and protection because of that. He drew this line in the streets and told them to cross.

Her spiraling ascent to the master bedchamber took Francesca past flitting views of the city below, each glimpse more distant and dim. Why Ciusa chose to find her rest at the top of a tower, Francesca did not know. The people of the sprawling capital seemed more eager to build upward than live outside the wall. She could see Amadore living in a tower—he'd spout some rhetoric about being farther from the city's damned lights and closer to the void of the night sky.

The more Francesca considered, the more innocent—naïve, even—Azran's outlook seemed. Like vampirism was just an extension of the life he led before, a staving off of the inevitable. He didn't understand that this was an existence all its own. Was that her fault? Had she, as blinded by him as he by her, failed to illuminate that?

He would learn. He loved to learn. But while he did, he would need whatever protection she could offer in the coming nights.

A short hall decorated with a fitting lack of modesty greeted Francesca at the last landing before the tower's roof. She passed a silver sculpture of a gnarled tree. Little dove figurines hung suspended from the branches by fine chains. The delicate birds looked small enough to pocket. Perhaps she would, on her way out.

She reached the chamber. One of two glossy, cherry wood doors was ajar. Firelight danced in the gap, casting a shadow when Ciusa crossed the room. Francesca knocked. Nothing out of place.

"Finally. Enter."

The room was almost the size of Francesca and Azran's entire flat. Den and fireplace to the right, canopy bed and half-dozen wardrobes to the left. Straight ahead, a vibrant fresco of a rose garden covered the wall. In the chamber's center stood a short and aging woman, her hair still not let down despite the late hour. Her face seemed to tighten as Francesca stepped through the portal. Even at home, in nightclothes, all the nobles of Aure looked the same. It was that mask of sophistication obscuring the naked hatred beneath.

Francesca curtsied conservatively, her eyes never leaving Ciusa. The lady sniffed, taking note of the small rebellion, but kept up the mask. The spy breathed slowly, but her heart hit an allegro. She had to remind herself the living couldn't hear it.

Ciusa reached out for the faceted chalice—and Francesca flipped the platter.

The glass shattered on the tiled floor. Gleaming, wine-soaked fragments settled in a pattern not unlike the fresco. The bottle only cracked, but liquid glugged out the neck, trickling around the shards and adding to the resemblance.

Francesca took only a moment to savor the image, and then the bewilderment on Ciusa's face that twisted to rage, before turning on her heel and strolling out with a calm smile. She barely heard the vitriol spouted after her.

• • •

Azran sauntered down the street, skirting its edge to keep well out of the late traffic. Here, in central Aure, most could only tell it was night by looking at the sky—avenues of blackness between buildings, sprinkled with scattered stars. Even without looking, though, he could feel the absence of the sun.

He played a harpsichord melody in his head, one he had invented the previous night. He didn't know the language of how it went, just the sound. He played, and music came forth, simple as that. Still, he did have some sense of the complexity. He knew he couldn't have played this melody when he had first pressed his fingers to the keys.

Night after night, from his perspective scrubbing tables across the common room of the Silver Sun, Azran had watched the old player. For reasons he still didn't know, the old player left, and Ria, the barkeep, said Azran would be the new player. Very quickly, he learned to go slow. He was shit, and patrons got mad when he hit too many bad notes. So, he hit fewer notes. Playing every night for two years changed that. It began as less than an hour—the most his stiff digits could manage. Then, it became two hours. Then three. These nights, he was up to five.

Azran loved to learn, to practice, to improve. And now, he had forever to do that. He sometimes thought about what he would master after the harpsichord. Not spells, certainly. He had never understood arcana, nor felt the power of his soul. He might start with other music. Francesca wanted to learn swordplay; maybe they could do so together. Or, depending on how tonight went, he could commit himself to Sevex's company and pick up tinkering— or "clockwork," or whatever his brilliant childhood friend called it.

Why not? Maybe that was why the old player left—she had finally chosen something.

"You look lost, brother."

The voice was strong, but tight. Constricted, maybe. Holding back. Azran slowed, turned away from the lights and toward the speaker in the dark. Even from several strides away, he could see the figure was tall, like a graveyard statue, shrouded in a thin silk cloak, face obscured by a cowl and veil.

Azran stood still, staring at the void beneath the hood. He was only vaguely aware the street was empty, but acutely aware of the silence. Even the harpsichord left his head.

"I know where I'm going," he replied.

The stranger hummed and came closer, showing himself taller still than Azran had thought. "Let me clarify—lost in thought."

The towering figure was a vampire, Azran could sense from the feeble amount of living blood circulating. He relaxed. "Guilty."

"Lost in spirit, too, I surmise."

A long arm rose from beneath the shroud. The fingernails were ebony. A light chain unwound from the closed fist, snapping taut from the black metal disk on one end.

"A peddling priest?" Azran asked with a doubting smirk. "At this hour?"

The arm retracted, whipping the cloak back around. "It is Tenebra's hour, brother. You share her blood. You share her spirit, as well."

Azran shook his head and started back on his way. The priest followed, a step to the right and two behind.

"Look," Azran said, "your temple's already asked. I'm not interested. Just not the religious sort."

"You will come around. All who stalk the night do."

"I don't stalk. I just live."

"Live?"

Azran laughed. "You know what I mean."

"I understand, brother. You are new. All the more reason to accept guidance when it is offered."

The priest was now only a step behind. Without looking, Azran could feel the looming presence.

"I'm not your brother," he said, quickening his stride. "And besides, I have to get to work."

His boots echoed on the flagstones. Why were the streets so empty?

The priest's height gave him longer strides. Still wrapped in the cloak, and with steps so silent, he seemed to glide in casual pursuit.

"Work," the priest echoed. "Yes, there is indeed work to do. Her hour is now, and soon it will always be."

"The fuck are you on about?"

The priest hummed again and stopped. Azran did not miss a step.

"You are right," he heard the priest mutter. "Too soon for such talk."

Azran glanced back to see the priest's spectral rush to catch up.

"Apologies. I owe you answers." The arm emerged again, along with the fist, chain, and black disk. "But in exchange, I need a promise, brother."

"I am not your brother."

The priest grasped Azran's shoulder with a second hand, this one gnarled and gangly, and stepped in front of him. For a moment too long, the face in the void—if a face there was—gazed into Azran's. The hooded head bent low and cocked, as though with curiosity.

"Are you not?" The question did not sound rhetorical.

"No."

Azran shrugged off the twisted hand and bolted toward a high wooden fence blocking an alley. He jumped, rebounded off an adjacent building, and used a hand to guide his flight over the barrier. He landed with a roll on the far side. Carefully, quietly, he pressed one eye against a gap between boards.

The priest stood in the middle of the empty street, staring at nothing. He shook his head and retraced their route out from view.

As Azran crept to the opposite end of the alley, he began to hear the sound of traffic once more. He hopped a similar fence, dropping onto a crowded avenue. Apart from a few glances for his mode of entry, he saw no indication from anyone that this was anything but a typical Aure night.

When he reached the eve of the Silver Sun, he paused under the familiar moon-shaped sign. The door was pushed open a crack.

"Look at his skin—I think he's living," someone said from inside.

"Aye. Been spending some time in the sun, have you?" Ria's voice asked.

"Smells like one, too," a third added. "Come to make a contribution, stranger?"

Azran rolled his eyes and opened the door. A man too clean for this neighborhood was standing just inside, with Ria and two bouncers forming a half-circle around him.

"That's a nice jacket, living," Ria said, sidling closer and reaching out a finger toward the white, silk garment.

The man started backing out. "Sorry—wrong address, I suppose."

Azran stepped up and draped an arm across his shoulders. "Sev? You found the place. Good. This one's with me."

"But not *with* you," Ria said, brushing aside a streak of blue in her midnight locks.

"No, but trust me, he's not interested."

"Damn. Got some dirt on your jacket." She smoothed Azran's hair. "Get in a scuffle?"

One of the bouncers scoffed. "Azran? In a fight?"

"Nah. Weird-ass walk over, though. I'll tell you about it later. For now, would you kindly get us a couple drinks? Sev, what you having? It's on the house."

Ria went behind the bar. "Hold up, Az. Free drinks come after you serenade us." She nodded toward a harpsichord near the west wall, opposite the black stone mantle.

"Yeah, get to work, you lazy bastard!" the other bouncer called out from the kitchen door.

"Look who's talking—I can see the stacks of dishes from out here!" Azran turned to Ria, painting a pleasant smile and producing a couple silver argi. "Fine. I promise I'll play plenty later. For now, a brandy and?"

Sevex glanced past the expectant faces to the disorganized rows of shelved vessels. He stared into the chaos, as though transfixed by it.

"Two brandies, then," Azran said at last, recognizing his old friend's urge to create order.

The voice broke the spell, and Sevex nodded. Ria eyed him curiously as she poured the drinks and Azran led him to a window table. The view through the glass was translucent and warped, sequestering Sevex even farther from his usual world—a world Azran used to share with him.

"Those are your friends?" Sevex asked quietly.

"Yeah. Don't worry. They just like to play games with new people."

They sat across from each other, allowing Sevex to examine Azran's face. It hadn't changed much, except for the red eyes. He had grown his hair out, parted it to one side. His clothes were rougher—common, Sevex's family might have said. But then, Azran could no longer plunder his friend's wardrobe.

Ria placed the drinks on the table, along with the coins.

"On the house," she said.

Azran winked. "I'll play a melody for the ages—or at least the week."

He reached for his glass but paused when he noticed Sevex staring at the tattoo peeking out from his jacket sleeve. He'd picked up the base ink, the dragon form of the sky god Caelix, when they were little more than boys, and since had it expanded. All these familiar things mixed in with the new must have been surreal for Sevex. "You seem distracted."

"It's much to take in." Sevex moved his hand in a reserved circle. "All of this."

Azran sipped his drink. "When's the last time you've been anywhere besides home and work?"

Sevex took a sip of his own.

Azran leaned back in his chair. "Well, nice to know I can still read you."

Sevex stared at the ripples in his glass. "Still with Francesca?" He nodded to Azran's ringless fingers. "You're not married."

"Not formally," Azran said. "But the feelings that prompt this kind of commitment don't flit away."

"It is true, then—the relationship between master and thrall?"

Azran chuckled and shook his head, bemused. "Well, yes, but she let me free the moment I woke. The trust we both showed means more to us than any verbal vow." He paused, remembering the act of compassion he hoped to one day repay.

"That's a lot of faith to put in someone."

"Too much?"

Sevex took a slow drink, the burn showing on his face before he swallowed. "I don't think I could."

"Neither did I."

"Please. You're a reckless man, Az. You always were."

"You're the second person to tell me that, tonight."

"That so?" Sevex was only half-listening now, some stray thought dominating the racing mind behind his darting eyes. Azran knew there was an empty pit in him, or perhaps a gnawing hunger. As much as he loved Sevex, as deep as the bond ran, they were different people. More so now, and not because of vampirism. Azran was the freest he'd ever been. Sevex, meanwhile, was…trapped? Yes, trapped. It was a familiar place.

"Tell me, what's Arcana and Technology got you working on these days?" Azran smiled as a bit of life returned to the man he'd forgotten in his new freedom.

• • •

A priest—a pilgrim—he was. Just then, he had trouble remembering what he was before. Before was bright, and he abhorred brightness. The hatred had begun with the sun but now encompassed all luminescence.

He slinked under the eaves of closed storefronts, detouring through an alley if a business was yet open. Most of all, he avoided the people. The living and the little candles they carried in their eyes, the marks of unmarred souls. Though now, even those who had been reborn repelled him to a degree. A few were fine—one or three. Not two; two brought conspiracy. But he could not withstand a crowd. That was beyond his power, for now.

They, those he served, and the One they served, promised to give him that power. Return it—yes, he could almost remember what it was to be a social creature. He had been so strong, then. But also weak—lost—without purpose. Mortal. He had chosen this path, this servitude. He had a sister—that detail, he remembered. To think dear Francesca might be the vessel She—the Goddess of Night, the Eclipse, Tenebra—needed. That was worth losing a few details.

Dear Francesca—she would be a spark this night. One of many. Horrible light would flood Aure, brighter than the uncounted streetlamps. Midnight vigils behind glass, mourners bearing white votives for the dead, lanterns in guards' trembling grips as they scoured the city for the perpetrators—he saw it all from above, a wraith in the smoke of riot fires. And then, darkness would consume. And with darkness, freedom—freedom for all the clan, all the temple, to carry out Tenebra's machinations.

He had a brother now, too—one yet lost in the light. Where was his brother? The priest had found someone earlier, but that was a mistake. He had never actually met his new brother—dear Francesca had some addled notion of keeping him neutral.

There could be no such thing.

The priest had searched, guided by the magic Tenebra gave him. He tried to recall the face of his new brother, but it was indistinct. He paused in a barren lane which defective lamps left in shade.

Perhaps a different tactic—he searched the memories of souls he had encountered. Their imprints were more tangible. He found one so deluded, it actually believed it was at peace in vampiric corporeality—believed the lie of neutrality. And it was tied to another—dear Francesca's. They were linked—if she followed this path, the new brother could yet be guided.

That soul, so deluded—it was the one he had spoken to earlier. Unmistakably. If only he had been more cogent, more aware—excitement had clouded his judgment, and deception was unexpected.

"I am not your brother."

Liar! He lied! How dare he lie to a brother, a servant—pilgrim—priest! How could one with the blood be so blind? How could one so entwined with them betray the family—the clan—the temple?

A thought struck—a dreadful one that halted all others—what if dear Francesca had lied, too?

He reached out to her consciousness—they were closer than she knew. He saw her spill the poison and turn her back on her quarry.

Despair drove out all other feelings—self-criticism, fear, doubt, confusion. Then came rage. Fury. Hatred. Dear Francesca was deluded as her lover. Part of him wanted to mourn his sister, now lost to him. But her arrogance—her smile as she walked away—filled him with wrath. She had spit in the face of the Goddess.

"Hey, tall and creepy. Oi!"

The priest opened his eyes—they must have been closed. Two figures stood before him—a dwarf woman and an orc man.

"Don't taunt him," the orc muttered through small tusks. "If half the Sunrise Chapter report is true—"

"I read the damn report," the dwarf said.

Both wore street clothes, but the priest sensed cold steel hidden within. Both were living, and they had the audacity to approach him now? Did they think the Godshadows would frighten him when he was shadowed by *his* deity? Had that organization forgotten the angels that created their shadeseers?

"Heard you know a thing or two about Angles of Shade, vampire," the woman continued. "Let's have a chat, shall we?"

He hated the living. And now, they addressed him as though they were equals—betters? He made a noise somewhere between a hum, hiss, and growl. A warning—he was beyond words. Tonight was meant to be glorious—a great beginning. He took a step back, leaned slightly forward, primed to charge.

The orc man ghost-stepped to the side. Out flashed a dagger, resting against Amadore's neck. "Hold it."

Now the living sought to command him?

The silken shroud and hood obscured the storm brewing inside. One hand—the twisted one—rose from the folds and clutched the orc's forearm. The priest was nearly as tall as the orc, but thinner. Slender. And yet, he pushed the heavy, muscled limb down with small effort.

The orc twisted free, pulled the priest's hood back, and launched a pommel strike.

Any remaining restraint snapped. Red eyes went wide. Shadows pulsed from the exposed face. The living fell to the flagstones, groaning, clutching their heads. Helpless. Blood-filled. He could drain them.

But there was other work to be done. Contingencies.

He pulled his cowl low. His form blurred—merged with the night—dashed through the darkness.

Nobody knew their place anymore.

● ● ●

"So, it's like a clock?" Azran asked. He glanced at a pair of newcomers, a dwarf woman and an orc man. He felt their living blood, out of place here.

"The mechanism is," Sevex replied. "The power is a tethered thread, like a runic spell."

"Well?" the orc muttered.

Azran switched focus, hair standing on the back of his neck.

"She's not here," the dwarf woman said, walking toward the side table. "But our cloaks did good recon."

At the bar, Ria cleared her throat. "Can I get you something?"

The living ignored her. Ria's bouncers stood straighter. The orc did the same, towering over them from across the room.

"And the brass conducts the energy...." Sevex's explanation trailed off as the dwarf invaded the space.

"Azran, right?" she said.

He looked at her sidelong.

"Mind having a quick word? Outside?"

"Kind of. In here's fine, though."

She chuckled through clenched teeth. "We'll see. Where's Francesca?"

Azran crossed his arms. "Work, I imagine."

"Where's that?"

"Who are you? Why am I running into the weirdest fucking people tonight?"

"Honey, don't get me started." The dwarf grabbed his collar and yanked him from his seat. "Let's go."

Azran pulled back, but she still made progress across the room. Sevex raised a hand in protest but did not speak out.

The two bouncers rushed forward, while Ria reached down. The orc engaged one, twisting out of an attempted hold. He

15

countered with a knee to the stomach and dropped the vampire with a heavy jab to the temple.

The second reached for the dwarf. She stretched out her left hand, exposing a painted rune. A wave of force blasted him through the air, back the way he came. "I got another one for you, barkeep. Best you put your hands in the open."

Ria complied, glaring.

Through it all, Azran feigned terror. He needed the right moment.

The dwarf glanced at him. "Think we should get a listener for this one?"

"No," the orc said. He drew a dagger from his sleeve. "He's got soft eyes. He'll point us in the right—"

Azran winked at Ria. He dropped to the floor, leaving his shirt in the dwarf's grasp. He rolled out of the orc's lunging reach. The dwarf leveled her rune hand at him, but gasped and jerked forward as a bolt punched into her back.

The orc whirled and charged Ria, who now held an empty crossbow. Azran leapt onto his back, using momentum to spin both to the ground. The orc wrapped one big hand around his throat. Azran pulled a stiletto from his boot and held it against the orc's, stopping the chokehold.

"Just do it!" the conscious bouncer shouted from across the room.

Azran knew he should, but he held the stalemate. The orc let go. The bouncer stepped up, closing a hand over Azran's. He let go of the blade and watched as it pierced the orc's eye.

Azran stepped into the flat not long after that. Within the hour? He wasn't sure. A low, flickering glow shone from the bedroom, silhouetting Francesca's profile. She didn't turn from the window.

"You're home early," Azran said.

"So are you."

"Didn't feel much like playing. You?"

"Think I told Filvié Noctirin to fuck off. At least, I told my brother to."

Azran hugged her from behind. The stars were shrouded now. The air was wet from impending rain. Occasionally, someone strolled past below, streetlamps casting many shadows across the stark white.

After a while, Francesca asked, "Have you ever met Amadore?"

Azran hesitated, remembering his walk to the bar. She'd always said her brother was strange. "I think I might have."

Somewhere, a bell began tolling.

"What did you do?" Azran asked.

"I decided not to kill someone."

"Oh. Well, that's good."

"I hope so. How's Sevex?"

"Hard to say. Living and working, I suppose."

Sevex had taken no action in the bar, was nearly mute in its aftermath. Was he turning into a cog, like those in his precious clockworks? At least he had offered Azran and Francesca a place to stay if the trouble didn't end at the Silver Sun.

The bell continued past twelve—not tolling the hours, but announcing something. Another joined it.

"I watched two people die tonight. Two people looking for you. Ria thinks they were Godshadows."

Francesca leaned into him. "And now, we've no one to watch our backs."

"Except each other," he said.

"Except each other." She reached into her pocket and retrieved a delicate silver dove. Even in the meager light, it caught a glare.

"That's pretty," Azran said.

Another distant bell rang, this one frantic. Smoke, darker than the rainclouds, rose over the far horizon of buildings. Azran hugged Francesca tighter. She squeezed his hand.

Lines were drawn that night, and they were drawn with blood.

2

Only Azran seemed free from the weight, free as his fingers dancing across the keys of an old harpsichord as he haunted the room with an improvised nocturne. He was always free, Francesca reflected. Always had been. Even back in Lunatel, in a town like a prison cell, devoid of any purpose or progression, she had met a man free.

She, on the other hand, felt the lingering pull of her family shackles, bolted to a wall a thousand miles away. The Darani name carried weight in the right circles—the ones that met at night or in heavily curtained rooms so the sun would not burn them. It was an old name, with many legends attached to it. Francesca and Amadore were born of vampires. This was rare enough on its own. But so were their parents, the whispers said, and their parents before them. And with that kind of lineage and singularness came expectations, and expectations became choking tradition, defined roles, social chains. The Darani children had a purpose, their parents had always told them. Soon, their family would be called to serve Tenebra the Eclipse, goddess of their kind. That, they said, was why Francesca could not remember ever basking in the sun. As far as anyone knew, she and Amadore underwent their awakenings as infants.

She had learned years ago that manse in Ostitel was not her home. Even from the beginning, she had to make her own way. She always had to seek and find love in other people. Whatever her family gave her was not love. Perhaps it was something adjacent, indistinguishable to someone on the outside, but to live it, to feel it, was not right. It never sat well with her.

Recent events brought these memories to the fore—tugged on the chains. Only in her husband's song could Francesca manage to find some freedom. She sipped her coffee along with the other patrons. The dark glass of the tavern's windows reflected faces shocked into impassivity. Many of them, the ones that paid attention, had seen this long night coming. But the chaos of this new present rendered any foresight useless—a burned home was a burned home.

Ria had sent word along her mysterious lines of communication that the Silver Sun would be a safe place. Those with no interest in the theft or the murder or the riots spreading like flames on oiled tinder—the vampires who just wanted to be people—could come and wait out the storm. The rest could be the night-stalking monsters the propaganda claimed if that was their desire.

Francesca and Ria shared the end of the bar nearest Azran. The barkeep had started with liquored coffee but soon moved on to straight booze. The women shared a look every time the door opened and another new refugee entered. *This is madness*, the looks said. Neither could quite understand what all the fighting was supposed to accomplish. Amadore knew, but damned if Francesca had any interest in seeing his veiled face or hearing his charged proselytizing anytime soon.

She reached for a ring-stained piece of paper on the bartop and pulled it closer. She had only skimmed the day's news pamphlet when they arrived, but now had the breathing space to read more carefully.

A Night Of Blood And Flame!

Citizens!

Our Golden City of Aure has come under siege from within. Yesterday eve witnessed an outbreak of murders and subsequent arson across the Rosaer Hills, home to some of the most prominent aristocracy in our great Empire. The perpetrators of these gruesome and deplorable acts are currently storming the streets. Yes—I speak of the dark legion of vampires now killing at will, drinking the blood of their victims and seizing, by force, once-peaceful neighborhoods in the north and east portions of Aure. Our wondrous lights are revealing the cursed nature they have sought to conceal in the shadows.

What hope we had in the coming dawn chasing these creatures away was smothered by the heavy clouds of this day, which had not the decency to wash the flagstones of spilled blood.

But take heart, dear citizens! All is not lost. The experienced Aure City Guard fights valiantly against this threat, and even now Imperial Legions are arriving through our gates. And yes, some brave citizens have taken up arms as well! I speak of the Solari, priests, acolytes, and templars of the Risen Goddess Sola, lending the very light of the sun to the soldiers' steel. Yes, I, too, pray the First Gods inspire their servants to such bravery, but for now, we will praise this lesser power. Indeed, I say few are better prepared to fight the degenerate denizens of darkness, these monstrous minions of Tenebra, Goddess of Shadows.

And just what, you ask, dear citizens, has prompted this uprising? Did the stars align such that the vampires' hidden lusts broke the flimsy shackles of their "self-control"? Look through the archives and anecdotes of history, and you will see the depressing frequency of vampires choosing fresh mortal blood over that of animals. Could it be the festering blight on our society, the so-called "sociopolitical alliance" of Filvié Noctirin, has planned this chaos from its inception? Or perhaps, they opted toward violence in lieu of civilized debate regarding the Senate's proposed action to legalize the slaying of these dangerous nightstalkers. The law, should it pass, is based on the Codes of Legex. Forged on the foundation of these divine dictates, it would allow living citizens to protect themselves from their vampiric neighbors without fear of unjust prosecution by the Empire. Recent events demonstrate how dreadfully, desperately, doubtlessly needed this proposed law is.

These creatures of the night are a menace to the peaceful Valentreid citizen. Stay in your home, lock your doors, watch over your neighbors. But once you are secure, rest assured, dear citizens—order will be restored. These insurgents will yield to the just might that birthed our great Empire.

—Scribe Director of the Printing Administration: Department of Current Events: Bureau of Culture: Autumn 1349

Azran often admitted to being rubbish at endings, but his music nonetheless came to some manner of conclusion. Few clapped. Francesca tossed the pamphlet onto the floor.

In the pause between songs, the door burst open. Two vampires hustled in, propping a third between them. All were armed with swords. Space cleared around them, and the carriers lay the third flat on the table. He was bleeding from a chest wound, and one side of his face and upper torso looked badly burned.

"You're gonna be alright," one of the newcomers said. "Is there a healer in here?"

"What happened?" Ria asked. "What in hades is this?"

"Bloody Solari are prowlin. They hit him with a false sun."

Ria grabbed the speaker by the shoulder and started shoving him toward the door. "You have to go. I'm not involving this place or these people in the fighting."

He pushed her hand away. "Look, lady, you're gonna be involved real quick anyhow. Guards are pushin, too, and you're gonna have a whole wave of us real soon." He glanced around the room and raised his voice. "You really wanna cross the clan at a time like this? Whole city's fillin with blood and flame. Ain't no neutral place gonna be left in the streets. I suggest anyone that don't wanna fight get gone."

Francesca felt Azran grab her hand. "I'll go where you go," he whispered.

There was a heavy pause before Ria addressed the crowd. "Sorry, everyone. I tried." She gave a nod to Azran and Francesca as a dozen people finished their drinks and exited, choosing to test their luck getting home rather than join a battle line.

3

A deep-cut shirt of blue silk covered most of his torso. The sleeves were torn off to display honed muscles and dark skin with sweeping patterns of darker ink. His ears were pierced, a gold stud in the left and a small shark tooth hanging from the right. He once traveled far to the north, past the end of Maceria, to a place where orcs rode drakes. The riders shaved one side of their scalps and grew the other long, sweeping the hair over. He thought it an interesting look and kept the cultural souvenir. Wavy, dark strands hid the gold stud except when it caught the sun. His eyes were a grey-blue seldom seen in southern lands.

Seneskar welcomed stares at his distinctive human guise, but here, he received few. This was Cruxia—after Aeribe, this city was home to more artists and creatives than any other city in the Valentreid Empire. All around the outlander strode poets and playwrights, painters and sculptors, actors and musicians. Many of them would stand out as much as Seneskar would in any other crowd, and some, even more.

The thought of reverting to his "natural" form, that of a storm dragon, in the street brought an amused smile to Seneskar's lips.

That would not do, though. He had come to the mainland with a purpose. He was supposed to be on the road to Aure. First, though, he had to gather allies. The news on the printed pamphlets—weren't those curious things?—reinforced his decision to wait. Seneskar read between the lines of propaganda, comparing this intelligence with his own. The fight was not over. The threat spoken of by the messengers of the Urathix— Seneskar's new gods, fire dragons of immeasurable power—would not be easily suppressed.

He wondered how many were vying for the Golden City. How much competition would the Faith of Fire face? He knew little about this Filvié Noctirin, these "Children of the Night," beyond what the sunathach—"priests" was the closest translation—who sent him on this quest had said. They were vampires, beings with corrupted souls that did not join the Eternal Fire upon death. And more recently, they were consorting with rogue immortals, angels that even the lost gods of the Pantheon had forsaken. Chief among these tainted creatures, the one who held the immortals' ears even above Filvié Noctirin's leadership, was an Ostiteli named Amadore Darani.

If this "outbreak of murders and arson" was Darani's plan for conquest, Seneskar was up against a violent-minded fool, a deluded madman, or a genius whose strategy he had yet to unravel. Any of those possibilities was dangerous to his gods' plans.

Music stirred Seneskar from his musing. The notes were familiar.

"Ah," he said, placing the sounds. It was that eastern girl with the oud. He had picked up on her unique style from the moment he first heard her play on a street corner.

The song emanated from an open window, filling the evening air around a tavern. He spotted the player as he passed, sitting on a stool on a small stage. She played slow, a ballad full of ringing strings and heavy with wordless vocals.

Something else broke him from his newest reverie. A woman crossed the intersection ahead. Her head was turned away, focused on a scuffle between street rats, but too many things were familiar for Seneskar's comfort. Judging by those around her, she was taller than him in this form. Heavy, defined muscles were visible beneath a light shirt. A sword was slung over her back—a large one, with distinct bronze accents on the crossguard and clasp of the sheath. The last detail, the giveaway, was a small, silver disk hanging from the baldric. It twirled on its leather loop, alternating between Chari sun and moon motifs.

Two thoughts reached the surface of Seneskar's turbulent mind:

This human nose couldn't smell a wet dog three strides away.

Is that who they sent after me?

Why else would Varja, his bastard second cousin, be in Cruxia?

She slowed, and Seneskar turned away. He walked around to the front of the tavern—Red Rocks, the sign said—past a pair of grizzly dock workers debating politics, and entered a common room decorated with the spoils of some old war. Swords and shields of every shape hung on the walls—straight continental arming swords, short choppers from the sea raiders, even a ten-foot althoch blade. Shields included everything from Chari wicker weaves to legionary kites.

He glanced back to make sure Varja hadn't followed him in—she hadn't. He stopped by the bar and ordered local rice wine before taking an open table near the window he had heard the music from. A server brought the drink, and he tipped with a Procumi copper. He sipped the warm wine, listened to the ballad, and wished he were in the country for pleasure.

The song ended on a lingering D chord. A few patrons clapped. One dropped a couple coins in the wooden bowl on the edge of the stage.

"Play something fun!" another man shouted.

The oud player smirked and swept long, dark hair from her face and tucked it behind the subtle point of her ear. "That's highly subjective. I'm having fun. Is anyone else?"

Those who had clapped did so again. After a second glance at the door, Seneskar added to the applause.

"Play something fast!" the same man shouted.

"That comes later." The player plucked out a scale. "Maybe it's not what you're used to here in the west. But in Astrellus, we ease into it, like a gentle rain that gives way to a storm." Her blue-green eyes swept the room. "I promise you a storm."

Seneskar grinned behind his tipped cup as he took another sip. If only he weren't an agent of the gods. He could do this for a thousand nights, and it still wouldn't get old. He decided he would go back to living for a while when this was over.

● ● ●

Varja felt the hair rise on the back of her neck and stopped. She glanced around the busy Cruxian intersection, but saw nothing that explained her sudden wariness. A few locals watched her with suspicion. Her eyes, the blue of a storm dragon's, marked her as separate from the brown- and green-eyed Zixarsi occupying the poorer quarters of the city. Neither side of her parentage afforded her much trust these days. She ignored the stares, as she had all the others. They were not her quarry.

She continued on for several hours until another long, fruitless day left her spent. Memories crept up around the edges of her mind, and she relaxed as she gave in to her wandering thoughts.

She had never truly belonged to the Stormblood clan— Kepeskeižir, in their tongue. She was a halfbreed, and her southern blood, her dragon blood, reminded her of that at every opportunity. To outsiders, she was just human. Among her mother's people, she looked Procumi; in Procumes or, as now, the Valentreid Empire, they called her Zixarsa, after the river. Ziach, if they were assholes. Ziak, if they were provincial assholes. There were many of the latter two.

In 1325, amid the chaos and confusion of the Faith of Fire's failed invasion of the Valentreid Empire, Varja's mother had used her dwindling influence to get her daughter to Procumes. As Varja heard it, her father was slain by a Chari fire dragon before she could walk, and the other Kepeskeižir had not known of Varja's existence. The elders eventually decided that, while she lacked any true claim to clan membership, they would not abandon a child.

This hunt was not Varja's first excursion from Procumes. When Charir mounted its second assault against the Valentreid Empire in 1338, volunteers from the rugged islands once again went to the aid of the legions. Unlike during the Rising Fire decades prior, the Kepeskeižiri remained neutral and forbade any clan members from fighting. A Procumi human on his way to join up reminded Varja she was not of the clan. She was seventeen when sailed north with a band of freelance warriors. They fought together throughout the conflict, bonding on the battlefield—and off, in the case of Varja and Kylan, the man who had convinced to leave.

She had searched for someone back then, too. She had ventured up the Muntherzix, seeking her human mother near its headwaters. She hoped for more success this time than that journey had brought.

The Second Flame ended, but Kylan wanted to keep fighting. Varja had a fair battle lust of her own, but four years had shown her a different perspective on war. They reached an impasse. He called her weak; she called him a monster. He called her a coward and a traitor like her mother; she nearly killed him.

In the intervening seven years, Varja returned home and fought for some semblance of respect among the Kepeskeižiri. Her chance came when Seneskar, a full-blooded dragon of the clan, was discovered to have joined the Faith and fled northward. Varja volunteered to find him and bring him in for justice. The elders took convincing but provided Varja with passage to Liore, and the trail soon led her to Lunatel.

Seneskar was fond of the human form. From what Varja gathered at the ports and waystations, he was wearing his usual guise. Either subterfuge was not his goal, or he sought to goad someone familiar into following him. Or perhaps he was just that audacious.

Varja first tried official channels—local guards, border checkpoints. But the atmosphere so close to Charir was less than welcoming. Though trade and travel continued between the empire and Procumes, and though Zixarsi had been in the southeast provinces for decades now, the sight of an armed "Ziak" built like a 13th Infantry legionary made lips tighten. The streets became Varja's friends, as the refugees and their descendants warmed up with the first Zixarsi word that left her mouth.

However, the trail grew colder the farther northeast it went and the larger populations became. Varja's funds grew thinner. Between bribing street corner informants—even kinship had its limits—and border guards—"non-citizen entry fee"—and the basic costs of travel, she was almost broke.

Fortunately, there was no shortage of cheap places to stay on the busy trade routes.

Varja paused at the doorway to the common room of a hostel. She hadn't paid much attention to the name. Something about birds? All she had latched onto was the cost—a silver coin a night. Sure, there were even cheaper places, but she had been on the road for months now. Beds were nice, and even nicer without fleas and rats.

One window at the far end of the room let in the late evening sun above the distant mountain ridge. Ten beds were divided along two walls, with a low table and lumpy cushions below the window. The innkeeper had said there were six others staying, but only one was present. A woman sat at the table, staring at the cityscape and absently plucking on what resembled a small lute. She looked to be near Varja's age, but the tips of her ears were pointed, hinting at elf blood—she could have been much older. Her white blouse contrasted with dark hair falling to the middle of her back.

Varja stepped into the room with heavy bootfalls. The woman glanced her way, nodded, and went back to her contemplation. Varja found a bed she figured was unoccupied and unshouldered her pack. She unfastened the baldric holding her sheathed longsword and leaned the weapon against the wall. The bed was hard, but not as hard as the earth of Charir. Most anything was softer than that.

She looked back at the other guest. Traveling musicians always seemed to know people. And from what Varja had gathered, Seneskar was quite the music lover.

"Are you a performer?" she asked.

The woman strummed a chord. "Aye. Why do you ask?"

"I'm looking for someone. I thought you might have seen him in the audience. He's quite distinctive."

"Maybe, but I've only been in town a week. I'm not exactly drawing crowds yet. Can't seem to find people here who appreciate a good Aurasi ballad." She played a short phrase of ringing, somber notes.

"Still, though," Varja said. "I'm losing the trail. He's a human. Dark skin but blue eyes. One side of his head's shaved, the other long and tangled. Last I heard, he was going by Seneskar."

"Well, apart from the 'he' bit and shave, I'd say I'm looking right at him," the musician said. "You related?"

"Distantly."

"Family matter, then. I don't envy you." She paused and thought. "You know, I actually may have seen him."

Varja stood. "Where? When?"

"Easy there. I was playing a street corner oh, three or four days back. He stayed and listened a bit, tossed me a silver, and left."

"Do you know where he went?"

"Couldn't say." The musician went back to playing, eyes on the neck. "That's a big sword. Can you actually swing that thing?"

Varja smiled. "Like you play that lute."

"Oud."

"What?"

"It's called an oud. This is what we play out east. It's a lot easier to carry around, and I could always get more intricate on this than one of those bulky Cortelli lutes."

"And what about you?" Varja asked. "What are you called?"

"Miranda." She set the oud on the table and walked up, hand extended. Up close, she was a good six inches shorter.

"Varja."

They shook hands.

"Varja," Miranda said, musing. "That's Draci, isn't it? 'Dance,' or something?"

"Dancer." She pointed her thumb back at the sword. "As I said, like you play that lu—oud."

4

"It's this way," Azran said, cutting into an alley.

"Are you sure?" Francesca asked, barely a step behind. "Have you ever been there?"

At the next thoroughfare, he stopped short but remained balanced. He pressed them both against the wall.

A squad of city guards hustled past, mail clinking and heavy boots tramping. Azran knew he and Francesca had nothing to do with the current state of Aure, but he also knew the guards wouldn't care. Tonight was a perilous one for vampires, whether they were involved with the insurrection or not. He didn't know what would happen if he and his wife were caught, but he had some ideas, and would rather not test any of them.

When the way was clear, Azran led their dash across the lamp-lit street, down a block of closed and locked storefronts, and into what was not another alley so much as a shoulder-width gap between buildings. As they squeezed through, Francesca repeated her question.

"Sure as I can be," he said. "Which will have to do. Just trust me."

"I do."

That was good, because Azran wasn't sure he trusted himself. Sevex had told him about the fancy house the Bureau of Arcana and Technology put him up in. Azran once again tried to overlay the description—gods bless Sev's obsession with details—with the mental map of the city he'd made over three years of midnight strolls. He was mostly sure of where he was leading them. It would have to do. *Nowhere else to go,* he thought.

Another street opened before them. A body sat propped against a lamppost with a crossbow bolt embedded deep in its chest—a guard, by the blue shoulder cape. He was dead, or close to it. There were dark stains scattered around the flagstones, but no further signs of a fight.

Azran heard hoofbeats not far away, growing louder. He spotted a smashed window and ran for it, pulling Francesca along. They hopped in, avoiding the jagged glass, and slid down in a clear spot. The place looked to be a ceramics shop. Vessels, dishes, and knickknacks lined shelves, and the smell of fresh clay was pungent. The only light came through the impromptu entryway.

The hoofbeats—those of many horses—slowed and ceased but for some restless pacing. Francesca tugged his sleeve, but Azran risked a peek regardless.

Mounted legionaries stood in formation. One called to the fallen guard and prodded him with a lance. The guard did not move. Another soldier gestured at the window, and Azran ducked back inside.

Feet, not hooves, approached.

Staying low, the pair crawled behind the counter. Another duo was already there—a living man and woman of middling age. A dumbfounded moment passed, then the potter man grabbed a knife from under the counter.

Azran held his hands up, while Francesca's went to the dagger on her belt.

"Wait," Azran whispered, glancing in the direction of the door. "We're just trying to get off the streets. We'll leave when they pass."

The potters glanced at each other and nodded, but the man did not replace the knife. The woman kept staring at the intruders.

A bulky shadow appeared on the back wall, then another.

The woman's eyes went wide. "Wait—you're with them. You're vampires."

The man looked over the counter and saw the legionaries. He pulled the woman up and back. "In here!" he shouted.

Azran and Francesca backed off as the potter waved his knife at them. Francesca drew her blade and interposed herself between him and Azran.

"Corp!" one of the soldiers called, drawing his sword.

He and the other had prepared to hop the window when a trio of cloaked figures dropped down to the street. Two dispatched the soldiers using long knives, while the third fired a bolt into the lead rider's face. The officer slumped in the saddle. The figures dashed toward the narrow gap. Riders shouted and gave chase, forced to circumvent the block.

It came and went fast. The four in the shop stood stunned. They almost didn't notice the fourth cloaked figure swing in through the shattered window. He pulled back his hood, revealing red eyes.

"Francesca Darani," the vampire said in a voice as quiet and fluid as his movements. "I bring word from your brother. He is waiting at the Ciusa estate."

Azran looked at his wife. For an instant, she wore the expression of a cornered animal. Her eyes met his, and she calmed. She faced the newcomer squarely.

"Tell him I'm already on it."

The cloaked figure hesitated, but nodded and leapt back out into the night.

"Leave," the potter said. He leaned forward, knife brandished and quivering. "Now."

Francesca looked him up and down, then said, "You wouldn't last a heartbeat."

Azran went to the window. Five more bodies littered the street, barely a block down—three soldiers, one horse, and one belonging to what he realized had been an ambusher. The dead guard was bait. He heard ringing metal somewhere in the distance.

"Come on," Francesca said, hopping back out. "Which way now?"

Azran took the lead once more. "What did you mean, you're on it?" he asked.

"I don't know. Just buying some time."

Azran wasn't sure they'd make it out of this, but he was once again grateful to be by her side.

For an hour that felt like five, they skulked through the city. The streets shifted between chaos and desertion. They passed few fires since they saw their burning flat, but smoke always lay heavy in the sky, like a reminder they didn't need. Likewise, they passed few corpses but could sense many more. They had to backtrack twice—once because a unit of guards had erected a barricade near a patrol checkpoint, and again because Azran took a wrong turn.

He slithered around the corner of a boarded-up inn. Brick houses lined either side of the next street, each with a black iron fence and trimmed, petit yard.

Left side, fourth from the corner, Azran thought. He pointed out the destination to Francesca, and she nodded.

"I don't like that," she said, indicating the clusters of people moving up and down the avenue. Some were hopping fences, returning with burdens of loot—heavy burlap sacks, rolled-up rugs and tapestries, reams of jewelry they now wore. Not all in the crowds looted, but all were armed with knives, staves, clubs, small axes, or even decorative swords.

Francesca gripped Azran's hand. "Just stay close, okay?"

"Okay."

A few bystanders stared as they passed, but the couple was dressed commonly enough and bore enough dirt and scuffs from their night of evasion that they walked unhindered.

Francesca leaned even closer into Azran. "What if someone broke into Sev's place?"

"Doesn't look like it," he replied, though he was concerned. Sev was a thinker, not a survivor. They paused to let a trio of looters pass, two carrying a large, embroidered rug between them, grinning at the prize.

"Good night for the low, eh?" the third said, winking at Azran and Francesca.

They each let their long hair shield their faces. "Sure is," Azran said.

A clamor rose behind them, rippling through the crowds. The couple looked back the way they came and saw a new group, garbed in yellow and sporting brass medallions of the sun. They sang a wordless hymn as the others parted to let them by.

"Solari," Francesca whispered. "Let's go."

But the crowd flowed away from their destination, moving to circle the clergy that now stood in a little circle of their own. The hymn faded. A word passed along—"vampires." They had three ready to execute.

"Aye, they're to blame for all the death!" the third looter shouted, raising his fist in the air.

Azran and Francesca squeezed through the tightening bunch, dodging around bodies and doing their best to stay together. Azran glanced back. Through a narrow opening, he caught a glimpse of a kneeling figure. A yellow-robed priest rested the tip of a sword vertically on the vampire's spine. Azran lost the view, but a tremendous cheer went up.

● ● ●

At last, they were free. Francesca spotted the house, fifty yards away.

"Where ya going?" someone asked.

"You're missing justice," a second voice behind them said.

"What, are ya vampires?" the first asked.

"Might be," a third said.

Three men broke from the edge of the crowd and began following Azran and Francesca.

The couple reached the gate to Sevex's yard. It was locked. Francesca nudged Azran forward, and they started climbing. A firm hand grabbed her foot and yanked her off the iron fence.

"Aye, they are indeed." One of the men loomed over her, a glare fixed on her red eyes.

Azran jumped down between them and pulled a stiletto from his boot. "Back off."

Francesca stood and drew her dagger. The man pulled a hatchet from his belt. The other two readied clubs.

The hatchet swung in at Azran. He ducked to the side, but the blunt backswing hit him square in the mouth. The looter followed with a kick to the shin that completed Azran's fall.

A clubber went at Francesca. She stepped in close and stopped his tight swing with her free arm. She stabbed twice into the attacker's abdomen, and he fell back with a choked grunt of pain.

She heard a footstep behind her and ducked. The second club still clipped the top of her head. Her vision flashed black, and she stumbled. With a cry of rage, the man she had stabbed came back and launched a vicious kick into her chest.

They were down. The hatchet man planted a foot on Azran's back. The clubbers prepared to bludgeon a barely-conscious Francesca.

"Pardon, but I believe those are mine."

The looters turned. Francesca followed their gazes to see a man coming around the corner of the property. He wore a red bandana to hold back shaggy black curls. Simple but solid swords, one longer, one shorter, rested on either hip.

"We saw them first," the hatchet man said.

The swordsman continued to approach. "No, no, I think I'm supposed to be helping these two."

Another roar sounded from the crowd down the street.

"They're vamps." The hatchet man gestured toward the vigilante execution. "They're the reason all this shit is goin down."

The swordsman raised an eyebrow. "These two, all by themselves? Impressive."

Francesca started to push herself up, but the man she had stabbed slammed his foot into her ribs. She gasped and hit the flagstones.

"Try that again," the swordsman said. That hint of snark was gone from his voice.

"Do ya one better." The looter raised his club to strike. At its apex, the swordsman was already there. In one continuous motion, the longer arming sword left its sheath and entered flesh, sliding up into the clubber's chest cavity.

Wood clattered on the ground as the looter stared at nothing.

The second clubber swung at the swordsman. He left his blade in the first, quickstepped out of reach, then back in with his shorter weapon in a reverse grip. He sliced up and across, opening the looter's face. The man joined his comrade on the ground, clutching at the wound and screaming.

A third cry from the crowd tapered off, replaced by alarm.

The swordsman faced the hatchet man, spreading his arms out wide and welcoming. The hatchet man glanced from the bloodied sword to the gashed face of one clubber to the still form of the other. He looked back to the swordsman, whose right hand was now limned in a soft white glow.

The hatchet man took his foot from Azran's chest. He whirled and sprinted back to the crowd. "Vampires!" he cried. "Over here!"

Dozens of eyes were now fixed on the scene. They rushed closer, parting to let the ten armed clerics reach the front.

The swordsman helped Azran to his feet, and he rushed to support his dazed wife. The wounded clubber scrambled away as the mysterious fighter planted a foot on the dead man and pulled his sword free.

"Release them to us," one priest said, breaking the tense hush.

"I can't," the swordsman said. "I made a promise." He held the short blade in his left hand, long in his right. The white light expanded to enshroud both weapons.

"You are a priest," another Solar said, pointing her oak staff at the glowing blades. "Surely you must understand how they corrupt and taint the very essence of the soul. The world must be cleansed of them."

Francesca, still recovering her breath, spat a glob of blood and saliva at the priestess.

The swordsman grinned. "Try it. I have Atora standing at my back. I'll show you what power a true god grants. Sola is a mewling child to a First."

The Solari bristled.

"Will you fight all ten of us, Atoran?" the priestess asked.

The swordsman laughed. "I'll fight this entire mob, and even if they do not all fall beneath my blade, enough will."

His eyes went white. He took a step forward, and the crowd shuffled back two.

"Walk off."

The priestess glanced at her fellows, who nodded. To the swordsman, she said, "Very well. But there will come a day when all who stalk the night must face the dawn. Sola will smile as they burn."

The clergy passed back through the crowd, which soon followed—after gathering the bits of spoils scattered about the street.

The glow around the swordsman faded. He gave a lingering glare after them, then wiped his blades clean and sheathed them.

"Thank you," Azran said.

"Quite welcome. Azran and Francesca, yes?"

They nodded.

"Good." He pulled a key from his belt and unlocked the gate.

"And you?" Francesca asked.

"Call me Luc. Come in, before they change their minds."

Francesca hesitated, holding Azran back.

"Sevex is inside," Luc said. "I'm just here to make sure that lot stays out. He also told me to keep an eye out for a pair of vampires."

He stood aside, inviting them to enter. Azran wiped the blood from his split lip and limped in. Francesca clutched her ribs, wincing with each step, but they made it to the mahogany double doors.

"Got a couple guests," Luc called.

They heard latches slide and click. Azran pushed one door open and hurried in.

Another mechanical slide and click sounded, and Sevex yanked Azran to the floor. A heavy, curved blade whooshed past, inches from slicing him. It swung back like a pendulum.

"Sorry, sorry," Sevex said. "I didn't think it was fully operational yet."

Azran let out a long sigh, part exhaustion and part exasperation.

Luc caught the blade—a gilded, ornamental thing—on the unsharpened side and held it back for them to get past.

A short woman with short hair, wearing a leather vest and several knives, entered the foyer and leaned against the frame. "I told him someone would get hurt."

"Yes, that's the point," Sevex said. "If Luc were bested, we would need a contingency."

"I'm hurt by your lack of confidence," Luc said.

"Hate to interrupt, or impose," Azran said, "but can we sit down somewhere?"

• • •

Des observed the vampires as they limped to the posh divan in the sitting room. They hardly seemed the bloodsucking monsters she heard about back in Equotel. Even Forente had its stories of urbane, seductive predators with fangs, and sewer-crawling abominations—never anything in between.

These two just seemed like ordinary people, as fragile as anyone else. They didn't look capable of instigating the chaos of this night. But then, Des had seen plenty of coups pulled off by the most unassuming agents of the Kraken.

The man was not a fighter. He walked with decent balance but didn't possess much in his upper body. His hair, though now a frazzled mess, looked taken care of in better days. If he worked, it was inside.

The woman, though hurt worse, had more steel. Even clutching her ribs, she refused help sitting down. And she had not sheathed her bloodied dagger. The man helped her down anyway.

Which is more stubborn? Des wondered. She would sometimes ask the same of herself and Luc.

They eased back on the divan, leaning against each other and sharing a long look. Des also wondered what passed between them. Had it been her and Ari, it might have gone something like, *"You're hurt." "You more." "But we're here. Are we safe now?" "Not yet. We Might never be." "I don't care. We'll protect each other." "You didn't protect me."*

Des arrested her thoughts. She didn't need that shit again— not now. The guilt was devious. So many innocuous images could make her mind betray her.

The vampires kissed. Des went into the kitchen. There, Sevex was pouring wine in the fifth glass on a tray. She noted how much was gone from the bottle—too much for the drinks.

"I assure you, they can be trusted," Sevex said, balancing the tray on one steady hand. "More so than a smuggler, I'm sure."

Des smirked. "I told you, I just kept watch."

"And I merely assembled Luc's hand, but neither entity would operate without us." He passed into the sitting room, and Des followed.

Luc was in there now, in a chair opposite the vampires. He had removed his sword belt and one leather gauntlet but still wore the left glove.

"I'm afraid my skill is not much in healing," the priest was saying. "I'm as disappointed in that as you, I'm sure."

"It's not that bad," the woman said. "Probably just bruised. Quit doting."

"Alright," her partner said, draping one arm around her.

Sevex set the tray of drinks on a low table, handing glasses to his latest guests. "Introductions," he said. "Des, this is Francesca Darani and Azran. Old friends of mine—quite old, in Azran's case."

"A year younger than you, ass."

"Ha, indeed so. And this is Desalie Vate and Lucian."

"No last name?" Azran asked.

"I never much cared for it," Luc said.

Azran raised his glass. "Cheers to that."

"Just Des is fine." She took the remaining glass. "So, word is you lot started this bloody mess."

Sevex nodded, swallowing a big gulp. "Yes, I was quite hoping you might illuminate this. All that with the Godshadows—"

"Doesn't mean we know any more than you," Azran said. He leaned forward. "And it's been fucking us over so far. By now, our flat is probably ashes."

"Easy," Des said. "We never accused you of anything."

"But she is holding something back," Luc said, staring at Francesca.

Azran followed the gaze. "But you said you didn't—"

"I don't," she started. "I don't know, exactly. But my brother is involved."

"Lots of people we know are," Azran said.

Francesca shook her head. "Not like he is. That thing with Lady Ciusa?"

"The person you didn't kill?"

"Yeah. It wasn't just because she was a bitch. The clan chose her carefully. Her death was important, and I'd guess it had something to do with this."

Azran sat back.

"What clan?" Luc asked.

"Filvié Noctirin," Francesca replied.

Sevex nodded. "As I thought. That has been the gossip among the government fellows. I suppose they could only be pushed so far before they struck back."

"No, there's more," Francesca said. "There has to be, otherwise Amadore wouldn't care. Tenebra must be involved for my brother to be."

"That would explain why the Solari are out in such force," Luc said.

"Great." Des rolled her eyes. "More priests."

Francesca sighed and chuckled. "You don't know the half of it."

"Her brother's a bit zealous," Azran added.

"But I don't know what his plans are. I never wanted to." Francesca took a long drink.

Silence stretched over the room.

"So, we still don't know anything," Des said after the pause.

"'We?'" Francesca asked. "And just who are you two, anyway?"

"Friends," Sevex said. He nodded to Azran. "I've been working at that. Turns out, favors are a good starting point."

Des looked away. She hated the word "favor." It took her back to Forente, where a lend always put you in debt.

Sevex stared at Luc. His eyes flicked to the priest's gloved hand. "It's alright, they won't judge. Believe me, they stand out more in a crowd than you."

"Chains, Sev, can you ease it back a bit?" Azran asked. "We almost get killed just trying to get to your house and—you're just making a rough night rougher, okay?"

Sevex stepped back and assumed the expression of a scolded dog. "Sorry."

"It's fine." Azran paused. "How much have you had to drink tonight?"

"Enough, it would seem."

Another silence stretched, broken by the cling of Luc's glass returning to the tray. He held up his left hand and pulled off the gauntlet. Beneath was what looked like another glove, but thin and made of dull metal lames. He clenched and unclenched, then spread the fingers apart. With each stiff movement, the metal clinked.

Azran and Francesca both leaned forward, peering at the appendage.

"What—" Azran started to ask.

"As I said, I'm not much of a healer. I blocked an axe with my wrist. My patchwork was so clumsy, every healer we went to said it was beyond repair. The nerves reconnected wrong. When we came to Aure, we heard about—"

"The clockwork." Azran looked at Sevex, who stood straight and smiled.

"I'm part of the anatomy team, I suppose," Sevex said. "I learned to build working hands—well, mostly working—for—it's not important. Secret projects. Anyway, I copied some notes for the soul magic component, took some spare parts no one would miss, and...." He gestured at the mechanical hand.

"Amazing," Azran said, still gawking. Francesca nodded.

"It's not perfect."

"I used to use both swords at once," Luc said. "I still do sometimes, but the left doesn't do much these days."

"Soon," Sevex said. "Oh, you should see the work we're doing." He stared through the wall.

"So, I owe Sevex," Luc said.

Des leaned on the backrest of his chair. "And I owe Luc. I started that fight."

Luc craned his neck. "I told you, it was my decision."

Des knew he wouldn't have been so wounded going up against that axeman if she hadn't first driven him into picking a fight with a whole den of thieves to prove his fucking point. She never told him she had considered leaving him to die. She didn't want her weight to be his.

"So, what now?" Francesca asked. "Are we just going to drink all night?"

"What else?" Sevex asked.

"Depends if the Solari come back," Luc said.

"I wouldn't put it past them." Francesca caught Des's curious expression. "They executed three vampires right out there."

"Chains of Crusix. Where are the guards?"

"Probably nearer the palace," Azran said. "But I don't think they'd stop some vigilante vampire slayers."

"Especially now that it's legal. There's a good argument for the drinking." Francesca finished her wine, letting the remnant drops run down the glass into her mouth.

"It hasn't been ratified yet," Sevex said.

"Doesn't matter. Just that it's on the table is—fuck. It's fucked."

Luc slid his gauntlet back on and picked up his arming sword. "I'll just go have a look."

5

The tenebrous priest glided across the floor. His feet skimmed the marble surface, barely touching. His body felt as elevated as his spirit. He felt his Goddess this night. The efforts of ascending and descending the stairs were reversed; up was the natural direction. And so, up he went. He longed for that newly vacant space atop the tallest spire of Ciusa's manor—one of the highest points in Aure, surpassed only by the Academy spires and the Tower of Solris at the Golden Palace.

He saw no other vampires as he spiraled up. Filvié Noctirin was hard at work in the city, securing the territory and stalking the few stragglers, deserters and enemies alike.

At last, he alighted on weathered stone beneath the cool night and basked in the glorious absence of the sun. The sky-light was gone, but the city was lit like the day. Lamps crisscrossed the scape like lines on a grid below the hilltop spire. And among and between the golden lamps was orange. From this vantage, the scattered fires danced like candles, their smoke rising like incense.

How the priest hated the light. But it could not dampen him— he knew darkness would soon follow. Like a dead forest burns before beauty can grow, so must the sun shine before the eclipse.

So soon. So many years of preparation. For a century, Tenebra's voice in the Mortal Realm had been silenced. Only recently had one of Her angels returned to speak Her wishes—and glorious wishes they were. A plot only the Shadow Herself could conceive. Her servants would draw Her through the Seal the other gods had placed between the realms. She would take a mortal vessel and, once here, no deity would be able to stop Her—they would be held captive by their own oaths. No other mortals had such a ritual at their disposal. The idealistic Godshadows would be helpless to prevent this transgression, for their precious shadeseers remembered the source of their clairsentience. They would not betray the angels.

Tenebra and the vampires—Her blessed servants, Her priests and pilgrims—would seize the Valentreid throne. They would take this dying empire and direct it to do what the aged, impotent Valentreid Dynasty could not—march west and destroy those dragon-worshipping heretics of the Faith of Fire. They would quench the unholy inferno of Darachzartha. They would restore faith in the Pantheon and raise Tenebra and all Risen Gods above their lowly status in the condescending eyes of those who served the First and the Interlopers. With a few steps into the light, the Shadow would cast Her presence across the world.

The other gods—the arrogant First, the many-faced Interlopers, and those Risen who remain their pawns—none would dare come for Her. A divine conflict would wreak havoc on the Mortal Realm. A lone divinity would rule uncontested.

The priest shuddered in anticipation—the power of a goddess on this side of the Seal, combined with the hidden strength of Filvié Noctirin. The living had no idea what the clan was capable of. They kept it secret, by Her command, until the time was right.

So soon.

"Amadore."

He opened his eyes. Zerexis lounged against the railing to his right, staring across the tower. Against the backdrop of the sky, the angel's dusky skin, black locks, and matching feathered wings made them indistinct. They were a void in the stars, and their eyes were holes to deeper nothing.

"Night," said the priest. "And such a wondrous one."

"And yet, there is a chain tethering you to the ground." Zerexis turned their inky gaze on the vampire. "Much as you might deny it."

The priest's lanky frame slouched beneath his robes. "My sister did not come when I called. She lied again—dear Francesca."

"And what does it matter? If she has not joined the Goddess's cause—"

"Yet," said the priest, leaning toward Zerexis, eyes cast down. "She is but lost. She must find her way back. I can guide her, I know it."

The angel's enormous wings fluttered in the open space—a tic of theirs. "But have we need of her? Her blood is as yours, and that would be a great boon. But Tenebra does not require a unique vessel. I have spoken with the Noblest of the clan. They think her a liability."

The priest stepped closer, looming. "You do not need her. But you need me, and I need her."

Zerexis straightened, now taller even than the priest. "You may overestimate your own importance, mortal."

The darkness around the priest deepened and solidified. His fraying silk cloak, little thicker than a burial shroud, swayed despite the still air. Red eyes became black as the angel's, and his voice like echoes in the pits of Tartarus.

"I disagree. She has chosen me to guide the ritual—me, above all Her other priests, above even the Noblest of the clan. I am as vital to its completion as you, immortal."

Zerexis backed off a step. "Very well. By all means, waste our resources to complete your hollow notion of family."

The shadows faded. Amadore looked out over the city once more.

Then, skipping the intervening space, Zerexis appeared on his left. The angel seized the vampire's arm and twisted it out from under the robes. The limb was a decrepit thing—pale, sharp, gnarled, curved in the fore and ending in fingers with jagged knuckles.

"But remember what you have already sacrificed," said Zerexis. "Angels of Shade are not charitable. Tenebra does not give, but takes."

The angel released the arm and vanished.

Amadore caressed the withered flesh with his good hand. He was well aware of the cost. Family was not hollow. Without it, what was the point of sacrifice?

He heard footsteps coming up the stairs. It was Alir, short and soft-spoken. Ex-Requiem. Few assassins who left ever killed again, but not even the guild's master dared to start a shadow war with Filvié Noctirin.

"More soldiers are entering the city," said Alir. "And the Solari are gathering quite the mob."

"We will retreat soon enough," said Amadore. "Did you breach the palace?"

"No. The Dragonblades killed the team we sent."

The shroud flared a moment. "Still a victory," muttered the priest. "I have one last task for you before the rest pull back. I believe it fitting for you, as you were deceived by her."

Alir bowed his head.

"Go, then."

The assassin hesitated. "Where is she?"

Amadore reached out with the gnarled hand. Alir recoiled, but the priest's reach was long. One bony finger touched Alir's forehead. Both saw a lane of looted houses, only a few untouched. The vision shifted to one, then inside, to a quintet in an immaculate sitting room. They saw Francesca.

The arm retreated under the shroud.

"Go, then." Amadore paid no heed as his thrall padded down the stairs. He had one other, minor task before the vile sun rose.

He projected himself into memories, first his own, then into dear Francesca's, and through her, brushed the faint soul of the owner of this tower—the woman his sister was supposed to have killed.

He had an end to tie, and a thirst to sate.

● ● ●

Luc had lost count of his laps around the house. Only the occasional, distant scream disturbed the still street. He yawned. Dawn was still hours away, but he wasn't used to being awake so late.

Des should be the one out here, he thought. She seemed more restless than him. Seeing a pair of lovers sometimes had that effect on her. She claimed to have accepted Ari's death, but clearly still held onto some grief. No, not grief—guilt. She lived in a world of guilt.

Luc flexed his clockwork hand, feeling the dull sensations the threads of magic provided. He hoped there was another reason Des hadn't left yet. He never blamed her, not after months of carrying a dead hand on his wrist, not even after his umpteenth drink on a bad night.

He yawned again, stretched, and took one last look up and down the avenue. He opened the door, waited for the blade to swing past, and hopped through.

• • •

Around the corner of the doorframe, Azran caught a glimpse of Luc resetting the trap and locking the door.

Sevex was passed out in a soft armchair, half-curled with his legs tucked close. The others were wide awake.

"Anything?" Des asked.

"No, it's clear." Luc unbelted his sword and sat on the floor, his back against Des's chair—the one he'd been sitting in earlier. "How are things in here?"

"We were talking about leaving the city," Francesca said.

"At least for a while," Azran added.

"And I might have a way out," Des said.

"How?" Luc asked. "Not Kraken connections."

"Not quite. Away from the coast, the guild's oversight is lax. You get a lot of adjacent groups, splinter factions, and such. They all do business with each other, but the Kraken's had a year to calm down since our run-in. And if there were a price on my head for killing Ecar, we'd know by now." Des looked back to

Francesca. "I can set up a meeting, but it won't be cheap. Smuggling people isn't easy."

Francesca tapped a pouch on her belt. "I kept a few souvenirs from my last job."

"You smuggle a lot of people?" Azran asked.

Des didn't meet his gaze. "I didn't smuggle. I was security. And that was mostly jungle goods, which don't include slaves."

"Mostly?"

She finally looked at him. "Mostly."

"Hey, fop," Luc said. "Des did more hurt to those bastards in Forente in one night than you have your whole life."

"Luc." Des put a hand on his shoulder.

"At least I never helped them," Azran said. "My coins are clean."

Luc stood. "Your girl's aren't."

Des grabbed his sleeve, but he pulled away.

Azran stood in response. "Just how would you know?"

"Azran, sit down," Francesca said.

He looked at her and pointed at Luc and Des. "They're killers. I don't know who Ecar is, but what kind of security work do you think the Kraken offers?"

Luc scoffed. "Forgive me if I ignore moral judgment from undead."

Azran snapped back to him. "We're not undead."

"Bullshit. Even I have enough sight to sense your unliving souls."

"He never said we were alive," Francesca interjected. "But we're not undead."

"I'm confused," Des said.

Francesca sighed. "My brother explained it like this. Undead souls are stitched together from the fragments left after someone dies, which is why it has to be done so soon postmortem. They're missing pieces of who they were. Back home in Ostitel, we heard plenty of night stories about the arisen soldiers of the Fated Legion during the conquest."

She paused to gauge their reactions. Azran had heard all this before but never felt like he fully grasped the information. Des looked curious, while Luc continued to sneer.

"Vampires are different. We don't die. Blood contains a physical essence of the soul. When a vampire drinks blood from a living person, it mingles with their own and picks up traces of the vampire's soul. The partial death...cracks the living soul. If the mixed blood is reintroduced into the dying person, the vampire's soul essence fills those cracks. That changes the imprint of the soul, and by extension, the new vampire's body. Maybe we aren't alive, but we're clearly not dead, and definitely not undead."

"Still not natural," Luc muttered.

"Not natural?" Azran repeated. "What do you call that glowing shit outside? Looked like soul manipulation to me."

"Nice tattoo," Luc said, nodding at Azran's outstretched dragon sleeve. "Pick that up in Charir?"

Azran brandished the ink. "It's Caelix, you imbecile, and it's art. If you think this makes me some heretic traitor, you'd lose your shit at the sleeves in Lunatel."

Luc took a step forward. Des stood and interposed herself between them.

"Luc, enough. You trying to start shit?"

He kept his gaze locked on Azran, who lowered his arm.

"Whas goin on?"

They all looked at Sevex, who was glancing from person to person with bleary eyes.

"Nothing, Sev," Azran said. "Just some tension snapping. Go back to sleep."

Sevex shook his head, but slowly. He held one hand to his temple, then moved it down to rub the sleep out of his eyes. "Can't. Headache. One cure for that." He grabbed his empty glass and headed for the kitchen.

Azran followed. "Sev, no. I'll get you some water, and you can go back to sleep."

"This will serve the same purpose. Besides, this is no night for sleeping."

Azran watched Sevex pour the remaining wine, and then, movement out the window caught his attention. "Sev, someone's out there."

Sevex started back for the sitting room, almost tripping on his third step. "Just the shrubberies in the wind."

Azran approached the window. He couldn't see details in the glare. He snuffed the lamp on the counter.

Those weren't shrubberies.

"Sevex, do you have some secret passages, by chance?" he called, leaving the kitchen. "The Solari came back."

"Shit." Des peeked over the sill of the sitting room's window. "Well, Sev?"

Sevex gulped half of his wine. "Fortunate that you ask now, rather than thirty years ago."

Azran pinched the bridge of his nose. "What?"

"After the Rising Fire, the empire became quite concerned with protecting—"

"Out with it!"

"Cellar. Door to tunnels. Locks from the other side."

The front doors banged and wood cracked.

"Let's go," Des said, taking Sev's glass and placing it on the table.

Francesca stood, answering Azran's concerned look with, "As long as I don't have to run."

Luc drew his arming sword and approached the foyer as the vigilantes struck the doors again.

Des touched his shoulder. "Remember Inks?"

An axe blade poked through with a crack. A mahogany splinter clattered to the floor.

"Yes. I killed fourteen."

"And you said you should have listened to me."

There was a pause in the blows, and then another struck near the latch.

"I remember." Luc followed her through the kitchen, joining the others.

At the door to the cellar, Sevex pulled up short. "My notes."

"No time." Azran pushed him forward.

"You don't understand. It's—can't say, but I need them." He went around Azran, who grabbed him and spun around him like a dancer back toward the cellar.

"Then I'll get them. Where?"

"Upstairs master bed drawing desk bottom right drawer."

"On it." Azran bounded off as Sevex and Francesca started down the steps. Behind him, he heard Luc ask, "Shouldn't we stick together?"

"Don't worry," Francesca said. The tremble in her voice was almost unnoticeable. "He does this."

"Always has," Sevex added.

Azran passed the foyer just as the doors burst open. As he ran up the stairs, he heard a cry of pain and a heavy thump. He grinned and shook his head—Sevex had thrown that trap together while drunk. Another thought crossed his mind, and he was suddenly much more interested in those notes—what could Sev do sober? Other than design a mechanical hand, of course.

Azran didn't take in any details of the second floor or master bedchamber. He focused on his task, and the rest blurred by.

Drawing desk. Bottom right drawer.

He retrieved a tall and thick book, bound in leather and tied shut. He turned to go, and a yellow-robed man with a crude mace blocked his path.

"Filthy bloodsucker," the man said, coming forward and reaching for Azran with a corded arm.

Azran launched himself past, ducking and using his free hand to keep wide of the man's arm. Then, like a spring releasing tension, he sprinted down the hallway.

Another priest topped the stairs and ran toward him. Azran hopped sideways into a guest room, getting between the door and the wall. Once he heard the footsteps reach the frame, he slammed the door into the priest, then slunk around the dazed man.

But the one with the mace was there, too. He grabbed the back of Azran's coat collar and swung the metal club. Azran went limp and dropped the book, sliding from the coat sleeves as both hit the ground. The mace struck the wall; Azran grabbed the book and kept running.

He reached the stairs. At the bottom, a third priest lay sprawled, bleeding from his throat. A fourth, also down, grasped the blade entering his chest and whimpered as he tried to stop it. A woman in a midnight blue cloak drove it in farther, but slowly.

Seeing this, hearing the two priests behind him, Azran hopped the railing. He dropped twelve feet, using his little forward momentum to roll. The hardwood floor still hurt, but not as much as stone streets and slate rooftops.

The killer ripped her sword out, whirling on Azran and splattering droplets of blood on his face. "Alir!" the woman, a vampire, called.

Azran kept running but couldn't help a glance into the foyer. A corpse with its torso nearly cloven clutched a woodcutter's axe. Two other bodies sported more mundane wounds, and two figures stood upright, both in dark cloaks and holding bloodied blades. One walked toward him.

Kitchen. Stairs. Cellar.

Without speaking, Azran waved the others onward. They entered the passageway. Sevex closed the door and flipped a lever. Dull sliding and thuds sounded from inside the steel plates.

"Is there no bar?" Luc asked.

"Five," Sevex said. "All set, on all sides. And, the other side's handle is retracted."

"That's even better than the Inks office," Des said.

"Blood." Francesca wiped Azran's face with her sleeve.

"Not mine," he said. "I think your brother's upset. I saw three vampires up there."

"How did he find us?"

Azran shrugged. He handed Sevex the book. "I hope these are as intriguing as I suspect."

Sevex breathed a sigh of relief and ran a hand over the cover. "Oh, I imagine so."

He picked up a lantern and descended. At the bottom of the steps, they started down a tunnel, double-file. They passed other stairwells, some with light leaking down. Apparently, Sevex's neighbors were content waiting by their doors. It was quiet except for their shuffling feet.

After a minute of walking, Francesca whispered to Azran, "Where's your coat?"

"Last I saw, in the hands of a very slow Solar."

She smiled and rested her head on his shoulder. "You're a fucking idiot."

He smiled back. "I know." A bit louder, he said, "This reminds me of the old days, eh, Sev? These passages are a bit bigger than your family's, though."

"Yes, but more straightforward. Remember when we got lost under the north wing?"

"All afternoon. I thought your mum was going to kill us."

Sevex chuckled.

"Speaking of the old days," Azran went on, "your family is quite welcoming. They never complained when I showed up and stayed the night. And they're all the way in Lunatel."

"You propose you and Francesca hide out there."

"I don't think it's a bad idea."

Sevex nodded. "I fear I may have to find new lodgings as well. It seems my home belongs to others, now."

Azran grabbed his arm, stopping him. Sevex turned.

"I'm sorry this happened."

Sevex gave a half-smile and shook his head, glancing at the tunnel floor. "I invited you. I knew the risks of that. That house was never quite mine to begin with, and, I must say, this is the most exciting night I've had in some time."

"Like the old days, huh?"

Sevex's face grew grim. "More like that night you helped kill a pair of Godshadows."

He started forward again. Azran followed after a moment's hesitation.

Des laughed softly. "I think we all have some stories to tell."

"He's oversimplifying the situation," Azran said.

"As you did to ours earlier."

"I didn't kill anyone. I just fought back."

Des's grin vanished. "So did I. That Ecar you seemed so concerned about? He had it coming. My fiancée and I left Forente. We got out. He got sore about it and ordered her death. I repaid the debt."

Again they walked in silence. Finally, Azran said, "Sorry I assumed. I can't imagine what that would feel like."

Francesca interlaced her fingers with his.

"No," Des said. "Neither could I, before it happened. I'm still not sure I know how it feels." She paused. "Just be prepared, you two. Seems like you're leaving someone sore, too."

The tunnel delved onward. The side passages, at first regular, became less consistent. Long minutes passed at a time without Azran spotting one. The stonework changed as they entered older sections, then newer. The old blocks were elongated, but thin, compressed over centuries. Some had been dislodged by the shifting foundations, leaving crooked, black gaps.

"Some of the passages are Antiqiri, they say," Sevex whispered. The sound of his voice broke the rhythm of their scuffing footfalls. "There are more below, but most have been crushed by the weight of the city."

The others found themselves suddenly aware of that weight. They followed each other's glances to the ceiling.

Undeterred, Sevex continued, "Amazing, isn't it, that even this much has held up over fourteen centuries?"

"Amazing, yeah," Francesca said.

Azran shared an uneasy, helpless smirk with her. "But where does this one lead?" he asked. He had hoped it would be apparent by now.

"West," Sevex replied. "So far, at least."

"And then?"

Sevex stopped, bringing them all to a halt. "Outside the city, likely. I know east leads to the palace, and I thought it best we avoid that. Most of the side tunnels are dead ends, for our purposes." He glanced between his companions' faces, which wore varying degrees of disbelief. "West."

Sevex continued onward. Des nudged Azran with her shoulder, nodding to drop back a few paces. Out of earshot, she said, "You've known him longer than me. Does he know something I don't, or is he making this up as he goes?"

"Sevex knows lots of things other people don't, but I'd bet on a bit of both."

"Right. Because I know a way. Maybe not the best way, but it's a path forward." Des gestured at the walls. "You catch any of those marks by some of the side tunnels? Smugglers' signs."

"Why didn't you speak up?"

"I haven't seen the right one yet."

Azran gave her a nod, and they quickened their strides to catch up. Perhaps another quarter mile went by before they reached newer masonry, an intersection with three side passages to the right and two to the left.

"Hold on." Des took the lantern—its oil was running quite low—from Sevex and examined the edges of the openings. Azran peered over her shoulder and saw crude pictographs etched into the stone. She glanced at the first left tunnel's signs, then moved on. The second held her attention longer. It bore a jagged wave pattern, a key inside a square, an eye, a stick figure sitting, and a group of four running.

"This will get us outside the walls," she said. "There's storage and a watcher's office. It looks like they have horses, too."

"Who?" Sevex asked.

"The Kraken," Luc said.

Des shook her head. "Not quite."

"Is this really the best option?" the priest pressed.

"It's what we were going to do before the house was compromised," Francesca said. She looked down the main tunnel. "Besides, if it's some kind of waypost, we won't get trapped between the sun and the tunnel."

Luc shifted. "What happens if you're caught in the sun?"

"We won't burst into flames," Azran said. "Despite what you may have heard. But it won't be pretty. It's like poison. And there's no cure but to get back in the shade before it kills you."

"A gift Sola gave us once Tenebra became a goddess," Francesca added.

Des met each of their eyes. With no one outright refusing, she led the way into the smuggler's tunnel. "Let me do the talking." She sent a hard glance back to Luc.

Unlike the main tunnel, this passage wound and curved, almost backtracking on occasion. At the extreme of each bend was a closed door. It seemed the tunnel was carved to have many access points.

"What was this place before the Kraken came?" Azran asked.

"There are always smugglers," Des said. "Always will be."

Eventually, the doors ceased. The tunnel straightened and sloped down gently. Another light appeared, but it did not flicker like the lantern; it glowed and bobbed like a wisp. The group stopped as the source approached, hovering just behind a woman in dark leathers. She was flanked by a forlire whose subtle tusks and dusky skin leaned more toward the orc side than human, and a man who seemed quite bored by the knife spinning between his fingers.

"Don't see sitter," the woman said. "Got some other carry, or just bogged?"

"Striding," Des said. "No cazzes here."

"Well, stride back the way you come. Gild's flinting, and so we're keepered till it ain't."

"Your lot looks nervous," the forlire said. "Bogged, too."

"You bring stows?" the woman asked.

The other man caught his knife.

"They got keys," Des said. "Enough to stride, at least."

"Yeah, from who?"

"Watcher Ecar, in Capital."

The woman looked to the knife-wielder.

"Dead," he said. "Inks Massacre."

"That so?" Des smirked. "Looks like we got more keys than I thought."

The woman cocked her head. "Might we can stamp. Gonna need heavy jingle, though. Ain't no dogs but our dogs tonight."

"Level," Des said.

The trio stepped aside, and the woman jerked her head farther down the passage. "After you, stows."

6

They entered the smuggling den through an open, ironbound door. Another agent, a man with far too many pockets, closed and barred it, watching the newcomers sidelong. Inside was a wide space supported by old pillars. Every inch of wall was hidden by barrels and crates. A motley workforce sat and leaned about. Some slept, though a few perked up or nodded at the woman, who now took the lead. Her magical light went out, its illumination replaced by glass globes hanging from the ceiling. They resembled Aure's streetlamps, perhaps too closely. Des snuffed the flickering lantern and left it at the door.

Another passage, almost a finished hallway, yawned at the far end of the stone warehouse. Doors lined either side. Here, the woman stopped and turned.

"You," she said, pointing at Des. "Follow me to my office. Bring whichever stow has the coin. The rest of you, take rest in there."

Without waiting for a response, she strode farther down the hall, turned a key, and vanished into a side room.

Des stepped forward, glancing back. Francesca followed. The knife man, hands now still, also came. Des could feel his eyes fixed on her back. The third man watched the remaining four enter something resembling a troglodyte's lounge, then left for the main chamber.

The office was large enough to squeeze perhaps ten people inside. A tarnished and scratched oak desk dominated the space, and like the shelves behind it, was piled high with papers and small parcels. A high-backed chair of pristine ebony, sporting silver trim and red cushions, was out of place by comparison. The woman sat there and motioned Des and Francesca to the worn and bare seats in front of the desk. The knife man closed the door and stood by it.

The woman swept back her light hair. "Now, then—business. Where you headed?"

Francesca looked at Des, who nodded. "Lunatel."

"Interesting. I see more people headed east these days. What's your name, stow?"

"Francesca."

"Hm. That's Ostiteli, yeah?"

She nodded.

"Not your first time on the road, then." The woman nodded in return. "Call me Sayel." She looked at Des.

"Ari," Des said.

"Well, Ari, Fran—Lunatel's a long journey. And judging by the size of your purse, you can't afford us to hold your hands the whole way."

"We'd be happy just getting Aure at our backs," Des replied. "Just a day or two."

"Whose days—yours or a forerunner's?"

Des saw Francesca's confusion. "Horse."

"How much would that be?" Francesca asked.

"For five?" Sayel paused. "Looking at ten argi a day, plus collateral, on top of stride fees."

"Stride fees?"

"We don't have to let you through. And really, we're taking a risk taking in two vamps." Sayel began counting off with her fingers. "So, we got routine passage, extra for risk, plus the horses for, aye, let's say two days. And, you're gonna need some kinda cover if you're going at night with this clusterfuck happening."

"How much?" Des asked, biting the inside of her cheek. She hated being at another's advantage.

"How much you got?"

Francesca reached for her purse, but Des stopped her.

"We have money, but money's not why you let us in."

Sayel leaned back in the ebony chair and interlaced her fingers. "Aye. Inks Massacre happened more than a year ago, and you say the watcher there is still alive?"

"Alive, but not there," Des said.

"This parch came straight from Capital."

"But Ecar's body was never found, was it?"

Sayel rested her chin on one hand, waiting.

"I don't know how detailed your news was. Don't know if it mentioned the boat by his escape passage was also missing."

"And what do you know of it?"

"I ran lock for him. He rose and fell pretty quick. Lived by his gut more than his brain, and his gut got him into a bad stamp. The merchant involved hired killers—some freelancers Requiem had yet to deal with. I know about the boat because I used it to get him and me out of Downing."

"And where is he now?" Sayel asked.

"Equotel. A town called Salles, where he's sitting on a nice pile he nipped in his wing."

Sayel waited a long moment, staring at her inkwell.

Des continued, "That ought to—"

Sayel stopped her with a raised finger, eyes still on the little vessel. Then, she looked past her guests to the knife man. He was so quiet, Des had almost forgotten he was there—and that quality, she thought, made him more dangerous than all his fancy knife tricks did.

"Aerna for your thoughts," Sayel said, snatching a copper coin from her desk.

The knife man held up a hand and caught the payment. He looked at Des and said, "We received a bounty promise with news of the Inks Massacre. The Kraken would likely have had no lead on the responsible party but for a turncoat who, given the right motivation, still played both sides. He told a story nearly as grand as your own—perhaps grander, as this one carried a hint of romantic tragedy. He gave two names—Arilysa Talbre, dead, and Desalie Vate, alive."

Des clenched one fist. The other eased toward her boot. She tried to appear calm, but a storm raged inside her, making her jaw lock and knuckles whiten. *Tiber, that rat-hearted son of a bitch!*

"Remind me to give you a gold one of these days," Sayel said. "Good gods, how do you remember all that?"

"I listen," the knife man said. "Desalie—you would be dead scarcely after your blade left its sheath."

Sayel laughed. "The bounty's long expired. And I'd rather not tangle with the Atoran you got waiting out there. I remember that part of the tale, at least."

Des said nothing, so Francesca spoke up. "Dare I ask where we go from here?"

Sayel, still bemused, said, "Lunatel."

Des's gaze whirled from the knife man to her.

"My offer still stands," Sayel said. "Assuming we got what we wanted?"

"How did you kill him?" the knife man asked.

Des hesitated but spoke evenly. "Salted him."

The knife man nodded. "You are capable of a powerful hate." Relaxed, he pulled a small blade and twirled it between his fingers.

• • •

The lounge was a makeshift affair, a spare room with furniture hammered together from old crates—a couple tables, four chairs to each, and a bench along one rough-hewn stone wall. A man and a woman sat at one table, playing cards. He wore a leather vest with no shirt; she, a skirt and blouse with hems that said expensive, but were soiled by dirt and dust. Neither acknowledged the presence of strangers. The only sounds were the light slaps of cards on wood and a door latching shut down the hall.

Azran sat at the empty table. He stayed upright a moment, then laid his head sideways on the cushion of his arms. His foot bounced, though, still jittery.

Luc sat on the bench, leaning back onto its rounded rest. He only half-closed his eyes. His swords protruded awkwardly to his sides, but he didn't seem to care.

Sevex sat at Azran's table, gingerly placing his leather-bound book on top. He watched the cards, counting to pass the time, until his eyelids drooped and he, too, buried his face in his arms.

At that point, Azran turned his chair to face Luc. "Is this going to work?"

"In the long run, I'm unsure," Luc said. "But I've seen Des talk her way into more dangerous places than this. This is her world."

"You said 'into.' We're not talking our way out?"

Luc nodded. The corner of his mouth lifted a little. "That's the hard part, and why I'm not sleeping just yet."

From his periphery, Azran caught the slightest glance from the card players. Their game slowed.

No more fighting tonight, Azran silently pleaded, closing his eyes. He remembered the soldiers falling, the looters going still, the Solar with a foot of steel in his chest, his blade entering an orc's eye by another's hand. He remembered hitting the ground, seeing Francesca there as well. It wasn't just images—the thuds, the scrape and hiss of blade on flesh. The smell of blood—something he knew well, but so rarely in the context of fear and pain, of anger, of violence.

The memories were hours old. They felt eerily present and as distant as his blurry childhood. Sitting in the quiet room, he felt both removed from and consumed by them, and he wasn't sure which he preferred. The few other times he had seen that much blood loomed on the edge of his consciousness. He wanted to scream.

Footsteps. Talking.

The card players left. Azran absently watched them go. At the door, he saw Francesca and Des. His wife came over to him. She smiled at the sleeping form of Sevex, then looked at Azran.

"Did you hear me?"

He shook his head.

"I said they'll let us stay until tomorrow night, then send us off with horses."

Azran nodded and rubbed his eyes. "How much did it cost?"

"Most of what we had. But Des says we made off as best we could." Francesca pulled a tiny figurine from her shirt pocket, a delicate silver dove on a fine chain. "Still have this, though."

Azran nodded again. "Still pretty."

"Your hands are trembling," Francesca said. "Are you okay?"

He folded his arms. "I'm fine. Just tired."

"Well, let's get some rest," Des said. "They're putting us up in the stable."

"Is that a joke?" Luc asked, standing and stretching.

"No, it's practical. It lets them keep us away from the real valuables."

Francesca snorted. "And according to the boss here, smelling like horses will help our story—we're to pass as private messengers until we're well away from Aure."

Azran shook Sevex awake.

"Shove off," he mumbled.

Azran began sliding the book away. Sevex bolted up, clutching the tome.

"Oh, are we going?" He yawned.

"Just a little ways," Des said, leading.

Sleep was restless. Comings and goings, people and horses woke Azran several times an hour—as best he could figure—until his mounting weariness allowed him to sleep deeper by the afternoon. He kept his shirt over his eyes to get some darkness but peeked out at every interruption to check the daylight under the doors.

His dreams were quick, fleeting things. He fought people whose faces he couldn't recall. And he ran—there was so much running. By the time dark came, he was a sweaty mess and had an ache in his shoulder from the hard, straw-covered floor.

Francesca lay near him, but with her back turned. She looked just as disheveled. It was autumn, but they slept at the mercy of lingering summer heat.

Azran rose and left her, heading back into the deeper caves. He carried his shirt over his shoulder until an odd draft chilled his damp skin and he pulled it on. He picked stray bits of hay from his pants and hair as he walked.

He caught the smell of smoked meat and followed it to a mess hall as crude as the lounge. Des was there, the remains of a late supper pushed to her side. She was talking with the forlire man from before. They sat on opposite sides of a long table made of several short ones placed end to end. The smell wafted from a small kitchen and pantry to one side of the room.

Des and the man both looked up as Azran entered.

"Good," she said. "About time one of you woke up. This is Galex—Gax. He's in charge of the horses."

The man nodded. "I need to know where you'll be taking my beasts."

Azran rubbed one eye. "Down by the Valla. I know the way."

Gax picked up a rolled-up map from the bench and spread it out on the table, using a knife and cup as weights.

Azran stared at the cluster of labels, then shook his head. "First things first—you got coffee?"

Half a cup and a few bites of meat later, Azran tried again. "Town's not on here, but it's just west of Dacaro, right on the Valla River." He pointed out the spot.

"Right," Gax said. "Most direct route's Elta, then south till you hit the latitude."

"There's a lot of big cities that way," Azran said.

Gax looked at Des. "I thought you said you were clean."

"Since when has that stopped the capes?" she replied. To Azran, she said, "It's easier to blend in when there's more people."

"Not the way I'm used to." He sipped his coffee. "Besides, Noctirin's looking for us, and they're in the cities."

"Look," Gax said, "I don't care which way you take once you leave the horses. Two days'll take you to Elta. A few miles southwest is one of our waystations, at this little crossroads. Rest is up to you."

Azran glanced at the brusque man, then returned to the map. The fingers of his right hand plunked out a tuneless melody on the table.

After the third repetition, Gax said, "You a musician or something?"

Azran stopped. "Something, yeah. My fingers get jittery sometimes. This is about when I'd start playing on a normal night."

A twinkle appeared in Gax's eye. "No shit."

7

Amadore again stalked the night. The streets were silent and empty but for scattered reminders of recent violence. A corpse lay here, another there. An odd light shone behind drawn curtains or tight shutters—desperate wards lit by desperate living. They were not his concern.

His quarry had hidden far from her home, placing her pride aside and fleeing to a servants' tenement outside the Rosaer Hills. But now, he sensed her moving through the open night. She fled for the guards' barricades. Two accompanied her. If he so desired, Amadore could call for a dozen vampires to cut off Ciusa and her bodyguards. But he wanted the chase, the kills. He needed the thrill and the satisfaction after the confrontation with Zerexis, after speaking to Alir.

Dear Francesca, poor, lost. His initial fury at her subtle blasphemy—ignoring the path Tenebra's highest servants had set for her—had faded. Alir would find her soon enough, and Amadore would guide her to penitence and redemption. She had never killed on command, never killed unless threatened. Perhaps it had been foolish to think she would change so suddenly. This was not the first time Amadore had to remedy her mistakes. He could forgive her this minor betrayal. When she became one with the Goddess, dear Francesca would see how little her meager principles meant in the changing world. It was all means to the end.

Until then, he would remember what he was—an enlightened being. Though he had reason to hate Ciusa, to seek vengeance—it was her who whispered into the ears of the Senate that vampires should be eradicated, even while Francesca served her wine every night—that was not why Amadore was so eager to find on her. Many vampires—perhaps even most, these days—refused to drink mortal blood, Marexuri or otherwise. They were like Francesca with her petty rules. Ignorance prevented their self-actualization.

Vampires hunted. Living died.

There—Ciusa, hooded, but with no cloak on her soul, walked between two swordsmen. The guards watched their sides, their backs, the rooftops above, but their false hope clouded their judgment—to them, ahead was safety, and it was safe ahead. They could not detect Amadore in the frame of a burned-out door. The smell of charred wood lay thick, but the scent of living blood, vibrant, rushed along by fast-beating hearts, was even stronger.

Closer.

He could hear the hearts beating now, louder than boots on paving stones.

"Hold on," said the nearer swordsman. Hand on hilt, he peered into the shadows of the eve. His eyes stared past Amadore's. "Never mind."

So weak, these living.

He took three steps away, and Amadore struck. Purplish-black sparks cracked between his gnarled fingers as his twisted hand clawed into the guard's face from behind. He pulled, tearing flesh and shearing bone. A gurgle escaped the blood filling the living's throat, and the faceless man fell. His heart raced, then slowed.

"Gods above." It was only a gasp from the other guard. He drew his sword and shoved Ciusa behind with his free hand. Eyes wide, sweat beading, he thrust at Amadore.

The shadows carried the priest out of reach. He crouched, then sprang forward, bloodied hand leading.

The guard put his blade between Amadore's thumb and palm, attempting to cut through. The sword slid across the twisted flesh without harm. Behind his veil, Amadore grinned. The guard deserved some credit, though—he pressed on, swinging at Amadore's exposed side. That impervious hand lashed out like a striking viper. He caught the guard's wrist and crushed it.

Now the living showed distress—a cry of pain and a feeble haymaker from his other hand that met only the night air.

Amadore circled around, clutched the back of the man's neck with his unmarred hand, and drove him face-first into the street.

He straightened and turned to his prey. She stopped backing away, held by the weight of his eyeless gaze. He glided closer, pulling back his hood and veil.

"Stop!" There was unexpected steel in her voice. "I am Lady Marcia Ciusa, Fourth of Rosaer and protected by the Valentrae. You will leave me be, beast. I command you leave."

She dared command him? Dared disguise her fear with aristocratic bravado? She had wealth, nothing more. That held no authority, not now, when she was so helpless to wield it. Her place now was to grovel and beg, or perhaps face death with honesty—dignity did not preclude fear.

Amadore reached out with his mortal hand. When he pulled her cloak aside, the contact with her skin, warm and flushed with blood, almost distracted him. But he felt her intentions and caught the stiletto before it pierced his ribs. He ripped it from her grasp.

She tore free of her cloak and turned to run. In the darkness, she could not escape. He rushed in front of her, wrapped his hands around her throat and thrust her onto the ground. Her skull bounced off the flagstones. He knelt and dragged the stiletto blade across her throat.

Amadore smiled again as the metallic scent of living blood flooded the little space between them. He did not take pleasure in killing. It was a simple act in itself. But letting her blood go to waste would be just that—a waste. He deserved to drink, to derive some pleasure from the experience.

He gave himself over to the taste of blood, letting it consume him. This was right, and it was good. She was too weak to hold him back, feebler by the second as he sucked her strength away.

Boots scraped on the flagstones nearby—the guard with the crushed wrist had regained his feet. He tore down the street, clutching his fractured joint, beyond conscious thought, driven by survival.

So be it—he could flee. If he was strong and clever enough to escape Filvié Noctirin's web to the guard barricades, perhaps he could serve well under Tenebra's reign. In the meantime, he could tell the empire what he had seen. Let them call Amadore mad—they would not be the first. The insects marching in their lines could not grasp his higher movement, and so they would call him a monster. They would hunt him.

Amadore wiped the blood from his chin and licked his fingers clean. He glanced at the flicker of the living rounding a corner.

Or perhaps another nightstalker would kill him. It mattered not.

• • •

Francesca shot up, sweating and thirsty. She wiped frizzy hair from her face. Azran was gone, but Sevex was curled up in the corner of their stall.

Of course she had dreamt of Amadore. She couldn't get him out of her head. As memory of the dream faded, she felt the absence of the sun outside without looking at the stable doors. *I can never forget what I am, can I? What we are.* She shook her head. These doubts were new. She had never regretted her nature because she never had a choice in the matter. *Never gave Azran a choice, either.* He would be disappointed in her for thinking that, but it was true. This whole mess with Amadore might always have been in Francesca's cards, but now her husband was as much of a runaway.

No, this wasn't her fault—it was Amadore's. She shouldn't have had to keep reminding herself of that, but decades of emotional manipulation had skewed her self-perception. She wished she could just be free. She was sick of fighting for it.

"Chains, I need some coffee," she mumbled. She belted on her dagger, picked straw off herself, and followed the smell of roasted beans to the mess. She heard her husband's voice chatting with a deeper, gruffer one.

"I remember the place," the rumbling voice said. "Went there years and years ago. I remember they had a pretty piece there, but you weren't the player."

"No," Azran said. "She passed it down to me a couple years ago."

Francesca stepped in. Azran turned to her, looking happier than she'd seen him since this ordeal began.

"Gax, meet my lovely Francesca. Cesca, this is Gax."

She waved, then leaned onto Azran from behind, clasping her hands over his chest.

"Gax plays the lute." He sounded like a delighted child.

Francesca kissed the top of his head. "Making friends, dear?"

"We were talking about the Silver Sun."

Francesca saw his empty cup. "Where'd you get the coffee? Is there any left?"

Des got up. "I'll get you some."

"Thanks." Francesca sat next to Azran.

"You think Ria's doing okay?" he asked.

"She's probably missing her prized harpsichordist."

Azran looked down, abashed, then back at her. "But really."

Francesca sighed. Des placed a cup in front of her, and she took a careful sip before answering. "She's good enough with the clan, I think. And she knows how to take care of herself."

Azran shook his head. "It's just now striking me that we might not go back there for a long time. Maybe ever. That would be sad."

"Ever's a long time," Francesca said, more out of hope than faith. "And that's what we've got."

"I watched a vampire die last night," Azran said. "And I can well imagine those other two going down the same way. And they cheered. Bloody living cheered."

Gax glanced at Francesca, then caught Azran's eye. "Hey music man, if someone wants you dead, you must've done something big. My da always said only cowards don't make enemies somewhere along the line."

He stood, taking his dishes to a pile of others in the kitchen. From across the room, he continued, "And if you're still raw about it, write a song. That's what all the bad shit in this world happens for—so miserable fucks like you'n me can write songs."

• • •

Ria thrummed her fingers on the bartop, bored by the bustle in the common room. With her other hand, she raised a bottle of whiskey to her lips. She threw her head back, took a swig, lowered the bottle, and swallowed only after a good burn.

A dull roar filled the bar—her bar, damn it—from a dozen shifting huddles of vampires. Ostensibly, they were all on the same side, but each group seemed intent on keeping its own secrets. Despite its proud declarations of unity, the clan was as quarrelsome as the Senate. The front door creaked open and closed as they came and went with news and orders. The Silver Sun had become a makeshift headquarters since the riots and vigilante executions began. Ria didn't understand why everyone seemed taken so off guard by the response—you can't kill a bunch of nobles and not expect pushback from the citizenry. It just perpetuated the otherness, deepened the divide between living and vampire. Neighborhoods were being separated, territories carved out, barricades erected. Maybe that was the point.

Ria was grateful for the protection—the barricades, and now patrols—as something resembling a structure returned to Aure. But she had never volunteered her bar for this. The higher-ups in Filvié Noctirin would say she merely managed the bar, rather than owned it. But Ria had paid her dues over the years—almost thirty of them.

She took another slow, methodical drink, recapped the bottle, and placed it back under the bar, next to her loaded crossbow. This arrangement made the Silver Sun a target, too. Bands of Solari, some dressed in plainclothes, still roamed the streets, putting vampire-owned houses and business to the torch, inhabitants to the sword. They didn't even bother to wait for the law to catch up to their prejudice.

Ria swept her gaze across the room. All these people, and she could count the paying patrons on her fingers. She only needed one hand for the regulars. Her eyes locked on the harpsichord. Azran hadn't shown up for work since this mess started. Francesca was gone, too. She could feel the liquor taking effect, thank the gods. The numbness was slight, but it was the only thing keeping her from sobbing. It helped her trap the worry inside. Many were missing. Many were dead.

The clan had warned of the coming conflict—said it was inevitable. Until it happened, though, Ria had given it as much credence as a doomsayer's date for the end of the world. It hadn't seemed so inevitable to her.

"You look ragged."

She turned to Alir. He slid a few coins to her and set his personal tankard on the bar. Ria retrieved his usual Caruse ale from a shelf and filled the cup.

"Are they working you too hard?" he asked.

"No," Ria said. "I'm just wondering where everybody's gone."

Alir took a drink. "Me too. They have my crew and me out searching the city. All we're finding are dead ends."

"Literal ones?"

"Often." He took another drink.

Ria hesitated, but the anxiety won out. "Have you seen—"

She trailed off as a hush overtook the room. Alir turned in his stool, and Ria looked past him. The whole crowd watched the door swing shut.

Amadore waded through the room, towering over most. A dark pallor seemed to follow his robes and shroud, transferring from face to face as he passed. All watched him. He watched Alir.

"I need a word," Amadore said.

Alir nodded and followed his master through the kitchen, heading for the back door. Ria did not protest. She knew well enough not to get in Amadore's way.

Eavesdropping was a different matter. As business resumed in the common room, Ria slipped out. She took a detour through the cellar, squeezed through the double doors into the alley, and crept to the corner nearest the kitchen.

"What was his name?" Amadore asked.

"Sevex Matias," Alir replied.

"Who is he to have such a passage?"

"All the houses in that neighborhood did. We got into the tunnel from another, but it turns into a maze if you leave the main stretch."

"Perhaps you should follow this name, then—Matias."

"There were others with them. We finally broke that Solar today. He said there was an armed Atoran—one with magic. Maybe that's what blocked your sight."

"No. I would sense if it were soul magic. I believe Francesca to be gone from Aure. She is beyond my range. Though, perhaps not that of—yes."

There was a pause. Then, Alir asked, "What's our next move?"

"Find the Matias family. The house was wealthy, and so his name has weight. I must confer with our allies."

Ria heard soft footsteps coming her way. She grabbed a small, empty crate from a pile by the cellar doors and placed it back down just as Amadore rounded the corner. Her chest constricted as he came far too close. She was unsure whether he felt less than mortal, or more. She could smell the iron tang on his breath from a recent feeding. She knew his palate; if his gaze hadn't held her frozen, she would have shivered.

"Fret not," he said. His voice carried unexpected sincerity. Ria told herself it was his priestly magic and ignored the sudden desire to trust him. "I want them found as much as you. More. They yet survive. I am sure of it."

The tall priest continued on, a shadow following the specter that cast it.

Ria let out her held breath and fought to control her shaking hands. She cupped one to her mouth to contain a whimper. She had spoken with Amadore before, but never felt so naked before him. He was different—more than mortal, less than human, she decided.

And he had his sister's trail. Ria was done waiting for answers.

She went back inside and told one of her bouncers to keep the bar for a while. She had some contacts of her own to meet. As she made her way down the darkened streets—the lamps were no longer lit in this part of town—she looked out over the depression just north of the neighborhood. Across the not-quite-uniform architecture of the lower ward, she spotted the Golden Palace on its hill, next to the eight-spired Academy and pillared Valentreid Mausoleum. Even at this distance, the gilded roofs of the palace dome and wings reflected their sheen into the surrounding night air. This business reminded Ria of the time she had been inside that 1,500-year-old monument of the conquered Antiqiri. Despite the thrill of that excursion and the wealth that came from it, she wished she had never taken that contract.

She kept moving, putting the palace out of view and out of mind. This carry would be different. She had worked too hard to divorce herself from the past.

8

A week became two, and Varja lingered in Cruxia. Only a dozen locals she'd asked had seen Seneskar, and perhaps half of those reports sounded reliable. But the trail was looking quite cold.

At least she was not alone anymore. She enjoyed Miranda's company, more than she had anyone's in a long time. The clan dragons kept her at arm's length, even the sympathetic ones. Sympathy—pity—that was worse than the open derision.

The last time Varja remembered anything better than sympathy occurred with her band of volunteers back during the Second Flame. During war. Even then, she knew that was a fucked up state of affairs.

Miranda was at the same time like and unlike those old comrades. In some ways, her confidence made Varja recall Kylan, but with a refreshing regard for others. And her music—"a storm," Miranda sometimes called it, and Varja could hear echoes of dragon song. So familiar, but also so foreign. It was free without slipping into chaos, and never quite the same two nights in a row. Each performance—and performance was the word— differed in length, in content, in mood. Miranda read the crowd and played for them. She took suggestions, but always added her personal twists, coloring each song with her own voice while making all look so easy.

The way Miranda talked about musicianship invited parallels with Varja's swordplay. She said it wasn't just about the final position, the moment of pick striking string. That moment was important, but so too was the movement between plucks. The way her fingers transitioned between chords, she said, determined the sound. Varja agreed, lacking the same eloquence on the subject, but understanding that what you get is decided by how you get there. The two of them shared a love of kinesthetic aptitude; footwork and fingerwork were not all that dissimilar.

Miranda described her style as "pale emulation of classic forms, shaken up by country bard yokelry." Her aunt had taught her the standard lute, but Miranda came into her own on the road, partnering or simply mingling with musicians from around the empire.

"Someone from Pastoratel sounds nothing like one from Forente," she said. "The Pastori like their strings to twang, when they even play strings. Most prefer winds—flutes, pipes, and such. They hold their notes long, like wind whistling through the highlands, you know? The Forenti play fast and hard, cause they're always in a hurry in that city. No one likes to sit and ponder too long when they live in that kind of cesspool. Those that do end up leaving."

Varja had considered launching into similar commentaries on the sword—the difference between Zixarsi longsword and Ternez broadsword. Or how so many people, especially in this country, thought of axes as primitive, but the Red Earth Chari had eleven tribal forms. Or the impact dwarven refugees into Procumes had on the southern schools of fencing. But she kept quiet. No need to bore her only friend in the city into leaving, she decided.

Other than continued promises to keep an eye out, Miranda only once commented on Varja's search for Seneskar. It was near the end of the second week. They were sharing an outdoor table at a Procumi restaurant for a late dinner. The patio was almost empty.

"Are you still looking for him?" she asked, breaking the silence as only she could.

"Of course."

"Dedicated to your mission, aren't you. I hope you come out stronger for it."

Varja had learned that Miranda was full of phrases like that—at the same time cryptic and uplifting. They always made Varja think.

The lack of progress was clawing at her spirits, dragging her down. She had never given up before seeing a task through, regardless of how it ended. Circumstances, or even just whim, could change her course, but she always reached some kind of closure. And all those times in the past, had she come out stronger?

"Mission." In Draci, the word was *njoagedh*, which literally translated to "worthy task." Perhaps she should consider the worthiness of this quest. It was naïve to think the clan's attitude toward Varja would magically change the day she tossed Seneskar at their feet. She had set out thinking this just one step in the

93

process of defying her perceived weakness. "Traitorous blood," they called her mother's side. None had ever articulated as much to her, but Varja understood she had to prove her loyalty.

But how many times had she done so? Was this akin to buying a position, like some nameless noble? Was that how she wanted to attain the clan's respect?

"Can I ask you something?"

"This should be good," Miranda muttered, watching an osprey alight on the kitchen's roof. "Ask."

"Why are you still putting up with me?"

Miranda turned an incredulous eye on her. "Don't put it like that. Believe it or not, I enjoy your company." She paused, her stare making Varja shift in her chair. "You're genuine—that's my answer. My whole life, I've heard Cruxia called the Western Aeribe. It's beautiful, people said. Full of art and cosmopolitanism." She shook her head and glanced at the terraced streets that surrounded them. "I suppose it looks that way from afar. But I'm disappointed. Everyone here just wants to walk the same circles in their safe little lives. They loathe risk. No one wants adventure—except you."

Varja looked away, letting her loosened hair hide her face. "I don't feel much like an adventurer these days."

"I don't think adventure is just running and fighting," Miranda said. "It's more doing something you've never done. Have you ever been to a Valentreid city?"

"I passed through a few in Liore years ago, and on the way here."

"That's not the same. These are cities you have to experience for a while to understand. Especially the ports. I've only formed my snarky opinion because I've been here long enough."

Varja faced her again, returning her smirk. "What path did you take here?"

Miranda laughed. "A circuitous one, you might say. I'm looking forward to some good old footwork or sailing in the near future."

Eventually, Varja's coin began to run out. She found odd jobs where she could—much as her old band did between contracts in Charir. Though back then, some of them thought looting villages to be a perfectly fine source of income.

Some days, Varja hauled crates and sacks on and off wagons or ships. Some nights, she bounced undermanned, overcrowded taverns. The pay was meager, but it was enough to sustain her. The bigger issue was that this took time away from her search. Guilt crept into her, flitting about the dark spaces. It seldom came into the light of conscious thought, but when it did, she questioned her task. Maybe it was the pace of her days, but she began to consider practical concerns she had initially pushed away.

How was she supposed to capture a dragon? Human guise or no, Seneskar was a shapeshifter. How could she keep him restrained for the long voyage back home? Varja had fought dragons before, and not just in familial sparring matches or hazing. Defeating Seneskar, even in his true form, was not out of the question. But then what?

Between work and sleep, Varja would continue her search. More and more, though, she hastened through that in order to follow Miranda each evening. They went to taverns and inns as varied as the neighborhoods of this colorful city. And rare was the night Varja left before Miranda.

• • •

Miranda sipped the blackest of teas from a rough ceramic cup under thatched shade out back of someplace whose name she had already forgotten. There had been so many establishments, so many names in the past few weeks. She wasn't playing here, so she didn't care. She remembered the name of that post-performance liquor the night before: "Chain the Moon." Some unholy recipe from Maceria. Or was that the name once it was mixed with brandy? Either way, the second shot had been a mistake.

They partied hard in Cruxia—on the whole, maybe harder than anywhere else she'd been. She couldn't quantify something like that, but after last night, it rang true. Like they were trying to forget how close they were to Charir and the Faith of Fire. From what Miranda recalled, this region had hardly seen war since its annexation over a millennia ago. Then came two major invasions within a few decades, shaking a society that had forgotten what war felt like. Were they drinking to forget what happened, or to forget that it would happen again?

A tame breeze carried the bow-drawn notes of a lyra from down the street. Miranda picked up snippets of "Red Runs the Sun" so perfect she wondered if the musician had trouped with Callistre herself. Of all the places to hear an Astrelli instrumental ode—maybe she wasn't so alone here as she thought. She could wait a little while to head back east, but once she had the coin, she was hopping the next ship out.

She knew she had wanted to go home for some time, even if she could not remember the place she had been before Cruxia. Hades must have been unwelcoming indeed if this city was homier. Or perhaps, like Varja, she had come here for some purpose. Of her recent journey to the Immortal Realms, she recalled only a few words from Mortis, the Severance, god of the dead. Whether they were advice or instructions, Miranda did not know.

"You are one of many now entwined. Time is a tangle of possibility, but the probable still occurs with preference. Immortals move on your realm—stepping through shadows, I deem. The roles of hunter and quarry mingle and twist, such that all are both. Follow the lines of blood, should you desire a role of your own."

Deliberate obfuscation irritated her to no end. Poetry was one thing; this was nonsense. Why had he been so cryptic? To make her aid him of her own volition? By her own initiative? Probably.

Don't send me to handle another bloody immortal, she thought. *Sure sounds like that's what this is. I barely survived a saead. I'd rather not go back to Hades just yet.*

A dwarven woman at another table caught Miranda's eye and moved closer. She had several thick braids and a complexion that spoke of Macerian origin rather than Procumi. But where had she—right, this woman was at the bar. Was she the temptress who had offered Miranda that liquid fire?

"Good time last night," the woman said. Her breath smelled of fish and weak wine. "You said you're from eastways, yeah? Never heard those jigs before. Good drinking songs."

"Sure." Miranda held the pitted cup under her chin, letting the tealeaves ward away the fish.

"You're a good player."

"Thanks."

The Macerian woman shifted in her seat, glanced right, then leaned closer and spoke lower. "You cavort with that Ziach woman, yeah?"

Miranda met her expectant eyes. "I wouldn't say 'cavort,' but—"

"Never mind the word. Listen. You're not from here, so maybe you don't know. Ziach are in the Faith. Even the ones who say they're not, don't trust them."

Miranda set her cup on the table. "Where are you from, then?"

The other woman straightened. "Born in the Wall, but mostly here."

"So, your family are refugees, then?"

"Forty years since, but yeah."

"So why should I trust you?"

The Macerian bit the inside of her cheek. The rest of her face went from curious to hard. "Because, elfblood, my folk fought the Faith. Died fightin the Faith."

"Some joined it."

She spat on the ground. "Blood traitors did."

"And your family fled."

She stared.

"Just like the Zixarsi down in the slums," Miranda pressed.

"The Ziach joined the Faith, but for a few clans. Opposite of my kin. We came here and work. They came, and they beg on a good day, steal and kill on the others. Don't you ever put mine and theirs together."

The Macerian woman stood and gave a long look of fury and disgust. "Stick around—cavort—and you'll come to see, elfblood." She left the back door of the teahouse banging on its frame.

Miranda shook her head at the door. One would think a city this diverse would be more inclusive, harmonious— "cosmopolitan," as it was sung in the east. Instead, everyone found a camp that looked like them and buried their head in its dirt. She had caught the looks directed at Varja, who herself either didn't notice or didn't care. If it was the former, she would eventually see.

The first ship out. Perhaps Miranda would bring Varja with.

9

The night ride west from Aure was exciting at first. Every band of soldiers and outriders presented the threat of capture. Every moving shadow was a vampire or Solar hunting them. But it soon became apparent that the soldiers were more concerned with what was happening inside the walls. The one sergeant who stopped them noticed the vampires' nature, but grumbled about his jurisdiction being Elta, not Aure, and seemed content with their messenger story. The shadows on the roadside belonged to nothing more dangerous than owls and hares.

The odd group stayed at a roadside inn through the first day. Sevex dropped a gold piece for the innkeeper's discretion. Francesca, verging on outrage, asked how many more of those Sevex had. "A few." She asked why he didn't pay for the horses—he never had the chance.

In a dark corner of the inn, they took stock of their resources. Azran had twenty-eight silvers and two gold—his entire savings since moving to Aure. Francesca had thirteen silvers, a pile of coppers, and a few remaining baubles and trinkets that likely wouldn't go far. Des carried ten silvers and not much else. Luc, nine.

All heads then turned toward Sevex. He leaned even farther over their table, shielding his contribution from outside view— twenty gold aurli. Even in the meager light, the coins shined in his companions' eyes.

"You just walk around with this?" Des said.

"I have more, in a hidden chest in my cellar."

"Why didn't you take it?" Azran asked.

Sevex began returning the coins to his pouch as quietly as he could. "I suppose, in all the excitement, I forgot."

"Lucky you didn't get your purse cut in that den."

"He wouldn't have," Des said. "We made a deal, and robbing clients like that is bad for business. The Kraken—and others like them—will swindle you sideways, but rules are what make it all work."

"We could buy the horses," Francesca said.

Des shook her head. "We'd get a better deal almost anywhere else."

"We'd save by just hitching with a caravan," Azran said.

"But we'd be easier to follow that way."

"We could walk," Luc said. "It would be no slower than a line of wagons."

Azran raised an eyebrow. "You want to walk four hundred miles, feel free. Me, I like my feet with skin on them."

Following directions from Sayel and Des's knowledge of "cant and scrawl"—as she called the spoken and written codes respectively—the group reached a nondescript shack in the hills outside Elta on the second night from Aure. As promised, they turned in the horses.

From there, they had originally planned to circumvent the city altogether, but the experience so far gave them a limited measure of confidence. Azran and Francesca stayed in another roadside inn for the day, while the others went in search of new mounts. After spending all but five of Sevex's aurli, they returned with serviceable horses—no steeds of legend, but healthy enough.

The road south soon grew dull. Their route through Cortellum had little in the way of landscapes. What forest there once was had been cleared centuries ago to fuel the growing empire's conquests and make room for grain fields. Towns were the most frequent landmarks, and the shelter they provided kept Azran and Francesca alive. Few in the province dealt in blood or other vampiric concerns, but they found one ally in a shack of a hostel.

The dealer was a tight-lipped gnoll vampire, one of the tall, canine natives of Sylgatum to the northeast. The door leading downstairs bore a sigil Francesca had seen a few times in her travels, always far from the clan's dominion. It was a red hand extended palm-up, welcoming. The blood cellar matched the building above but had the necessities. The dealer led Azran and Francesca into a cold room of shoddy brickwork and shelves that were no more than stacked planks and blocks. Arcane runes tethered threads of power to keep the ice frozen, and thus the vials chilled.

The selection was limited. The pig blood ran an exorbitant price, so the couple settled for goat. It was better than snaring rodents. They also bought tents of thick black canvas for the daytime camping and curtains of the same material for inns.

On the eleventh night from Aure, they saw the Valla twisting through its shallow gorge.

The final stretch to the Matias estate was a blur. They rode hard to make it before sunrise—harder than Azran and Sevex had since their race to make the final night of *The Cavalier* at the Theater of Lights. It was the last performance before the Bureau of Culture arrested the playwright for his accurate—flawed—depiction of Empress Mirena. Azran told the tale as they paused to water the horses at a stream. Sevex had never been in the saddle that long before and had spent the performance standing bow-legged. On the final note, before the photoeffects faded, the playwright, Usul Aracas, ran onstage to deliver the news and lament that art and history die before frightened governments. When the guards led him away in chains, he bowed at the edge of the stage. Twenty thousand spectators chanted his name over the guards' orders to disperse.

This time, the haste proved unnecessary. A storm came up from the sea, keeping the sky dark and drenching horse and rider alike by the time they left the stone road for the muddy path to the estate.

Fields of wheat awaiting harvest swayed in the south wind. At the lane's end, overlooking the river valley, stood a manor of grey stone. A wing sprawled to either side of the central hall, connected by closed second-floor walkways held aloft by arches. A large, timber stable stood out front, but no servants came to take the horses.

"I don't see any lights inside," Des said over the storm.

Sevex didn't respond. He dismounted and led his horse to the stable, fishing a set of keys from some pocket. The first didn't fit in the padlock, but the second did. Only two horses were inside, watching and snorting at the newcomers.

"Both Valen's," Sevex said. "My brother's." He held his hand out to the one with a white diamond on its brown face. The horse sniffed him with recognition.

They put their tired mounts in empty stalls—there were plenty—and gave them feed. Water trickled into the troughs from collectors on the roof. Sevex went around and pulled a stiff lever in each stall. The troughs slowly filled, and excess drained back outside.

"Sevex made that setup when he was, what, thirteen?" Azran said.

Sevex glanced away sheepishly. "Fourteen."

They headed for the house and ascended a carved façade. Weathered faces of nameless figures and beasts stared out into the rising mist. Sevex raised his hand to knock, hesitated, and then clasped the brass loop of one door and rapped twice.

There was no response.

He retrieved the keys once more. The first didn't work, but the third did. "What is the first for?" he asked, pushing the tall oak door open.

The front hall was dim. Grey light filtered in from a series of windows near the thirty-foot ceiling. A row of pillars lined either side of a dark carpet running from the doors to a grand staircase. The landing continued forward, wrapping the pillars with a mezzanine. Banners and tapestries hung above two cold fireplaces on each side of the hall. The hangings waved in the sudden draft.

"Who's there?" a voice called from ahead and above.

A man with a lamp entered the landing from the side. He shared Sevex's straight, jet-colored hair and thin build, but stepped and spoke with more confidence despite his nightshirt and bare feet.

"You used to be up this early, Valen," Sevex said, removing his muddy boots.

"Gods have mercy." A grin spread wide across Valen's face. He hurried down the stairs, set the lamp on a table, and wrapped Sevex in his arms.

Sevex hugged back. "When I tell you about the journey, 'I'm glad to see you' will take on new meaning, as it has for me."

Valen stepped back to arm's reach. "I am glad to see you." He looked past his brother. "And Azran! How many years has it been?" He buried Azran in another hug.

"At least five. You were still in Aure last time I was here. I guess we switched places."

"Well, this is a pleasure. I haven't heard from Sev in quite some time, but that's my brother, is it not? And who have you two brought along?"

Azran stepped aside to present. "This is Luc, Des, and my wife, Francesca."

The nightshirted aristocrat bowed and took Francesca's hand. "Valen Matias, at your service. It's an honor to meet the person capable of meeting Az's standards."

Francesca smiled. "The stars must have aligned, then, because I never felt I had to try."

"Well, come on all, our home is your home," Valen said. He picked up the lamp and started toward the staircase. "I believe there are some coals going yet in the south den. Let's get you lot warm and dry."

"Where is everyone?" Sevex asked.

Valen stopped at the bottom step and turned around. "It's a bit of a tale. One that, frankly, Sev, you would already know if you'd ever given us your address in Aure. Now come along, brother. And everybody else."

Valen led them through the walkway to the south wing, then down a less-grand set of stairs to a cozy sitting room with plush furniture. He took up a poker and stirred the ashes under the mantle, adding some kindling and frayed birch bark to get a flame and thick logs to build it high. He checked a kettle for water and hung it over the fire.

"Tea's in the cupboard," he said. "I'm going to dress more presentably, and then we'll all get caught up."

The drenched travelers stripped off their jackets and other outerwear. They lay the garments across the oak tables and crowded close to the growing fire.

Azran felt at once comfort and discomfort. He was no stranger in this house. He had spent half his childhood and adolescence here. It would have been all if he'd had his way, but the elder Matiasi had insisted he try to have a relationship with his own family. While the warmth and light of the fire brought him closer to those memories, Valen's cryptic words colored the atmosphere with unease. The present emptiness of the place was alien. Azran could see Sevex's eyes shifting and calculating as he tried, in his own way, to understand this state of affairs. The dampness and stench of horses and road clung to them all, and reminded Azran that he wasn't here to visit, but to hide.

The kettle boiled before Valen returned. Azran got up and brewed the tea. He heard footsteps down the hall and hurried to make a sixth cup for Valen before passing out the others.

"Sorry for the delay," Valen said as he entered with an armful of clothes. "I noticed nobody had packs, so I assumed you only have what you're wearing." He tossed the bundle across a divan.

"I raided Sev's wardrobe. Az, it should still fit you, and Francesca seems about the same size."

Azran chuckled and held up an embroidered shirt. "Just like the old days."

Valen turned to Luc. "I hope our elder brother's fit, because we've nothing larger." To Des, he said, "The only thing I could find for you was our mother's dresses. Fret not, she is quite stylish."

Des hid a sour look by glancing away. "I appreciate it, but I don't wear skirts. Does she have anything for riding, maybe?"

Sevex shook his head, and Valen said, "She doesn't ride. And Alessa—our sister—took everything of hers when she left."

Des walked over to the pile of Sevex's clothes. "I'll roll the sleeves back."

"Fair enough."

Azran handed him a teacup and asked, "Don't suppose you have any coffee?"

"That, I'd take," Des said.

"I'm afraid I don't drink it," Valen replied.

Azran raised his eyebrows. "Since when?"

"I've sworn off the stuff. If you drink it every day, pretty soon you can't go a day without it."

"You could say the same about tea. Or food."

"Or blood?" Valen took a sip, letting Azran flounder a moment. "I've been to a few cities. Don't lump me in with the folk around here. You had brown eyes when last we met." He sat next to the clothes, brushing a few garments out of the way. "And given the news trickling down from Aure, I imagine those eyes have something to do with your presence here."

Azran sighed and nodded. He figured this was coming.

"Well, go on, then," Valen said. "Get in some dry clothes. Then, as I said, we'll all get caught up."

• • •

Des returned first, wearing the same pants but now with an oversized, red, silk tunic. She put her wet clothes near the fire and her weapons next to her on a divan opposite Valen.

The wind shifted outside, and fat drops began pelting the small, high window of the den. Distant thunder clapped.

"I don't know what you heard," Des began. "But we didn't have any hand in the shitstorm in Aure."

The corners of Valen's mouth turned up. "Between Sev and Az, I would be genuinely surprised were that the case." He studied her a moment. "Are you a friend of Azran's, then?"

"I only met him and Francesca a couple weeks ago. No, I'm here because of Sev."

"You don't seem like his usual company. And I mean no offense by that—in some ways, it's a compliment."

Des looked at the blue-grey windowpane. "I owe him. He helped out me and Luc. Put himself in some risk to do it, too, he said."

"And how much do you owe my brother?"

Des looked back at him, expecting an expression she knew well—that of a businessman wondering just much leverage he had. In Forente, it was all favors and debts, leverage and business. Aure hadn't seemed that much different. Sevex was an anomaly. So was his brother, it appeared—Valen's face was curious but otherwise neutral.

"I'm not sure," she said. "He says we're even, but we aren't by my reckoning. Besides, at this point, I'd call us friends."

"So why are you tagging along? For the friendship, or the debt?" An edge crept into Valen's face, if not his voice. Protectiveness hedged out the curiosity.

"You can relax. I'm not going to hurt him."

Valen sat back and nodded. "So, no dresses? Never?"

"They never seemed to suit me," Des said. "And they aren't practical in my usual line of work."

"And you're always working, are you?"

Des laughed. "Luc says so."

Valen shared a chuckle. "Maybe you and Sev aren't such an odd pairing. He's much the same way."

Des stopped. "We aren't—"

"No, I didn't mean to imply," Valen said, waving a hand. "I know an engagement ring when I see one, and Sev would never choose one so—so natural."

Des reached one hand up to the silver ring hanging around her neck by a fine, black chain. It was normally hidden under her leather vest. She fiddled with the band, feeling the engraved vine pattern and small emerald. The metal was cold to the touch.

"Yeah," she said, forcing a smile. "His would probably have a winding key and sprout legs."

"Will you wear a dress for the wedding?"

"Why are you so obsessed with putting me in a dress?"

Valen shrugged. "I've never met a woman as adamant as you on the issue. Curiosity, then, I suppose. I'm afraid it runs in the family."

"We used to argue about it. She said she would, so why couldn't I? It's pointless to question now, anyway. She never even got to ask me."

"She?"

110

Des nodded. "Arilysa was her name. You know, for a self-proclaimed city guy, you seem awfully sheltered right now."

"No, I've met plenty of couples like yours. But marriage? Amalus's priests only perform that rite for man and woman."

"Head out east sometime. Or just farther north. Liba's a lot less stodgy."

Valen paused for a long while. "I'm sorry. I must seem terribly naïve, not to mention intrusive."

Des smiled. "It's honestly better conversation than I'm used to from your family."

• • •

Valen sat unspeaking once his guests concluded their tale. His eyes stared at some place beyond the warming den. Then, he sipped his tea and started, "The Night of Blood and Flame, they're calling it. A bit grandiose, if you ask me." He focused on Francesca. "You're certain you don't know why Filvié Noctirin—"

"Went bats?" She shook her head. "I wish I did."

Azran glanced at Sevex, who watched his brother. Valen remained distant.

"Your turn," Azran said.

Valen met Sevex's gaze for the first time since he returned to the den and took a deep breath. "You remember Father sheltering those actors after the *Cavalier* fiasco? Well, he made that something of a habit, shielding people who got on the Bureau of Culture's bad side. It wasn't a problem for us—until Usul Aracas himself escaped imprisonment and got a tip this way from one of the old troupe."

He paused to drink the last of his tea. "Aracas was followed. Some bastard spy from the Unseen. Aiding a traitor—that would

111

have been crime enough. But somehow, the bureau found out about the others, too."

"Wait," Des said. "The guy who wrote that play was charged with treason?"

"And convicted," Valen replied. "The only reason he lives is his popularity."

"That's fucked."

"Godsdamned right," Azran said.

"What happened to Father?" Sevex asked. "And Mother? And where are Alessa and Ocasi?"

Valen held up a hand. "Easy, Sev. Father isn't a traitor himself. They took him, and Mother, too—she had enough of a hand in it. They took both to Lunatel. They aren't in a common prison with murderers and all that, but they are locked away. The bureau wanted the estate, too. Ocasi is in a legion, and can't inherit property until he retires in a decade or so. Like Father said, in that time, the crats could shuffle papers and pass it off to some senator's cousin. Alessa—Sien knows where she is. She heard what happened and disappeared worse than you.

"When this all occurred, Father wrote me. I was in Astrellus for a holiday with some colleagues. It seems Father got one of the decent barristers, because, well." He gestured at the walls around them. "She's still in the family. Most of the fortune's gone, though. I'm afraid I had to send the staff on their way. Some folk from the farms nearby are supposed to help with the crop soon. They'll split the bigger share, but at least it won't go to waste."

Valen covered his face, then stared at Sevex and shook his head. "You might well be the wealthiest one of us at this point."

"Assuming my house stands."

"Of course." Valen let an awkward pause fill the room. "Where were you, Sevex?" He stood and left.

10

After a much-needed day of rest, they reconvened in the Matias dining room for a simple dinner. Valen and Sevex spoke little, the initial warmth of their reunion chilled by the Sevex's attitude toward what had happened. Their father had broken the law, he said. As much as Valen might disagree with it, so it was. Valen then broached the subject of visiting their parents. Sevex gave no answer.

"It has been a while since we've gone to Cruxia," Azran said, trying to turn lead to gold. "You could see them, then we could see a few plays. Hit the taverns for some local music?" He put a hand on Sevex's shoulder. "When's the last time you saw the sea? It's been far too long for me."

Sevex eyed him, then the hand, and then went back to his plate.

Azran let go. "I miss the sea."

Sevex dropped his fork, letting it clatter on the ceramic dish. "Your nostalgia is for a time long gone, Azran. Things have changed. The world is falling into madness and you're treating this as a—a fucking holiday. Vampires chased us out of Aure, chased me from my home. Stop trying to recapture some old camaraderie. It is gone."

Everyone stared at Sevex.

"The camaraderie is gone?" Azran said. "What are you talking about?"

Sevex sighed. "The old is gone. The dynamics of our relationship have changed. I no longer feel compelled to let myself get dragged along on midnight rides to outlawed cultural events."

"I didn't realize you were so reluctant. 'Dragged along' isn't the phrase you used back then."

"Must I repeat myself a third time?"

Their eyes locked. Sevex's carried unusual anger, tempestuous enough to match Azran's.

Azran shoved his chair back and stormed from the dining hall.

He stalked the long halls of the manor, passing many dark rooms. He knew things were different. Of course he knew. *Look at this empty place.* Sevex acted like he possessed some unique insight into people, but he didn't. He never had. He was brilliant in many ways. A genius, even. But Azran was the one who understood people. He talked to them.

Things had changed, and that was why he had suggested the trip to Cruxia. Gods forbid he try to lift the mood. *Not in this house.*

Azran kicked a doorframe as he passed. "Fuck him."

He kicked another but lost his balance. He recovered and spotted something he hadn't expected. Low light from the corridor revealed the first twelve keys of a harpsichord.

He took a piece from a candelabrum in the hall and lit another in the music room. He had forgotten about this place, tucked away in the north wing. It was large enough to hide a grand harp, a couple empty lute stands, a few stools, and the deep red harpsichord. He remembered Alessa playing the keys while her mother accompanied on the lute.

Azran slid two fingers across the keyboard without pressing down. He had never shown much interest in the stilted, imperious songs the Matiasi would perform. He figured out why a few years ago—he was an improviser. Still, he wondered if that early exposure had given him his ear for music.

He pulled a stool over and sat at the instrument. He had learned that playing could be cathartic. He pressed a few keys.

"Still in tune," he muttered. "Shame there's no one here to play you anymore."

A low, fat chord rang off the curved ceiling, then another. Lighter notes from Azran's right hand joined them, frantic. His anger had been subsumed by surprise, but now it billowed forth like black clouds and thunder. It passed through his shoulders and down into his forearms, wrists, fingers, channeled into what some people called art.

To Azran, at that moment, it was not art. Art was something to be observed and reflected upon. There was no analysis in this— only raw emotion. Only the present. There was the next note, the next chord, and nothing more.

But even so, three years as the player at the Silver Sun meant his muscles remembered no pure chaos. High and low played off one another. Harmony emerged ex nihilo in this dance. Breath shallow, sweat coating hands and brow, he carried the song to someplace far from its origin—to the sea, maybe. Yes, the sea. He found a resolve reminiscent of wind and waves, sails and salt and gulls.

Notes faded. Air returned to his lungs.

"Better?" Francesca asked.

Azran jumped and turned. His wife leaned in the doorframe. He hadn't even seen her shadow just to his left, covering those first twelve keys.

"I think so." He stood and went over to hug her.

"It took me a while to find you. Even after you started playing."

"It's a big house."

"It reminds me of my parents'."

Azran wasn't sure how to respond to that.

"In a good way. I used to love running up and down the halls, playing hide and seek with Amadore." She laughed. "How's that for irony?"

Azran smiled. "Were you good at it?"

Francesca shook her head. "He always found me." She slipped around Azran and grabbed him from behind, poking two fingers into his lower back. "Unless I found him first."

Azran spun away from her. "So you found me." He tilted his head. "But can you catch me?"

He sprinted off down the corridor. She laughed again and gave chase.

● ● ●

Francesca stared at the white ceiling. White rooms were always brighter, night or day. The walls were paneled with pine, but the ceiling still filled the chamber with the pale afterglow of the sun creeping at the edges of dark, doubled-up drapes. The bed was large and almost too soft. In the rising heat of the late morning and lingering sweat of her and Azran's coupling, they had kicked the blankets, rope, and even sheets onto the floor, lying naked and separate.

She turned her face from the cloaked window and into the guest room, one of six in the manor. Her family's had nine, but who was counting? Stale furniture lacking taste or form lined the walls—a squarish vanity, a tall box of an armoire, a desk with no drawers. A blurry painting of a woman on the riverbank hung above the desk. Francesca had seen that style before—more cultured types called it "impression" or something. It was all the rage in Astrellus these days. To her, it just looked like splotches of color.

She realized she hadn't thought of Amadore in a while, and then he was there. Even through the hood, the shroud, the manipulated shadows, she could always see his face. It looked so much like her own.

Behind her, she brushed the back of Azran's calf with her toe. The simple touch banished her brother's hold over her. It was ridiculous to think Azran could overpower Amadore, but in this instance, his presence was enough to protect her. She rolled over to see his back with its subtle definition and less subtle ink. The draconic tail of his Caelix sleeve curled over his shoulder and transitioned to a maelstrom of dark clouds, pale blue heat, and purple lightning that covered half his back.

Much better than a blurry clotheswasher, Francesca thought. But her observations were attempts to avoid the issue. She didn't relish bringing it up.

"Love," she whispered.

"Hm?"

"You know, he wasn't totally wrong about our situation. Prick though he may have been in his words."

"Who? Sev?" A pillow muffled Azran's response.

"Yeah. We should lay low for a while."

Azran's back heaved with a sigh. "I know."

"I'm just worried is all, that someone's going to get hurt because of us. Because of me."

Azran rolled halfway over. "I'm fine never having someone lift a hatchet or a mace over my head again."

Francesca nodded. "I don't think a little paranoia is wrong here. Sometimes it pays off. Maybe we could stay here through the winter, then see what's what."

"I wonder, though—is the fear worth it? Forever's a long time and all, but is it worth it if you spend the centuries hiding?"

Francesca grabbed his hand. "It would be a lot shorter if you weren't there."

He looked at her, blinked, and swallowed. "I know. You know I understand that. I'm only afraid to make a habit of not living. Holed up in one place or another is not living to me."

"I know."

"I want to see the sea again."

"You will. Just a little patience is all I'm asking. Prudence isn't fear."

"I wonder what the ocean is like. The big one beyond the straits. I want to see that someday."

Francesca smiled and pulled herself closer to him. "I can't give you an inch, can I?"

Azran put an arm beneath her neck, around her shoulders. "Don't worry. I'm not going anywhere without you, nor you without me."

• • •

The music room was not the only place of interest in the north wing. Valen said Ocasi would practice with weapons in the training room, years ago. The rest of the children had some rudimentary instruction at their father's insistence, but Ocasi, the soldier, was the only sibling who had kept up with it.

Francesca's parents would have found such an arrangement common, or even barbaric; perhaps that was why she had always wanted to learn swordsmanship. She had some friends show her footwork and forms over the years, and rapiers did not feel alien in her hand. But still, it was nothing compared to what she had seen Luc do. How he had moved when he rescued them, or every morning on the journey south—she wanted to move like that, too. Sometimes, she would glance out the window of an inn or the flaps of the tent before the sunlight grew too steady and see him transitioning through stances and positions with the same fluidity as Azran's hands across a keyboard.

The second night at the estate, she approached Luc after the evening meal. "How long have you been fighting?" she asked, walking with him through one of the connecting walkways, pretending to be more interested in the moonlit river through the windows.

"Many years," Luc said. "Almost since I could walk." He tapped the pommel of his arming sword—he wore it everywhere. "But if you're asking about this, I became an acolyte of Atora at thirteen. That's when they started me on swords."

"So, you've been schooled."

Luc nodded. "You haven't."

Francesca slowed, now looking at him. He stopped.

"It's in your stance," Luc said. "I caught sight of you with the looters just before you went down. You're a scrapper, not a woman of the blade."

Her cheeks reddened. "Yeah, well, I—"

"You want me to teach you?"

"Um." Francesca glanced away, scratching at the back of her head. "Yeah. Yes. Please."

Luc started walking again. "Well, let's scout that practice room."

She hurried to catch up to his longer strides. "Was it that obvious?"

"You hid your excitement poorly. But mostly, you seem like a fighter. Something in the way you're always guarding Azran, I suppose. You are the protector."

"You're perceptive."

"I am a priest, you know. In any case, I could use a new practice dummy—I mean, sparring partner, of course."

Francesca laughed. "Yeah? We'll see about that."

We'll see about how much this is going to hurt, she thought.

The practice room was below the ground level and had its own staircase. The floor was wood, but Francesca could feel the firm stone underneath. A few notched poles and more elaborate, battered dummies were lined up on one wall. The opposite held racks of wooden training gear—polearms and blades of every shape and length, as well as shields from buckler to kite. The entire space was perhaps thirty feet either way. The ceiling was high enough to swing a halberd overhead.

Luc blew a low whistle, his gaze sweeping over the racks. "A shame only one of them used all this. I'd quite like to fight Ocasi one day." He unbelted his sword and placed it on a bench by the door, then went to the practice weapons. "Pick up whatever feels comfortable."

Francesca went to the "blades" and selected a narrow rod about two feet long past its plain guard. She stood in the center of the room as Luc followed. He held a slightly longer, heavier pole. He spun it a few times and went on guard.

"Show me what you know," he said.

Francesca took a deep breath and assumed the stance her friends had shown her—straight-backed crouch, right foot pointed forward, left pointed outward two lengths behind, heels and lead arm in line.

Luc showed no signs of approval or disapproval. He stood still.

Then, like a coiled spring, he closed the gap between them. Luc veered to her right and cut down. Francesca scrambled to reposition her feet while throwing her blade up to parry. Her right leg hit a barrier as she blocked. Luc's free hand went under her main and shoved. She tripped over his leg and hit the floor.

Luc backed off, composed. "I used to prefer that stance myself."

Francesca sat up.

"But I found it has weaknesses against fighters who don't also use it," he continued. "If I were wielding two blades, that push would have been a thrust. Maybe not fatal, but good luck continuing. Going at your left would have been even easier."

Francesca shook her head. "I think you could take me even straight on."

"True. But not everyone attacks in a straight line. Remember the thug who flanked you?"

She ran a hand over her scalp where the club had clipped it. "I asked you to teach me."

Luc gestured with his weapon for her to stand. She did. He moved next to her, facing the same direction.

"Go into that same stance," he said. "Now, turn a bit—just a bit, like this. Put your trailing foot a tad farther out. Blade a couple inches in—you still have a center line, it's just moved. There."

"I thought sideways was better," Francesca said. "It presents a smaller target."

"That it does. But this lets you cover more angles, especially if you use your off hand. For a rapier, I recommend a buckler or parrying dagger. Or, there's always a use for an empty hand. Your choice."

"I think I'll keep the one blade, for now."

Luc nodded, going back in front of her. "Now, you attack me."

Francesca took a few advances and retreats, watching her feet and testing the new stance. Then she looked back up at Luc. His weapon was in a high guard, so she kept low, stepping forward and lunging with a thrust.

Luc's pole swept down, knocking hers out wide. His wrist rotated as he continued the motion. Francesca pulled back and settled into a neutral position, avoiding the disarm.

"Good," Luc said. "But you're linear again."

He circled around to her right while she pivoted to keep up. He quickstepped back left. He struck her on the hip, then her left shoulder as she was still moving to parry the first hit. Francesca recoiled from the growing stings.

Again Luc backed off. "Perhaps this will help. One of my masters told me to envision a circle between myself and my opponent. Follow the edge of this circle. A skilled foe will do the same. A mediocre one will rotate, either too slowly to keep up or too fast to stay balanced." He moved around an imaginary enemy as he spoke. His stance remained wide, and his legs never crossed for long. He reversed direction, just as he had moments ago. "Even with the skilled one, you might still find an opening. This gives you more angles to look for one." He spun back to Francesca. "Understand?"

She nodded. "I think so."

"Good. Show me." The pole went back up.

That became their routine. Evening after evening, Francesca would wake up and "spar" with Luc—his joke about a practice dummy was not far off.

It was difficult with the forced nocturnalism, but some measure of fellowship developed between the vampires and their new companions. Des kept late hours out of habit. She enjoyed listening to Azran play the harpsichord in the music room. Along with Francesca, they would converse between songs about every subject save one—Des would not speak of her lover's death. She shared the stories of their time in the Kraken, or how they met, or when they moved to Equotel—nothing beyond that point. When Des spoke of Ari, she displayed genuine joy and even grew comfortable with Azran and Francesca's affection toward each other.

For their part, the couple told of the nightlife in Aure—the music, the people you would never experience during the day, for better or worse.

Valen sometimes joined them for a while before retiring, but Sevex remained distant. He said little, least of all to Azran. According to Valen, his younger brother had taken to restoring his old workshop a few doors down from the music room. The dusty space was adjacent to the library where Valen worked on his arcana when other business did not demand his attention. There was little other business of late.

A week passed in this fashion. Autumn storms rolled upriver, the last deluges before winter's dryness took over. On days when the weather was clear, neighboring farmers came to help harvest and left with wagons full of their take. It was a strange arrangement to Francesca's experience; at her parents' estate, the masters took the lion's share and doled out what was left. Despite the circumstances that prompted it, she thought the Matias system much fairer.

• • •

On the twentieth evening since "the Night of Blood and Flame," their ninth at the estate, Valen intercepted Azran and Francesca on their way to breakfast. He held an envelope with the back facing them while he examined the front. "I believe this is for you two," he said.

The couple looked at each other.

"A private rider delivered it today. It's addressed to 'the harpsichordist of the Matias estate.' And it came from Aure. There's no magic or arcana on it that I can perceive."

"But someone knows we're here," Francesca said.

Valen nodded and handed the envelope to Azran, who ripped it open with his finger. A letter was inside. He moved closer to a candelabrum to read it aloud.

"Azran, Francesca, my friends,

"I hope you are the ones reading this—I've been stumbling about in the dark for some time now. But if Amadore is to be believed, you two are still alive and this letter will find you. He is many things, but I do not call him a liar.

"Aure is no safer than when you vanished. There is a measure of order, but Solari still carry out their brand of justice. More importantly, Amadore is involved in some darker plot. That night was only the beginning. He speaks of 'allies.' I don't know who he means. I am frightened—not just for you, but of him. He wants Aure, to claim the city in Tenebra's name. I wish I knew more, but I do not. He wants Francesca—you would understand why better than I.

"He knows where you are. Alir—that old Requiem bastard—and his band are on the job. I believe you met once already. Be ready for them.

"I send my love.

"Ria."

Without looking up, Azran said, "Remember when you said we should stay here?"

"Yeah," Francesca replied.

"I'm still thinking Cruxia. It's a big city. We can blend in." He raised his gaze.

Francesca stared at the floor, shaking her head. "They're coming here either way. And if they don't find us—" She nodded to Valen, letting the implication hang.

"So, what, then?" Azran asked. "We just wait?"

"We can end this here. I know that band. There's five of them, six of us."

Valen stepped closer. "I object to you assuming my involvement." He grinned. "But damned if I haven't tested my mettle in some time."

"They're killers," Azran said. "Trained, experienced. And we don't know how many they might bring."

"And I have some wards yet to be tested on flesh. I suspect the results will be as vicious as any assassin." Valen put a hand on Azran's shoulder. "Besides, what manner of host would I be to let my guests come to harm?"

"We've got this," Francesca said, following Valen to the dining room.

To the ceiling, Azran said, "We're going to fucking die."

• • •

Valen sat cross-legged on a stool in front of one of the library windows. One hand steadied the other wrist as he painted an ink pattern on the sill with a thin brush. A worn book sat nearby, opened to a page filled top to bottom with diagrams and notes. Peering over his shoulder, Des examined the sweeping, hyperbolic letters of the Arcane Language. She looked at the deliberate, layered sigil on the wood, growing more complex with each stroke of the brush.

"Kinetic," she said.

"Very good," Valen replied. "Are you familiar with runes?"

"I've seen a few in my line of work. Luckily, they were either from our side or I had a chanter with me to do something about them. Damned if I know how they work."

"They're reservoirs." Valen's script continued to spiral inward, each concentric line of letters connected by matching esoteric sigils. "Just like the Arcane Language serves as a conduit and focus for a cast spell, a rune forms a maetrïz—matrix. Thus, you can store energy to be released later. The rune keeps the thread tethered and lays out what it will do, when, and how." At the center of the pattern, he painted a simple circle, then leaned back to assess his work.

"Right," Des said. "I remember a comrade of mine saying he'd set one to go off in an hour. Sure enough, I'm looking out over the East Docks and see his handiwork blow a ship in half."

"Gods, if only. I'm attempting to preserve the house, so these aren't quite so large. Little stingers, set to go off when a person passes through the target space." Staying back, Valen blew over the ink, then placed a book over the rune.

"I'll mark that."

"Good plan."

11

The Lieutenant pulled her cowl back, revealing cropped hair and eyes that glinted like her naked sword. She needed her periphery as she crept up the steep bank to the manor. She paused to check her belt—yes, her knife was still there. She did not check the positions of the others. Gear failed; companions didn't, and Alir least of all.

The Arcanist followed her, muttering dead phrases to check for wards. Alir would wait for the Arcanist's signal to enter. The Sniper sat in a tree on the opposite bank.

The Lieutenant's mind strayed forward in time, to the impending bloodshed. They only needed two alive. At least three others would bleed and die.

Focus.

She clutched an exposed root with her free hand and rolled over the lip. The Arcanist soon joined her under the wooden frame of a balcony.

"Well?" the Lieutenant asked.

"All the doors. Windows are clear, but some threads run through the whole place. Alerts, maybe."

"We move fast. Alir's on the north side. Tell him to make for a window. You take care of the ward on this door."

The Arcanist nodded and whispered. A dull flash emanated from the manor's north side, signaling. The Lieutenant and Arcanist climbed the balcony's frame. Crouching, the Arcanist slinked up to the oak doors. He stopped three paces short and fixated on the bottom of them.

"As mort in akir maetrïz perkotak," he intoned. He then curled his fingers around the latch. It was unlocked. He nodded to the Lieutenant.

She joined him, ready to sprint inside. Her mind was already there. Perhaps that was why she didn't notice him hitting the ground until some invisible, soundless push rocked her off balance.

The Lieutenant caught herself and glanced back. The Arcanist lay sprawled on the balcony. One hand reached down to his leg. Blood oozed from a dozen holes as if he had been shot by a dozen tiny bolts. His other hand waved her onward.

She stood at the top of a grand staircase overlooking a luxurious hall. A corridor led to the wing on either side. North, her instinct said. Alir was that way. No one was in here.

First blood to the prey, she thought. *Last will go to the hunters.*

She moved with grace, quick and cautious like a prowling cat. A door creaked down the hall. A man—living—put one foot out and pointed. The Lieutenant ducked, and a bolt of kinetic force took a chunk out of the wall inches from her head.

The living retreated.

The Lieutenant spun into an alcove, behind a pedestal and bust. Following him was a trap—or a diversion?

Something crashed on the level below, muffled through the floor but echoing up a stairwell just to her left. She grabbed the bust and tossed it into the dim corridor. A wider blast sent it careening back and rattled loose ornamentation. In the spell's wake, she rushed out, pushed off the opposite wall, and bounded into the stairway.

In a spacious library, Alir dodged a rapier thrust and batted the blade wide with his short sword. The rapier, a gaudy, decorative thing, was wielded by a vampire woman—Francesca, one of those who should not die. Another vampire picked himself up from the floor, wiping blood from his nose—Azran, also, was not to die.

Judging from the trail of debris, the fight had spilled in from another room. Then, from that other room, a living swordsman charged Alir. The Lieutenant intercepted with her thirsty steel. The living spun, backstepped, and parried her middle thrust. He countered with a basic diagonal cut from high. She blocked. The bind was strong from both sides, but he had the height advantage. The Lieutenant gave, then came back, rotating her wrist for a thigh cut.

Parry, riposte, retreat—a kinesthetic rhythm built. She was on the defensive, where she felt her power over the situation wane. The swordsman's eyes and blade exuded a faint but brightening glow. The Lieutenant spotted the medallion with Atora's grinning face. A Blade—she could not win through technique. Trickery, on the other hand, she had in spades.

Another crash sounded as Alir rolled backward over a table and flipped it in Francesca's direction.

The Atoran pressed on. The blades bound again, this time his strong on the Lieutenant's weak. He swept her sword out wide, and she let go, feigning fear. Her right side was wide open, and the priest took the bait. Eyes on the opening, he did not see her draw a knife in her off-hand. She turned sideways and leaned back, avoiding his thrust. With a flick and swipe, the knife sliced into his elbow.

The Lieutenant latched onto his sword with a gloved hand and pulled it from his weakened grip. He punched with his left. She rotated back, but even the glancing blow to her shoulder staggered her. Something about that hand wasn't right.

The priest kept coming, growling like a wounded beast and swinging that too-heavy fist. When he launched a hook, he leaned too far. The Lieutenant went under, wrapped his arm in a hold, and flipped him onto his back.

The living arcanist appeared in the door, bleeding from his forehead and scorched across his shoulder. He looked at the Lieutenant and started a spell, but the team's own Arcanist veritably fell down the stairs and interrupted.

"Ichnir vesnis parotak!"

The effect was weak, general, and lacking focus—but still, a burst of dull flames erupted over the living arcanist before dissipating in a flash. The living covered his face and cried out, whirling on the Arcanist. After the first word, the Arcanist started his counter.

"Ïs andeves mort parotak."

"As mort friŋatar nist."

A blurry beam fired from the living's fingertip but deflected into the ceiling. Splinters of wood rained down.

In her distraction, the Lieutenant missed the priest's heavy hand chopping across her ankle. Teeth-clenching pain shot up her bones as her leg gave. She fell, and he rolled over her, pinning the knife with his main hand and raising the fist to strike.

"Stop!" Alir shouted. "It's over."

He had Azran likewise pinned to the floor and looked prepared to cut the target's throat. Francesca rocked on her feet, one of her eyes swelling shut.

The Lieutenant knew Alir was bluffing. She prayed the prey did not.

The glow faded from the Atoran's eyes as he watched Alir. How the Lieutenant wanted to pull free and drive her knife into his neck, to open his vessels and soak herself in his warrior blood.

"Get off her," Alir said.

Wary, the Atoran stood. The Lieutenant followed suit. They each put a pace between them.

"Francesca Darani, you're coming with us," Alir said. He pulled himself and Azran to their feet. "Your lover, too. You misled us back in Aure, so we're done being civil. Amadore demands a reunion."

"You can tell my brother to go fuck himself."

Alir chuckled. "No, I can't. I've yet to meet someone who can."

Francesca straightened a bit. "You can't kill us, either."

The Lieutenant weighed her knife, then whipped it at the living arcanist. It stuck in his abdomen, and he grunted and doubled over.

"True, but we can kill everyone else." She shrugged. "Your call."

"Everyone...fall," the living arcanist growled through grit teeth.

"Yes," the Lieutenant said. "You're—"

"Son us foriz apaza ilir parotak."

A horizontal pulse of sonic energy distorted the air in a disk several feet off the ground. It struck the Lieutenant and the Arcanist, but everyone else hit the floor before it went off.

Dazed, head splitting, the Lieutenant struggled to focus on distant and dull images and sounds. Vibrations in the floorboards indicated an ongoing struggle. Some came near, and she swept an arm out, touching something tangible. Her ears popped after what felt like minutes. She opened her eyes. The Arcanist crouched over her, mouth moving as the volume of his voice returned to that of normal speech.

"They went through the window," he said. "I hit it with fire."

The Lieutenant craned her neck. Tiny licks of flame danced on the drapes.

"I saw a new one," he continued. "She was already outside."

The Lieutenant sat up. "Alir?"

"He followed them."

"They can't have gone far." She hurried to the window but stopped when she spotted the Sniper, face-down on the riverbank. She then vaulted onto the grass and followed the trampled path around the manor. Deranged, Alir called her grin. Also sadistic. Once, fucked up. Her outlook was a problem on hunts, only just outweighed by what she brought to the table. It wasn't a problem she had much interest in fixing, however.

He would have to be quick to stop her from killing every one of these bastards.

"Where is Darani?" she heard Alir ask. She rounded the corner to find him once again holding Azran hostage, facing down the Atoran. The target in question emerged from the grass behind

Alir. The Lieutenant opened her mouth and flexed, ready to shout and rush forward.

A hand clamped over her mouth and a blade dragged across her throat. At the same time, Francesca drove the Lieutenant's knife into Alir's lower back. He tensed, and Azran twisted free. The Lieutenant's vision spun as she twirled to the ground. She struggled to remain on her hands and knees. The reddening dirt was calling her.

She looked back to see the Arcanist clamber through the window. A woman with hair like hers and a leather vest took hold of him and, with fluid movement, spun and threw him into the next window over. The Arcanist's head broke the glass, and then gore splattered what remained as some unseen force spiked vertically through his skull.

The Lieutenant heard Alir struggling. Then Francesca said, "You were clever to get in on your own. Hades, you almost screwed our whole plan." There were a thump and a grunt like she kicked him. "But all that skill don't mean a damn thing when there's a knife in your back, does it?"

The Lieutenant tasted blood, but it was her own. She was growing numb at the same rate as the world around her.

Last blood still went to the hunters; it was then that she realized they had let themselves be the prey.

$$\bullet \ \bullet \ \bullet$$

Azran rounded the corner of the manor first, the others following behind. He saw Sevex already leading the prepped horses out of the stable.

They boosted each other into the saddles and rode the remainder of the night. Des said she took out a crossbowman across the river but admitted that tracking wasn't her strength. There was no telling how many assassins there were. Valen's wounds called for an easy pace, but his obstinacy set a hard one. Even more than on the journey from Aure, they avoided the main roads. They crossed the Valla at a weathered, toll-less bridge a dozen miles downriver from the estate, ignoring the first two they passed.

"There's an inn not far from the western bank," Valen said once they crossed. He straightened in the saddle, grimacing.

"I know," Azran said. "But it's too close still. We should make for the one in Calle."

"That's another twenty miles. How many hours till sunrise?"

"Enough." Azran turned his horse and kicked.

Calle was one of the dozens—perhaps hundreds, only the bureaus cared to count—of farming villages dotting the Lunateli countryside. The sky grew grey behind the riders as they galloped past fields and huts. The earliest risers watched them like silent ghosts.

The owner of the lone hostel gave them a long appraisal but rented them the beds. A party of six, some armed, would no doubt fuel gossip. Azran counted on the remoteness to shield them from prying eyes.

They were the only guests, so drawing the curtains of the shared room was no issue. The drapes were thin, so Francesca hung the thick black ones over the rod. An oil lamp sat on a round table, casting broad shadows onto the walls. A white glow doubled the shades for a moment, then faded.

Luc stepped back from a shirtless Valen. "They're sealed and won't get infected, but you should have a real healer or physician treat you."

Valen gingerly touched the red and white, seared flesh of his bony shoulder. "Thank you."

"No, thank you. You got us out of there."

"Not bad for two days' preparation, eh?" Valen wrapped a bandage acquired from the innkeeper about the closed wound in his abdomen. Sevex helped him tie it.

Then, the six of them sat around the table, half laying their heads in their arms and the other half slouching back in the chairs.

Azran sat up. "So. We need to take stock of our situation. We need to get to Cruxia. What then?"

Valen shook the exhaustion from his face. "If Francesca's brother is making a bid for Aure—if I understand your friend's letter—someone of authority needs to be informed."

"Shouldn't Ria have already done that?" Sevex asked.

"I wouldn't count on it," Francesca said. "It's not a safe time for a vampire to bring attention to herself. And with Ria's connections, I doubt she'd risk being arrested."

"He's a priest, yes?" Luc asked. "That sounds like a task for the Godshadows. We're not too far from the Crescent Chapterhouse, I think. They may help with the assassins, too, should more come for us."

Azran covered his mouth with his hand. "Right, about that. Just before all this started, a pair of agents came for me, looking for Francesca, to get to Amadore."

"And how did that go?" Des asked.

"It ended with two dead agents—not by my hand," Azran said. "Point is—"

"They're already after him," Des finished. She paused. "Did they follow up on that mess?"

Azran furrowed his brow. "No. I'm not sure what it means, but they didn't."

Des let out a breath. "Sounds to me like we've stumbled into something bigger than us. It's best if we just back out while we can." She met Francesca's gaze. "Unless you're feeling responsible for him."

Francesca did not answer.

"Right, then," Valen said, putting one hand on the table. "You lot hole up somewhere and wait for this to blow over." He stood and retrieved a large satchel, leaning to one side under the weight. When he plopped it on the table, the shadows cast by the lamp danced. Muffled clinks sounded as the bag settled. "As I said, we lost most of what we've got. But a tenth of what we still have to our name is enough to last a long while in the city. Not extravagant living, but comfortable."

"How much is in there?" Des asked.

Valen dropped a hand on the bag. "Gold. Three hundred aurli. Some trade bars and merchant checks worth another five hundred."

"Sailae's fucking fortune," Des muttered.

The others, except Sevex, mirrored her amazement.

"That's generous and all," Azran said. "But—"

"Some, not all," Valen said.

Azran nodded. "But I doubt Amadore will give up because his thugs were defeated. How far can we run?"

"What if—" Francesca stopped, glanced at the table, and rapped her knuckles once on the wood. "What if we don't run? I don't want to run from my brother anymore." Azran saw something long pent up within her break free, and it fueled her verbal momentum. "I've avoided him as much as I could. I never wanted him to have power over me the way our parents—but you know what? I can't avoid him. I never could. The more I push him away, the more I run away, the more control he gets. He's sending godsdamned assassins now. Valen almost died because I chose to run. All of you almost did.

"Fuck Amadore. The most sure of myself I ever am is when I stand up to him. Fuck. Him. I'm done running."

Five stares met her from around the table. Luc's was blank. Des's carried a sort of reserved support. Valen's admired, like a child gazing upon a hero. Sevex was confused, at a loss. Azran's grin faded to worry.

"But then what?" he asked. "What can we do?"

Francesca's fire diminished.

"We aren't warriors," Azran said. "We aren't arcanists, or priests."

"We are," Luc said. "It's rude to exclude people from conversation."

"You've put yourselves at enough risk on our behalf," Francesca said. "All of you. We can't ask for more."

"Can't, or won't?"

"Luc," Des said. "It's not our fight."

"No fight is yours until you join it."

"We have someone else to think about." Des jerked her head toward Sevex.

Luc followed the gesture. "What say you, then?"

Sevex sank back in his seat. "I—I think we should let the authorities handle this. I mean, what exactly are you proposing, Francesca?"

"I don't know. I still need to come up with something resembling a plan. No matter what, we need more to work with."

Valen cleared his throat. "Well, Sevex, if you aren't on board with this, we can see about getting you back in the safe hands of your employers."

Sevex gave a weak smile and nodded at that.

"You needn't worry about my brother," Valen said, looking at Des. To Francesca, he offered, "And should you need me, don't hesitate to ask. We've a few favors left to call in."

"But then what?" Azran asked. "You always say he never listens to you. Are we fighting Amadore? As in, physically fighting him? What if it comes to that? Because I think that's a terrible idea."

"I don't know," Francesca said. "But whichever way we go, getting to Cruxia, getting off the road, is the first step."

12

"I don't like the look of this place," Varja said.

"Which is why we're on our way out," Miranda replied. "I'm sorry it wasn't a more fruitful visit."

Varja just nodded, eyeing the ramshackle neighborhood around them. Coraea, it was called. Broken and pitted streets filled the narrow spaces between hastily constructed tenements. The residents eyed her back, sitting in the curtained doorways or leaning against rough timber walls. The complexion and features of the dwarves and humans were familiar—Macerian refugees and their descendants. They didn't want her here.

Varja tried not to blame Miranda. It had been a promising lead on finding Seneskar. She supposed that man's eyes might have looked more blue than green—if the beholder were colorblind. A few minutes' conversation had dispelled any lingering suspicion in Varja. That was not him.

"Elfblood."

Varja and Miranda stopped. A dwarf woman with her brown hair in several thick braids stepped away from one of the shacks into the street.

"Thought I warned you to keep away from that Ziach filth," she said. "And instead, you bring her into our home. And armed, no less?"

Varja glanced around. No one else was moving, but their eyes hadn't left her. They almost seemed too calm.

"We had someone to meet," Miranda said. "We're on our way out. No need for trouble."

The dwarf woman scowled. "Oh, we've a need."

Flat metal slid against Varja's back, then pulled away. The weight of her baldric vanished. She whirled and caught it on instinct, coming face to face with a short, wiry human. He held a knife in one hand and her sheath, its strap cut, in the other. Another local leapt onto her back, wrapping arms around her neck. She let go of the sheath, intercepted the grappler's hold, and threw him to the ground. The thief bolted with her sword.

The man on the ground rolled back to his feet and came on with raised fists. Varja barreled forward, blocked a jab, and got inside his reach. She took a second, shorter jab to the cheek, but willingly paid the price to lay a forearm across his collarbone, grab his knee with her free hand, and drive his upper body into the cracked stone. She bounded on past the dazed man and into an alley in pursuit of her sword.

Three more Coraeans stood between her and the man with her sword.

The thief held up one end of the cut strap and examined the silver sun-and-moon disk hanging from it by a leather loop. "Nice trinket," he said in Zixarsi. "What clan you from?"

"My mother was of Naryk," Varja replied through clenched teeth. The disk was her only physical connection to her mother. It was all she could do to size up her opponents before she charged into their midst.

The thief glared at her. "Naryk, is that so? We were only going to take your sword as recompense for your people turning to the Faith and driving our parents from their homes. But the warriors of Naryk slaughtered a lot of Macerians before they were brought down. And we've had no shortage of trouble from all you that came as spies among us. You heretics, you blood traitors just can't get enough, can you? Give her what she deserves. Give them one less soldier for their next crusade."

He stalked toward the far exit of the alley. The other three Coraeans stepped forward with fight in their eyes.

Varja grinned in response. She doubted she could explain how wrong their assumptions about her were. Part of her didn't want to, and that was the part in charge now. "You first, then the thief."

She went to one side of the alley to guard her back. The nearest attacker, the most nervous and likely inexperienced, launched a left-handed cross. Varja bobbed out of the way. One hand caught his extended elbow and pulled, the other clamped his throat and pushed, and she planted her left leg behind his. In full control, she threw him in front of the second attacker's punch. It connected with the first man's neck, reversing his direction again. He hit the ground, devoid of his bearings.

The third hooked Varja's left shoulder with both hands and dropped, pulling her ribs onto his knee. Grunting from the pain, she struck with her free hand, but the angle left her punches weak. He planted a foot on her side and pushed, attempting to dislocate her shoulder. Meanwhile, the second attacker kicked her other side viciously.

Varja flexed her chest and pushed off the kicker with her feet. Roaring, she launched herself over the control point and drove her first two knuckles into her holder's eye socket. She couldn't quite free her left arm, but it was enough to get on top of him and throw a straight punch into his nose.

She was unbound for just a moment before the second man hooked both her shoulders from behind and tried to pull her off. She kept her joints from locking back and followed him willingly. She pumped with her legs, taking control of the movement, and slammed him against the opposite wall. She spun around with a haymaker to the temple. His eyes rolled, and he was out.

The third man recovered his feet. Blood dripped from his broken nose, and one eye wouldn't open. Nonetheless, his fists were up. He and Varja squared off, both heaving from exertion. He feinted a right, but Varja knew he wouldn't go with his blind side. She dodged the expected left jab, quickstepping out of his sight. Before he could follow around, she put her thigh against his hip and her forearm across his opposite shoulder, so her hand was against his neck. With three points of control, she threw him to the ground. She followed, reversing direction and clipping her elbow across his lower jaw.

She stood and turned to the first attacker. He held one hand to his neck. Pain, fear, and hate mingled in his grimace.

"Varja, are you—whoa."

She didn't turn to look at Miranda. She asked, "You alright?"

"Yeah, fine. I could ask the same of you."

The unconscious man was rousing, and the half-blind one rose to one knee.

Varja smiled. "Fantastic."

"Here."

The hilt of Varja's sword appeared in her periphery. She pulled it from the sheath and went into an ox guard, pointing the blade at the trio. "How'd you get this back?"

"He wasn't watching where he was going and took a trip to the dirt," Miranda said. "He had a knife, so I didn't feel bad about pulling mine."

The nervous attacker's grimace deepened. "You killed—"

"No, of course not. Easy, man. There he is."

The thief entered the alley behind the beaten group. He opened his mouth to speak, but Varja interrupted.

"I'll say this once, so listen. My mother was Naryk, not me. Her clan was converted by sword and claw. She came as a spy, yes, but defected to the Valentreids. The Faith found out, and sent her back to Muntherziach as a hostage, to keep the clan in line. She never wanted me to live under the Faith. I grew up with my father's people in Procumes. The best I got from them was pity, and most didn't even afford me that. You're far from the first people to call me a traitor for the circumstances of my birth.

"And yet, against their wishes and all common sense, I went back to the continent. Do you know why? To fight the Faith. I bled and killed so people like you would be safe from them. But by all means, keep blaming me."

They refused to meet her eyes. One by one, they shuffled to clear a path back to the street. Varja rested her blade on her shoulder and walked out. The memories had killed her lust to beat them even more senseless.

Miranda walked backward behind Varja, her condemning gaze passing from man to man.

When they were out of Coraea, Varja slumped onto a bench. She stretched her left shoulder. It was strained, but not dislocated.

Miranda sat next to her and offered the sheath. Varja scabbarded her sword and stared at the silver sun-and-moon disk.

"Fucking pricks," Miranda said. "That dwarf showed me there was ignorance and a lot of bad blood around here. But if I'd thought they would pull something like that, I would never have—"

"It's alright. It was nothing I haven't dealt with before. Lucky for me, they can't wrestle worth shit." Varja leaned forward, putting her elbows on her knees and hanging her head.

"If you don't mind me asking, where's your mother now?"

"I went to the Naryk seven years ago, looking. She was already dead. The local sunatha found out she was still feeding intelligence to the Valentreids and had her executed." Varja tapped the silver disk. "This was all she left behind. It was a gift to her from the Silver King of the Chari tribes near Ternezorak. The Naryk said it was in case I came back. She's probably dead. Let's go get a drink."

"Don't have to ask me twice."

•••

Cruxia. It had been a long time since Azran was last here. 1344, maybe? Something like that. He had accompanied—no, back then it was followed—Francesca after she passed through his shitty hometown.

The streets were lit, but dimmer than Aure's. They were sparser, too, now that the evening tavern rush was over and everyone had settled into their cups. Most of all, they were calmer. Even so much closer to Charir, Cruxia strolled on, night and day.

Azran hadn't realized how much he missed his walks. Away from the nightlife, there were no crowds and little noise beyond the dull rumble of the waves down the hill. A chill, salty breeze tousled his hair, and he flipped it out of his face. He wished Francesca were here to enjoy it, as well. Work was important, sure. Her brother was a fucking madman, true. She needed to deal with that, yes.

But walks were important, too.

His feet, wandering independent of his thoughts, led him to a rocky shore. The city sat above, casting a pale glow down. The harbor lay to his right, dark masts cutting lines through the rippling glare on the water. Below the outcrop, waves rose and fell with the wind. Farther out, the sheen faded into the inky sea.

Azran tossed a rock over the edge and heard a muted splash. He picked up another stone, but as he cocked his arm, he heard a similar disturbance. He looked over and saw a sturdy figure throw again. Even in the scarce light, he could make out the vibrant sapphire of her eyes as she glanced his way.

"The Imperial Sea," she said. "The ego of this empire never ceases to amaze me."

"I'm sure it has a more fitting name, lost to the ages," Azran replied.

"The Cloud Sea, the Alturi called it. Or the Misty Sea. I don't remember the translation. That was before the dragons came, back when the Marexuri dwelled in the north."

"North? Our ancestors landed on this very coast."

The woman looked at him and smirked. "Is that what the Valentrae teach?"

Azran gave a half-smile of his own. "Where are you from, then, o sage?"

"Procumes."

"No shit? Ever meet a dragon down there?"

"A few."

Azran turned back to the silver-black waves. "It must be beautiful, surrounded by all that water."

"Yes. The mainland has its own charms, though. I've never heard music like I do in this city. The island I'm from is a bit stagnant. Slow to change. But there's so much variety here."

"You a music lover?"

"I seem to be turning into one. Are you?"

"It's one of three things I live for—music, my wife, my friends. I've only been playing a few years now, but I've always had the passion."

"Do you fancy a drink, zikochir? I have a friend you might like to meet."

"Zikochir?" Azran asked.

"It means 'sea gazer.' It's a compliment, I promise."

The Procumi woman said her name was Varja. She led Azran to a tavern that looked trapped somewhere between rustic and urbane. Tables were round, built of pale birch planks, but the edges seemed gnawed. The surfaces bore dark stains. Chairs had thin cushions, but the padding was worn almost to shreds. Graffiti was carved everywhere, in every form—initials, dates, vulgar invitations—tables, chairs, walls. Across the half-full room, a light-haired antileri woman dressed for the road but too clean for that spotted Varja and raised her glass.

Varja introduced Azran to Miranda, who called for a round.

"Not playing tonight?" she asked.

"Just enough for the drinks," Miranda replied. "I have to be careful. I think I'm starting to garner a reputation among the locals."

"You mean like those men who went up to you between songs last night?"

Miranda nodded. "One just wanted to fuck. Whatever, that's normal. But the other asked me to join his shanty crew."

Azran chuckled, but Varja cocked her head.

"They get a troupe together on a boat and sit in the harbor. It's basically busking, but you get paid in fish."

"Well, aren't you popular?" Varja said with a wink and sip from her drink.

"And then tonight, I met a band who invited me along to tour Pastoratel. No thanks." Miranda finished her original glass and grabbed her fresh one. "So, Azran—what's your story?"

"On holiday. The wife and I wanted to get out of Aure for a while."

Miranda painted a serious expression on her face. "Watch it, Varja—he's a married man."

Varja's eyes darted between the two. "What? I know. I—that's not why I invited—"

Miranda shook her head. "So easily flustered. I'm just poking some fun."

"How about your story?" Azran asked. He nodded at the head of an oud peering over the table. "You seem familiar. Ever been through Aure?"

"Not in a couple of years." Miranda studied him a moment, tapping a finger on the table. "I get what you mean."

"Silver Sun?"

She lit up. "Harpsichord?"

"That's right, shit, I did play that night." Azran winced. "I was not very good back then, and I apologize for any damage to your ears."

Miranda laughed. "I won't argue with that. Skill comes with time."

Azran lifted his glass in toast. "You should see me now. I wish there were a harpsichord around here. That's the only thing—you can't take them on the road with you."

"I might be able to locate an open one. I've seen a few since I got here."

Azran had a sudden notion to keep a list of every harpsichord he encountered on this journey. He wondered if they were always this common, and he just hadn't paid attention before. "Well, other than my shit playing, I remember it was a good night. Good week, really. You missed Ioran Delosa by a day."

Now Miranda winced. "'Missed' is a strong word. He gets more talk than he deserves."

Azran stopped halfway through taking a drink. "The man singlehandedly responsible for bringing together riverfolk and Astrelli jaunt gets too much credit?"

She laughed. "Right, okay. I'm from Astrellus, and I'm telling you there was nothing singlehanded about it. His old partner, Carus, lost his pick and started plucking riverfolk-style to keep up his speed."

Azran leaned forward in his seat. "Alright, but still, you can't deny—"

Miranda plowed on. "After they parted ways, what happened? Ioran reinterpreted every folk song from here to Septrion, but Carus continues to pen new melodies to this day. Have you heard a master play 'Blood for Blades'?"

"Yes, and it's just a Shallows ballad, except with arpeggios out the ass."

Miranda matched his posture. "You dismissing arpeggios? Of course you are, you're a keys player from Aure. Let's put a fingerboard in your hands and see how far your precious scales get you when you have to hold a fast beat alone in front of a room."

She chuckled and shook her head. "You sound like a raven mimicking its master's words. I've heard all this out of every dandy bard from here to Libre."

Azran eased back into his seat, Miranda into hers a fat moment later.

Barely able to contain his grin, he asked, "What's your opinion on Tall Renden?"

"Fuck him, and fuck you."

"Finally—something we can agree on!"

The pair broke out laughing. Varja followed their lead, but admitted, "I have no idea what just happened."

13

Francesca tasted the dirt of the warehouse floor. Like everything in this city, it carried a tinge of salt and dead fish. The ground was cool, smooth, dry—a contrast to her sweat-soaked clothes.

Flat metal rapped her shoulder blade, making her shirt cling to her skin.

"Up," Luc said. His footsteps receded.

Francesca blinked, spit, and pushed herself up, grunting at aching muscles. She turned to see Luc already back in his stance. She took a breath and found her own.

They raised their swords in unison. Now bereft of the fine sparring weapons of the manor, they had taken to wrapping thick cotton around real blades and being very careful with thrusts. Luc held his arming sword, while Francesca wielded the first work of an apprentice smith deemed worthy of sale. It was slim, nearly a rapier, and sported a basket hilt hammered with little finesse. But it was cheap, and it worked.

They faced off in a small, abandoned warehouse Azran had found one night walking alone. When Francesca asked him how he had stumbled across it, he replied that he was exploring. "You never know what you might find—a makeshift sparring ring, for instance."

Every morning before dawn and every night after dusk, Luc gave his lessons. Francesca took to the routine with spirit. She could never handle idle days. She needed something to work at. Even before heading to the warehouse, she would move through forms and footwork; afterward, she was too exhausted. Luc had offered to ease back on the pace, but she refused. She had found a challenge to overcome—lose that moniker of practice dummy.

On the walk there or back, she would ask her teacher about the intellectual side of swordsmanship, the storied side. Where did the circle school come from? What was the difference between coastal and heartland rapiers? Was it true that Sanna Arelli killed an armored knight with a wooden sword? Yes, it was.

Francesca knew she should have other concerns on her mind, but she wanted to obsess over something other than her brother. Every day, she would find a solution tomorrow; today, the training was her focus.

Twice she had lingered too long to beat the sunrise back to their inn and slept through the daylight hours on that smooth, salt-tinged floor. She did not complain. The training was her focus.

Focus.

Luc stared her down from five paces away. He moved in by one, then two. Three. Four. Still, he stood relaxed, poised for no obvious move. Francesca's mind raced, predicting half a dozen cuts and lunges he could launch.

"Right!" he yelled.

Two weeks prior, she would have fallen for that. She pivoted left, bringing her sword in for the parry. Steel met steel below the cloth wraps, near the crossguards. Luc pulled back to disengage, but she advanced and kept pressure on the bind. Though he was stronger, Luc could not overcome the leverage. She forced his blade down, then reversed and slashed up at his face.

He ducked backward under the swipe, rotated his grip inward, and blocked her following cut. This time, Luc pushed Francesca's blade low and cut up. She attempted to mirror his dodge, but the strike was a feint. Luc's wrist made a small circle as he went wide around her head and connected with her neck on the opposite side.

They each backed away.

"Better," Luc said. It was the highest his praise went.

"But I could do better still," Francesca said once she recovered her breath. What amazed her most about fencing was how much energy she could expend in just a few seconds.

"You have to give yourself time. We've only been at this a few weeks. Feinting, and especially how to recognize it, comes with years of experience."

Francesca allowed herself a small smile. "I did catch that first one."

"You did. That trick's more focus than anything. You watched me instead of reacting blindly to my voice." Luc walked over to a warped door. A rush of sea air blew in as he poked his head out and checked the stars. He began unwinding the cloth from his blade. "It's late. We're done for tonight. For the next session, I want you to meditate on how not to get tripped. You need to spend less time on the ground."

He sheathed and belted his sword, then left. Francesca lingered a few minutes, reenacting her successes and reworking the failures from tonight.

When she returned to the inn, a calm place called the Broken Arrow, Azran was not there. Francesca changed, washed her face and hands, and then began the nightly quest to find her meandering husband. She hoped he was at a nearby tavern, not gods-know-where along the shore.

As she passed the sixth establishment eastward, she spotted him through a paneless window. A smooth tune from a lute carried into the street, and all inside—including Azran and some tall Zixarsi warrior he shared a table with—seemed enraptured by the fingerpicked ballad.

Follow the music, Francesca thought.

When all that red is spent,
When it floods moor and fen,
And rivers run with rust,
We'll wade through e'ery glade,
With no more blood for blades....

She entered as the musician sang the final lines and flicked a series of ascending chords with her middle finger. A dense crowd cheered and sent coppers sailing to the floor around the player's stool. Francesca weaved her way through the patrons, coming up close behind Azran. "Found you."

Azran jumped and jerked back, sighing as he settled. "Chains, woman, why'd you do that for?"

She moved to his side and leaned on the table. "The mood struck me," she said, raising her voice to stay above the tumult. "Why'd your tongue slip for? Drunk already?"

"Not yet, but Miranda just bought us another round." He gestured with his glass to the musician, who was now picking coins off the floor.

Francesca turned to the Zixarsa. Her gaze lingered on the hilt of a longsword up against the wall before bidding the stranger a good evening.

"Right," Azran said. "This is Varja. Varja, this is Francesca."

Varja nodded. "Have a seat."

Francesca settled into the empty spot between Azran and Varja, just as Miranda sauntered in across the table. This time, Francesca introduced herself, almost yelling over the crowd.

"So, are you two related?" Varja asked, pointing at Azran.

"What?" Miranda and Francesca asked at the same time.

"What?" Azran asked a second later, leaning over the table and cocking an ear.

Varja looked confused. "You have the same eyes, and you're the only ones I've seen here so far with red eyes."

"Oh." Francesca broke out laughing.

Azran looked at her, then Miranda.

"Varja thinks that's your sister," Miranda said.

He chuckled and shook his head. Varja still seemed lost.

"No," Francesca said. "We're just both vampires."

"I thought so when I saw you, and when you mentioned the Silver Sun," Miranda said to Azran. "But I thought it crass to blurt out."

"Vampires?" Varja asked. "As in, blood-drinkers? Nightstalkers?"

"Have you never come across one?" Francesca asked.

"Campfire stories. Maybe in a bestiary once or twice."

Now Azran laughed heartily. "We're in bestiaries? What monsters we are."

Varja held up a hand. "No, I didn't mean to call you—"

"Relax," Miranda said. "Here come our drinks. Ale tastes better than your foot."

A server placed three foaming glasses on the table and took the empty ones. Miranda handed him some coppers and ordered a fourth.

"Loud bunch here," Francesca said.

"But generous," Miranda replied.

Azran cut his sip short, and then set his glass back down and caught Francesca's eyes. "You want to step outside?"

Francesca knew that look—time for serious.

The couple exited the tavern and used the mouth of an alley to shield themselves from the ruckus pouring onto the front porch. They leaned against the wall, shoulder to shoulder.

"Have you given more thought to our next move?" Azran asked.

"It sounds like you have."

He shrugged. "I want to play music. I've been talking to Miranda—"

"That woman you just met?"

"I met her once before, actually, when she played at the Sun." He sounded almost defensive, and definitely on edge. "Anyway, she knows where I might get my hands on a harpsichord around here."

"You have one waiting in Aure. And a job with it."

"I know." Azran scuffed the ground with the bottom of his boot. "It's not like I never want to go back, but." His voice trailed off in the face of Francesca's incredulous stare. After gathering himself, he continued, "This place she mentioned is looking for a new player. I think I have what it takes. And then, we could make our way in Cruxia a while. Let your brother's obsession cool down to a simmer before we return."

Francesca shook her head. "It won't. No matter what happens or when, it's going to be painful. Dangerous. That's why I've been doing what I have—so when the time comes, I'll be ready."

"When will you be ready?"

"I don't know."

Azran rolled his eyes, and the conversation paused at that dead end.

"What if we just don't go back?" he asked after a while.

Francesca shot him a burning glare.

He stepped away from the wall and faced her. "I'm just putting the idea out there. If you're not offering anything solid—"

"And you are? You haven't thought it through either, have you?"

"Chains, Francesca, give me something then. When do you want to do this?"

"I don't know."

Azran paced down the alley, then back up and onto the street.

"Soon!" Francesca called after him. "Shit," she said, more quietly.

He was forcing her hand, forcing her to confront the reality she sought to ignore twice a night while sparring, and she had nothing to play in return. Part of her resented him for it, but she resented the situation more. This conversation—and its outcome—had been inevitable, and that was frustrating.

Neither of them liked decisions with consequences—which, they each often pointed out to the other, were all decisions. But where Francesca would stand and stare at the possible doors until sunrise, Azran would grow impatient and kick one open.

Ponderous and impulsive all wrapped up in one—the blessing and curse of her husband.

She followed the alley to the opposite end and stopped. Across the street, in a gap left by two dead lamps, she saw Amadore. He held out his unmarred hand. Francesca recognized this for what it was—a choice. She had spent the past weeks convincing herself there were no choices left in her life, that she was coerced to act and wait and act again at the whim of the world around her.

But that was erroneous thinking. She could go to Amadore. It would be as simple as crossing the street. It wouldn't be surrender if it were on her terms. She still didn't know what he wanted her for so badly. It couldn't just be about his mad revolt in Aure. He wasn't sane, but his obsessive nature gave him an uncanny intellect for scheming. There had to be more to his actions than Francesca knew.

Across the street, the shadow continued to beckon. She took one step closer. Going to him would allow Francesca to find answers. And once she did, she could choose what to do with them. She had resolve now. Her refusal to kill on his order showed that. Being near him might not rob her of agency the way it used to. Might.

She took another step, staring at the apparition. She felt stronger. She felt confident. She told herself she could handle him. But was that her speaking, or Amadore? She knew how he deceived—not through lies, but by fostering just this sort of self-assurance. His psyche was a snake in the grass, waiting to strike when Francesca took one confident, mistaken step.

One of the arcane lamps flickered back to life, and Amadore was gone. Francesca blinked and rubbed her eyes. Her racing mind cleared, becoming a calm stream. A question surfaced that she should have asked several minutes ago—was that beckoning shadow her mental projection, or was Amadore himself somehow reaching into her psyche?

• • •

It was dawn when Azran returned to their room. Francesca already lay in bed. She was on her side, facing the wall opposite the door. He couldn't tell whether she was still awake. She'd been taking to bed early lately.

He hesitated—he had something to say but didn't want to start the argument anew and ruin this peace. He peeled off his fog-dampened shirt and tiptoed over. He lifted the blanket a few inches and slid in. Underneath the coverlet, he eased one arm around his wife's middle. She breathed calm and slow, regular, but as Azran lay his head down, she took a long inhale.

"I just want to take charge. I'm so exhausted of reacting. He acts, I react. I run. You can't imagine how exhausted. Sometimes, I don't even know what thoughts are mine or his anymore." Her hand closed over Azran's. "I want to look my brother in the eye and tell him to fuck off. And if he then tries to force anything, I want to punch his smug fucking face. Kind of want to do that just because. And I want to be strong enough that you need not fear for me."

Azran squeezed her hand back. "I'm not afraid for you," he said. "It's for me—I fear for myself. You are so much stronger than me. That you want to go back at all is proof."

Francesca rolled onto her back, still tight against him. "Not strong enough."

"Not yet." He touched her shoulder, tracing past her breast and down the side of her chest. Her ribs were more hidden now as firm muscle built on top. His other hand let go and traced up her

161

arm, now denser, toned tight. Against his leg, her bare thigh had less yield. She had always possessed tangible strength, from the first time their bodies met like this. Weeks of sparring twice a night built upon that foundation. The occasional fight for life likely helped, too, but Azran didn't want to follow those thoughts now. He wanted to think about Francesca—think about her strength. Feel her strength, which he did at every contact point. Eyes closed, his tracing ceased. Appreciation settled into contentment.

She shifted, and he felt her lips on his.

"I'm sorry," he said when the kiss ended.

"So am I. We'll figure this out."

"We will."

•••

Despite her fatigue, Francesca lay awake long after Azran began breathing the slow, uninterrupted rhythm of sleep. Light peeked around the heavy, black curtains, but not enough to cause discomfort.

She couldn't get Azran's words out of her head—he was afraid, and she was not. He had no idea how backward that was. She put on a show of determination but remained terrified of what would happen if they returned to Aure—to her brother. She recalled the hallucination in the alley—if that's what it was—and how even considering going back led her mind astray.

Even if she could manage to return, face down those doubts, fear remained. Maybe not for herself, but if anything happened to Azran because of her actions or her family's—well, perhaps she would at last comprehend his despair those years ago. Not for the first time, she regretted making him a vampire.

She looked at the edge of the curtains. This state of being brought more curses with it beyond that of Sola. Azran deserved a better existence. He would insist that she gave him the best he could ask for, but doubt still clawed at her. If they made it through the inevitable reunion and the conflict it walked arm in arm with, that would be Azran's test. Their test together.

Amadore was ruthless, odd, even deranged when last they spoke. Part of her—the youthful part that still loved him—had difficulty accepting him as the architect of the terror, fire, and death in Aure. Perhaps he was finally, truly broken. He'd had cracks in his reasoning since they lived on the estate in Ostitel. Those unsettling obsessions seemed to be consuming him—had consumed him, if Aure was his doing.

Even being born a vampire had not prepared Francesca for this.

14

The last time Des passed through Cruxia had been years ago. Now, she headed for the only part of it she remembered—Fishers Harbor, a series of rocky isles connected by wooden bridges of varying integrity. Thick morning fog rolled in from the sea, wrapping about the outcrops and masts of passing boats.

That previous passage had been a routine carry, apart from the distance involved. Slith, nip the sitter, caz. As usual, Des was a lock. Her role was easy. Among the fisherfolk, few were out past midnight.

Des sought that same isolation. She found it on a ledge between a steep basalt face and the grey shroud. The fog bank deadened sound, as well—she could not hear the bells or calls of the rising day. There was only the gentle, windless surf and the shifting of her body against the hard seat.

As her thoughts meandered through other last times, she realized she hadn't been seaside since her visit to Forente. "Visit" sounded casual. Dishonest. She'd gone there to kill a man; she ended up killing several people. Afterward, she barely saw the water as she and Luc hurried out of the city. That meant the last time she sat and watched the waves, her hands had been covered in Ecar's blood.

Des looked at her rough hands—a bit of dirt from climbing down here, but no blood. Was that her problem? Was she only sure of herself when—when killing? She hesitated to even think the word. She didn't want to end the thought with it.

No. She felt purpose when fighting, when struggling and striving for something. So did everyone else. She was like them—normal.

That last time in Forente, she didn't kill for pleasure. Ecar's death gave Des pleasure, but she had killed him for Arilysa. Justice for her fiancée, not revenge for herself. Why else had it felt so right, were it not the right thing to do?

That begged the question, then—what did Des fight for now? Ari would know. At the very least, she'd have a direction to offer. She always had.

The Cruxia carry happened before Des had met her. She didn't think Ari had ever been this far down. She would have enjoyed this city. Des had heard music around every corner as she walked alone the night before. The Kraken, or some affiliated guild, had a presence, but it was more hidden than in Forente. No watchers strolling down open streets, or cazzes around every corner. Cutters, sure, but the city would be more suspicious without pickpockets.

"You would've liked it here," Des said. "It's familiar, but without so many bad memories."

Damn it, she was talking to her fiancée's ghost again. Her hand reached up and pulled the emerald ring from inside her collar. Her fingers moved across the vine pattern, but her eyes never left the hazy sea.

She had to stop talking to a ghost. People might think her mad. Des was wondering herself.

"Nobody's here," she said. Then she understood the dual nature of that statement—nobody was there to think her mad. Luc always said voicing one's problems was better than keeping them silent.

"I—" Now that Des was conscious of it, she found it difficult to start. She took a breath. "I feel like I have no direction. Without you, now that all is wrapped up, I don't know where to go, what I want. I keep saying I owe Luc a debt, but he denies it, so how long can I harp on that? How far can guilt carry me? I can't go back to the Kraken. I don't have to tell you why.

"I could stick with these vamps, but I don't think they know what they want, either." She paused. The water lapped the rock. A little bell rang three times in the distance. "I hesitate to say I want something bad to happen, but it seems like those are the only times I have answers. Or maybe I just don't have time to question myself. What's better—having no answers or having no questions?

"I'm so tired, but sleep seems like such a waste. I just want *something*." She threw a stone into the sea. "I want to bleed."

• • •

Varja staggers out into the rain. She stumbles not from pain, but from muscles starving for reprieve. The pain will come soon.

Duck a wild haymaker. Counter to diaphragm.

The drops, chilled by the night air, send a shiver through her nerves, which fire as though she is still under attack. But the flinch passes, and serenity ensues.

Fall prey to the feint. Miss counter. Buckle from an elbow to the back.

She reaches her right arm forward and left, stretching the bruised shoulder blade. Here comes the pain. But it is a good pain.

Keep moving. Roll out of reach and regain feet. Brace to receive.

She shuffles in small circles, facing the black sky. It is a good pain not for itself, but for what it means. She is alive. She fought. Win or lose, she struggled, and there is accomplishment in that.

Rain washes the sweat and blood from her features. There is forward motion in struggle. Even if you do not move, there remains the illusion of motion.

Clash. Tackle. Wrap limbs around joints and throw.

The damp air amplifies the smell of salt. Sea and sweat. There has been almost no motion since Varja came to this city. Not even the illusion. She only waits and asks and waits for answers that bring more waiting.

Follow to the dirt. Hold arm and legs. Put weight on the chest and hold.

She stretches other limbs before they stiffen from fatigue. In a fight, waiting is a mistake. You don't miss opportunities—you give them to the other person.

Take reverse headbutt to the left eye. Slacken grip. Lose hold.

She closes her right eye. She can still see through the left, from which a dull throbbing begins to spread. The pain is a reminder. She is alive, but forgot for a moment. She waited, and so collected another bruise.

Stand. Ignore slow left hook. Follow eyes low instead. Catch low kick.

She smiles. The rising downpour cleanses the blood from her split lip. She revels in the vitality only combat can bring—combat or a storm.

Don't wait. Don't pin. Strike with free hand. Penetrate off-balance defense. Punch again and again and again. Don't wait.

She runs one hand over the scabbing knuckles of the other. Her callouses have grown soft. More pain. Further reminder.

Thunder rumbles, starting somewhere far off and echoing through the streets. Varja's smile turns into laughter. A fight *and* a storm? The weather bathes her in water; the new surge of adrenalin bathes her in ecstasy.

The laughter subsides into energetic reverie.

• • •

Des slipped around a monolithic bouncer and out the back door. A second peal of thunder confirmed that she had heard a first. No matter—she could use some cool rain after the sweaty basement arena. And if that Zixarsi fighter went outside, so would Des.

She wasn't sure why she was doing this. Every time she got too close to another woman, Ari's ghost would halt Des's pursuit flat. But despite knowing what would happen, she wanted to spit in the face of her better judgment. She had to meet this fighter, this westerner who stood at least half a foot above her, who moved like a dancer even as she bashed her opponent's face in, who grinned through a bloody lip, who roared like a beast and then walked up the stairs without a word.

This woman had fight in her, the vital spirit Des feared she was losing. Watching that fight made her feel more alive than she had in a long time.

And then, there she stood in an alley lit only by the streetlamps at either end. Rain soaked her fast as she gawked at the Zixarsa. The fighter faced the tavern's back wall, forearms and forehead flat against the brickwork.

Des almost turned and left. But she didn't run. She, too, was a fighter. Heart pulsing faster, she leaned her back against the wall a few feet from her quarry. "Good fight," she said over the rain, before wincing to herself. Was that the cleverest she had?

The Zixarsa eased into a more vertical posture and looked at Des. Her bottom lip was scabbed, and her left eye was swollen not quite shut. She blinked a few times. Her demeanor was that of someone waking from deep thought.

"I thought so," she replied.

"You okay?" Des asked.

The Zixarsa grinned, and her lip split open once more. "You should see the other guy."

Des smirked back. "I did."

The Zixarsa started toward the door. "I should go thank him."

"Might want to wait till he's conscious," Des said. "He's awake, but just barely."

Lightning flashed, thunder following a second later. The Zixarsa glanced up. "Nice night."

"Oh, yeah," Des said with a chuckle. She looked at the fighter's serene expression. "You're serious."

"Nothing better. The sky right now is the only thing stopping me from drinking the rest of it away." She went back to the wall, letting a meager eve shield her from the rain as she watched for more lightning.

Des spent the next minute shifting her gaze between the sky and the fighter—from her loose, wavy, black hair, past her statuesque, exposed shoulders and arms, lingering probably too long for subtlety on her ass, and finally to her bare, muddy feet. She cast a hell of a profile. Not all women with power like that retained such.... *Breasts, yes, Des, you're staring at her breasts and her body and her whole everything, now say something before she notices or leaves or notices and then leaves or who knows—*

"Well, when you do, let me buy you one."

"What?" the fighter asked.

Des swallowed and managed to meet her eyes. "Let me buy you a drink."

"Oh. Sure, I appreciate it."

Does she understand? Des wondered. *Godsdammit, not this time, please.*

"Did you, um, want to do that now?" the fighter asked.

Des shrugged. "Whenever."

"Now. I could use one now. The pain is good at first, but—"

"After a while, yeah. I know the feeling. I think I saw some northern whiskey behind the bar. That should do the trick." Des winked. *Fuck it, I need a drink either way.*

"You fight?"

"Hey, don't let the height fool you. I've been in more than a few scraps." As she led the way back inside, Des could have sworn the Zixarsa's gaze lingered on her—perhaps not ogling, but not far off. They sidled around the bouncer, who may very well have been a breathing statue. "What's your name anyway?"

"Varja."

"That's pretty."

"It means 'dancer.' What's yours?"

"That fits. I'm Des."

"What does that mean?"

"Nothing, really, as far as I know. It's short for Desalie, but no one calls me that."

The fights were more or less over when they reentered the basement. Varja's was the last good one, or so the passing patrons kept saying as she and Des drank Pastori whiskey at the bar.

"Did you come to fight?" Varja asked.

"No, not really," Des replied. "Just wanted to see what the rings are like in this part of the empire. I'm a street scrapper from out east, so my tactics probably wouldn't go over well here. You're all so honorable in this city."

Varja took a shot. "I'm from Procumes. I'm just here on—I'm looking for someone. Ostensibly."

"No luck?" Des said.

Varja shook her head.

"There's an art to it, some of my colleagues used to say. But it's mostly about asking the right people the right questions the right way."

"Is that what you do?" Varja asked. "Find people?"

"I'm—in between careers right now." Des slammed a shot. The liquid burned away her anxiety. "I was in security work. Being a bodyguard for merchants and such. Sometimes, that meant having to find people, but the last time I did that was freelance." She saw the question in Varja's eyes. "Who are you looking for?"

After Varja gave the description, Des said, "Sounds like the sort you'd see in Cruxia, as long as they aren't looking for a government job."

"Your government seems—"

"Strict? Demanding? Labyrinthine?" She nodded. "You learn to work around it. So who is this guy who's got no right blending in?"

"He's, ah, family. Sort of. More my clan." Varja sighed. "I was supposed to be taking tonight off. Anyway, I hope finding him will help me get in their good graces. I don't exactly...fit in."

"So what? Fuck that. Look, I know I don't really know you or this whole story. Maybe this is the whiskey talking, but it's never made me lie, so listen." Des leaned forward, putting two fingers on the bartop. Varja did not recoil. "Have you ever been happier, been stronger, been more you with them than you were in the ring tonight?"

"I don't—I'm not sure."

"Worth considering. From where I'm looking, I doubt it. What I saw tonight was genuine. I saw fire and spirit and it was beautiful. Don't let anyone take that from you."

"You seem passionate about this."

Des poured herself another drink. "I guess I'm just trying to keep moving forward. I don't like what happens when I wait."

Varja held out her glass for a refill. "I'll drink to that. Next one's on me."

And no sign of a ghost, Des thought. She smiled, praying she hadn't just jinxed her luck.

15

Seneskar hated to linger in Cruxia. He knew his clan's stance on the Faith of Fire—that it was a despicable show of arrogance. Meeting with the sunathach proselytizing in Procumes was another black mark on Seneskar's deviant reputation. And now that he had disappeared afterward, the clan leaders would have been foolish not to surmise his conversion. In short, he was a traitor and a fugitive. They were quite formal when it came to that.

The clan's choice of retriever was curious, however. Seneskar had kept an ear to the streets since that close encounter, and had heard tell of a tall, blue-eyed Zixarsi woman with a longsword searching for his human guise. She was still here—Varja, the halfblood. How the clan expected her to be successful, Seneskar could not guess. Perhaps they did not. Poor thing.

Still, one as rash as her could compromise his agenda, even accidentally. If, by some miracle, she did find him, his cover could be blown. He had to move on.

However, getting in contact with his potential allies had taken longer than expected. The sunathach had told him that certain members of the Godshadows, the Valentreid magical and religious peacekeepers, were uncovering the same conspiracy as the Faith's triumvirate. If Seneskar could hide his allegiance, he had a chance to recruit their help. If they discovered his secret, it would be quite the challenge—they specialized in finding heretics. He hoped they were desperate enough for help that they wouldn't delve into his motivations.

Given the delicacy of this maneuvering, he had implored himself to be patient. But now, on the cusp of contact, nerves set in.

Seneskar scanned every inch of the quiet tavern. The Hanged Sorrow often hosted such clandestine meetups, from Kraken smugglers to Airin cultists. It filled a niche, and no faction wanted to see this neutral ground compromised.

Thin shafts of light entered through shutters on the west wall, catching suspended motes of dust. Candles burned on a few uneven, splintering tables. Seneskar sat in one in a far corner, away from the illumination. His gaze flicked over to the other two patrons across the room as one slid a lumpy purse to the other. His eyes swept right, lingered on the reinforced door, then continued to the antileri bartender reading an almanac by the light of a brass lamp. He looked back to the door, then down at his clasped human hands.

The door opened, flooding half the room with orange before closing. Seneskar watched as a silver-haired elf took quick stock of the interior. The newcomer was too pale to be from the coast. He wore a ragged grey cloak over a decrepit, dull, and motley outfit of fabrics and leathers. An arming sword hung from his left side. Eyes the color of his hair absorbed the room, and the elf glided across the floor toward his table.

"Seneskar?"

He had thought it best to be truthful about one thing. Doubtful diviners always seemed to start with names. He nodded to the creaky chair opposite him. "The Shadows?" he asked as the elf sat.

"Yes. I'm Exus. And ex-Shadow, if we're to be honest. But I still have pull with some, shall we say, sympathizers. I'll spare you the politics."

"I'll thank you to do so, unless it involves our business. Now, I've heard you discovered something troubling in Oretel."

"That's one way of putting it."

He's not sure how much I know. Seneskar realized he'd have to be the one to say it. "You found a man practicing soul magic on other people, a crime against gods and mortals alike. Do you know where he came by such knowledge? And why?"

"A rogue angel. For what purpose, though, is yet unclear."

"Not to all," Seneskar said. "An Angel of Shade known as Zerexis. Its agenda goes far beyond making a few heretics." He paused, gauging the elf. Exus's eyes did not go wide; he did not lean forward over the table. If Seneskar had to guess, Exus had expected such an answer. He still had the elf's attention, though, so he continued. "Whether Zerexis still serves Tenebra or not, it has designs that very much reflect her old schemes, but are more brazen. It wants the throne of the empire. It wants to shroud the land in darkness. Classic story of myth, I know, which is why my sources tell me there is more to it. But it and the bulk of its allies

will be in Aure. We will go there and ensure it does not spread its
heretical will."

Without hesitation, Exus asked, "Who's 'we?'"

"All who are willing," Seneskar replied.

"Who are your masters?"

Seneskar attempted a disarming smirk. "Masters? I have
sources, but—"

Exus cut him off. "You speak as an agent would. I could hear
the deference in your tone."

Seneskar leaned back in his chair and entwined his fingers.
"Let us say they have a vested interest in the status quo of the
empire. In truth, even I have not met them in person, only
messengers. I'll spare you the politics."

Now Exus hesitated. After a long, discerning look Seneskar
had seldom seen from a Marexuri, the elf said, "I have three
Godshadows willing to follow me. Each is skilled and has contacts
across the empire. What can you provide?"

Seneskar let out a small sigh, relieved. "Just me, but I can fight.
More importantly, only a handful of people in the empire know
my name. Fewer still know my face, and this is one of many I can
wear. I am well versed in glamors."

Exus lay bare another hard gaze, this one accompanied by a
muttered spell. Seneskar held the look, desperate to hide his inner
panic.

A raised eyebrow indicated Exus's first hint of surprise.
"That's no glamor. What are you?"

Seneskar chuckled and folded his hands on the table. "That
was quick. A touch paranoid?"

"The last time I followed blind faith, I—nearly died. And I
failed someone. So, before we go one step farther, you will answer
my questions."

178

Well, that is curious, Seneskar thought, taking a new measure of this elf. "It seems we both have our secrets. You have a strange air about you. I can't place it, but you don't feel quite…alive."

That struck a nerve. Exus was tapping one finger on the pommel of his sword and seemed ready to pounce.

Seneskar did first, continuing, "I could ask you the same questions. What are you? Who do you serve? Or, we could each agree that our goal is more important than our reasons. Do you still wish to pursue this alliance?"

In Exus's silver eyes, Seneskar saw a maelstrom of fear and spite. That soon passed, replaced by calculation. After a long while, during which the other two patrons paid for their drinks, left a generous tip, and exited, the elf gave a slight nod.

"Agreed, then," he said. "On the third dawn from now, meet us the northeast road, in Quarrytown. From there, we go to Aure." Exus stood and left. He flipped a coin to the barkeep, who barely looked up from her book to catch it.

Seneskar remained as the light through the shutters faded. Many thoughts passed through his mind, but most were a variation of *I'll have to be careful with this one.*

16

"Fuck me," Des mumbled with a groan. "And fuck whiskey." She cracked open one eye and found herself in a familiar inn room. "Ah, hades, I didn't mean that." At least she had found her way back. She checked her surroundings more thoroughly and discovered she was backward in the bed, wearing her full clothes and boots, and alone. She'd expected the last part but figured there was no harm in hoping.

The rest of the night came back to her. She and that fighter, Varja—such a pretty name—and woman—and—

Des shook her head, then regretted the motion. Anyway, the two had stayed at the bar until everyone else had left. They talked about where they were from, their time so far in Cruxia. Des made some drunken suggestion that the night was young and they should see it through. Varja declined, likely with more gentleness than Des remembered. So, Des bought the rest of the bottle for the road, and left it lying empty on said road.

Up until the end, it had been a good night. But Des, in her state addled by both alcohol and the thrill of connecting with such a woman, had also suggested something else.

Damn, what was it? I said—no, offered to—

She snapped her fingers. She had offered to find that cousin or whatever Varja was looking for.

Shit, why did I do that? Who do I think I am, Lockiron? I don't know this city. I don't have dogs here, and even if I do, can I trust them anymore? Des still didn't know if word got out about the precise events of that night in Forente. She'd given the Kraken too wide a berth to find out. The cazzes in Aure seemed to have an inkling even before she gaped.

What was the man's name? Sesker? No, Seneskar. Some Procumi name, or maybe Zixarsi.

Des sighed. She supposed she could poke around a bit. She would get to know Cruxia. If nothing else, it gave her something productive to do.

Not much of a carry, she thought, *but it'll do. Later.* She kicked off her half-laced boots, removed her leather vest—gods, she was sweating—took a swig of stale water from her canteen, and collapsed back into bed.

Some hours later—no more than two, she guessed—Des roused again. She finished her canteen, re-dressed, checked her boot knives, secured her fighting knife under the back of her vest, and smoothed her bedhead. She needed to cut her hair. But first, she had a fugitive to find.

She made her way past Luc's room, then Azran and Francesca's, and down the stairs to the common. It was almost noon, but to Des's surprise, she smelled fresh pastries and frying eggs. The tavern area was nearly empty, but a few patrons were eating breakfast. Her stomach growled.

Leaning on the bar, she asked, "Can I get coffee. And, are you still serving breakfast?"

"Well sure, honey, we just started." The innkeeper, petite even for a dwarf, gave a warm smile. She went to a kettle at the edge of the open kitchen and began straining some coffee. "Not from Lunatel, are ya? Never heard of a Cruxia day?"

"In passing."

"Well, dawn's at noon, luncheon at dusk, and festivities end at moonset." The innkeeper placed a steaming clay mug in front of Des. "My night keeper says you got in a bit later than that, even."

"Yeah? Guess I wasn't paying attention."

The other woman laughed. "He said that, too."

Des perched on a stool. "Everybody gets up at noon?" Where she was from, only two kinds of people kept such hours—city guards and their opposite.

The innkeeper put her elbows on the bar. "Well, not everybody, but lotta folk. Cruxia's a city of people too close to conflict for comfort, but doing their best to forget that."

Des took a sip of coffee and tipped the mug toward the innkeeper. "I like that. You know the city pretty well?"

"Only been here a few years. I think that's why I can sit back and see something like that. As I said, most folks do their best to forget what's on the other side of the mountains."

"Right. I've only been through once, and that was a real stride. I wager you know this place better than me, at least."

The innkeeper nodded. "I wager."

"Well," Des said, edging forward. "I've some business with a man fresh from Procumes. A quiet man, if you get me. I hear he's fond of music, too. Know where I might find such a man? What neighborhood he might hang in?"

The innkeeper rubbed her chin. "You might try Agora, specially if he's a trader. But that night man of mine, Theod—he'd know better. He's got these streets and everybody in them tattooed on his brain, I swear by the gods. Tell him Serile pointed you his way."

"I think I will. When does he come in?"

"Oh, you don't have to wait for that. He don't sleep much. Should be down on Painters Row, working a place called the Autumn Flower. Insists on working more, but I can only pay for so much time, you know?"

"I think I know the type." Des finished her coffee and passed two silvers to the innkeeper. "Tip for a tip." Just as she stood to leave, her stomach growled again.

Serile laughed. "So sorry, dear, you asked about breakfast and I just started rambling. Coming right up, you just have a seat. Theod can wait."

Des chuckled, both at her haste and the innkeeper's demeanor. She sat down. *Good to be on a carry again,* she thought.

Painters Row lived up to its name, as did several blocks to each side of the thoroughfare. As opposed to the whitewashed or dull brick dwellings of most residential Cruxian neighborhoods, the buildings here were vibrant reds, blues, and yellows, many decorated with murals and frescoes. In place of buskers, streets corners featured canvas artists vending economical pieces, or even doing on-the-spot commissions with performative flair.

A passerby at one crowded intersection bumped into Des. She caught his wrist before a tiny blade between his fingers could find her purse string.

"Excuse me, ma'am. Should've been watching better."

Des released the cutpurse, and he retreated down a side street. *New city, same amateurs.*

The Autumn Flower was airy, with a lattice door, wide windows, and large back patio perched on a sheer drop to the next street. Long pots rested in the windows and edged the patio with blue- and white-flowered caryopteris in full bloom. Smoke from more practical herbs mingled with the sappy aroma of the plants. The inside was blue-green and accented with horticultural still lifes between the windows.

Des dodged a gesticulating orc's sweeping mug on her way to the bar and found a seat. She spotted the keep, a sallow-faced young man sporting a short beard, and hailed him. "Don't suppose you have any good tea here?"

"No call to be coy, ma'am. Chamomile and blackcurrant right from Forente. Straight, enhanced, or dirty?"

"Blackcurrant, dirty," Des replied. "But brandy. I can't think about whiskey right now."

"Thought you looked familiar," he said, wagging a finger. "Coming right up."

When he returned, Des said, "Theod, right? Serile mentioned you could help me. Said you know the city."

Theod glanced around to ensure no one was waiting, then lit a pipe and sat behind the bar. "New to town?"

Des sipped the mixed tea, enjoying the fruity notes. "Took a stride through once, but that was years ago. I'm looking to reacquaint myself."

Theod took a pull and exhaled a grey cloud. "Stride on a carry? How many dry?"

Oh, shit. Des knew she slipped into Cant on occasion, but it was rarely an issue.

"You on a carry now? I'll be slippish."

"No carry," Des said. "Not for Cap or Cross. Just a stow with an innocent wink. I'd make us level."

Theod nodded. "What you dredging, then?"

Des hesitated, making sure she wasn't misremembering what Varja had said, then repeated her description of Seneskar.

Theod snapped his fingers and took another long draw. "Blue eyes—there's the ringer. Now, where'd I see him? I'm having trouble remembering."

Des took a small handful of silvers from her purse and passed them over the bar.

Theod glanced at them, then chuckled. "Hang onto your jingle, stow. I wasn't making a ploy. Where might I have seen him?"

Des sighed. "That's what I'm asking you."

"Right, right. But if you had to loose an arrow in the dark—"

"Chains, I don't even know his business. He's Procumi, he's spring from seaside. He likes music, I think?"

"Ah, why didn't you say prow? Right, I've seen him in a couple drowners on the Song Streets. Red Rocks and the Coin Stage. Red Rocks twice, now I think about it." He swept up the coins, holding one between his fingers. "Drink's covered. And no worries, stow. I didn't glance your blue-eyed stranger was looking to bog. Or else, he's cracked at it."

"Thank you," Des said, both frustrated and relieved. That could have gone better, but she still got more than expected. And, she still had some anonymity. "Remember—slip."

Theod, making his way to a patron at the end of the bar, turned his head and held a finger up to his lips.

She finished her dirty tea and left, pondering her next steps. Varja had neglected to mention where she was staying. Des could try the ring again, but chances were Varja was taking a couple nights off. And from what she had said, it wasn't a venue she planned to frequent while here.

Ari would know what to do, Des couldn't help thinking. *She was always better at planning than me.*

After a casing excursion up to Song Streets—another apt moniker—Des returned to the inn. Over an "early" lunch, she put a smile on Serile's face by saying Theod was helpful.

Then, sitting in her room for a much-needed rumination on her circumstances, Des heard a knock on her door. She had been wary ever since unknowingly meeting a Kraken informant that afternoon. She pulled a boot dagger, held it reversed inside her sleeve, and padded to the door.

The floor creaked on the other side, and knuckles rapped three more times. "Des?"

She opened the door. "Evening, Luc."

The priest's eyes flicked to her left hand, hidden by her sleeve except for her curled knuckles. "Expecting somebody else?" he asked.

"Guess you learned something in Forente after all." Des flipped the blade around and sheathed it. In response to Luc's inquiring stare—*godsdamned priests*—she said, "Simple caution."

"You were gone late last night, and most of today," Luc said. "Most days we've been here, when I think about it."

"Been doing a lot of thinking."

"Have you?"

"Yes."

"Just thinking?"

"A bit of doing, too, I suppose. Found some work."

"What kind of work?"

"What do you want, Luc?"

He continued his priestly stare, then said, "Well, I hope you don't have any crime bosses to kill tonight. Azran and Francesca invited us out for drinks."

17

"Fuck me," Varja mumbled with a groan. Despite the post-fight high and long night that followed, she was in more pain than she wanted to admit. Lying in bed, she stretched her arms with care. She was sure that elbow to the back had left a bruise, and her muscles were stiff, but nothing alarmed her there. She felt around her left eye—swollen, but a bit less than last night. She sighed. Minimal damage, considering.

Still, *fuck,* everything hurt.

With another groan, she sat up and cracked open her eyes. Tousled, frazzled locks shielded them from the late morning sun flooding the hostel. She heard a cup clink on a saucer and turned, brushing the hair from her face.

Miranda sat at the table by the window, sipping what smelled like strong black tea. Her long hair hung loose but was tamer than Varja's. She wore a thin nightgown, blue-green—like her eyes—

with lines of white that rippled like waves when she shifted. Varja gazed less than usual, though—for some reason, looking at Miranda made her thoughts turn to the woman from last night.

Desalie—Des. No one calls her Desalie.

"Good morning," Miranda said with a glance her way. "I was surprised when I got back before you last night. Have a good time?"

Varja pulled herself to sit on the edge of the bed. "Oh yeah."

Miranda did a double-take. "Chains of Crusix, Varja, what happened to you?"

"Got in a fight."

"Oh, good. At least I know you're not dangerously clumsy." Miranda rolled her eyes. "What in hades happened?"

"Don't worry. The other guy got the worse end." Varja displayed her scabbed knuckles with a proud grin. "I needed to let loose. I heard about a ring bar from a worker in Shippers Harbor, so I checked it out."

"There are other ways to get rid of pent-up energy." Miranda counted them off on her fingers. "Singing. Dancing. Running. Drinking. Fucking."

Varja laughed. "Well, I did a bit of the last two."

"You did?"

"Yeah, I fucked that guy's face with my fist, then had some drinks with a generous spectator."

"Oh," Miranda said. The humor dissipated her remaining shock. Then she gave a sly look. "Just drinks?"

"Yeah. She insisted on buying me one, then I bought her one, and so on."

Miranda mumbled something, but Varja didn't hear. She was busy reliving the night at the bar. Des was nice. She kept paying for drinks even as Varja started to put her under the table. And they talked more like old friends than new acquaintances. Des told tales of old "scraps" in Forente, which Varja traded with war stories—the lighter ones. She wanted to keep the night fun, after all. Des sounded like a good fighter. Varja hoped she could see her in action sometime. Gods, Des was nice. She sounded like she'd been through a lot but still had a strong heart. And she had such a cute—

"Varja? Hello?"

She shook her head. "Sorry, what?"

"You sure you didn't get kicked in the skull too hard?" Miranda asked. "You were staring at the wall like you wanted to snog it."

"Snog it? No, I'm fine. Just a little hungover maybe. What were you saying?"

Miranda sipped her tea, giving Varja a look she couldn't read. "I said I was going to play at the Coin Stage tonight, and our new friends will be there—Azran and Francesca? Good place for a relaxing evening. Unless you have other plans?" Again with that look.

"Sure. Sounds like a good time. What other plans would I have?"

"You never know. Alright, then. They mentioned they have a friend who's skilled at finding people. I thought that might interest you."

"Oh? Yeah, sure," Varja said. *Back to the impossible task, then.* "I'm going to find some food."

● ● ●

Des told herself it was her paranoia acting up again. This wasn't a fisher. She was with her friends. *Friends that Kraken agents would have little trouble manipulating,* something in her said. No, they were canny enough to make it this far. And how would any agents here recognize her from whatever half-forgotten description Laryn, Sayel, or anyone else may have delivered?

Still, she stood outside the Coin Stage—one of two bars Theod had named—as Azran said this was where they were meeting his and Francesca's new friends. This was a touch unsettling.

Des swallowed her misplaced apprehension and followed the others—Luc and the two vampires—inside. The common room was round, with a bar straight across the far end like an arc and a raised stage in the middle. Around the stage, there was space enough for dancing before circular tables filled the remainder. The platform stood empty, but every table looked occupied.

"Let's hope they snagged one," Azran said, scanning the carousing crowd.

"There they are." Francesca pointed and started maneuvering over.

Des followed the line of sight and, again, questioned her agency in the cosmos—only for a moment, though. In the next instant, the questioning, the paranoia, even the lingering vexation from Luc's earlier rebuke all faded from mind. Because, somehow, sitting next to some dolled-up antileri was Varja. And she saw Des. And she smiled at Des and gave a small wave.

Des's feet started working again, and she arrived at the table as the others were pulling out chairs. Azran reached for the one next to Varja. Des gently but insistently tapped his shoulder. He looked at her.

"Can, uh. Can I sit there?" she muttered, just audible for him.

Without so much as a glance at Varja, Azran winked and replied, "Sure thing." He sat on the other side of Francesca, shifting Luc over a place.

Des took her seat. She gave a sheepish look to Varja, then cleared her throat and mustered her courage. "Hi."

"Hi, Des."

"You two have met?" Francesca asked.

"Yeah, last night at a ring," Varja said.

"Your eye looks better," Des added.

"Ah, I was wondering what happened," Azran said, nodding. "Well, glad you're in one piece."

"Can I buy you another drink, Varja?" Des asked.

"Already coming," the antileri woman said. "I'm Miranda."

"Des." She nodded. Another possibility for Varja's mixed, even contradictory behavior entered her head.

"So, she's the one?" she overhead Miranda say.

Varja gave Miranda's tone a puzzled look. "Yes?"

A server delivered a bottle of local wine and six glasses. "Anytime you're ready," he said to Miranda.

"Be right up there. Keep it coming for this lot and take it off the top." She poured herself a glass. "So, Des, and?"

Des blinked. "Oh, sorry, this is Luc. Old friend of mine."

"And my new fencing teacher," Francesca added.

"It's a pleasure, Ladies Miranda and Varja." Luc gave a slight bow. He gestured with his glass at the sword leaning against the wall. "I can't help but notice that hilt next to you. Not many in this land use the longsword."

Maybe he didn't learn in Forente after all, Des thought.

Varja smirked. "Not many know how to. It takes more finesse than the foppish swashbucklers claim."

"I've no doubt. Though, I don't know what Des would say about me carrying such a blade. She complains that even my arming sword is too brazen for the street. Eh, Des?"

"I think swords of any length are fine," Des said.

Luc cocked his head at her.

"I've never heard you claim otherwise," Azran said, following with a long sip of wine.

There was a pause, and then Miranda finished her glass and stood, withdrawing an oud from under the table. "Well, I've got to sing for sup. Varja, don't be shy. I hear Des knows who you're looking for." She gave Varja a tap on the arm, shot a wink at Des, and made for the stage.

Des, who prided herself on reading others' unspoken intentions, felt lost in subtext.

"Ladies and gentlemen of fair Cruxia, your evening entertainment starts now!" Miranda announced. She hopped the stage, accompanied by a chorus of cheers. Instead of taking the stool, she circled the perimeter, in complete silence as the crowd hushed. She reversed direction and launched into a tune. It started with full chords, then transitioned into a staccato melody.

"So, should we talk business?" Varja asked Des after the first verse and refrain.

I'll talk anything you want, Des thought. "Let's."

"Well, I'm looking for someone named Seneskar. He's—wait, did we talk about this last night?"

"Yeah, I said I'd poke around," Des replied, covering a wince by taking another drink.

Varja looked mortified. "I'm so sorry, it was just—"

"Just a long night. It's okay." Des glanced at Miranda, who had transitioned into an extended instrumental section, then examined the crowd. About half clapped in rhythm. A few of the early drinkers made their way to the dance area. The rest carried on private conversations. She saw nobody matching Seneskar's description.

"So, how should we go about this?" Varja asked.

"Well, funny enough," Des said, giving the room one more sweep before turning back to her. "We're in one of two taverns I heard he's gone to in the past few days."

"Really?" Varja nearly leapt from her chair, looking.

Des hooked Varja's elbow—fingers grazing a solid bicep—and pulled her back down. Or tried to—it took Varja relenting to get her seated.

"If you know what he looks like, my guess is he knows you," Des said, now on the carry. "If he spots you, he could bolt, and we won't catch him in this crowd. Besides, I don't see anyone near that description in here. I'll go ask the barkeep. You said yourself this isn't your specialty. Follow my lead."

Varja just stared, taken aback. "Okay." She shrugged off Des's grip.

Des held that hand suspended, half-closed, before putting it down and nodding. "Sorry. It's just, I've seen people get killed from habits like that."

Miranda's song finished to rousing applause. Des gave a couple claps before standing and heading for the bar.

• • •

When Des left, Varja turned to Luc and Azran. "Is she serious?"

Luc nodded. "Very serious. Though, I can't say I've ever heard her apologize after one of her reprimands."

"A night of firsts for her, it would seem," Azran said.

"Indeed." Luc glanced to Des at the bar while Azran whispered to a curious Francesca. Something dawned on his wife's face. Then, Luc turned back to the group. "She's a creature of habit, so it worries me."

"It shouldn't," Francesca said.

Varja was used to not catching every nuance of a conversation, but it seemed like everyone at this table spoke two languages at once. No matter where she went, she was the outsider. The foreigner.

A song later, a server delivered a second wine bottle, and then Des returned. According to her, the barkeep had no idea who she was asking about and assured her he was keeping every night. Either he, or her contact, was misremembering or misleading.

Of course, there was another possibility. Varja debated telling Des the nature of her quarry. But saying "dragon" might scare off the first person who seemed to have a shot at this. And besides, Seneskar was probably keeping his usual guise. He was vain enough to. Right?

She kept quiet as Des explained that Red Rocks was a better shot anyway. Unless her contact was, as she said, "Full of shit, in which case we're fucked back to scratch."

Des paused to drink and listen to Miranda's rendition of "Angels Just Upriver." Azran remarked that she was nailing Carus's stage presence, and maybe had a point about him and Ioran Delosa.

"What did Seneskar do, anyway?" Des asked Varja.

"He never much liked to austras'akunsak mirt ach eiẑir pek. Follow the clan, essentially."

"Isn't that what you said about yourself, though?"

Varja glanced at the glass between her hands. "Sort of, but I would never join the Faith of Fire."

Luc perked up at that. "Bela's blood, I'll help you take this man down for that."

"He's not been sentenced to death," Varja said, staring hard at the priest. "Not yet, anyway. I'm not an executioner. He ran off, but I'm to make sure he returns to present himself before the elders. Then, they'll decide his fate."

"And after that, you'll be in these elders' good graces?" Des asked.

"I hope so." Under her breath, Varja said, "Nothing else I do seems to put me there."

"Is that what you really want, though?"

I want to belong, she thought. "Yeah."

Another song ended. Another cheer. Another glass of wine.

• • •

It wasn't difficult for Miranda to reserve the stage at Red Rocks. She was fast establishing a reputation on the south end of Song Streets, and the aging place was desperate for new talent. It was also easy to get the barkeep talking about this blue-eyed Procumi who'd come in several times and had promised to once more before he left town the following day.

Convincing Luc to sit this one out was more of a challenge. Still, between Des's ambiguous references to Forente and Francesca all but begging him for a lesson—even one night off seemed too much—he relented.

Azran, after assuring his wife he would stay safe, later told Des he could keep watch, and even keep up with a runner. She believed him and would have him on a roof across the back alley.

"But if it gets too rough, you run," she warned.

Des would watch the front from a low-fenced dining patio across the street. If Seneskar bolted that way, she'd intercept with her body or a blade, depending on traffic.

That left Varja inside to make her move, and Miranda to watch her back.

18

Amadore knelt atop the tower under an overcast night sky. He pulled back his left sleeve, exposing his withered, twisted arm to Tenebra's gaze. He closed his eyes and centered himself, using his desire for Her successful reincarnation as a focus for the communion.

She could see him, he believed—he knew—even through the Seal. When night fell, it encompassed all, even those meek and misguided who carried their terrible lights—their blasphemous illumination. All. She saw him. She saw him but could not speak to Her chosen servants—Her priests, Her pilgrims. How wrong that She could not speak to Her future vessel, could not guide her into Her embrace. But if She could, there would be no need for a vessel—no need for dear Francesca. And so, the priest found gratitude for this reality.

But though Her voice in this realm was silent and though his beloved sister so confused, Tenebra's faithful pilgrim knew She would approve of the choice—he could feel Her pleasure at the shape of this future. A beautiful redemption for one so blessed at birth coincided with Her return to Her native realm.

Dear Francesca—so broken, but soon enough to become so perfect.

The priest—he would be nothing more until this task was done—looked upon his gnarled limb without opening his eyes. He needed not—he witnessed the warped flesh with every sense, every nerve. Every shallow beat of his heart that sent blood back into his torso reported how broken and strong and wrong his arm was. There was a time he had thought himself Tenebra's chosen vessel. He understood now that could not be. This arm—the price of power—such power—made him imperfect. No, his place was not as the vessel, but as the wise priest, the faithful pilgrim, the guide. The guide to the one who was—

"You call to Tenebra, and I answer."

Yes, She was constrained to silence, but She had gifted Her followers with a herald—a voice. Wings fluttered behind him.

"What do you seek, Amadore?" asked Zerexis.

The priest opened his eyes, lowered his twisted arm and re-covered it, then stood and pivoted to face the Angel of Shade. Such darkness—dark garb, dark skin, dark wings, dark eyes. The angels needed no light, desired no light—they were strong.

"I wish to discuss the retrieval of my sister," said the priest.

Zerexis wrapped their wings about their body. The black pupils of dark eyes jerked south, then back to the priest. "Your methods have failed?"

The priest bowed his head. "Yes, and so I request—"

"If your methods have failed, then you have failed. Your sister is not necessary. There are others within this very city."

The priest glanced up, then bowed again. "Please, herald, understand that I have only Tenebra's wishes in mind. They consume my being. This is not a selfish request. Dear Francesca was born a vampire, as I was. Our souls were cracked from conception, and we drank of our mother's essence in the womb. And she will trust me. No conversion of body or mind will be necessary, only the joining of a soul."

"She will trust you?" echoed Zerexis. "If so, why has she fled? She does not wish to be part of this. When she refused to kill Lady Ciusa and be the spark of the Night of Blood and Flame, she also refused the Goddess. She is forsaken."

"No!" The priest trembled with a sudden fury. His gnarled hand clawed at his thigh. Zerexis was the herald, but only the herald. The angel was the lesser authority, and not above error. She had gifted the priest with authority, as well. The angel needed him to carry out their goddess's wishes. They would listen to him—must listen to him. "She is lost. Misguided. Her lover—her deluded lover who thinks he stands in neutral twilight. He is to blame, not dear Francesca."

He paused. Zerexis's wingtips fluttered in agitation, but they remained silent.

The priest outstretched his good hand—his pure hand—with palm up in supplication. "I can save her. I can guide her to glory—Tenebra's glory."

"No," said Zerexis. "We will use the emperor's daughter. She already desires war with Charir. All we need do is convince her this is the path to her goal—one shared by the Goddess. She will require only minor deception to accept Tenebra's direction—much more expedient than your 'guidance.'"

The angel strode right up to the priest, leering over his averted face. "And if you continue to squander your talents, you will have no part in bringing the night." The dark wings spread as Zerexis approached the edge of the tower.

"What would you ask in exchange?" blurted the priest, stopping them.

They turned an intrigued eye.

Was it a sin to tempt an angel? The answer was irrelevant here—this was guiding a fellow worshipper back to Tenebra's will. The priest knew the tale of Zerexis and their two siblings—how they first taught soul magic not to fulfill Tenebra's desires, but to placate their own lust for power over mortal souls. He thought of how wretched this arm was, but it had paid for his soul-scrying ability. That was not enough—it had not allowed him to save dear Francesca. He needed more.

"I will sacrifice more of my flesh to bring her to me," said the priest. "Such is my surety that this is the best path for our Goddess."

Zerexis faced him. "You have already given up much in exchange for great power. You would lose another arm?"

"Arm? No, I must have a hand to present. I will—I shall sacrifice a leg. The same leg, my left leg."

"Remember, the limb will be strong, but also broken. You will be lame except under Her sight."

The priest nodded. "Yes, yes. But the power—"

"Will be worthy, as always." Zerexis gazed over the cityscape, contemplating. They turned back to the priest. "Very well. For the vitality of your leg, I will bestow upon you the power to weaken the Seal in concentrated spaces, even at a distance. You will be able to call immortals through—to an extent. They will be more than ghosts, but only just. Reaching further would draw unacceptable divine attention. For that reason also, do not use this power more than you must. However, with your soul-scry, you can arrange retrieval of your sister and removal of any, as you call them, deluding influences."

"But I cannot scry her from so far away—however far away she now is," said the priest.

"I do not grant paltry boons. If you have difficulty, you are being too weak. Now, shall we proceed?"

Calling immortals—even other angels? This was more than the priest had hoped for. This was power worthy of sacrifice—the power to ensure Tenebra's return and rise. And to save dear, lost Francesca.

"We shall proceed," replied the priest, bracing his body and will for the coming agony.

Zerexis raised a taloned hand that bled black in the night. The claws struck, tearing through the robes over the priest's thigh, lacerating the skin and muscle beneath. The priest fell to the stone.

Lines of freezing fire and burning ice raged across his flesh, scarring, deforming, taking, and giving. Flesh crawled. Muscles twisted, knotted, and ripped free. Nerves shattered. Power seeped into his blood, a conduit to his broken, vampiric soul. His heart raced, but the angel's gift outpaced his coursing blood. Energy suffused him, and when it reached his brain, he recognized it for only an instant before the agony drowned out any coherence. Only a primal understanding made him smile, made him laugh through the withering of his limb.

Zerexis articulated what the priest could not. "The sacrifice is honored." With a hadean grin of their own, the Angel of Shade basked in the mortal corruption. Dark wings spread and Zerexis took flight. Their voice lingered on the tower, echoing in bleeding ears. "Crawl into the dark, priest, and master the pain."

The priest needed no telling; he had done this once before.

19

Red Rocks—Seneskar would miss this place. It was not grand, not luxurious, not artsy. A bit garish, really, with the antique armory strewn across the walls. But it had good wine and better music. When he arrived, he was delighted to see that eastern girl tuning her oud to play. A fine serenade before his departure, he thought, bringing his glass to his lips.

There was a woman at a table between his and the stage. Her back was toward him, but he noted her hair and physique—and the sword below the table, bridging two chairs.

Seneskar paused mid-sip. The wine burned until he swallowed.

The player lifted her eyes from the neck, met Seneskar's, and then angled down a hair, at the swordswoman. Varja—it had to be—shifted and nodded.

Seneskar elected to act first. He stood and took the seat adjacent to her. "Evening, Varja," he said in Zixarsi.

She went for her sword. He caught her wrist, and he saw her contemplating a test of strength.

He led her vision around the room. "Here?"

"Why, you have somewhere else to be?" she asked in the same tongue.

"Varja, I am sitting right here, and not about to leave when such a pretty girl is playing such pretty music. Rest easy."

Varja relaxed her arm, and he let go.

"The clan chose you? Truly?" Seneskar asked.

"The choice was mine."

"And they were glad to be rid of you."

Varja stared long at him, but not hard. Her gaze then drifted to the table.

"I know the feeling," he said. "I'm likely more an outsider than you."

She looked back to him. "Don't start. We're not alike. I did not betray the clan."

"Betray the clan? I followed my beliefs. A clan whose mores are at odds with my own heart is not one I wish to remain part of."

"Your heart told you to join the Faith?" Varja leaned one elbow on the table, blue fires dancing in her eyes. "The Faith that brought the Rising Fire? The Second Flame? If you saw what I saw in the wake of those wars, perhaps your heart would tell you something else."

Seneskar watched the oud player and took a gulp of wine. "You are young. No revolution is peaceful. Not even the good ones. The world is full of festering wounds. The rot must be burned away. Did the Urathix personally kill every dead human or charoch you saw?"

Varja started to respond, but he continued, "Do not mistake me for a mindless zealot. I understand my religion is not innocent. No religion with power is. But the future my gods promise—that is what I wish to be a part of."

He turned his face toward her, and she retreated from his conviction.

"You would do well, Varja, to find what it is you want. It is the greatest feeling in this world to know who you are. Where you belong."

"I know where I belong. And I will drag you back there in chains."

Varja's hand shot under the table, closed around the grip, and drew her longsword.

Seneskar spun out of the chair. He searched the walls for a suitable blade as Varja assumed a high guard. He knew his talented cousin, Mirricix, had trained her in swordplay. Still, even in this smaller form, he could overpower her—it was not built like most human bodies.

He took a Valentreid legate's sword from its rack, ripping the pegs from the wall in the process, and faced her.

The thin crowd skirted to the edges of the room. The barkeep almost shouted but kept silent. The oud player mutated her song into a faster, jauntier tune.

Varja took in the tight quarters between tables and shifted her stance. She held her weapon in a half-sword grip, one gloved hand out on the blade, hilt at her hip, tip pointed at Seneskar.

"You know I could take on my true form and eviscerate you with one swipe," Seneskar said in Draci.

"In here?" Varja responded in kind.

He chuckled. "Sassy bint."

He snarled and nearly took a step forward, but Varja came on first. Guiding the strike with her forward hand, she thrust up from her hip. Seneskar stepped back and parried down. The upper half of his blade struck the lower of hers. He felt the angles and force—his weak against her strong.

Varja drove his blade up and brought hers back, shifting her off hand back to the hilt. She cut up from her left, pulling short to slash rather than chop. Her blade opened his shirt and skin in a diagonal line across his abdomen.

The pain registered, and Seneskar started to reel back from the fire. But Varja's dance continued.

She took the half-sword again and bashed her pommel into his chest, knocking him to the floor. The legate's blade clanged onto the hardwood. Seneskar gasped and coughed. He put one hand to ribs he was sure had been broken. His other went to his stomach, coming back red.

The onlookers gawked. From that first step, it had all happened inside a three-count. Even the minstrel stopped playing.

Varja looked down at Seneskar with something near pity. If not for the pain, he would have contemplated that irony.

"You haven't seen me fight since before the war, have you?" she asked in Draci.

He shook his head weakly as he squirmed, willing his shapeshifting flesh to repair—a slow and taxing process.

The door slammed open.

"Drop the sword!"

A quartet of armored guards rushed in, pushing patrons aside with blue-caped shoulders. Shields forward, swords drawn, they fanned out around the pair in the center.

"Stormblood business," Varja said, switching to Serma. "This one is a fugitive from the clan. A criminal."

"Only criminal I see is you," the guard with the shiniest armor said. "Drop the sword and come with us."

Varja did not move. Seneskar sat up and tore off a strip of his shirt.

"Don't worry, Ziak," the guard said. "He's coming too."

Seneskar stopped in the middle of tying his makeshift bandage. "She attacked me."

"It's true!" an onlooker shouted.

"We'll get this all sorted at the post. Last chance—drop it."

Never taking her eyes from the guard's, Varja wiped the bit of blood from her blade, sheathed it, and placed it on a table.

• • •

From across the way, sipping tea and nibbling hard bread with olive oil, Des caught glimpses of the ruckus through the tavern's front windows. She wasn't the only one—other diners and passersby took an interest. One streetwalker exclaimed, "They have swords—call the guard!"

Echoes of the cry traveled fast, and within moments, four mailed men in green tabards and blue shoulder capes hustled in from around the block.

Shit. Shit, shit, fucking chains of Crusix. Des had no pull with the guards here. She didn't even know if the local Kraken did. *Why'd she have to draw that horsecleaver? What is it with fucking swordsmen that makes them so street-stupid?*

Before she could figure out a plan of action, the guards were entering the tavern with their own blades drawn, shouting the typical arrest orders.

Des dropped an uncounted palmful of coins on her table and hopped the short fence surrounding the patio. She could try to explain the situation. No, the guards wouldn't care, especially with it being a foreign affair. She could do something really stupid to get their attention, then bog them once Varja got away. Wait, how would a six-foot Zixarsi woman with a longsword and no training escape on these streets? Would she even think to run, or just rush in to help Des?

The guards exited the tavern, one holding Varja's sword, two in front and two behind their prisoners. Des's instincts took over. She hid her face by brushing her hair and walked behind a cluster of spectators. Through shifting gaps, she watched the procession head toward Cruxia's administrative district.

Once they were far enough, Des followed the curious passersby into Red Rocks. People inside were recounting the sudden duel and loosing exasperated oaths about foreigners. Miranda stood near the back door, talking to Azran. He spotted Des and waved her over.

"Which way did they go?" Miranda asked, glancing between the two lookouts.

"North," Azran said.

"Admin," Des added. "If I had to guess."

"Damn. Figures."

"What now?" Azran asked.

"They won't be fast," Des said. "If we go now, follow parallel on another street, we can cut them off and spring them. Duck through alleys, lose them in the night and crowds."

"Whoa, easy," Miranda said. "No one died, so they're looking to show their peacekeeping chops. Our pair will probably just be fined and released. Maybe roughed up a bit, but Varja can take it."

Ari's ghost flashed into being. Only this time, she was more visible, more tangible despite her broken visage—bleeding nose, red-splotched temple and matted hair, lifting her shirt to expose bruised ribs. Scrapes from where her elbows and shoulder hit the stone floor.

The thought of fucking capes laying their hands on Varja flooded Des's vision with red. "And how do you know that?"

"I've been taken in before. Not here, but I don't imagine it's much different. Bureaucrats want two things—money, and a system that gets them more money."

Des told herself to calm down and listen. After all, she'd never been caught. There had been close calls, but nothing bribes, fast talking, or fast feet couldn't solve.

"You were arrested?" Azran asked. "What in hades for?"

"The crats in Cruxia are a lot more lenient about music and entertainment than some other places," Miranda replied. "I bet Filvié Noctirin keeps you lot in a nice bubble in Aure."

"Everything's got an upside, I suppose."

"So what do we do, then?" Des asked after a calming breath.

"Go see if we can get them released with the least hassle," Miranda said. "And by we, I mean you two. I've got to keep up appearances if we're going to have another shot at this."

"The barkeep said Seneskar was leaving tomorrow," Des reminded.

"Then get him now," Miranda said. "But I'm not going near another fight with those two. Not my fight." Her voice dropped even lower. "Besides, something's not right about that man. The way he moves. The way he gets hit. There's something both animal and unflinching. I've had a bad experience with that shit." She grinned. "Good luck."

• • •

How's that new life going? Azran asked himself. His words to Francesca the other night echoed off the inside of his skull. It wasn't that he craved a boring existence—he sought vivacity and experience with this second chance his wife had gifted him. But tonight, hustling to a city guard post to retrieve a person who had nearly killed someone—apparently, a religious nut—in a tavern with a fucking sword? It felt like the same shit with different faces. He was ready for Cruxia to erupt in anarchy any moment now.

Of course, he didn't have to do this. He could have agreed with Francesca's concerns and sat this ordeal out. She was right—he was not a fighter, he was a runner. But Des seemed to have had a good plan. Since they met in Aure, she always knew what came next. She understood these situations. She could handle them, or at least adapt faster than the rest of them.

But now, watching her from the corner of his eye as they passed in and out of lamplight, he could see past the façade. Des's face was forward, focused on their yet-invisible destination to the exclusion of all else. *No, not all else,* Azran decided. Something happened back in the tavern. Some chain snapped taut and kept pulling. She had been through this before, and unlike during their flight south, Des was not in control. Her heart was beating faster than even their brisk pace should require. Anger. Frustration. Fear, for sure. Somebody had been hurt before, and Des feared somebody new would be hurt. It wasn't hard for Azran to determine each person in question.

"Hey," he said.

"What." She did not shift her gaze.

"We got this. We're nipping the bud."

"Sure."

Azran stopped and grabbed her shoulder. Now she shifted—she spun, one hand going for Azran's wrist and the other for a blade on her vest. She stopped short of both and took a deep breath.

"Don't listen to me," he said. "Listen to Miranda back there. She knows way better than I do. We got this."

Des shook her head, out of amazement rather than denial. "How the do you stay so fucking positive all the time?"

Azran chuckled. "I don't, except when I know something will work out. Eyes forward." He started walking again, and Des was soon at his side. After a couple blocks of internal debate, he asked, "Was it Arilysa?"

Des seemed to expect the question. "Yes. Not much gets by you, does it?"

Azran shrugged. "Just some extrapolation."

"Some what?"

"Using logic to build on what I knew for sure. You seem quite taken with Varja."

Des turned her face away. "Suppose it's obvious."

"Not to her, I think. But she can be oblivious, I've noticed."

There was a lull, and then Des asked, "Think she feels the same?"

"If she does, I'm not sure she knows how to proceed. If you're asking my advice, cut the subtlety. I think she really has no idea why you bought her all those drinks."

"I'm probably wasting my efforts," Des said. "She was telling war stories from Muntherziach—Muntherzix? Whatever. She mentioned this guy. Kyland or something."

"Did it sound like she was over him?"

"Absolutely, but—"

"Then it don't mean shit. Not everyone sticks to one shore. There's a whole river in between."

"True. I mean, Arilysa was…in the river?"

"You're right, not my best metaphor," Azran said. "But the point stands."

"It's just, what are the chances? Two in a row?"

"Better odds than many expect, I expect. I think more people are in the middle than care to admit. Or maybe can admit. I'm certain I caught her checking you out."

"She—oh." Des took a moment to digest that. Then, her bashful look became a grin. "I knew it. So, you think she's oblivious, or in denial?"

"They probably go hand in hand. Either one, the only way to go is forward."

Des eyed him sidelong. "You've thought about this a lot, huh?"

"Are you surprised?"

"If I still thought you were on dry land."

"As opposed to wet? Ugh, it was a shit metaphor, Des. Let it die."

Her laughter died as two separate guard patrols crossed paths in front of them.

Must be getting close, Azran thought, looking to Des for direction.

"There." She pointed over a row of townhouses to a looming, battlemented, square structure flying Valentreid, Lunateli, and Cruxian banners at every opportunity.

Like the compound outside, the interior was well lit. There was something resembling a foyer, with a long table and four guards. One asked Azran and Des to place any weapons on the table. Also, no magic or arcana inside. Des, with noticeable reluctance, surrendered the knife across her back, two daggers from inside the front of her vest, and one of two Azran knew were in her boots.

Whether lethargic or buying her performance, the guards did not pat her down. Azran, they did.

Past the foyer was a wide floor with a counter along the far wall. Benches hugged the others, interrupted by sturdy doors. Three stone-faced clerks in mandated, white attire sat behind the counter in varying states of uprightness. Other than them, two standing guards, and one passing through from side door to side door, Des and Azran were the only people in the room.

Azran chose the most awake clerk. As he reached the counter, she gave him a practiced smile.

"Good evening, citizens. How may I be of service?"

"A friend of ours was taken in, oh, not even an hour ago," Azran said. "Could you tell us the charges and fees for Varja—" He glanced at Des. "What's her last name?"

Des shook her head. She said to the clerk, "Procumi woman. Tall. Came in with a sword and a Proc man named Seneskar."

The clerk rifled through some papers. "From Red Rocks in Song Streets?"

They nodded.

"Both foreigners you speak of were brought in less than an hour ago. A charge has yet to be delivered to this desk. You may wait while they are processed." The clerk gestured at the benches.

"How long will that take?" Des asked.

"That depends on their charges and cooperation. But I imagine no more than three hours."

Azran scoffed.

Des leaned in. "Is there any way to speed this up?" She tapped her purse with two fingers.

The clerk painted on that false smile again and clasped her hands in front of her. "Bribes are illegal."

Des stared a long moment, then raised her eyebrows, stalked thirty feet to the nearest bench, and sat with her arms crossed. Azran thanked the clerk and followed.

"Bribes are illegal," Des mocked.

"You're not in Forente anymore," Azran said.

"Don't matter. The Kraken has business in Cruxia, so I know these crats are greedy as the rest."

"Maybe they're just quieter about it here."

"And maybe they're buying time to 'discourage' these foreigners from staying."

"If anyone can handle that, it's Varja. Just the other night she was volunteering to get punched."

Des shook her head. "That's not the same as three guards slugging and kicking your manacled ass onto the floor."

"They do that?"

"They did to Ari."

"The fuck. Well, we're not in Forente."

"Keep saying that like it means something, sunshine."

20

Varja sat in a dim cell with five other waiting "criminals." One stared at the wall, another at her own bare feet. One slumped, drunk to unconsciousness. Perhaps the remaining two, both staring at Varja, deserved the moniker. The dwarf looked like he wanted to kill her. The half-orc mordiri looked like he wanted to fuck her, then kill her.

A half-hour passed. The barefoot woman was escorted out, praising the True Deity Airis and the four prophets as she went.

Another half-hour passed. Two more prisoners left. Finally, another guard entered and pointed at Varja. "Her."

The absent-faced jailer unlocked the cell and Varja walked out. The escort led her to a room that was empty except for a table and one chair. A sharp-dressed man with a sharp-tipped mustache and slick hair sat there. The escort closed the door, standing behind Varja. Two more guards watched from the other side of the room.

The man at the table shifted through some papers, dipped a quill, scribbled something, and then looked up.

"When you entered this post, you gave your name as Varja Stormblood. Is this accurate?"

"Yes. And who are you?"

The man jotted a line, then paused. "My name is Salgi Ixos, Chief of Guard for Patrol Section 6 of Cruxia, and henceforth I will ask the questions. Now, the arresting officer claims you mean the Stormblood clan of Procumes, the Kepeskeižir. Is this also correct?"

Varja grit her teeth. "Yes."

"Do you claim any blood ties to Valentreid citizenry?"

"No."

The pen scratched on paper.

"Why did you instigate the quarrel with this…Seneskar?"

"As I told your officer, he is a traitor to my clan. I was sent to find him. He didn't want to come with."

"I see. Would you call this a matter of blood feud?"

"I guess that's one way to put it."

"It will do." The chief made a mark. "Since no deaths occurred, this will be counted simply as unprovoked assault—"

"Unprovoked?" Varja took a step forward.

The chief heaved a sigh and interlaced his fingers. "Yes. You drew steel on an unarmed man. Therefore, you will be charged two aurli for the crime—that's gold, barbarian. Five silver argi for civil fees, and since you are not a citizen, another aurli for the return of your sword. If you cannot pay, you will remain imprisoned until someone does, or until you work off your debt."

"Are you serious? Three gold?"

"And five silvers. Only two gold if you leave the weapon, but I understand you people are quite fond of your ridiculous blades."

"And what of Seneskar?"

"He committed no crimes in my eyes. He will walk free—after civil fees, of course."

"He's dangerous. He's in the Faith of Fire. I don't know why he's in Lunatel, but it can't be good for you."

The chief tapped his fingertips together. "If that is the case, then he is a foreign threat and out of my hands. Others will handle him. Now, can you pay?"

Varja shook her head, exasperated at this prim little man. "Yes. Or I could, if I had my purse."

The chief took another piece of paper and jotted down a few lines. "Good." He handed the paper to a guard, who left the room. "Your money will be sent to the front desk. Your sword will be returned upon exiting the building." He nodded at Varja's escort, who led her from the room.

• • •

Azran and Des waited. Time passed, but whatever clock this place ran by was not in this room. Guards and officials proceeded in and out. Occasional civilians came through, but they seemed to have a better sense of when to retrieve their deviants. Every time papers were exchanged behind the counter, the principled clerk would answer Des and Azran's expectant looks with that fake fucking smile and a head shake.

Then, finally, she nodded. They rushed over.

"The woman is charged with unprovoked assault. Fines and fees come to three aurli and five argi. The man, however, will be transferred to the provincial offices."

"Why?" Azran asked.

"He must have committed some transgression beyond our jurisdiction. It has been omitted from the report."

"Okay, fine," Des said. She slapped the coins on the counter. "Fine."

The clerk gathered, counted, and stored the money in a lockbox under the counter. "Thank you for your cooperation with our municipal system." She stamped the arrest report, then took it through a door marked *Holding*.

"The provincial office is in Fort Mirena," Azran said. "Thirty leagues from here. Varja won't be happy about that."

"We'll deal with it," Des said, finally returning to a semblance of calm. "The important thing is that we've got her."

• • •

Two guards, one before and one behind, escorted Varja through the narrow hallways. Her hands were still bound. These were not the same corridors as when she was brought in. The guards made several right-angle turns and passed many doors, some open and some closed. One of the closed doors muffled the sounds a beating and unintelligible, shouted questions. Varja tried to pause, an angry curiosity coming over her, but the guard behind gave a hard shove.

"What's that about?" she asked, continuing forward.

"Who knows," the guard replied. "Uncooperative, maybe. Maybe just a troublemaking barbarian. Count yourself lucky, Ziak." He shoved her again, this time unprompted.

Varja stopped and half-turned. Her raging glare met a smug smirk.

"I dare you," the guard said. "I could use some exercise."

"Let her be, Rin," the guard in front said. "Shift's almost over. I don't need this shit."

"It won't take long. I ain't got my hands on one of these slum rats in a while."

Varja turned to face him fully.

"Won't take long? Motherfucker, she's taller than you. I will give you three silvers to not start this."

Rin continued to match stares with Varja, who was trembling, on the edge of an explosion. She pictured slamming her forehead into that smug mug, hooking his leg with hers, and beating her bound fists into his breaking nose.

Finally, Rin blinked. "Four."

"Three."

Rin shrugged. "Deal. Turn back around, Ziak, and you can get back to your deadbeat father and whore mother."

Varja spat in his face.

A leather gauntlet with knuckle studs slugged her cheek. She staggered a step, but only one. Numbness yielded to the burn of broken skin.

"You can take a punch, I'll give you that, Ziak," Rin said, shaking his wrist.

"Good hit for having to reach so high," Varja countered. She turned around and nodded past the guard in front.

They continued into a spacious, barren room with a counter and benches along the wall. To Varja's surprise, Azran and Des stood near the middle, arms crossed. When they heard the door creak, the pair spotted Varja and hurried over.

"Are you alright?" Des asked while the unnamed guard unlocked Varja's bonds.

"More or less."

"You're bleeding." Her concern took on a hard edge.

"She asked for it," Rin said.

"So did you," the other guard said. "Get outta here." He and Rin exited the way they came.

"What happened?" Azran asked.

Varja wiped the blood from her cheek. "Fighting words. That's not important, though. They're taking Seneskar somewhere else."

"Fort Mirena, yeah," Azran said. "So we heard." Varja started for the clerks, but he stopped her. "They won't help. Let's leave and figure out our next move."

Varja nodded, already with a backup plan in mind.

Her sword was waiting in the weapons check. She unsheathed and examined it while Des repacked her own arsenal. The blade was fine. Varja checked her purse and found it eight coins lighter. "Can you believe they fined me to get this back?" Varja asked as they exited.

"Right?" Des said. "I'm gonna have to find real work at this rate."

"Wait, they fined you, too?" Varja asked. "What for?"

"It was for you—to get you out. You saying we both paid?"

Azran laughed. "Incredible."

Varja went back. She tossed her sword on the table and strode up to a clerk.

"Is there something else I can help your party with?" the clerk asked.

"There's been a mistake," Varja said. "My fine was paid twice."

The clerk hummed as she glanced through some papers. "The record states it was only paid once."

"Well, your record is wrong."

"I assure you, miss, we keep impeccable records of our transactions. There's been no mistake."

Azran appeared next to Varja. "Come on," he said. "It won't do any good."

"But Azran, she said—"

"There's been no mistake." He looked Varja in the eyes. "Let's go."

Varja gave the clerk's faux-pleasant smile a parting glower and followed him.

"Was that it?" Des asked when they met her outside.

"Yeah," Azran replied. "Won't take bribes, but they have no problem robbing you and your friends."

She started down the street. "Let's get the fuck out of here."

Once they had gone several blocks and no guards appeared within earshot, Varja asked, "Where is this Fort Mirena?"

"Straight north," Azran said. "Two days on a hard ride, but slower for prisoner transport."

"So if we're fast, we could cut them off and get Seneskar in our custody," Varja said. The other two stopped and looked at her. "Right?"

Azran shook his head. "They'll be expecting his arrival at the fort. If they haven't sent a resonance yet, they will soon."

"A what?"

"An arcane device that lets you send short messages fast over long distances," Des said. "Expensive, but useful."

"Very expensive," Azran said. "Not many besides the law and army have them. They run on special crystals or something."

"Point is," Des said, "if he's important enough for province level, and he doesn't show, they'll come looking. And besides—" She stopped to let a patrol cross an intersection. "And besides, you're talking about taking on a highway escort band, maybe even legionaries."

"I'm not saying we kill the guards," Varja said.

223

"How do you expect to snatch a prisoner out of an armored wagon without steel being drawn? The capes already showed they don't care about your agenda."

Azran nodded. "She's right. Our best bet is to go to Mirena and try your pull there. Provinces can deal with foreign matters. Evidently, cities can't."

Varja wasn't satisfied. She'd already let Seneskar slip through her grasp once. And now, he would be going outside the city—how easy it would be for him to massacre his escort and flee. And then, even if he returned to Cruxia, he would be more careful about his appearance.

"No," she said. "We need another solution. There are things about Seneskar you don't know. He's much more powerful than he lets on."

"From what Miranda told me, you kicked his ass in the bar," Azran said.

"He was holding back. He didn't want to expose what he can really do. What he really is."

"And what's that?" Des asked. "What have we been trying to drag?"

Varja stared at the cobblestones and said, "I mentioned doing this for my clan. They don't much care for me. That's because I'm a halfblood." She flicked her eyes up. Des and Azran watched her with rapt curiosity. Varja licked her dry lips and looked back down. She almost didn't continue. She wasn't ashamed of what she was—she was guilty for getting them involved without telling them the full risks.

"My mother was a human from Muntherzix. The other half—the half my clan cares about—is Kepeskeižir, the storm dragons of Procumes."

She stood with her eyes closed.

After a long hesitation, Des broke through the silence. "Wait, so you're half-dragon? How—what? How does that even. What?"

"Dragons are shapeshifters," Azran said. "It's not unheard of. I've no problems with dragons in general." He pulled back his right sleeve to reveal a tattoo of Caelix. "If they're much in spirit like their god, I'd say they're alright. My only concern is what this revelation implies for Seneskar." He stared hard at Varja with a mixture of worry and accusation.

Des's eyes went wider. She looked to Azran, then back to Varja. "You mean—"

Varja nodded. "Seneskar's full-blooded storm dragon. If he gets beyond the eyes of the city, even legionaries won't be able to hold him. That's why we have to—"

"No, no, hang on," Azran interrupted. "You dragged us into this without telling us we were trying to catch a dragon? Are you stupid, or just a deceitful bitch?"

"Hey—"

"Fuck you, Des, this is some bullshit."

"I knew he wouldn't use his true form in the city," Varja said. "I wasn't going to ask you to help any further."

"You knew, or guessed?" Azran asked. "People in corners lash out."

"I knew. He snuck away. He has some agenda he needs to stay low for. I don't know what, but he needs his disguise."

"And then what?" Des asked. "There's a lot of empty between here and Procumes. You have some way to restrain a dragon?"

"Did you plan any of this?" Azran added.

"No," Varja admitted. "I don't know how I'm going to do this. But I'll figure something out. The clan sent me, so there must be some way."

Azran walked in small circles, hands on his head and muttering to himself. Des looked like she was considering walking away without another word. Varja just kept thinking, *I really fucked this up. Every part of it.*

"Is there, though?" Des finally asked.

Varja looked at her.

"Is there a way for you to succeed, I mean."

"There has to be," Varja said.

"There doesn't have to be shit," Azran said, calmed somewhat.

"Then why send me?"

"You said they didn't care about you," Des said.

"No, they just—well, yes. But this is a test. To earn their favor."

Azran tapped Des's arm. "Remember what I said about subtlety."

She glanced at him, then refocused on Varja. "Maybe they're not sending you to retrieve a traitor—maybe they're just sending you away."

Varja's mind whirled. This thought was not novel to her, but she had chalked it up to self-doubt. To hear someone else say it— that made it real. Des was right, but there was more still. The elders held Varja with the same regard as they did a heretic and a traitor. No, it was so much worse. If Seneskar was not to be punished—not so much as scolded for his transgression—then they had allowed him to leave of his own accord. Varja was more an exile than him.

The weight of this sent her slumping into a wall, then to the gutter.

Even during her journey through Muntherzix years ago, Varja enjoyed the delusion that the clan cared whether she returned. Now, she was sure that had she died then—or on this fool's errand—and she was such a fool—they would never know. And they would be fine not knowing.

A word came to mind that Varja first learned from reading about sea dragons—*thr'ochaz*. Because sea dragon clans roamed together, exile from a territory was an unfit punishment. Instead, one who was enough of a disappointment would be ignored by the clan, no matter where they met. Varja was exiled without being banished. She was thr'ochaz'akuns—shunned. And they let her think it was her idea. They hadn't lifted a foreclaw to get rid of her, just fabricated some cruel fantasy to lead her away.

She shut her eyes tight, squeezing out tears. She was numb, distant from sensation. Salt was deposited in the cut on her cheek. Her chin was tickled before the drops hit her chest. An arm was placed around her shoulders.

She blinked through the moisture. Des was down in the gutter next to her. Varja let her head fall onto her.

Azran was hunkered down nearby, arms on his knees and an apologetic look on his face. "I'm sorry for snapping earlier. And for calling you a bitch. I didn't realize how important this was to you."

Varja just nodded. She didn't want to talk.

"Go tell Miranda Varja's out," Des said. "No need for the rest yet."

"Sure." Azran stood. "For what it's worth, Varja, I know what it's like to have a family like that. It's no use trying to please them. You never can." He walked away.

When he was gone, Varja's ragged breaths became sobs. Des reached with her other arm and pulled her into a gentle embrace.

"You were right," Varja managed through her broken voice. "I don't belong there. I don't belong anywhere."

Des pulled her closer. Or maybe Varja tightened her grip.

"I think you fit in fine right here."

21

Seneskar stood against the wall, avoiding the damp, stagnant floor. The dungeon reeked. He was told an armored wagon was waiting to take him north in a few hours. "Just finalizing the paperwork," that official—Chief Ixos—had said. This was an unfortunate circumstance. Seneskar was to meet Exus and his companions at dawn. How many hours that was from now, he could not say. It had been a distracting night.

He slid his fingers through the long tear in his shirt and touched the scabbed wound running across his abdomen. Even with his regenerative abilities—thanks to the same divine ancestry that allowed dragons to shapeshift—this cut would take less than a day to heal. He wanted to stretch the muscles and scratch the itch but refrained. Instead, he focused on the one who had cut him.

Varja Ziacheižir, Ziach-blood, the clan used to call her when she was around. When she wasn't, they called her Ziathrixturoz—

the Ziach bastard. Seneskar would do the same. He did a lot of things back then he would now condemn. Even so, he counted himself among the few who took pity on this forsaken child. Not that she knew—one habit he retained was acting without acting. The right quiet word in the right ear could accomplish much—like encouraging Mirricix to teach her niece swordplay.

And did she ever learn. Seneskar traced the wound again.

The real pity was the death of Varja's father. Before she could walk, he was slain in Charir by an athir, a fire dragon considered an angel by the Faith. Though, given his flightiness, he may have paid his daughter no more mind than the rest. From every angle, it seemed Varja was fated for rejection. She would have to find her own way. Seneskar's words in the tavern had been sincere. That was perhaps the Faith of Fire's greatest appeal—it called its adherents to light and carry their own flames, rather than count on others to bestow purpose.

Varja seemed to be taking her first steps. She had found at least two companions in that lovely minstrel and the woman watching from the street. She had hunted him down, no miracle needed. Seneskar hoped his quiet words had been the right ones at the right time.

Down the hall, keys jangled to the beat of footsteps. He shook his head. *Enough of that. I have to find a way out of here, thanks to that reckless thrixturoz. That wagon is probably my best bet.* He had pored over maps in preparation for this quest. He knew he was going north, and he knew just where to make his move. *Exus strikes me as a patient man,* he consoled himself.

The footsteps stopped in front of Seneskar's cell. That same official stood with a pair of armored guards and another man in a green, tailed uniform.

230

"The wagon has arrived, accused," the officer said, stroking his waxed mustache. "Just a final security check and you'll be on your way."

"Excellent," Seneskar said. "It's a bit dank in here. You might want to consider renovating your dungeon."

The officer's mouth did not so much as twitch until he said, "I do not know what law enforcement is like in Procumes, but here, we treat prisoners as prisoners. Arcanist, if you would?" He stepped aside.

The man in the green coat stared hard at Seneskar and spoke in an arcane language. "Mor skidak arkana ud animavi makus ors ravar." Then he said, "No present spells, although his soul casts a mighty aura."

"Are you a priest, foreigner?" the officer asked.

"No, just a pious individual."

"Very well. Your hands will be bound and mouth gagged. Any sign of magic will result in severe punishment." The officer turned to one of the guards. "Load him up with the others."

• • •

An hour north of Cruxia, a team of eight horses pulled a large, ironclad wagon at a slow gallop along a stone-paved highway. Six riders escorted the rumbling carriage. The sun rose over the open, rolling landscape to the east. The last farm estate was over a mile back south, and the next lay a mile ahead.

Commotion beneath him prompted the driver to yank the reins and call out to the escorts. The horses slowed, then stopped the heavy cargo as the riders converged. One of the prisoners had started flashing magic.

Two escorts dismounted and opened the rear doors. A guard inside threw the perpetrator onto the stones. The prisoner, a dark man with a torn shirt, started to push himself up. An escort planted a boot on his back but found he could not push the bound and gagged man back down—no, not gagged. The gag was burning away, as if from the breath forced from the prisoner's rapidly expanding ribcage.

His limbs swelled, too. His whole body, tearing already ragged clothes. Shackles bent and broke. The other dismounted escort kicked the prisoner's face, but sleek silver scales protected a lengthening muzzle. Others drew swords and bows. The guard in the wagon attempted to close the doors.

With incredible speed for such bulk, the thing that was not a prisoner, that was not Marexuri, spun and spat a bolt of lightning into the terrified guard. A severed arm tumbled to the road, followed by its owner as the draft horses panicked forward. Screams of men and beasts rent the still countryside.

Two mounted escorts fired arrows. One missile glanced off spreading scales. The other sank into the thing's back. It fell to all fours, the shifting bone structure seeming more appropriate for such a stance. The dismounted escorts ran for their horses, which reluctantly circled back to their masters. The remaining two charged the monster with swords.

Like a many-armed beast breaking the water's surface, two leathery wings and a powerful tail burst from the creature's form. The tail whipped one rider from the saddle; a taloned forelimb gouged the other into a lacerated mockery of a man.

More arrows, to no avail.

A longer neck. Miniature fins shaped like a flying fish's. Another bolt of lightning. A bloody pounce.

The driver of the wagon urged the team onward. A surviving prisoner pulled the doors shut. The driver looked back and saw only the silhouettes of corpses. He looked side to side, then forward.

He should have looked up.

• • •

Winging his way back south, Seneskar allowed himself to enjoy the rush of warming air under his wings. It made him forget the arrow in his muscled flight shoulder and cut across his belly. Falling onto the highway had reopened it, and though his shifting would normally have fixed that, the violence of the transformation tore it open and closed. It was like stitches being ripped out and re-sewn with each passing moment. That had been perhaps the most painful transformation of the storm dragon's life.

Top five, for sure, he thought. *Probably leave a scar.*

He flew between low cloud banks and high fog rolling in from the sea. No survivors would report what had happened. With luck, it would be hours before anyone even stumbled upon the carnage.

Smelling the sandstone and cooking breakfasts of Quarrytown—it was good to smell again—Seneskar descended into a muddy ditch surrounded by laurel trees. He sensed nothing warmer than a few startled rodents in the copse. Shifting back into human form—this time with shorter hair, lighter skin, and brown eyes—snapped the arrow shaft and pushed out the head. Soon, a grimacing, naked Valentreid man stood knee-deep in stagnant water.

Blood of a thousand dead gods, that fucking hurt.

With as much haste as his growing fatigue allowed, Seneskar stole a simple, brown and grey outfit from a clothesline and reached the road to Cruxia. He saw the expected morning traffic, but not the paranoid elf or anyone who looked like they kept such company. He started walking toward the city, watching the shrubs and rocks just off the road, cursing the limited senses of this form. They were sharper than most groundlings', but there was just nowhere discreet to put a set of thermosensitive pit organs.

"Southerner."

It was a whisper, but he heard it. Seneskar rounded a crag. Exus and three motley yet somehow orthodox strangers waited for him—two women and another man.

"You're late," the elf said. "And you changed your face."

"I'm surprised you recognized me," Seneskar said.

"Different face, same soul. I don't forget anything that peculiar."

Seneskar gave a half-sincere bow. "Well, my apologies for my tardiness. I ran afoul of an old acquaintance and landed in a guarded wagon headed north. All's well enough, though. None will report my absence for quite some time."

One of the women, a hooded human with a drab robe under a drab cloak, leaned toward Exus. "Can we trust this man?" she asked.

"Trust no one on this venture, Daia," the elf replied. "We're out of the sight, now." He looked directly at Seneskar. "We'll all leave some dead by the time this is done."

No use hiding it now. "Speaking of, we should avoid the northbound highway."

"Understood." Some brows furrowed at Seneskar's words, but not this elf's. That cold demeanor was beginning to worry him.

"We have horses waiting at the north end of town," Exus went on. "But we'll be tracking more eastward. And if you've a new face, we should have no trouble reaching Aure."

"Famous last words," Seneskar said.

"Not my first," Exus muttered, heading for the road. None of the other Godshadows seemed to hear it.

More and more curious, this elf.

22

Des perched on an outcrop, arms around her knees and resting her chin on top. Ahead of her, light surf crashed on a rocky beach painted orange by the rising sun. Varja was still a silhouette casting a long shadow. She was facing south and a bit east—her best guess at a straight line to the place that was not her home. Not anymore, if it ever had been.

Home is a strange thing, Des thought. Forente used to be her home. Born in Upping, raised across Downing, Waft, and Hawk's Nest. Her mother's luck with employment had been abysmal. The first four taverns she served at had closed by the time Des was fifteen. The fifth gave Des her first coin-paid, steady jobs—the serving gig, as well as passing notes, then packages from one patron to another. Her mother caught her once and had a word with the barkeep regarding his clientele. Des overheard the conversation. Back then, the Kraken was truly a leviathan, a many-armed monstrosity lurking in every shadow. At the end of that exchange, Des's mother chose to keep her job rather than protest further.

As for Des, she was at the height of her audacity. If Luc thought her heedless now, he should have seen her then. Despite her mother's cautionary tales, she not only kept passing messages and satchels, she began demanding more coin. Most Kraken agents laughed. Some laughed and complied.

One day, a stow who felt marked decided to take it out on the messenger. Des showed the stow and his two companions firsthand what kind of girls the lower neighborhoods produced. It was an impressive display involving a pitcher of ale, a dining knife, and a surprisingly fragile table. Des had to pay the barkeep back for the broken pitcher and furniture, but she had the coin. The more important takeaway was the attention of a low-level caz who was short on locks. By eighteen, Des was working the tavern in the afternoon and the docks at night. The Kraken's illusion of monolith faded. It amazed her the whole thing hadn't dissolved years ago from the internal backstabbing.

Those last two years were hard on Des's mother. She couldn't appreciate it at the time, but looking back, Des realized how hard her mother had fought to keep her away from such a life. If they could have left Forente, they would have. But the city had a way of trapping people, especially those born amid the web of clandestine deals and structures designed to control the chaos.

And no matter how steady your life seems to be, Des reflected, *things can change without warning. You're always one bad day away from losing it all. It might not even be* your *bad day.*

Des was twenty when her mother died. She still didn't know what the sickness was, but it struck fast and ugly. All the bloody money from Des's lock job couldn't save her.

She almost left after that, but there was nowhere else to go. And thanks to her employers, the web was tighter than ever. Forente was her home.

But then, years later, home became a person. With Ari by her side, Des could go anywhere. They could escape, and they knew it. It took time, calling in all their favors and settling all their debts, but they did it.

Or so we thought. That ache, that voice in the back of Des's head returned. She could smell Ari. She could smell home. *And now I'm homeless. Just like her.*

Down on the rocky beach, Varja turned and walked back toward Des. The scab and bruise on her cheek had faded fast. Des wondered if that was the dragon blood. She had dragon blood. At first, Des had been shaken by that. What did it mean moving forward? What did it mean for them? But soon, Varja after had gone from a half-dragon warrior to the lost, confused, rejected person hiding just under the surface. Des shoved aside her own confusion, born of the hegemonic purity the bureaucracy crammed into every aspect of life. Because at that moment, Varja needed someone, and who was Des to push away the woman she was falling in love with?

Varja was next to her. Her eyes were bloodshot, and tearstains lined her face. She gave one more heaving sigh and said, "I'm hungry."

Des stood and stretched, yawning and rubbing her eyes. "Let's find some food, then. After that, sleep?"

Varja nodded. "Hopefully I don't collapse on the way."

Des hopped down from the rock. "We both know you're stronger than that."

"It's not the physical fatigue I'm worried about." Varja started toward town, but Des got in front of her.

"And it's not what I'm talking about. It takes a powerful spirit to make it as far as you did."

Varja shook her head. "Or just a powerful foolishness."

"That's one way of looking at it, yeah. But given the road that brought you here, I'd call it determination." Des took Varja's hand—holy gods, she was holding her hand—holy fuck, she had spent the night hugging and comforting her—and led her along. "You'll feel better after food and rest. It won't make this alright, but it'll help."

The handholding didn't last. After letting go to climb back to the street, Des saw no window to reinitiate contact. But they did have breakfast side by side at the end of a dock, near one of the few vendors open at this hour. Des finished scarfing down grilled sea bass, then leaned against Varja as she nibbled hers. She wanted to fall asleep there, against Varja's muscled side and shoulder, under the early morning sun. It felt right.

But then, Varja stood, tossing the bones into the harbor. Gulls dove and squabbled, and the romance was broken.

"I need sleep." Varja wrapped Des in a hug. "Thank you." She let go. "I'll catch up with all of you wherever Miranda's off to tonight."

"I'll walk you back," Des said.

"You don't have to do that."

"I want to. I'm sure you'll be fine, but we don't have to part yet."

For the first time since before the arrest, Des saw Varja smile. "Okay."

They talked on the way to the hostel—not about anything relevant to recent happenings, but sights of the streets, anecdotes about other cities. An armed passerby allowed Varja to segue into swords, and traveling with Luc allowed Des to keep up. Mostly. Both avoided any mention of home.

At the door, Varja turned to say goodbye. On impulse, Des wrapped her arms around her, and she returned the hug. Then, the same impulse told Des to go tiptoe and kiss Varja, and she did. It was quick. Varja stood stunned. Des said, "Goodnight," turned, and put a façade of confidence into her stride as she left.

Gods, I hope I didn't just fuck it all up. That was her first thought while walking away and her last before hitting her bed and crashing into sleep. Somewhere in between, she annotated an earlier reflection: *Damn, I am in love with her.*

● ● ●

"So, let me get this straight," Francesca said, sitting up in bed. "You want to settle down, and you tried to help capture a dragon? Without this bitch even telling you—or Des—it's a dragon?"

Azran sat on the other side of the bed. "More or less. I can't say I entirely blame Varja, though."

"No, blame her. You're lucky you aren't dead."

"All of us are, at this point."

"I thought you didn't want any more of this."

"So did I. We're in it now, though, right?"

"Forget it, Az. We've got enough problems already."

Azran shook his head. "I can't. I want to help her. I don't want her going down the same road I did."

Francesca's visage softened. "You think she will?"

"Not sure, but it looks a lot like where I was. Grander, maybe, but a shit family's a shit family."

Blood. He stares in numb amazement at just how much blood there is. Not astonishment, though—he has not the energy for such a taxing reaction.

241

The adrenalin has flowed out, and his heart beats slow, and the cold they always talk about is settling in.

Azran didn't know why his unconscious chose that instant to bring up that memory. He hadn't done it because of his family. They didn't help—they shaped part of his perspective, as the present mind is chipped and polished by every experience prior. But no, the root cause of his action that day went deeper. Something he tried his damnedest to bury had broken free, and his response was the sort that took a moment to carry out, but forever to see to the end.

Black spots obscure some of that blood, heralding the unconsciousness he is there for. You fucked up, *says a voice in his head with startling clarity.*

In the room, dim from sunrise edging around black curtains, Azran touched the faded scar on one of his wrists, then the other. They were more difficult to see than they used to be.

He had hated his family, in that life before. But even then, he had realized he hated himself more. And whenever he would leave, that was the hate he brought with him. Even in the good times.

The spots swim and swim. Where are they going? He needs them here. They swim, and they coalesce into faces. Some laugh, some scream, some sleep, all without sound. The only sound is fuzzy, crackling echoes like distant thunder heard from inside a cellar.

He walked over to the curtains. Francesca, having seen this before, sat quietly. Azran considered stepping out into the sun. How long would he last? He'd never tried.

He huffed and smirked without humor. There it was again. His mind was in that place, so that's what he thought about. He still hated himself on some level. He no longer listed the reasons why, which he supposed was a kind of progress. But the feeling was still there. He doubted it would ever leave; he'd just forget it for a while.

One of the void-motes becomes her face—F-r-a-n-c-e-s-c-a. It takes a long time to think her name. His mind is mud. Some indeterminate period later— in the midst of which he feels a dull, sluggish piercing on one bleeding gash or the other—he realizes what the noise is. First, it was her footsteps. Now, the thunder is closer and it is her voice.

He stepped away from the curtains and lay back on the bed next to his wife. Yeah, he knew Francesca back then. Loved her, too, and she loved him. Life was good, both in the relative and culturally recognized objective sense.

But there were times. Unwanted times when unsought notions would enter his head. Notions of achievement and failure, of what defined his own worth—and it was always about him, wasn't it? Even when he saw his experiences reflected in others.

Now it is him swimming and morphing among the blackness. He hadn't known dying would take this long. How his body must be fighting to correct his mistake. The cold is long gone. Temperature is no longer relevant.

And yet, he almost feels warm.

He reached up a hand and cupped Francesca's cheek, drawing her down. It was not a deep kiss, but a held one; dry, not casual, but familiar.

"Wife" was not a worthy enough name for her role, Azran had decided years ago. It did not encompass what she had done for him. She became his savior, the one who believed he was worth another chance when, even in the gentle throes of death, he did not.

Yes, it is warmth. It starts in an extremity and spreads to his core, a reversal of the natural order of things. Blood—so much blood. Except now, it is inside him. It is his own, and yet it is not.

Their lips parted. She lay next to him, head on his arm lain across inadequate pillows, her arm across his bare chest. The slight pressure let him feel his heartbeat.

She had drunk his blood that day—right off the ground. Then, she cut her own flesh and willed the mixed blood, hers and his, back into him. Azran remembered waking, as if from days of sleep, in her arms. And all of this recollection in no more than a minute. His mind could race with the best of them.

"Never regret what you did," he said. She never out and said it, but from the tones and fragments of unfinished thoughts, he had pieced together the only doubts she refused to voice in full.

Her hand closed into a ball on his chest.

"It was worth it," he said.

Another shallow, but far from meaningless kiss.

He didn't want to ever trade this for the alternative. *But never say never,* he thought. It was a road fraught with temptation to turn off or turn around. Sometimes, he didn't know whether he was going toward or away from the end. He didn't know what the end looked like. He might never get there. Varja still had time to step off that road. If Azran could help her find a different path, then he would.

Of course, the real irony of all this resolve was the way vampiric existence always ended—murder or suicide.

23

It was a burning cold, like standing on the north side of Hospent Montes. Like exposure to the winter wind of Glacire Mare and Infinitir, if there were no skin to shield the muscle and bone. He shivered in the wake of his sacrifice, but it did not warm him. He dared not rub life back into the limb. Touch would renew the slow flensing of mortal flesh. It was too soon, too raw. Nor did he look at the leg, now—like his arm—that frightful combination of withered and strong. It was not as mortal corporeality was meant to be. This process was against nature, an affront to many gods—but not his.

He felt the vile sun rise and set three times as he lay in the searing chill that subsided to mere numbness. Then, he stood. Using the rough brick wall as a crutch, he limped from the vault hidden beneath Aure's vast blood cellar.

The moon was wan behind the fog and blackened by clouds more often than not. This was good. Even Itera's faint sun he abhorred. When Tenebra came to reign, there would be no lights watching and burning from the sky. That moment of arrival, an eclipse greater than any sign of favor since Her ascension, became his focus. He called upon a loftier servant to descend from the void and aid him, and so his litany was:

"By the pilgrim's hand, by his sister's holy blood, the Eclipse will paint a shadow upon the earth. By the pilgrim's hand, by his sister's holy blood, the Eclipse will paint a shadow upon the earth."

Again and again, he recited, meditative, on top of the tower. An onyx-tipped ash cane lay on the weathered planks next to his kneeling, bowed form. Someone attempted speech with the pilgrim, but without success.

The interruption was hours gone when the keen edge of his consciousness cut across seals and planes like a ghostly arrow. His call spread in his wake, audible only to select ears.

"By the pilgrim's hand, by his sister's holy blood, the Eclipse will paint a shadow upon the earth."

"And it shall be my shadow." A reply resounded in his opened soul. *"But only my shadow. The Eclipse is yet to come."*

"Sooner now, by my hand, her blood, and thy shadow," said the pilgrim, now receding into his coil. *"But we must first retrieve the vessel."*

"The vessel will be retrieved," said a voice in the pilgrim's ears, faint yet tangible, a whisper from all sides. "Send me to her."

24

Varja seldom remembered her dreams. They were distinct from her waking mind and lost within minutes. Those she did recall were usually the ones she'd rather forget, memories of horror and pain twisted further by her powerlessness to intervene. She was never lucid. So, this was a strange experience. She could not distinguish between her racing, heated reflections on what had happened at the door and her languid, heated dreams.

She lays in bed, naked or near it—she isn't sure. Neither bothers her because the hostel is empty. Empty and bright from the daylight. Hers is the only bed in the spacious room. She does not look to make sure, but she knows. The place is empty but for one bed, Varja in it, and Des next to her. Des is there. Did she follow Varja in? Or was she there waiting?

Des is clothed, which lends credence to this being a dream. Though Varja cannot remember her dreams, she knows they are composed of fragments of memory—or so said a desert ascetic in Muntherzix.

But then, Varja sees the other beds. Someone is walking through the room, and it is not Des, and Des is gone.

And then the beds vanish, one blink after another. And then Des is there. "It doesn't have to end yet," she says. She kisses Varja again. Varja is sweating. Des is sweating.

"I've never kissed a woman before," Varja says. "I kiss men. I fuck men."

Des rises, smoothly, effortlessly, and perches on her knees. Her quick fingers fiddle with the ties on her vest. "Do you want to fuck me? To kiss me?"

Varja does, but she says, "I don't know."

Des pulls one tie, and all the clothes slip from her torso. Her body does not look as Varja expected, but rather some amalgam of other naked women Varja would sneak glances at without ever asking why.

"Well, we don't have forever," Des says.

There is an emerald ring on a delicate chain around Des's neck. Varja had noticed her fiddling with it the night they met, when Des was well into her cups. Now, it hangs between Des's foreign breasts.

"Whose ring is that?" Varja asks.

Des breaks the chain and pockets the ring. "No one's anymore." She leans forward, over Varja, and puts one arm and one leg to either side of her. She is completely naked now, and so is Varja. "Do you want to fuck me?"

Varja wants to fuck her up and down the room but doesn't say it. Cannot say it. She wants to fuck Des until that glaring sun sets and lie back, Des against her, clothed or not, but dozing as they sit on the rocks and listen to the crashing tides and know that moment—they—will last as close to forever as they can grasp.

But she does not say this, either. She cannot.

Someone is in the room again. Somehow, it's darker now. Did it already happen? Then where is Des? There's just a chilly draft and music. No, wait—Varja is asleep. She knows it now.

Varja opened her eyes. Sweat dampened her clothes and the blanket she had rolled herself in. Orange light slanted into the fully furnished room, but she was in shadow. She heard Miranda picking gently at her oud.

She sat up and wiped heavy gunk from the corners of her eyes. Des was not in Varja's bed, and that made her sad. Why did that make her sad? It was just a weird dream. She'd forget it soon enough. She always did.

"Hi there," Miranda said.

"Mm. Hi." Varja stretched and disentangled herself from the blanket. She suddenly became conscious that Miranda could see the contours of her body. "Sunset? I'm surprised you haven't headed out yet."

"Soon enough." Miranda went halfway down a scale, then jumped to the bottom and started back to the middle. "Soon as you're ready. We need to meet and discuss our next moves, according to Azran. Glad to see you're not in chains, by the way."

"Me too." *Damn, I slept from dawn to dusk. Or near enough.*

"Sleep well?" Miranda asked.

Varja hesitated. "'Well' is—a word."

Miranda raised an eyebrow. "Your tone says it was something more than the sun in your eyes."

Varja wiped her face and arms with a spare shirt, gathering sweat with more success than she was gathering her thoughts. The dream still ran through her head—not flashing, but a slow retelling. She dropped the shirt on the bed and started tying on her boots. "Where are we meeting the others?"

"Place called the Broken Arrow. It's where their lot is staying."

Varja fastened her sheath onto her baldric and slipped it over one shoulder. "Let's go."

Miranda placed her instrument in its burlap case and led the way.

Several blocks in, as they cut down a side street with fewer visible eavesdroppers, Varja decided, *Fuck it. I clearly need help.*

"Des kissed me this morning."

Miranda stopped and turned, the knowingest grin splitting her face. "Wonderful." She started forward again. "About fucking time," she muttered.

"What?" Varja came up next to her. "You knew she'd do that?"

"Oh, don't say it like she stole your purse. I saw the way you looked at her. Honestly, I got a little jealous at the shift in your attention."

"Looked at her how? I don't—it's not like—I only ogle men, thank you."

Miranda laughed. "And I only play for the money." Then she cocked an eye at Varja. "You're serious?"

"Three lovers, all men."

"Well, not everyone sticks to one or the other."

Varja paused. "Really?"

"Chains, woman, what do they teach you down there? You speak five languages, for Nab's sake."

"Four. Most things, I had to learn on my own," Varja said. "Or else beg someone to teach me. Blood, the only thing they offered me was swordplay." At that, she remembered her aunt. Strict, but a good teacher—a mentor of not just how to fight, but when. Varja excelled at the former; not so much that latter. A cloud passed over the memory. Did Mirricix know about Varja's impossible quest? Had she been in on it?

"And you never knew anyone who'd been with both?" Miranda asked. "Not at the same time—though that's also a thing. It just doesn't seem like you. But, a woman who loved another, then they split, then loved a man? Any combination of those elements?"

Varja thought back. After twenty feet of walking, she shook her head.

"That's wild," Miranda said.

"So what?"

"So I'm saying, just because you've only fucked men so far, it doesn't mean you only love men. I don't know, though. I'm not you. Maybe you're right, and the rest of us are just misreading this."

Varja's cheeks turned ruddy. Everyone else had been expecting that kiss.

"So, were we misreading?" Miranda asked.

"I—don't know. I should know, though, shouldn't I?"

"Should, maybe. Would, maybe not. Not if you're from such an apparent backwater and had no one to help you figure it out."

"What about you?"

"Men, all day, all night. So maybe I've been speaking out of turn. But damn if I don't love seeing love, no matter who it's between."

"I meant, can you help me figure it out?"

Miranda took a breath. "Well, okay. Okay. When Des kissed you, how did it feel? How did you feel?"

"Which one?"

"Both."

"It felt—I was surprised. I felt like I was on fire but that it was alright. I got a little dizzy. I wanted to talk, but I couldn't, and she was already walking away. I felt drunk."

"Did it feel like when you kiss a man?"

Varja thought. "Yes and no. It was different. It was a woman, and I don't—I don't know anymore."

"How about the 'yes' part?"

"It was short, unexpected. But I had these dreams all day."

"Sexy dreams?"

"Confused dreams, I guess."

"Are you glad it happened?"

"I think?" It hadn't felt wrong. But Varja could only take so much shattering of her worldview in one day. "I need to think."

"Well, you can always talk to Des about it," Miranda said.

Shit, that's true. Blood of the dead, she's going to be there. I'm not ready. Shitfuck. Okay, easy, Varja. Courage facing the wall of the storm. Just like Mirricix taught you. Breathe, and meet the thunder with your own. When it roars, roar back.

"Oh, shit," Miranda said with a sympathetic laugh. "I just realized how awkward this is going to be now."

When it roars, roar back!

$$\bullet \; \bullet \; \bullet$$

Des sat in the common room, foot bouncing to a nonexistent, frenzied beat. She'd slept a dead sleep, and with her restored energy came renewed nerves.

She'd done it—she had actually kissed Varja, someone Des wasn't even sure wanted her to. *That's why I never do it first.* She thought she had seen the signs, but how much could she trust her perception? She talked to an imaginary ghost, for the gods' sakes.

The ghost of the last woman she'd kissed with passion. Des had come close a few times in the interim. One time, she even fucked, but it wasn't making love. Those kisses didn't count—not even the ones up top.

So, that's where I'm at, Des thought. *Where you at, Ari? I know you're around. Do you approve?*

Maybe Varja wouldn't even come tonight. Des couldn't decide whether she wanted that. *Quick answer and an awkward evening? Or keep waiting and twitching till my leg falls off?*

She became aware of cool metal and a faceted stone among her fingers. She knew what it was, but looked down anyway. *So that's where you are.* Des had caught herself fiddling with the ring— her engagement ring—of late. It had ceased to be conscious. She needed something to distract her.

"I think all we need is a senator," Azran was saying from across the table.

Francesca, next to him, shook her head. "We need more than that."

"Well, as a start. It doesn't matter what province. They just need someone in the room who knows what we are, instead of the caricature in most people's minds. I mean, you heard Varja."

"We're in a bestiary." Francesca gave a humorless laugh.

Des's eyes widened. "What?"

"According to Varja, the night we met," Francesca said. "We'd be, where, just after tritons?"

"And you know there are way too many people in that chamber who think we belong there," Azran added.

Francesca nodded, staring off. "True. I've had people on the street beg me not to drink their blood."

"That, I find understandable," Luc said. "We used to tell monster stories as kids, and more than a few had vampires. People let fear rule them."

"Happened to me once," Azran said. "Fucking Department of History bureaucrat. Educated government official. It's not a matter of courage—it's a matter of ignorance."

"Where do you think fear comes from?" Luc asked.

"I think a lot of people are scared after what went down the night we left," Des said.

"Yeah." Azran sighed. "But we almost got a mob execution. That night was bad, but it doesn't excuse a witch hunt."

"Maybe," Luc said, taking a swig of ale. "But it explains one. They're still calling it the Night of Blood and Flame."

"This started well before that night," Francesca said. "Filvié Noctirin's been fighting a movement to make hunting vampires legal. Forget riots, if you hate your vampire neighbor, you can stab her in her sleep."

"So you respond by confirming all their fears?" Luc asked.

"Us?" Francesca almost jumped over the table. "*We* didn't do shit. If that's how the cabal wants to do things, we want nothing to do with them."

"But you could do something to stop them," Luc said.

"Such as?"

"Stop fearing your brother."

Francesca slunk back down. Azran glared at the priest and put an arm around his wife's shoulders.

"Luc, you're being an ass," Des said.

Luc swallowed his ale. "How?"

"By assuming you know what's happening better than the people it's happening to. Get off the horse and walk around for once. Listen to more than your bloated fucking ego."

Luc stared at her for several heartbeats, then stood and headed for the door.

Azran and Francesca turned to Des, who said quietly, "He's had it coming a long time. I still owe him, but godsdamn am I running short on patience."

The door opened in front of Luc, and in walked Miranda and Varja. They greeted each other—Luc stiffly, from the look of it—and approached the table.

This is shaping up to be a Rixian night, Des thought.

• • •

Again the priest's soul cut through reality, but now only across the mortal night. Sure as a hunter's arrow to a stag's heart, it sped toward dear Francesca. She had gone so very far—not far enough. With the angel's gift—no, the reward of the pilgrim's sacrifice to Tenebra—he could again find her. Her blood was the same as his. It was so simple a matter, and yet he could not follow her so far until now. All he had to do was open his eyes—when upon a time he closed them to scry her soul, now they shone black as the angel's—blacker than the heavy night curling around his flesh atop the tower.

He saw a city, a crescent sprawl at the crossing of many roads. He saw a building, an inn, a warm common room. It was all so bright—the city, the room—such abominable illumination. Focus. Follow the path of shadows through the glare. Yes, there was dear Francesca. She looked well. She looked strong. She looked up. She shivered and sensed something close, but he knew she couldn't see him. How could she, one so misguided?

And there was her tempter, her corruptor, next to her—touching her! And there were others, one with the stench of the

First Gods, one an Interloper's halfbreed descendent, one who had been to Hades, Realm of the Dead, and last, one haunted by the dead. Such corruption at one table, and all around his dear Francesca.

"Where?" inquired the whisper from all sides.

"There," said the pilgrim. "We need her. The other vampire dies. The rest may die."

Following the path left by the scrying soul, almost like energy along an arcane thread, the ghost of an Angel of Shade flew to the city, the inn, the light, the sister, the blood.

And angel-black eyes watched.

• • •

"Can't say I expected that," Miranda said once the tale was told. "But I knew something was off about Seneskar."

"Azran already told me about him." To Varja, Francesca said, "So that makes sense about you."

"I missed out on dueling a dragon," Luc muttered to himself.

"You're all taking this better than I expected," Varja said.

Miranda raised her glass. "Honey, we all followed some bizarre road to this place. You found the right crowd."

"So, why was I not brought along?" Luc asked.

"Because I knew you'd do what she ended up doing," Des replied, gesturing toward, but not looking at, Varja.

Luc sat back. "You don't trust me."

"I do, but it's a prudent trust." She did not have the capacity to deal with Luc's shit right now. Varja was sitting right there and hadn't said a word to Des except a hello and now that reality was here Des found herself wishing Varja had not come because to have her within arm's reach and be unable to touch her or know if she wanted Des to touch her was ripping her apart and *godsdammit Luc of course you weren't brought there was already a wild card even if she was hot and strong and gentle she had a temper to match your own you fucking berserker.*

Des took a breath. "So, how do we move forward?"

There was a quiet moment. Varja shifted like she was about to speak, but didn't. She seemed surprised at Luc's, Francesca's, and Miranda's relative indifference to the full story, and now was clearly contemplating. But what was she contemplating—why she had kept those things secret, or something about Des? She kept stealing glances when she thought Des wouldn't notice.

"Well," Azran finally said, "Seneskar's probably busted out by now and started off wherever he was going after this. Varja, do you have any idea?"

"I don't know. He's been heading northeast since he landed on the mainland."

"Northeast," Francesca said. She looked at Azran. "You don't think?"

"Aure's a mess right now," he said.

"Quite the opportunity for the heathens nipping at our flank," Luc added.

Des rolled her eyes. "That's a big leap."

He glared at her. "It's something."

"What do you think?" Varja asked.

Des almost got tongue-tied. She thought a lot of things. "We ask around, like we found him the first time."

"He might be in a different skin," Azran said.

Silence stretched across the table. Other patrons went about their business and conversations. Des's eavesdropping habit picked up happy tidbits—a good job, a love rekindled, fair weather on the voyage here. It felt like their table was in a world all its own.

Then Varja said, "What's the point anymore." No one else spoke, so she continued, "We lost him. I lost him. I was never supposed to find him in the first place. And—and it's not like they'd want me to come back even with him in chains. 'Oh, look at that, the Ziathrixturoz actually did it. What do we do now? I know, we'll have her go to Darachzartha and kill the Urathix!'" She pounded the table, rattling drinks, and dropped her face into her palms.

Des gingerly reached out to touch her arm. Varja recoiled from the contact. Her expression was torn, confused, and dejected all at once. Des was aware of how much Varja was struggling to make sense of this. Her life as she knew it was over. But after last night, because of that ill-considered kiss, all Des saw in that expression was rejection. *No,* it said, *I don't want that. I don't want you.*

Her hand fell. She stared through the bottom of her glass.

"If anyone's interested," Miranda said, "I've been saving up for a ship's passage back to Astrellus. Might be nice to...get away from unpleasant reminders."

Why east? Des thought. *Not east, please. I can't. She's there—that's where Ari is.*

"That doesn't sound bad," Azran said. "It might be good to keep moving." He looked at Francesca. "Until, you know."

"It's crossed my mind."

No.

"Varja?" Azran asked. "Des?"

"Never been east," Varja mumbled. "Why not?" She was giving Des that look again. What was behind that look?

I can't go east.

"Des?" Miranda asked. "You in?"

They were all looking at her. Even Luc.

"I—"

25

The lights—candles, oil lamps, the glow from the streets—dimmed to the level of a pale, weak moon through mist. Miranda pulled a strange, crystalline compass from her pocket. It spun, then stopped with its arrow pointed at the center of the tavern.

"An immortal," she whispered.

A thing appeared in the room. It coalesced from the space where light once was. It was tall—taller than Varja, taller than an orc or any mortal creature that yet wandered these lands. It had two arms and two legs and two wings, but its whole form was indistinct. Its skin swirled like smoke, here thicker, there only vapor, always shifting. In place of eyes, set within a face that did not exist in as many dimensions as it should, in that wrong visage were two holes to a world where light was not, had never been, and never would be. Even in the ink of that smoky skin, the not-eyes were darkest.

All this Francesca saw, though not a second had yet passed. It was more a premonition—she knew what she would see when she looked. In the same way, she knew what this was and why it was here.

Others—those at the table, those within the tavern—now became aware of the alien presence. Shouts and shrieks of surprise and terror rang out. Then the thing—the angel—moved, and the cries became pain and horror. The darkness pulsed, and shards like polished obsidian flew from its outstretched hands. In the gloom, blood was not red but black.

Motion erupted. Des rolled out of her chair into a low crouch, dagger drawn as she coiled to spring. Varja rose and kicked her seat behind her, pulling her long blade from under the table. Luc drew a pair, his arming in his right hand and short in his stiff left. He chanted as a faint, sharp glow emanated from his swords and eyes. Miranda scrambled back from the thing, oud in her hands and fucks flying from her mouth. Azran grabbed Francesca's arm, ready about to flee.

"What is that?" he asked.

"Angel of Shade," Francesca answered.

At the sound of her voice, those holes in the spectral face fixated on her. Yes, it was here for Francesca. It came from Amadore.

It charged, legs pumping but feet not touching the floor. It sprang to summit the table. At the same time, Des launched forward. She thrust off-center into what looked like an abdomen. The vaporous flesh disentangled itself from the steel, but the angel still stumbled to its knees, momentum interrupted.

Before it could stand, Varja swung down in a diagonal arc. The angel bent sideways, spineless, and shifted to its feet. Luc came from the other side, a cry on his lips as he loosed a flurry of strikes.

"Atora, make my blades laugh! Make them sing!"

Because his left was slow, Luc used the short blade to set up strikes from his right. He threatened and herded the dodging creature into thrusts and cuts—and that glow left its mark.

Varja and Des, working the flanks, had a harder time of it. Sword high and dagger low, they struck but left no more damage than pricking needles would.

Francesca gave Azran a look.

"Go," he said. She started for the exit, pulling him along.

But those not-eyes still saw their quarry. The hands became more solid. One snagged Luc's left wrist and pushed it wide. His right, withdrawn for a thrust, could not intercept the other. The angel slugged him in the solar plexus. Luc staggered over double but kept his feet.

Des attempted an arm lock, but the towering figure shrugged her off.

An obsidian shard struck the wall in front of the vampires, stopping them short for an instant. The angel lunged in behind the missile, blocking their escape. It reached for Francesca.

A body-block from Varja bashed the angel into the wall, cracking the vertical boards.

Azran and Francesca retreated, finding cover under two pushed-together tables while the melee continued behind them. Miranda was down there, too, tuning her instrument. Then Des joined them, tumbling and sliding across the floor. Her dagger skittered just out of her reach.

"Motherfucker," she growled. She looked at the other three. "The fuck are you doing? Help kill this thing!"

"Working on it," Miranda said, turning keys. "Trust me. Trust me and cover me."

"Right." Des pulled a knife from each boot. She rose, threw one blade, and charged back in.

Francesca glanced around and pulled a rapier from the belt of a dead man. "Stay here," she told Azran. Then she, too, seized the situation.

Azran watched from under the table. The most light came from Luc's blades. As he danced about the angel, the glow shifted and blinked—when it came to that, the form was opaque.

Varja bled from three rakes in her shoulder. She held her longsword in a half-grip, thrusting and pommel striking, which at least seemed to budge the creature.

Francesca picked her moments but served best as bait. The thing wanted her, and this gave the others openings.

Des hopped onto a table, flipped her knife into a reverse grip, and leapt onto the angel's shoulders. She wrapped her legs around its torso and drove the blade into the base of its neck. It did not scream—it had made no sound at all this entire time.

The shadow-body twisted and tightened, becoming almost serpentine. It flowed up, through, and beyond Des's grip. She hit the floor. The angel resumed its normal proportions, roiling forward to land in front of Francesca. It knocked her rapier flying and grabbed her with an oversized, taloned grip. Luc came on, then fell back with a black dart in his side.

Azran saw all this in the moments it took to occur. Within the next, he had grabbed Des's lost dagger and launched himself at the angel. He made contact as it lifted Francesca, kicking and choking, by the neck. Azran stabbed furiously, once, twice, three—

The angel's free hand twisted around its back. A cold sliver of the void pierced Azran's ribs. White-hot pain exploded in his chest and spread. He coughed blood, saw black, and fell. Somewhere, he heard faint and fading music.

Varja chopped into the arm holding Francesca aloft. It released her before finding its strength again. Francesca rasped and crawled to Azran.

A wing lashed out, knocking Des through the air. She landed on her feet next to Luc, her gasping and him grimacing. She thumped his shoulder.

"Come on. I've seen you bleed harder than that."

"It's not just the puncture," he said. But he advanced with her regardless.

Varja did her best to keep the thing occupied. She parried and dodged talons that swung with frightening speed. Her counters did almost nothing. Then, as it reared back for a double swipe, she snatched an opening. She launched a half-grip thrust, shifting her left hand back to the hilt as the blade passed the dodging angel. She hooked one muscled leg around the slender shadow-leg and kept her other rooted. She reversed direction, planting the pommel on the angel's chest. She flexed every muscle in a line from her forearm to her foot, going for a tripping takedown.

The angel, impossibly slick, rotated out and around Varja. It hooked her with an arm and a wing and continued the spin. Something sharp protruded from that driving hand and into Varja's back. She had no time to acknowledge the pain before she was thrown across the room. She crashed into the wall and bounced to the floor, dazed beyond sense.

"Motherfucker," Des growled again. Something primal welled up in her. Without a thought, she took the short sword from Luc's bad hand and charged.

The angel loomed over Francesca, who guarded the bleeding form of Azran with her body and a small knife.

But Des did not see them. She did not see Luc's confused shock, or Miranda emerging from her cover. Des was blind to all but the thing that had tossed Varja like a giant ragdoll.

She jumped, clutched the shoulder of one wing with her free hand, and hacked the other with the glowing sword.

The angel spun and flailed, trying to throw her. Des coiled her abdomen and hooked her legs on the wounded wing. Now closer, her sword hand went around its neck. She grabbed a handful of tangles that might have been hair and let her weight fall. The head jerked back, and then Des dragged the soul-charged blade across its throat.

She landed and rolled back, preparing to charge again. The angel convulsed but turned to meet the combined assault of Luc and Des. A hand caught each around the neck and upper torso, held tight, and began to crush. But before their bones could snap, the angel froze. Des became aware of a song.

Miranda stood on a table, playing her oud. The music was gentle, but increasing in speed and volume. She struck a full chord, and blue sparks jumped between her fingertips and the strings. Faster and stronger and heavier, power rose with the crescendo and allegro.

The angel dropped its prey and, for the first time, it screamed. The sound echoed as soon as it originated, hollow as those twin voids in its wrong face. The scream came from all sides at once, ringing in ears and minds alike.

The thing staggered toward Miranda, gaining momentum as it went. She continued her dance on the strings, her face composed. The notes ascended to a peak. Grey flames engulfed the angel. It screamed again, reaching out one clawed hand that closed over the air in front of her. Then, like some vile drink spiraling down a drain but faster, the Angel of Shade was banished from the Mortal Realm, taking the darkness with it.

There was not silence in its wake. Des had expected silence. But she panted, exhausted. Francesca sobbed while Azran took ragged breaths. Miranda stepped down from the table. Luc muttered as he pulled a sliver of shadow from his side— something had remained behind, it seemed. Across the room, Varja groaned and used a toppled chair to pull herself up.

Somewhere far away, a bell rang.

Luc paused next to Des. The bare skin under his torn shirt was sealed, but still scab red.

Des glanced at the short sword. Its glow was gone. She offered it hilt-first to Luc. "Sorry."

He stared at her not with offense or irritation, but awe. "Don't be." He continued forward and knelt next to Azran.

"Help him," Francesca said. "Please. It's my fault, help him. It's my fault that thing was here."

Luc put a hand on her shoulder, then went to work on Azran, clutching his medallion and praying.

Varja sat down and began wrapping her own shard wound with the bottom half of her shirt. Des went over to her but stopped when she saw the wracked body of Serile, eyes frozen and a shard in her forehead. Then, Des noticed the many other corpses in the room. She recalled a few patrons making it out the door early on, but she had thought they were more.

Behind, Azran coughed and propped himself on his elbows.

265

"Thank you," Francesca said, hugging him. "Thank you," she repeated, this time more pointedly at Luc.

"He'll still need a real healer," the priest said. "He had at least one broken rib and could start bleeding internally over the next few days."

"What do you mean it was your fault?" Miranda asked, staring hard at Francesca.

"I think my brother sent it. It was here for me."

"It did seem that way," Luc said.

"Then why are all these other people dead?" Des asked, roused from her corpse-induced fugue.

Azran coughed and lay back down. "Because he's an asshole."

"And because you shouldn't fuck with immortals," Miranda said.

"Seems you have before."

"That's how I learned not to."

"And who taught you to banish them with music?" Luc asked.

"Mortis. Met him in a bar once. Though, I suppose the song belongs to Musymph. Long story."

"Can I learn to do that?" Azran asked.

Miranda smirked. "Keep practicing, young'un. But enough of that. We need to move. Now. Unless any of you want to explain this to the authorities."

As if on cue, a rough cry of "Make way!" sounded outside. Dozens of heavy boots pounded up the block.

Des was already moving. "You okay?" she asked, handing Varja her sword.

"Well enough."

"Out the back," she said to the rest.

Azran struggled to his feet, his breath heaving. Francesca and Luc helped him walk.

266

Miranda perched herself on a table near the front entrance as the others reached the kitchen.

The guards were drawing close.

"Let's go," Des said.

"Miranda," Varja said at the same time.

"You go on," Miranda said, smiling. "Seems you all have some important business to take care of. I'll catch up down the road. Best of luck."

"But—"

"Don't worry about me. I'll lead them on a merry chase. I've done this before."

"Thank you," Varja said, brows arched in concern.

Des just gave a nod, pulling her along.

Miranda gave them a salute as they vanished around the corner.

The front door burst open, and half a dozen armored guards poured in, swords drawn.

"By the gods," several oathed.

"You could say that," Miranda said.

The guards spun on her. "On the floor," one ordered.

Another went with, "What in hades happened here?"

Miranda winked and went through the open window. Outside, a dozen more stood ready.

"I strike again, and so I will again, by the Chains of Crusix!" she shouted at them. She laughed maniacally and bolted.

"It was her!"

"Get her!"

"She a mage?"

"Someone get the Godshadows!"

Eighteen sets of feet—so she hoped, she wasn't slowing to check—pounded after Miranda.

I'm gonna need a quiet drink after tonight.

26

The others heard Miranda's shouts amid those of the guards. They did not pause—Des wouldn't let them stop—but Azran said, "That's a brave woman."

"Mad, I'd put it," Luc said.

"Aren't we all?" Des muttered.

"She's roaring back at the storm." Varja gave a sad smile.

"Where do we go?" Luc asked.

"Aure," Francesca replied. Her free hand pawed at the looted rapier on her belt. "Amadore. He won't stop coming, so I'll stop running. I won't let my fear kill anyone else."

"Healer," Azran said. "I can't ride like this. We'll need new day supplies, too. Can't go back to the inn."

"I could," Des said.

"They'll have it under guard while they investigate," Francesca said.

"I've slipped into more secure places."

"That's true," Luc affirmed.

"With Godshadows, given what happened," Francesca added.

"I stand by my words," Des said.

Azran coughed trying to speak, then managed, "We could get in touch with Valen. He could help us."

"If he's even still alive," Francesca said, quieting the discussion for a moment.

"Well, for now, there was a healer staying at the hostel," Varja said. From what little she had interacted with him, he seemed a crotchety sort. But he knew his trade. He had commented on the speed of Varja's recovery from the ring fight and the guard's sucker punch, and correctly guessed it was due to her ancestry.

"Is that safe?" Azran asked.

"Should be for now," Des said. "We just can't stay long."

The others nodded and trudged on through dark alleys. Despite their state, no scavengers attempted to pick at them. According to Des, there existed a threshold of don't-fuck-with-us that they had crossed. Wounded or not, that many armed people, alive despite the fight that caused the wounds, would deter harassment.

"That's how Luc and I got out of Forente."

• • •

"It's three cracked ribs," the physician said in a grumbling slur. "They're not out of place, so they'll heal with time." As he spoke, his reedy natural voice became more apparent. "I am no priest. I don't—*vhsht!*—magic bones back together."

He perched on a stool beside the unclaimed bed where they had placed Azran. The physician was tall, but spindly, and sat

270

hunched forward so he resembled a scarecrow in an old nightshirt. "Now, may I return to sleep, or will you be discussing the cause here?" He gestured to Azran.

"A bar fight," Varja said.

Azran's laughter turned into a groan, then a hiss. "Ah, fuck me."

Francesca looked to him, then to the physician. "Is there nothing else you can do?"

"We have an urgent need to travel," Varja explained.

"We can't take weeks to—"

"Won't take many weeks, lass," he replied, interrupting Francesca. "Well, to fully heal, perhaps. But he should be able to travel in two weeks or so." He saw the helpless expression on her face and her hand clutching Azran's. The treelike man sighed, stood, and trudged to an organized mess of luggage. After some rummaging and more grumbling, he returned with a small, leather pouch. "You're vampires, yes? Yes. Well, this is powdered bone, mixed with an herb called osgra. Stir it in with blood and drink it. All of it. That should mend you faster."

Francesca took the pouch and examined its contents. "That sounds like alchemy."

"Suppose it is. The mixture will blend with the soul essence in the blood you drink, and then guide your own soul into healing your injury."

"What kind of bone?" Azran asked.

"Cow," the physician said. "So, cow blood will work best."

Azran made a disgusted face. "Hate cow blood." He nodded at the physician. "Thank you."

"How much?" Francesca asked.

271

The physician waved a hand. "Nothing, if you take your business elsewhere now. I've had some wild nights in my day, but I've no desire to relive them. Goodnight, you young shits."

He paused as he passed Varja and looked at her reddened makeshift bandages. "Bar fight, eh?" He tossed her a palm-sized vial. "Smear this all up in there, once the bleeding stops. You heal fast, but infection can always be faster."

He lowered himself into bed and rolled away from them.

• • •

Des and Luc waited outside the hostel, keeping watch for guards with a purpose. At least, that's what they were supposed to be doing. Instead, Des watched her hands tremble. As the rush of the fight faded, she noticed this phenomenon and became fascinated by it. She was fine when the danger was still right around the corner. She always had been. She could not recall the last time her hands shook like this. They hadn't after the assault in Forente, even as she left Ecar to die the most torturous death she could arrange.

She followed lines of thought by association, tangent to tangent, and then it came to her. The last time her hands shook this much was the night Ari died in them. That night at Inks and the breakwall, Ari was there, but she wasn't *there*. Not like Varja was tonight. There was no threat of loss then, and now there was.

Des hugged herself, just so she had something tangible and still to hold. She looked at Luc, then away. "What? You've been staring at me for the last hour, what?"

It wasn't an angry stare—if Luc was still pissed from the conversation before the thing appeared, he did not show. It was an inscrutable stare, the knowing gaze of a priest.

"You used soul magic," Luc said.

Des turned to him. "What?"

"When you took my sword, the energy should have faded. But it didn't."

"I'm not a priest."

"Clearly, but you don't have to be."

"So what does that mean?"

"It means you believed hard enough, felt something strongly enough. I've been thinking." He shifted his feet. "I don't think you could have conjured that power."

"Thanks for the confidence."

"Same to you for yours last night. But you sustained the charge, and that is not nothing. Even with the myriad of soul energy filling that room—a chaos through which I had difficulty focusing—you managed to fight through. Just what did you tap into? What did you feel?"

"Anger," Des said without considering. Then, she considered. "And fear."

"At what?"

Des sighed and paced out and back, hands still grasping the opposite elbows. "It hurt Varja."

"Ah." Luc pondered, a half-smile forming. "Desalie, are you in love again?"

"Don't take that tone. But yeah, I must be. For all the good it does me."

"What do you mean?"

"I think it's one-sided." Des leaned against the wall, slinking under the shadowed eve.

Luc joined her. "You think, or you know?"

"I fear."

"Have you told her?"

"No."

"You should tell her."

"It's not that easy."

"It's easier than living in fear."

Des leaned her head on his arm, remembering why she ran with a fucking priest. Sometimes, she needed him to say things like that out loud, things she ignored when they were spoken in her head. "I'm sorry for snapping at you earlier."

Luc didn't say anything, but she felt some tension go out of him.

"Hey, Luc?"

"Yes?"

"How the fuck are we friends."

Luc laughed. "I believe we're both trying to be better people. But we don't always want to, because it's hard. So we each found someone who would push us."

"Hm."

"You disagree?"

"I thought it was because of Arilysa."

"At first, sure. But I think this is what keeps us going now."

"Makes sense. I guess you can only ride grief so far."

● ● ●

It didn't work—*it did not work*. Such power, and it failed.

The angel had lusted too much for blood. They had been so eager to feel the Mortal Realm again—thus why they heeded the priest's call. But the eagerness was too great. The priest had tried to direct the immortal but to little avail.

And that musician. She was no immortal, nor even a mystic, and yet she banished an Angel of Shade beyond the Seal. Dear

Francesca had surrounded herself with mighty allies—mighty tempters.

The priest limped around the perimeter of the towertop, cane in hand, gnarled knuckles strangling the smooth onyx. His unmarred hand clutched a black disc on a chain with equal fervor. He brought the amulet to his lips, begging for Tenebra's guidance on this matter. His path was ordained, but it was a heavy burden to try and fail again and again. This was a test, but Tenebra could still guide the guide.

The scriptures—stories. When Tenebra walked as a half-immortal. She would one day wield the power to eclipse the vile sun, power so great that Sola, in fear, cursed all vampire flesh to reject the light. But back then, before Her ascension, before even Her vampiric awakening, Tenebra was an assassin. She had skill in stealth and the bow, but the scriptures told also of Her guile. Deception. Expectation and irony. Enough to outmaneuver the gods themselves—ancient Firsts, clever Interlopers, and tenacious Risen alike.

The angel had failed. Perhaps force was not the way. Perhaps a lure. But who? One dear Francesca would trust, and yet one the priest could rely upon.

If only that deluded Azran held faith. The priest would confirm his death, but across such a distance, only his sister's blood shined in the dark. And the priest was spent. For now. He kissed the token again, praying for the sinner's demise and judgment.

"Ria," said the priest aloud, stopping mid-stride. He stumbled, still unused to his lameness.

Ria—yes, the barkeep. She knew Francesca. They were friends, the whispers told him. They also said she had experience retrieving people at the behest of a many-armed beast. And he could control her—through pressure, through aimed threats—yes, the whispers told him much—and through rationed information, half-truths.

Dear Francesca was important—true.

Dear Francesca was troubled, lost—true.

Dear Francesca had been led astray, manipulated, and had left not of her own accord—half-true.

That was deception, the scriptures taught—to lie by speaking the truth. This was Tenebra's guidance. Her wish, Her way.

• • •

Varja, Francesca, and a slow but independent Azran walked out of the hostel.

"You're looking better," Luc said.

"The edge is blunted," Azran replied. "And, I've some medicine to speed things up."

Des gave him a nod—she was happy he would be alright. But her eyes were drawn to Varja. She had a bag slung over one shoulder, over her baldric. Her makeshift bandages had been changed, but oh gods, of course her abs were still showing. Varja looked at Des, and Des resumed keeping watch. It was that or stare.

"We need somewhere to lie low for a few days," Francesca said. "Somewhere far from here and the inn."

"The Cruxian blood seller," Azran said. "He said there's a travelers' house in Quarrytown. Vampire-friendly, and the owner even sells curtains and day tents."

"Where's Quarrytown?" Luc asked.

"Northeast of the city proper," Francesca said, nodding. "Past Coraea. It's far enough. But we'll have to move now."

"Anything at the inn no one can part with?" Des asked. "Last chance."

276

"You said you could get in there?" Francesca asked.

Des nodded.

"Then save yourself for Aure. We'll need you."

"If you're coming," Azran added.

Des rubbed a bruise on her shoulder. "Your brother just threw an immortal at us, and that thing threw me across the room. Twice." *And hurt Varja.* "And something I've learned—deal with your past before it can deal with you. Sure as shit I'm going."

"Then let's go," Azran said, turning north. He pointed with intrepid flair, then groaned, "Onward."

"Easy, dear," Francesca said. "It's still hours before dawn. Nice and easy."

"Good plan."

Luc and the couple led the way. Des and Varja followed after an awkward moment.

"We should talk," Varja said quietly.

"Yeah, we should." Des said nothing further. Now that the moment was upon her, she was looking for a way to avoid it, despite Luc's attempt at inspiration. She wanted to believe this hesitance was just Ari's ghost breathing down her neck, but the presence was so inconsistent that Des couldn't tell where the haunting ended and her own ragged heart began. Whose doubting voice was she hearing?

You know this will not end well. It will end in death. Just like before. You're not cursed—that would be too convenient, leave you with unstained hands. Not cursed, but evil. You're a wicked person. How many men and women did you kill that night you got vengeance? Have you felt a moment's remorse for any of them?

They deserved it.

Justification, or rationalization? Cali was a sadistic bitch, and Ecar was the cause of all that bloodshed—well, the immediate cause. But did the others deserve murder? Do you even remember how many it was?

Six. Or seven.

You don't know. And there were more.

Luc killed those ones.

You brought him there, even knowing how fucked he is. But did any of them deserve it? The low-tier locks?

They were with the Capital Kraken.

So were you, once. Then, you convinced Ari the two of you could leave.

We convinced each other.

Wouldn't have happened if not for you. People die around you. That's the truth you're trying to ignore. Ecar died paralyzed and bleeding into salty shark water. And you felt nothing but peace. Do you think you're the kind of person Varja would love?

Ari loved me.

And now she's dead. Some people just are not meant to be happy.

Des saw Varja in the ring again, then out in the rain. She saw her beauty, heard her vitality and honesty in their conversations, felt an echo of that protective rage. The shivering thrill of that kiss.

I was happy.

And after all that, you're just going to give up. You fucking failure. You don't deserve happiness.

Five blocks later, Des had still not said another word aloud. Varja touched her shoulder, and Des spooked like an animal. The two stopped while the others continued down a crowded bar street.

"I'm not angry," Varja started. Then, she paused.

Des stared, mortified at the expected "but."

"It felt good," Varja blurted. "It's just new to me, because I thought I loved men, and I think I still do, and Miranda said there are people like that—who love both—but my clan never told me that. Which isn't surprising, since I guess they don't give a godsdamn about me. But I'd never kissed a woman, and it was good—I said that—and after, I had really confusing dreams, except sometimes I was awake. But I couldn't stop thinking about you, and I don't know if that's a good thing or a bad thing. I'm leaning towards good, but it's new, and I don't really know how to handle this. I know this is a weird time to say all this because we almost died. But that's why I have to say it—not because of fearing regret, but because my nerves are completely shot and I can't hold it in."

By the end, Varja wasn't out of breath, to Des's amazement. What she found more amazing was that the best-case scenario was the reality. She wanted to sigh in relief, cry from joy—or some raw emotion—and pounce on Varja all at once. Instead, she just slammed into a hug, barely avoiding Varja's wound.

"It just seemed like the thing to do," Des said, meaning both the hug and the kiss. She let go and looked up. Varja's face bore similar mixed emotions, wrapped up in something else holding her back. Des should have held off on kissing her—she knew a person could only take so much change at one time. "We'll take things as they come."

This won't end well. Soon enough, she'll see who you really are.

She has some conclusions to make yet. Let her decide what she sees in me.

Evil.

Maybe, but right now, I don't feel evil. I feel needed.

279

27

The priest was a pilgrim again, journeying through a land of sinners to deliver a call from the Goddess. The moon had waxed a sliver, and no fog now eased the glow. White light and stars flooded the world, and he hid from them. The streetlamps cast pale, yellow light, and he hid from them, too. He passed a shattered and charred storefront where white candles, votives of Mortis, burned in remembrance—he hid from these, also. Alleys and eves provided succor. As night fell and he awoke, he had worried the corrupted—no, sacrificed—leg would slow his flight through the shadows. Not so. Rested and refreshed, the pilgrim traveled with Tenebra's grace, as always. The twisted arm held the cane, and both lay beneath enshrouding vestments.

His path was barren, devoid of all but those living who heard not the gods. The others knew without knowing to make way. The pilgrim halted when he saw a face on a news board—his face. On a wanted poster, bordered by warnings and crimes. "Inciting civil disobedience" was among them. "Murder," too. Perhaps Ciusa's guard had been strong enough to make the barricade. They knew much, and too many knew for Filvié Noctirin to silence them all.

Haste—they needed haste. The urban authorities were pinpointing the key figures, and the shadeseers could not hold back the Godshadows forever.

The pilgrim's hood was low. He breathed and pulled more shadows into the space where his face should have been, where light dared not pass. Then, the gliding passage resumed, eve to alley, alley to eve, through the blind places.

The tavern—the Silver Sun, that brazen metaphor for the moon. This was the one. There was a perimeter—a front where guards and vampires stared across at one another as both awaited permission for bloodshed—not that blood wasn't shed every night interim. But neither force hindered the pilgrim. He crossed the line in the streets, then the threshold of the tavern.

Bright—it was bright in there. Why was it so bright in there? With enough faith, even the common worshipper would be granted Tenebra's sight. But, the pilgrim reminded himself, one should not expect too much of them. Every clan needs its expendables.

Past the initial glare—which banished the shadows from beneath his cowl—the pilgrim saw the tables, the windows—boarded but for slits—the hearth, the harpsichord, the bar, the vampires—militant and otherwise—and the one called Ria.

All heads turned when he let the cool breeze in, then all eyes fled to surfaces and drinks. Only Ria watched the pilgrim. She knew why he was here. He limped to the bar but did not sit. Those nearby mumbled unacknowledged excuses to relocate.

Ria was southern, and she looked it. Perhaps she was from Cruxia herself. But she was older than she looked. Her long history demanded that be true. The pilgrim fixated on her dyed silver hair, short and asymmetric, and her clothes—solid ink-blue with patches of sheer, two belts, also asymmetric. She would not mingle with nobles of the old country, nor the elegant Noblest of the clan. But she would be known to dear Francesca.

"Can I help you?" asked the one called Ria. She appeared calm but was terrified beneath. Good.

"You may serve me, but not with drink," said the pilgrim. "A task, sister. A journey and a retrieval."

Ria shook her head. Her fingers curled. "The higher-ups want me here, to run the place when the endgame comes."

"I promise you, Sister Ria, the night will not fall until your task is complete." The pilgrim leaned over the bar and still his height was great enough to loom over her. "And I am higher than those coordinating such petty considerations."

She swallowed and glanced left, to a burly pair at the end of the bar—her bouncers, her people. Back to the pilgrim, said she, "Very well. What do you ask?"

Like all the others, the bouncers avoided the pilgrim's gaze. "Ask," said he. "Ask is a word, a good word, sister." He spoke more softly, his head cocked a bit, but still he loomed. "For you see, without cooperation, we cannot succeed. You know my dear sister, my born sister, Francesca. She is not here, and I—we—require her cooperation."

Ria took a step back from the leering shadow. She crossed her arms. "You said 'retrieval.'"

The pilgrim twisted his head farther. "Did I?"

"Yes. 'Journey and retrieval.'"

The pilgrim's head righted itself. "Ah, so I did. And so it is."

"If I recall," said Ria, "Ces left of her own accord, as did Azran."

The traitor, the tempting sinner!

Ria took another half-step back. The pilgrim must have let the fury bleed through.

"Yes, sister, I am sure that is what you were told," said the pilgrim, calm. "I am also sure of a fondness you possess for your harpsichord player. But he is no brother. He does not believe as we do. He holds no reverence for Tenebra, you know this."

Ria mulled. She did know this. Then, said she, "Perhaps. But what's that got to do with Francesca?"

Curse the blindness of commoners.

"Do you not see?" asked the pilgrim. "His faithlessness has deluded dear Francesca. She is misguided and needs to return. She has a higher purpose."

"So hire a messenger," said Ria. Her heels dug, and she stood on the cusp of flippancy. "I'm sure you can find one faster than me."

She needed to remember who the pilgrim was, and who she was to him.

"You have a good life," said he, glancing around the establishment. Like a cat's, his gaze jumped back to hers. "But it was not always so. Once—or many times, I am sure—you retrieved people, even when they had real reason to flee. Which dear Francesca does not. You carried shackles and chains, and you ran and rode and sailed, one arm among many."

Ria's arms uncrossed. One hand gripped the liquor shelf behind her mismatched belts. Her eyes were now averted.

"You retrieved many, ignoring tears and oaths and bribes and the scars upon their backs," said the pilgrim. Not just the force of the words, but the will of his soul made Ria shrink. The light came from the side, but his shadow fell squarely on her. "All that you pushed aside whenever it confronted you. Dear Francesca is no slave, no debtor. She is merely a wayward sister who needs to come home. It should not be so hard."

"I'm not that person anymore."

"But sister Ria, you are. What we are is in our blood. This, too, you know."

Her pale knuckles grew whiter as she clenched the shelf. "And if I refuse? What will you do?"

"It was not always slaves and debtors," said the pilgrim. "Once, it was a senator. He vanished. Such a crime would yield execution, should the culprit be discovered."

"You bastard," came her low growl. She may have looked young, but she had been a vampire long enough to fear the true death. Thus, her prayers to the Goddess. Yes, the whispers told the pilgrim much.

"To me, and to dear Francesca, the rest of you are the bastards," said he. "And so, again, I ask—I call you to serve."

The tension slipped from Ria. She almost fell but resisted. And he knew then she was his.

"She is in Cruxia," said the pilgrim. "Bring her home. Leave the others."

As he turned to go, loosening his mental grip, Ria found the courage to ask, "What is her higher purpose?"

His head turned—almost too far—and said he, "You need not know."

"But what do I tell her?"

"If you must speak, tell her—tell her I know why we are. I cannot explain with words, but I can show her how beautiful our existence truly is. Tell her she will soon understand why I have done these things."

It was more than he had intended to say in answer, but he had not expected such questions. Ria knew her place, but she pushed at the boundaries. He left, back into the night, where Tenebra granted him grace.

In an alley, the pilgrim shed his mask. A bat flitted from a perch beneath an eve. In an instant, the twisted hand dropped the cane and plucked the animal from the air.

None know their place—their purpose. They push at the boundaries, or break them. And thus, I must explain, as if to children!

The captured bat's squeaks reached a new pitch as lacerations opened its flesh. Blood poured over the withered palm and gnarled knuckles. The pilgrim screamed at the sky, and then the bat fell apart in his hand, and then the pilgrim laughed. Shrouded in darkness, eyes closed, he came close to seeing the face of his Goddess.

It was all for her, all for Her—the façade of civility, the sacrifice of flesh, the strain of mortal communication, all the pain and struggle inside and out. It was all for Tenebra, it was all for Francesca. He longed for the night they would become one, and his sister would understand.

• • •

Quarrytown was indeed far from where they were—or so Azran thought, once again brushing the place where he felt his cracked ribs. A rough patch of what felt like old scab covered the spot. He had never been healed through magic before—well, not that kind of magic.

What he found most worth pondering as they walked was the claim of all priests—that inborn talent played a part, but it was faith in the gods that allowed them to use such gifts. Some said "gods," but all—even an Umbriri mystic that once blew through the Silver Sun—all used the words "faith," "belief," or some synonym. And if one had to be born with the potential, did one need religion to use soul magic? The gods had been absent from the Mortal Realm for a century, it was said. And yet, as tonight reminded, people could still use such powers. The enigmatic Seal between the realms was either weaker than dogma stated—tonight evidenced this, as well—or it was largely irrelevant to mortal life. People still believed in the divine and acted as though the gods would intervene. When a miracle did happen, was it by mortal or immortal hands?

The moon was long set when the beleaguered quintet reached quiet streets edged by workers' tenements, vagrants' shacks, and shabby storefronts. They found Floodplain Lane, a dirt track on the north side, opposite the dark lumps of sandstone cliffs. The ground was broken by stagnant puddles and creeks that only ran when it rained. A humble, two-story structure bore the sign they were looking for—a red hand extended in welcome. The stylized letters of Filvié Noctirin were nowhere to be seen. A lamp burned in the front window of the house.

"Wait here," Francesca said. She adjusted the unfamiliar blade on her hip and ascended the creaking, weathered porch. She knocked, and a shadow crossed the wall behind the lantern. A man opened the door. A vampire—Azran could see his eyes as he looked around. He couldn't make out the hushed conversation with Francesca, but the man waved them all to come in.

"Living too, eh?" the man said as they crossed the threshold. His accent marked him as Septri. "Lucky we got too much room late, or the old lady'd knock ya back way ya came."

"We normally wouldn't ask," Francesca said. "I know we're many, but we're in a bind."

"Long night, ya said, aye."

Azran studied his surroundings. The ground floor consisted of two rooms—this one and a kitchen visible through an empty doorframe. The first room had two low tables, with the lamp and an unfinished card game on one. A staircase as cracked and rickety as the floorboards rose to the left. Heavy black curtains, now open, hung at every window. A faint smell of stew and smoke filtered from the kitchen. Otherwise, the house smelled old—not musty, but the dry scent of sun-soaked deadwood.

"Name's Dario," the Septri man said. He was not tall, but heavy, solid, the little pudge just a blanket thrown over the muscle beneath. His head and face were free of hair, but thick, black bushes grew above his eyes. "The old lady's out back havin smoke. She don't like folk doin in here, n'even herself. I'll introduce ya."

Dario led them through the kitchen, where a wood stove still simmered the contents of a large pot. Nearby, wooden bowls sat stacked and drying. The back door opened onto another weathered porch, this one overlooking a wooded basin. An elf woman old enough to show crow's feet sat on a bench. She wore a brown tunic and fraying, white skirt and held a long-stemmed pipe. Smoke curled up like the grey hair hanging down her back. Her sharp, green eyes took in each of the strangers at a glance. She took a pull from the pipe and exhaled.

"This is the old lady," Dario said. "Lucina."

"Motley bunch," Lucina said. "Who are you two?" She pointed her index and little fingers.

"Azran."

"Francesca Darani."

An eyebrow twitched. "Now there's a name," the old lady said. "I notice you aren't up in Aure, causing more nonsense."

"We thought it best to get out of town for a bit," Francesca said.

"Trouble with Filvya Noctern?" Dario asked.

Francesca hesitated. Azran replied, "You could say that."

Dario grunted. "Good. Any'd piss them off are okay by me."

Lucina's eyes never blinked nor left Francesca during the exchange. "You know, they're looking for a Darani. So I hear. He's wanted for the whole mess. Might want to hang onto your last name." She looked at Dario. "Her brother's the one dancing with angels."

Dario nodded solemnly. "Well, if y'ain't part of it, that name don't leave this porch."

"You lot look like you crawled off a battlefield," Lucina said. "Been a quiet night in Quarrytown. Where you walk from?"

"A place in Cruxia we can't stay," Francesca said. "I wouldn't say we have no part in—in the mess in Aure. My brother is trying very hard to drag me in. I intend to address the issue, but his, ah, last visit left us banged up. We just need a few nights and some supplies, and we'll be on our way."

Lucina nodded. Then, she jumped up, emptied the pipe over the railing, and rushed inside, bare feet slapping the wood. From within, the others heard, "Ha*ha!* Top *that*, Dar!"

Dario sighed and cursed. The newcomers followed him into the main room, where a smug Lucina stood with her arms crossed by the card game. Dario searched the layout, then cursed again under his breath and scratched his head.

"Ocassra," Azran said, recognizing the aged strategy game. Each card represented a fortress, a famous commander, or an army. They were laid out on a marked mat—or carved table, in this case. After each player chose starting positions on their side, the cards moved turn by turn according to their kind and captured or killed opposing cards based on strength and positioning.

Dario's forces looked to be in a tight spot. He sat down and started plotting a move to save his right flank.

After a couple minutes of silence, Francesca spoke up. "As I was saying, we need maybe three or four nights, some black curtains, and a day tent. We can pay—"

Lucina, still looking at the game, shushed and waved her hand. "For the stuff, sure. I'll price you later. But we have free beds, and beds are free. So don't you worry about that. Oh, feeling risky, are we? No? Ah, I'll leave you to it, Dar." She started toward the stairs. "I'll get the guests settled."

The upstairs featured a short hallway with three doors. The one at the end was Lucina's, while the other two led to a pair of large, shared quarters. The right was full up, or near it, so the left was theirs. There were six beds for the five of them, and Azran felt his insides drop as he thought of Miranda.

She chose it, he told the rising guilt. *If we went back looking for her, it would defeat the purpose.* He rubbed his face. *She's a badass. She'll be alright.*

As Lucina bid them a good rest and Francesca pulled the curtains closed, Azran lowered his fully-clothed self into a bed. His wife soon followed, removing only her shoes and belt. Sleep nipped at his heels, but he whispered, "We've met some lovely people."

"Yeah," Francesca replied, also groggy and quiet. She held his hand under the blanket. "I feel bad pulling them into this."

"Don't," Des said from across the room. "I haven't had a right reason to do anything in far too long."

"Happy t'help," Azran mumbled as he passed out.

28

V arja did not sleep so easily. Her wound itched like mad. She scratched the skin around it, a trick she learned on campaign west of Maceria. It helped, but not enough. She may have dozed off for a bit, but was awake to see the sun start to peer around the curtains. Her stomach growled, and she realized she hadn't eaten in a full day—not since fish breakfast with Des.

Des—she was asleep in another bed. She was small enough to squeeze into Varja's. She had even paused to see if Varja would offer, but she did not. Not yet. She didn't know when. If. She didn't know what she wanted, and thinking about it was worse than thinking about the itch in her side.

Everything she had said, the whole stream of word-vomit she had unleashed on Des, she had meant. But Des's response—not the hug, the hug was good—what had *she* meant? *"We'll take things as they come."* What the fuck did that mean? Did Des still want Varja? It seemed that way. Did she expect Varja to do something? Make a move? What move?

If I don't do something soon, my head is going to fucking explode.

Varja threw off her blanket and stood. She couldn't keep lying and thinking. Not with an empty stomach.

The main room downstairs was vacant. Lucina and Dario seemed to have finished their game. Varja could not decipher the final arrangement, but she imagined "the old lady" had won.

The smell of frying bread wafted from the kitchen, and she heard a spoon stirring a bowl. Peeking in, she saw Lucina smear a thick mixture of sauce and shredded meat onto flat bread in a pan on the stove. Sunlight flooded the kitchen, blinding after the gloom.

"Well, come in, then," Lucina said. She took a spatula and folded the frying bread. "You hungry? Want some kosdra risvak?"

"Oh, gods yes." Varja hadn't eaten "drake shell" since she left Muntherzix. "Please."

Lucina's amused hum became a tune as she flipped the risvak. "Well, get a plate, what's-your-name."

"Varja."

"Get a plate, Varja, dear. Lovely name, that."

Varja took a premature bite and worked to keep the food from burning her tongue. Once it cooled enough, she savored the spice blend and the crunch of the bread. "This is perfect," she said once she'd swallowed. "It's just like in Muntherzix."

Lucina put one on a plate for herself and left the remaining two with the previous batch. "Well, where else would you go to learn em right? You know, the borders weren't always so tight."

"Before the Rising Fire, you mean?" Varja asked, taking another bite. *Damn, this might be better than the ones back west.*

"Well, before Liore was a province," Lucina said. She held her plate, letting the shell cool. "That's when I learned this recipe. Back when it was just a bunch of cities, and trade was trade, and travel travel."

Varja thought back to the Valentreid histories she had read growing up. The time Lucina spoke of was almost 250 years ago. She was used to dragons speaking in such timeframes, but she had met few elves. Just how old was Lucina?

"You know, when the conquest happened," her host continued, "most of us down here didn't think Emperor Ialid could pull it off—two campaigns on opposite ends, both in bad terrain for marching legions. Never been to Ostitel, that's just how I hear it. But then, that's the empire for you. So many people with so much strength and talent." She sighed and looked out the back window. "That's why all this division of late is a shame."

Varja, leaning against the wall, licked the remaining sauce from her fingers. "I thought everyone here was pushing for unity."

Lucina scoffed. "Nah, they're just taking one way of being and saying it's our way—'our' meaning only the types they want around. And it just makes us weaker, cause you snuff out the strengths you don't like." She held the back door open. "Let's sit outside. I'm afraid you'll knock my wall down doing that. And grab another risvak."

Varja did, and the two shared a bench on the back porch. In the daylight, Varja saw a muddy pond at the basin's trough and recognized the trees as laurels.

Lucina finally bit into her risvak. "You know, best thing about these is they stay good all day. They'll make a nice breakfast for the rest."

They munched for a few minutes, listening to marsh birds. Then Lucina said, "You don't like sleeping or something?"

"Just a lot on my mind," Varja replied. "I feel like a bad prophet, with too many revelations and no way to sort through their meaning."

"Well, like they used to say when I was young, the world cannot sleep if a priest wakes."

"What?"

"Ah." Lucina waved a hand. "I can never remember which ones you pre-centennials know the context for. Guess that one made more sense back then."

"So, am I the priest or the world?"

"Well, which do you reckon?"

"I'm awake, and the others sleep, so—"

"No, you're the priest," Lucina interrupted.

Varja blinked at her, lost.

Lucina put her plate on her lap and gestured while she spoke. "What's on your mind? Thoughts. Dreams. You can't make sense of them because you're still sleeping, and the world's waiting. Wake up. You see?"

Varja didn't. It was a strange metaphor, like poorly translated poetry or something from a dead language. She nodded anyway.

"It's a dry day," Lucina said. "No fog in sight. Suppose it's making up for the other morning." She packed her pipe and lit it. "You don't get thick fog like that out west, do you?"

Varja shook her head, finishing her second risvak. "No, but I'm from down south. Sometimes it's so dense, even the stormwings won't go out."

"Stormwings? Ah, dragons who chase gales, yes? Craziest bastards I ever heard of." Lucina blew a smoke ring that dissipated quickly. She made a sour face. "Though I think I saw one in that bank the other morn."

Varja almost choked on her last bite. "A dragon? You saw a dragon in the fog?"

"Sure did. Storm dragon, even. Hard to see him through the soup, but these eyes are sharper than they are old, you know. Landed right in that mud and turned into a naked man."

"You're fucking with me."

Lucina gave an earnest sidelong look. "I don't do that, dear. I give it straight."

"But you seem so calm about this."

She took a long drag and blew a more solid smoke ring. "When you get to my age, you've seen a lotta crazy shit. More coincidences than you'd think fate would allow. But then you remember, even gods can love a bird's rhetoric."

Varja ignored the metaphor—more dated nonsense—and asked the next burning question. "What did the man look like?"

"Well, that I couldn't much tell." Lucina shrugged. "Dark, but not too. Short hair."

Damn—he changed. If that was even Seneskar. But who else?

"Which way did he go?"

"The town, I imagine. He came out from the north country."

That's him. Shit. Varja wasn't sure what to do. She'd heard Seneskar meant to leave soon. The day this strange anecdote happened, in fact. Could she pick up the trail again? She knew she couldn't capture him and had no interest—well, less now—in going home. But she wanted to talk to Seneskar again, about what he had said in the bar. She felt foolish for interrupting him, given what she knew now. Maybe things with the clan were the same for him. Maybe she owed him an apology.

"You're dreaming again," Lucina said. "I know that furrow-brow look. You listen to anything I say? You can always run in a swimming city, girl."

Varja threw her hands up. "Guess I need more Serma lessons."

"Well, I'll spell it for you, then. It means impulse exists for a reason."

Varja considered that. She'd always been told she was rash— impulsive. But there were times it had been her greatest asset. She acted when others waited. She'd been so stuck on pondering and agonizing of late, she hadn't realized the solution to it all was right in front of her. She just had to act. *Can't always take things as they come,* she thought. *You face the storm, and sometimes you have to fly straight into it.*

"You're right," she told Lucina.

"I'm old."

Varja stood and hurried back inside. Before the door even swung shut, she backtracked and said, "Thank you for the kosdra risvak."

"Anytime, dear," Lucina said with a smile and a wave.

Varja took the steps two at a time, then padded as lightly as she could across the creaky room. She only wanted one person awake.

"Hey," she whispered, nudging Des.

Des's eyes fluttered open while one hand jerked an inch toward her pillow—but just an inch. "Varja?" she slurred.

"I need to talk to you."

"Okay." Des rubbed her eyes and sat up. She looked an unholy concoction of hopeful, apprehensive, and groggy. "What is it?"

Varja's eyes flicked to the other side of the room, where Azran and Francesca slept. "Can we go outside or something?"

Des blinked. "Okay." She slid from the bed and flexed her spine.

Neither bothered to put on boots. They stepped out the front onto a sparse street. Varja led Des to the space between the house and a neighboring tenement.

"What's going on?" Des asked, waking more and more.

"Lots," Varja said. "Lots is going on. First, Lucina saw Seneskar land in her yard and turn into a different man."

"What—"

"But don't worry about him. I'm done with that. I'm still going to Aure with you. Because the other thing is I've made a decision."

"Okay, what—"

Varja leaned low and kissed Des, heavy, long, forceful. After an instant of surprise, Des threw her arms behind Varja's neck. One of Varja's lifted Des up, wrapped around her more slender, but still tight midsection. Her other hand explored upward, to running over the back of Des's neck and then holding her short, dark hair. Des's nimble fingers worked their way into Varja's tangled, black waves. Des was so strong, seemed so hardened much of the time. But she could be so gentle, too.

When their lips finally separated, any hint of sleepiness was gone from Des's face. Her smile was small—not one of excitement, but of quiet joy. Her excitement showed in her breathing, which seemed to match Varja's racing heart.

Des went in for another, this one shorter, and then started laughing. Her smile cracked wide, and Varja returned it.

"I figured out a while ago that you can't always take things as they come," Varja said. "Sometimes, you have to go to them."

"Yeah," Des said, burying her head in Varja's shoulder before letting herself down. "So, what you figure? You like this?"

"Feels pretty good."

"Damn right it does. And, you don't want to go after Seneskar?"

Varja shook her head. "I just want to move on."

Des nodded. "Eyes forward, Az says. It's something I could stand to practice."

"You know what helps with that?"

"Yeah, I do. Come here."

• • •

The emotional high didn't last long. After a sleep made peaceful by sheer exhaustion, the weight of the previous night and dread of danger to come pulled at them all like rocks chained to a bogged corpse. The urge to run off sang to Des. She could pick up with Varja where she had left off with Ari—far and free. But they had promised to help Azran and Francesca, their new friends. Whether on a watcher's carry or a dog's lend, Des had always stayed loyal. It was the one virtue she had, and she didn't want to lose it. Besides, Des liked those two and thought they'd die taking this road alone.

And this feels right. They've given me something good to fight for. Don't need an excuse or justification. I like this feeling. The voice telling her to run grew silent, but not before it asked, *Are you just making the same mistakes all over?*

Varja shifted in the bed next to her but was not yet awake. She lay on her stomach, head facing Des and one muscled arm cradling her. It was early evening on the first day at Lucina's. Neither Des nor Varja had been keen on talking, so they experienced the presence of one another now that all was in the open. Well, not all. Des hadn't told her of Ari's death or planned proposal. That morning, it had seemed too dark, too heavy. But the shifting atmosphere could change that.

Azran and Francesca had roused a few minutes ago, which was what finally woke Des. "Evening," Azran had whispered, casual as could be. "Hey," Des had whispered back. The couple then went downstairs.

Luc had been more surprised. He opened his mouth to speak half a dozen times, then gave up and also went downstairs.

Des's mind turned to their next move. They had to contact Valen and send for horses, since their collective funds were too exhausted. The ones they had ridden in on had been left at the Broken Arrow. Des was good, but not enough to get back out of there with five horses in tow.

She wanted to go with the others. There was a carry. But more, she wanted to be there when Varja woke. It had been a long time since she'd experienced that with someone.

● ● ●

Azran almost coughed up the first gulp of his blood-and-bone mixture, and chains, coughing just made his chest ache more. "Gods, that's awful. Like drinking mud."

"Physician's orders," Francesca said. Azran watched with envy as she sipped hog's blood.

Maybe I could just not drink it, he thought. *Let myself heal on my own. Put off this whole ordeal.*

Reading his face, Francesca said, "We have to do this. Waiting only gives him time to formulate a more deranged plan than the last."

Azran took another long, viscous swallow. For the sake of his ribs, he kept himself from coughing. "I ever tell you your brother's fucked up?"

"Several times."

"What do you think his next move is?"

Francesca shook her head.

"Maybe he'll call down Tenebra herself," Azran said with a wry smile.

"Azran, enough." She slammed her glass onto the table as if his joke had struck close to her fears—or her intuition.

"Sorry. Just how I respond to insanity. You know how I am."

She sighed. "Yeah. And I respond by going mad myself."

He grabbed her hand. "I think you've been handling this very well."

Francesca looked out at the twilit street. "But you don't want to do this."

"Of course not." Azran gripped her hand tighter. "But I will for you." He finished his painful elixir. "Ugh, okay. How are we contacting Valen?"

"Imperial Messenger Service seems like our best bet," Des said, entering the room. "Think I saw a local post on the way in." She took an uneasy glance at the traces of blood in the empty glasses. "As much as someone like me would rather avoid the government, they're fast and reliable. I wouldn't suggest asking for night riders, though. That would mean the letter switching more hands, easier for cutoff."

Azran located a pen and some paper in the sitting room. "Just us? Or are Varja and Luc coming?"

Des paused at the doorway. "She seems tired still. I think healing that fast takes a lot out of her."

"I heard Luc mumble something about—dueling her?" Francesca said.

At Francesca's half-question, Des sighed and rolled her eyes, seeming to know what that was about. Azran did recall an exchange a few days ago where Luc mentioned that desire.

"He's an Atoran," Des said. "I imagine he wanted to do that the moment he saw her sword. Past day or so likely exacerbated that."

Azran nodded, trying again to understand the priest and the ex-smuggler's relationship. Both seemed to simultaneously loathe and defend each other—as if no one could abuse them but themselves. They were rather like siblings, he thought. And now, Luc was going to put Varja through his version of interrogating his sister's new flame.

"He's such an asshole," Des said.

After a few moments' consideration, Azran started writing. The envelope called them business partners in Cruxia. The letter inside requested five horses be sent to the edge of Quarrytown. The signature read only: *Regards, your harpsichordist.*

29

Varja lay in bed after Des left, awake, digesting all of the past few days. The low hum of voices downstairs lulled her into dozing, but the sharp rap of a closing door jerked her back. The hum was gone. So was her sword.

She rolled out of bed and checked underneath—just her pack and boots. She didn't see it anywhere in the room. She pulled a spare shirt over her torn one and took long strides downstairs.

Luc stood in the sitting room, facing the front window. He turned as he heard Varja creak in. He held her scabbarded longsword and wore his own blades on his belt.

"A fine weapon," he said. "Well crafted." He held up the silver sun-and-moon token with curiosity.

"Give it back."

"Of course." Luc held the sword out hilt-first.

Varja took it, her glare alone warning him to never do that again.

"I found a little space by the sandstone bluffs," he went on. "Let's go have a spar."

Varja drew back, suspicious. "Why?"

"I got a glimpse back at the inn, but I want to see what you can do with that fine weapon. We may find ourselves shoulder to shoulder soon. Get your boots, and let's see how you can handle yourself."

"A challenge, then?"

"Make of it what you will."

Varja could not deny a similar curiosity toward the priest. And she always found pleasure in shoving condescension back down the speaker's throat.

She nodded.

Sheer sandstone rose above three sides of the makeshift arena. A dirt track ran from the open fourth back to the shantytown. Two borrowed lanterns provided flickering illumination. It had been a long time since Varja last wrapped her sword. She finished the final, tight pass of dirty cloth Luc had "acquired" and stood to face him.

Luc removed his weapons belt and held only his arming sword, likewise wrapped. He took an eastern fencing stance, body a quarter-turn from the front, knees bent deep, ready to move side to side. His sword pointed forward. He was three paces out of reach.

Varja went into a middle guard, hilt to the right side of her chest and blade pointing straight up.

"Aggress—"

Luc bit off the word as Varja closed the distance, striking down and to her left. He cross-stepped back, voiding. Varja transitioned into a plow guard—hilt by her hip. She thrust at Luc's upper torso. He continued to his left, keeping her sword outside, and parried. At the same time, he stepped closer, inside her longer reach. He went for a riposte to her leading arm. Varja pushed out with her left hand, tilting her blade up.

The swords met in a bind, her strong against his weak. She used the leverage to push his blade high while she switched to a half-sword grip and bashed her pommel into his arm.

Luc retreated, angling right from Varja. She went back into a middle guard and advanced. He moved for a parry, but she switched to a high guard and launched down from above her head. He was forced to let her open lower body go, instead stepping left and parrying.

In lieu of a riposte, he grabbed her leading wrist with his free hand and continued around her. Sensing his strategy, Varja rotated the opposite way in a fool guard—hip height, directly in front of her. She spotted Luc's high cut and parried.

Another bind, this time with Varja on the weak. She raised her hilt, inverting the contact points, and thrust over Luc's blade.

Luc dodged low, closed, and went for a draw cut across her abdomen. Varja pushed back off her lead foot and felt the cloth brush her without impact.

He pressed onward, gripping with two hands and levering Varja's counter wide. He let go with his left and shoved her open shoulder. Varja kept her balance and half-gripped to parry the downward cut that followed. But Luc pulled back and flicked his wrist around, coming from the side instead. The blade rapped her left ribs, just above her still-bandaged wound.

Both froze, eyeing each other, then stepped apart and caught their breath.

"You're faster than I expected," Luc said after a few seconds. "I admit, my experience with longswords is limited."

"I haven't seen many here," Varja agreed. "You're not the first Valentreid to underestimate it."

"It's not that. I've heard plenty of the exploits of the Dragonblades, the emperor's seven most elite guards. Each wields an ancient longsword said to contain the bound soul of a dragon. Alas, I've not seen them fight. I wonder how their style compares to yours. Most here who use such blades are more defense-focused—make the sword a wall your opponent cannot get past. Avoid binds, strike and retreat."

Varja shook her head. "The Zixarsi way my aunt taught me is to stay on the offense. If your opponent is busy defending, they cannot attack. Every move should be both an attack and a defense."

"That seems difficult in a fight—too much thinking."

"So don't think. Practice until it's natural."

Luc went on guard again. Varja chose the ox, bringing her hilt up by her right ear and pointing at Luc.

He began circling to her right. Catching on to his style, she did not pivot, but rather circled left and closed the gap. She caught an arch of surprise in his brows before she launched her thrust.

Luc's hand dipped down and his blade up as he made a vertical parry, continuing his circular footwork. Varja tried to work the strong-strong bind, but Luc's free hand pushed the flat of her blade. Feet gliding, he went underneath to the other side.

In the winding, Varja freed her blade, switched her ox guard left, and thrust again. But Luc was too close now and easily parried. He countered with a short fencing cut. Varja dodged inside, throwing her body into profile and striking up from a plow guard.

With surprising flexibility, Luc bent back to avoid the rising strike. He cross-stepped back, then forward and right as Varja readied a downstroke from a high guard. She managed to parry his cut at her left, but he was too close now, and her back was nearly to the wall.

She went back to half-sword. She held the hilt near her armpit, tip forward, putting her whole body behind. She thrust once, twice, driving Luc back.

He tried to angle sideways, but her footwork kept him in front. He feinted a step left, then went right. Varja didn't quite fall for it, but the moment of hesitation allowed Luc to brace a leg behind her lead foot, get his free hand inside her grip, and push her into tripping.

As she rolled to kip up, Luc pounced with a thrust. Varja let go with her right hand, rolled back toward him, and grabbed the back of his knee. Her sword, now held by the blade, bashed pommel-first into his gut. There was little strength behind the blow, but enough that she could pull him off his feet.

Varja got on top of Luc, holding her hilt high in her right hand and blade low in her left. If she were fighting to kill, she would have performed a murder-stroke. Instead, she went to put the wrapped middle of her blade to his neck.

Luc got his sword over him and grabbed it near the tip, blocking. His knee connected with Varja's abdomen, and he twisted out from under her.

Before he could stand, Varja perched low on the balls of her feet and punched with her blade hand, catching him in the face. He let go of his sword tip and hooked her arm as they rose. He sprang diagonally, trying to spin her back down. Varja went with

307

the momentum, put her left hand on the back of his head, and threw him back to the dirt. She went into an ox guard and thrust at the prone priest. From so low, his parry was ineffectual. Varja's blade stopped inside his guard, inches from his face.

Again they froze. Luc released his weapon. Varja lowered hers and offered a hand. She pulled him to his feet.

"You are relentless," Luc said. He picked up his sword.

"Not so bad yourself."

"Don't get too cocky." Luc gave her a hard look. "Once I get this off hand working, I'll be able to dual-wield again. All those shoves will be replaced by thrusts." He sat on a rock and started unwrapping his sword.

"What's wrong with it?" Varja asked, doing the same.

He shook his head, looking down. "It was almost severed. Nerve damage, they told me. I would need a specialist and a lot of money before I could do more than open and close it. A friend back in Aure made me a metal replacement, but it's only a little better. He says he's working on an improvement. I paid the axeman back, though, I assure you." He forced a smile.

"Sounds like a story."

"Sure is, but not mine to tell. I was there because Des was." Luc looked up at Varja. "Take care of her. She's been through torment enough already."

Varja nodded, now understanding the purpose of this test. "I will."

Luc stood and approached, extending his good hand. Varja rose and clasped it.

"She's opened her heavy heart to you," the priest said. "She'll never ask you to help carry it, but know that her burden is not light." He released, clapped her on the back, and retrieved a lantern. "It was a real pleasure. Let's do that again sometime."

Varja took the other lantern and followed, contemplating his ominous words and pondering what she thought a strange custom of this land.

30

D ay after day, night after night passed with neither sign nor word of Valen. The messengers had promised delivery in three days, but there was no way to confirm that. And those were the fast riders, the professionals. It had taken Des and the others four days and then some to reach Cruxia from the Matias estate. And from there, Francesca lamented, it was more than ten for a straight-shot, highway ride to Aure.

Time, with naught to do but dwell and agonize.

Des spent most of her evenings in a small pub at the north end of Quarrytown. It was cheap enough to not strain her dwindling purse, and the glassless front windows looked out at the road where Valen would enter town. And more, it gave her a chance to keep up on rumors. Some patrons were there to watch for their own business; the rest watched for everyone else's.

The first night after sending the messenger, Des sat, ordered some of the thin ale from the one-eyed, one-handed barkeep, and immediately overheard something good to know from the next table.

"The Broken Arrow, it was," a tattooed and sun-weathered greybeard said. "Whole common room. Keep, too."

"So you said," a companion grated. He had different tattoos and facial hair, but the same complexion. "A massacre, aye. But who they lookin for?"

"That's where it gets into the wild," the first said. Retired sailors, Des decided. He leaned over toward his two tablemates more out of showmanship than subterfuge. "A twain got out when the blood started. Found the guard, right?" He paused, and the other two nodded. "Hysterical, they were. Screamin about some beast. Guards hustle—whole squad—and open the door. Whole room's dead but for an antileri woman. Dark hair, them eyes like a green sea. She runs off, wailin and braggin."

The greybeard settled back and lifted his mug. "Deadly angel-woman, right out of a song. That's what did it." He took a swig.

"That's a load," the third said. He was not quite grey yet. "I heard it were vampires. They found vampire sign in one of the rooms and no dead ones. It's that Aure cabal stretchin their reach."

"And what, pray, is vampire sign?" the first asked.

"I'm drowned, but that's what Aller's boy says."

"Aller's boy says the emperor's dead, and the crats are puppeteerin his corpse by magic," the second said.

"Angel-woman, mark me," the first said.

"That's what I heard, too," Des said. "Without the angel part, though. Just a bloody howler chanter."

The second looked at the third and raised his mug to Des. The first repeated, "Angel. Somethin beyond our ken is brewin. Been lots of Godshadows about of late."

"Aye," the second said. "Whole crew goin north on that very road out from the city, rathern the highway."

"They goin to fix up Aure, at long last?"

"Better be. Draggin their damn feet, they are."

Little else of use was said after that. Most of the succeeding nights, the talkers—sometimes those same three—rambled about ship crews, quarry crews, screwing, and weather. Des kept her ears perked but zoned out for long stretches. She thought about Varja, and how she wished she could at least sit with her here.

But her new woman was with Luc and Francesca at night. The latter had resumed training—Des couldn't blame her—and Varja was lending her own experience. The couple still had time together, but it wasn't enough for Des. She had suggested finding a private room, just for one night, but Varja wanted the group to stay together. Des couldn't condemn that, either. And that was frustrating. This had to go somewhere. They—she—had to go somewhere. Move. Move on.

The ring was cold as her fingers rolled it back and forth under the table. It always felt cold, even when she fiddled it around for an hour before pocketing it. She had stopped wearing it around her neck since her first kiss with Varja. She hadn't talked to Ari in days but feared it would happen again soon.

Eyes forward, she thought. *Easy for you to say, Azran. Francesca didn't die because of you.*

A week passed. As the sun set on the seventh day, Des finished her warm swill and prepared to leave. Azran would come soon for his shift. She stood against the wall outside, waiting to pass the baton. At last, she spotted him coming up the street—if it could be called that—joined by Varja. Des smoothed her short hair with a casual brush of her hand and started toward them.

"Evening," Varja said.

Azran gave a friendly salute.

"Hey," Des said. "This is unexpected."

"Luc and Francesca are getting deep into one-handed fencing," Varja explained. "He suggested I take a night off."

"Oh, so when he suggests it, you listen." She was aware of Azran slinking into the pub without a word.

"I'm sorry. I didn't mean to be—"

"It's fine," Des said. "Sometimes you have to hear it from someone else. I'm just glad you're here." She tiptoed and gave Varja a peck on the lips. "Let's go for a walk. I'm sick of staring at this neighborhood."

They meandered around Quarrytown. There was a surprising amount of beauty hidden among the dirt and broken brick and cracked timber—little gardens and flowery groves, the occasional clear stream. They found their way up the bluffs and stood admiring the backlit sprawl of Cruxia sloping down to the black water. To the west, behind the high seating of the Theater of Lights, blue, white, red, and more alternated to the narrative beats of a dramatic performance.

"So," Varja said after a long time, "what's that ring you carry?"

Des's stomach lurched. "Why do you ask?"

"I've seen you fidget with it. It's pretty."

A suspicious thought struck Des. "Did Luc say something?"

Varja did not meet her gaze. "He mentioned a—a burden. I thought maybe they were related."

Des sighed and sat on the hard, scrub-dotted earth.

"If it's something you'd rather not talk about, I understand."

Des considered taking the out. "Sit," she said. "You've shared yours. It's only fair."

Varja joined her. Des pulled out the emerald ring. It was cold in her palm. "This belonged to my fiancée. I found it in her drawer, back in Equotel. I know she was going to propose marriage, but—she died with this ring in her pocket."

Varja said nothing, and her face was inscrutable. Des imagined the swirl of emotions her words prompted. She imagined most weren't good.

"So, I carry it," Des said. "My only keepsake, apart from the memories. Sometimes I wish I could get rid of it, but I can't."

"Because you still love her?"

Des looked at her with her own mixed expression. "I don't know what I feel about her anymore. I don't want to feel her anymore." She shifted over to Varja and leaned on her. "I just want to move on."

Varja put an arm around Des and held her close. "What was her name?"

"Arilysa."

A gust from the sea tousled their clothes. Varja let her hair loose.

"She died because of me," Des said, out loud for the first time. "And I didn't stop it."

"What happened?"

Des swallowed—gods, her throat was dry—and told the story. She explained how they met, how they were lovestruck fools who believed they could run off together. The walk through the vineyard. The poisoned bolt. Feeling Ari's last, shallow breath. Who did it and why.

"It was my fault," Des repeated.

"That's not how it sounds to me," Varja said. "It was this Ecar."

Des shook her head, leaving tears on Varja's shirt in the process. "We convinced each other we could leave. We should have been more careful. I should have. I was right there, Varja. Do you know what that feels like? To hold someone you love as they bleed and die?"

After a pause, Varja said, "Yes. I lost a few comrades in Muntherzix."

Des lifted her head to see Varja's face. "I'm sorry."

Varja kissed her, slow and gentle. "Don't be. You have enough guilt."

"Do you ever…talk to them?"

Varja stared out over Cruxia. "I used to. I still have dreams. Sometimes they're alive. Sometimes dead. On a bad night, I watch them die." Her voice cracked for a moment. "And I can't do anything to stop it. Just like it happened."

"But you stopped talking to them."

She nodded.

"How?"

Varja took a long, shuddering breath. "Time. Life brings new woes." She looked at Des. "And new blessings."

Des made a small, scoffing noise. "I'm no blessing."

"To me, you're a godsend. Without you, I'd have had no one when I had my—revelation. I might never have had it on my own." Des didn't respond, so Varja added, "Closure helps, too. With the dead."

"Oh," Des said. "I got closure. The only time I returned to Forente in the last three years was to kill Ecar. And Luc and I killed a lot of people getting to him."

"I see," Varja said, piecing that together with whatever tidbits Luc had fed her. Des wasn't sure if she was mad at him or not for that. This was a conversation that needed to happen. At the same time, though, this was not the kind of night Des wanted.

"I felt nothing when I killed them," she said. "And I felt good when I killed him. They say vengeance destroys you. I felt complete that night. Looking back, I don't like what I became. I was monstrous. I was death. I'm not a blessing. You should know that."

"We've all done things in anger," Varja said. "I went through war and discovered my mother, whom I hadn't seen since I was a girl—she had been killed years before. You think I didn't lose my temper? For a long while, I became monstrous."

Des chuckled without mirth. "You saying we deserve each other?"

"I think we do, but not because of that. You survived that ordeal, as I did mine. Cracked, broken in some way, but alive. Don't let the monster rule you, but accept the things that give you strength. I do."

Des held the ring before her eyes. "So, you don't think I'm crazy for talking to ghosts?"

"Sure, but who isn't?"

An impulse to chuck the ring down the dark hill flashed through Des's mind. She arrested it and replaced the cold thing in her pocket, out of sight.

"You're the first I've shared my heart with since Ari," Des said. "You haven't run away like I feared you would. But most of all, you're the first person I've met who understands. You are a blessing, Varja. The only one I've seen in a long while."

Des pushed off the ground and kissed her, forcing her down. The contact was broken only to breathe, and after a short respite, they resumed the passion. Varja rolled, and Des let her—wanted her to—pin her to the ground. Hardly thinking, Des put her nimble fingers to work on the ties of Varja's shirt. She pulled it wide, and Varja pulled it back. Des traced the fading wound from the angel with one hand, while her other followed tight abdominals down. Varja's eyes closed at the light contact. Then she opened them and started on Des's vest. She helped with this, throwing the armor, her shirt, and hidden blades to the side. Varja explored Des's breasts with curiosity, her advance slowing.

"I've never done this with a woman before," she said, numbly, needlessly. "I don't know what to do."

Des undid Varja's belt and the tie of her pants. "That's okay. I'll show you."

• • •

A ninth morning passed, then an afternoon. And then, from her window table, Des saw seven tacked and packed horses trotting through long shadows. Two bore riders; the rest were led.

"That's him," Des said to Varja, who had taken to joining her these last two days. Des sprang up and juked through the half-open door. "Valen!"

The elder Matias eased the horses to a halt. The beasts huffed but did not appear overexerted. Valen dismounted and walked over to Des, taking stretching steps.

"Desalie," he said, doffing a wide-brimmed hat and sweeping it in a bow. "Glad to see you in one piece."

Des shook his hand. "I could say the same to you. You left in rough shape. Thanks for coming."

He bowed again. "Nothing time couldn't mend. Where are the others?"

"Most are back at the house. This is Varja."

She stepped forward and gave a nod.

"Yet more new friends," the arcanist said with a pleasant smile. "Valen Matias. It's a pleasure, Varja…?"

"Kepeskeižir."

Valen raised his eyebrows as they shook hands. "Quite a name." He gestured back to the other rider, a bearded and wiry fellow in drab travel garb. "This is Inen. He's an old hand from the estate, and one of our few remaining friends."

Inen tipped his hat and dismounted.

"So, what news from Aure?" Valen asked.

"Let's walk," Des said. "I'll fill you in."

● ● ●

"I see," Valen said inside Lucina's sitting room.

The others were present, and Francesca had helped fill in details between sips of functional coffee.

"I would dearly love to know the specifics of your brother's plan," the arcanist said. "Why does he desire you so?"

"I'd love to know, too," Francesca said. "Maybe he'll tell me. Once I give him *my* words, of course."

"He plays with dangerous powers," Lucina said. She drank from a cup of cheap wine.

"He doesn't play," Francesca said. "He knows exactly what he's doing. But damned if I've known in the last ten years. He wasn't always like this. A bit of an obnoxious zealot, but not—"

"Wait," Dario interrupted. "He called down an angel?"

"Part of one."

"An he coulda done it again anytime in the las week?"

319

"Ease, Dar," Lucina said. "This bunch is many things, but not stupid. I'm sure they thought of that." She shifted her aged gaze to Francesca.

Francesca hesitated, conscious of all the eyes on her. "I'm not sure how, but I—I *know* he won't. He tried it once and failed. He won't let loose that power again soon. He has other things he needs it for. Somehow, I know that." Her mind flashed back to her brother's ghost on the streets of Cruxia. "Intuition, I guess."

Lucina stared. She took another drink of wine and said, "You got special blood, and so does he. It's plain by your name. That's how you know. And how he found you from so far away."

Dario settled back, content with her judgment.

Francesca returned Lucina's gaze. "Who are you?"

She blinked and padded her bare feet back to the kitchen. "Just someone who's seen a bit of the world," she called. "Pay attention, children, and one day you, too, can be as wise as I."

Francesca wondered at that—at how many people knew her family's secret. Even Azran did not. And what did it have to do with her brother's schemes? There had to be a connection.

"You're welcome to join us," Azran said to Valen, bringing the conversation back to the matter at hand.

"I must decline. A week is long enough to be away from an empty manor. Inen and I will find an inn for the night and return. I didn't run the horses hard. A few hours' rest and they should go till dawn. They're the best I could get outside Equotel—on short notice, anyway." Valen stood. "Gods be with you. Except the one, of course," he added with a wink.

"We don't know when we'll be able to return them," Des said.

Valen waved a hand. "Worry not. Keep them. I'd rather they go to friends than a government auction."

Francesca rose and walked over to him. "You've been so generous. Sorry for dragging you into this." She gave him a heartfelt hug.

"I have an out still," Valen replied, returning it politely. "And I'm taking it like a dissident playwright when the crats show up."

Azran chuckled at that. "Send Sevex our best."

"Take them yourself. He returned to Aure already under imperial protection." Valen snapped his fingers. "Dear me, I almost forgot. Luc, he has something for you when you arrive. He said the secret project's done." Valen gave the room one last bow. "Lady Lucina, you have a lovely home. Farewell, friends."

He turned and made his exit.

Luc stared at his gloved left hand. It trembled slightly from the wrist.

"I swear forgetfulness runs in that family," Azran said.

Lucina reentered the room and waved goodbye to Valen's back through the window. She turned to her remaining guests. "There, now, you lot leaving soon?"

"This very night," Azran said.

"Finally." She addressed Francesca. "You have a generous definition of 'a few.' Not that I don't enjoy the company, but I'm starting to feel like a god listening to a bird give a speech."

Many puzzled glances were shared, but Varja just nodded and said, "Understandable."

31

It was an eleven-night ride to Aure by the highways. The time between dusk and dawn was growing longer but still constrained travel. Packed to camp if need be, Francesca led the others northeast out of Quarrytown as the waning gibbous moon started across the sky. However, they made it only twenty or so miles before the east grew grey over distant, rolling hills.

The first highway formed part of the border between Lunatel and Scissum. It was nearly empty, except for the forts and occasional patrols of outriders that kept their eyes on the west.

The border with Cortellum, where the three provinces met at Lassaer, was a different matter. Early on the fifth night, they walked the horses through the city, garnering only a few curious looks at what appeared to be a mercenary band. The border checkpoint was on the other side of town, past the outskirts. And here, the sentries' eyes went in all directions.

Legionaries, clad with blue tabards over mail, guarded a small, stone fort that spanned the highway with a half-open gate. Low walls, just high enough to bar a leaping horse, stretched several hundred yards into the countryside. Floating lights out in the dark indicated mounted patrols.

"We should have taken a side road," Varja whispered as the group approached the fort, still on foot.

"I'd rather deal with gate guards than risk outriders," Des said. "Here, there are civilian witnesses."

"What's our strategy?" Azran asked.

"The truth," Francesca said. "Just not the whole truth."

"Right," Des said. "We're returning home to Aure."

Azran took a deep breath. Varja followed suit and noted the flying banner—a rearing, maneless hunting cat, cobalt on white. "The Blue Lions," she said. "We met a company of them during the Second Flame."

"Do you have a rapport?" Azran asked.

Varja grinned. "Oh, no. They hated us barbarians, even as we fought beside them. Thought we would steal their glory."

"Did you?"

She grinned wider. "A bit."

"Halt and be recognized." A pair of legionaries stood on the road. Azran was acutely aware of a dozen more watching from the battlements and towers flanking the gate. "Five riders, four armed, traveling at night," the soldier said.

"What is your route?" his companion asked.

"Cruxia to Aure, sir," Des said.

"And your business?"

"Returning home from a personal visit, sir."

The first soldier pointed to Varja. "Her too?"

"A new home," Varja replied.

The second stalked closer. "Why continue at such an hour, when Lassaer is right there?" He saw Azran and Francesca's eyes and answered his own question. "Vampires." The word fell like spit.

"Have you a writ of passage, vampires?" the first asked.

"Since when do they need that?" Des asked.

"Since the Senate passed emergency measures following the Night of Blood and Flame."

"You two may pass," the second soldier said, pointing to Des and Luc. "The vampires and the foreigner stay on this side of the border."

"This is ridiculous," Varja said. "I fought beside your legion as a free company auxiliary in 1340. And I vouch for these two— they are no danger."

The soldiers did not so much as blink. "So thought the capital's citizens until a few weeks back. A mercenary's word does not absolve them of their kin's misdeeds."

Varja shrugged an apology to her friends. Azran patted her shoulder in thanks anyway.

Des glanced around, her gaze lingering behind the group. Azran followed the look and saw six armored riders ascend the raised road from the fields behind them. Lances stood silhouetted by the lights of Lassaer.

Des turned back to the pair in front of them. "There's no need for hostility. How much for a writ?"

"They are given, not sold."

The hoofbeats clattered to a stop behind them. The riders formed a half-circle. Each infantryman put a hand to his sword.

"Remove your weapons and relinquish your mounts, vampires. You are under arrest for suspicion of treason."

"On what grounds?" Francesca asked. "We weren't even here on that night."

Azran took stock. They couldn't run—he saw archers above. Luc and Varja's hands inched toward their weapons. He knew Des could find hers in an instant.

"Don't," he said to them. "We'll figure a way through this." He swallowed his fear, willing his voice steady. "But I would appreciate it, sir, if you would answer my wife's question."

"You're vampires. The Senate's measures give us authority to arrest your entire wretched species. None can be trusted."

"You two *citizens* may pass. Watch your company."

"And me?" Varja asked.

The first soldier glanced at the second. "She vouched for them."

The second nodded. "Arrest the foreign bitch, too."

The butt of a lance whacked Azran in the back. He staggered forward.

"Step to it," the lancer said.

Des gave Azran the slightest of nods. *She bragged she could dance past Godshadows,* he thought. He prayed that was not an empty boast.

They were ushered in irons through the gates, into a passage bordered by looming, curved walls to either side. An identical gate stood at the far end. The legionaries turned them left, through a solid, iron door. Beyond was a longer, walled courtyard with three low buildings—barracks and an armory, perhaps. A trio of soldiers leaned against one, smoking and drinking.

"Oi, watcha got?" one called out.

One of the escorts shoved Azran forward—though he had already been walking—and replied, "Two bloodsuckers and a tanglehair."

"Aye, a Ziak by her look," another soldier said, wiping whiskey from his beard said. He hooted and added, "And lookit her. Think I could tame that beast, boys?"

"Wait'll they're processed," the escort said. "Then, I don't care what you do with your time."

"Eh, and you, pretty one," another smoker called as the group passed around the corner. "You suck blood, eh, what else you suck?"

"Hey, dear," Francesca whispered to Azran. "Next time Varja and Luc look like they're going to kill these pricks, don't stop them."

"Noted," Azran replied through gritted teeth.

"I think I hate this country," Varja added.

"Well, no worries, Ziak," their other escort said. "One way or the other, you won't be here long."

On the far end of the courtyard was a rectangular keep anchored by a tower at each corner. A soldier opened an ironbound door, and the prisoners were led through, single-file. Then, Varja was separated and brought down a flight of stairs while Azran and Francesca were shackled to chairs in a small chamber. A table sat before them with a more elaborate, cushioned seat on the far side. There was one door, which the escort closed behind them.

This was what Azran imagined an interrogation room looked like. He watched the door, waiting for the torturer to arrive. Francesca grabbed his hand.

After an indeterminate period, the door opened. A soldier and a man wearing white and blue bureau robes entered. The robed man carried a ledger, pen, and ink. He sat in the cushioned chair while the soldiers stood guard.

"Good evening," the robed man said politely, if not pleasantly. He produced a pair of spectacles from the folds of his garments, balanced them on his nose, and flipped the ledger to a blank page. "May I have your names?"

"Francesca Vate." She said it without hesitation. "This is my husband, Azran."

The questioner wrote in the ledger. "Ostiteli first name. From where do you hail, Mrs. Vate?"

"Equotel, originally. But I've lived in Aure for ten years now. My mother was Ostiteli."

He scribbled some more. "And you, Mr. Vate?"

"Lunatel," Azran said. "Though, Aure since we married."

"Very well." The man looked from one to the other over his drooping glasses. "Now, the men who brought you in said you claimed to have left Aure before the…unpleasantness. Is this true?"

"Quite true," Francesca said.

"Do you know any of the perpetrators or their agendas?"

"No," the couple said together.

The robed man sighed and looked at the soldier. "You may leave us, legionary." Once the door closed, the robed man removed his glasses and turned back to them. "Sir, ma'am, I realize this may be difficult given your circumstances, but I ask you to trust me. I am with the Bureau of Law, not Military Affairs. My job is to have your best interests at heart. You want to get out of here. I want that, as well. But I cannot help you unless you tell me everything you know."

As a rule, Azran did not trust the bureaucracy. However, as this man said, they were in a tight spot. They didn't know much, but what they did might be enough to get them released. The only problem was, how much did the law already know? Did they know about Francesca's brother? What would happen to her because of that connection? Was there a way to satisfy this man without telling everything? It was all so intertwined, Azran wasn't sure there was.

He didn't know what to do, so he looked at his wife. She shook her head as she turned back to the robed man. Slumping her shoulders and lowering her face, she adopted a crushed tone and said, "I'm afraid we really don't know anything, sir."

"Nothing but the rumors that reached Cruxia," Azran added, putting on an equal show of helplessness.

The robed man jotted a few notes. "Well, that makes this more difficult, but let us see if I can yet help you. Else, I am afraid we shall have to give you over to the Godshadows' listeners." He let the threat hang in the pause before he continued. "What do you both do for a living?"

"I'm a harpsichord player, a house musician at a tavern," Azran said, wondering where this could possibly be going.

"I do a variety of work," Francesca said. "Latest was serving in a manor."

The man nodded. "And in these occupations, are you well paid?"

Azran covered his exasperated laugh with a cough. "Excuse me," he said. *Chains of Crusix, everyone here's suspecting us of treason, and he's looking for bribes.*

"Enough to live," Francesca said. "But as your men may have informed you, we are returning home from a long absence. Our funds are scarce."

"How much do you have?"

"I don't know about Varja, but we should have maybe fifteen argi?" She looked at Azran for confirmation.

"And some coppers."

The robed man made a show of his disappointment. "This is not enough for me to help you." He jotted something in the ledger, closed it, and stood. "You will be held until tried. But I must tell you, it does not look in your favor."

When he exited, Francesca screamed at the closed door, "Fucker! False-faced, moneygrubbing piece of shit."

"Des will come for us," Azran said. It was all he could hold onto at the moment. He had expected danger, but not here, not yet, not this. A maniacal brother-in-law he could handle, but this system wielded more power than any priest. It was a monolith, slowly crushing everyone beneath its immensity. For a brief, sick moment, he looked forward to Amadore's revolution. Or whatever he was doing.

Before long, a pair of soldiers entered, unshackled them from the chairs, and led them down the same stairs they had taken Varja. As Azran expected, it led to a row of damp, stinking cells. Most were empty, but the soldiers still escorted them to the farthest one.

They passed Varja, who was refusing to sit in the filthy film of the floor. "How'd it go?" she asked.

"One chance left," Azran replied.

"Don't you be trying anything now, bloodsucker," one of the escorts said. "You won't get far."

"I was referring to our trial."

The soldier laughed like a jackal. "He told you there'd be a trial?"

With heavier, grimmer mirth, the other escort said, "Come noon, we'll be taking you out for some sun." He veritably threw them in a cell and slammed the door. "How's that for a trial?"

The soldiers walked out.

"Des will come," Azran repeated.

This was a mistake, he thought. *Better to be free and on the run than trapped and waiting for death.* He hated feeling helpless, more than anything. Even when he had tried to kill himself, it felt like an out, like he had some agency over his own fate.

"I won't die to the sun," he said. "Whatever happens, not that."

"Nor will I," Francesca said. "I can't. You know, I never understood why Amadore so abhorred light—not just the sun, but any light. I've seen him get violent if he isn't expecting it. But now, I wish I could tear this prison apart and hide under the rubble."

They leaned on each other, silent. After perhaps an hour, the same pair of soldiers came down and removed a ragged orc man from his cell.

"Can we have some water?" Azran asked. The moldy air and the trepidation had parched him. "Call it a last request."

"If you're thirsty, cut yourself and drink!" That jackal laugh disappeared up the stairs.

32

Des lay on her belly in a copse of shrubs, too far off the flat fields for the riders to venture at night. From the movement of their lights, she had found an excellent blind spot. The only other illumination was the moon above her and the lanterns of the fort before her. She watched the patrolling figures on the walls—their routes, how well they kept them—and filed it all in her professional mind.

Lucky for her friends, the fort was a perfect copy of several border checkpoints Des had carried in her past life. She knew where they would keep prisoners, where they would keep contraband and other seizures. She even knew where they would build a postern gate. This was one area where the drive for efficiency and uniformity betrayed the authorities—making it easy for any trained soldier to work any fort also made it easy for anyone else.

The hard part would be getting those three out without being spotted. Des's confidence getting in came from her solitude—more people, more chances for something to go wrong, regardless of skill.

To avoid suspicion, Luc and Des had to take the horses over a mile down the road. Slipping that far would take time. Azran and Francesca had mentioned sunlight would not kill them immediately. Des hoped a low sun would prolong that time. Clouds would be better, but the autumn sky was clear.

Luc, of course, had suggested simply busting them out and riding hard—lose the soldiers in the darkness. Des reminded him that any violence would draw many more hounds than some missing nobodies.

On the walls, the guard changed. The new ones followed the same paths with similar pace. Finally satisfied, Des eased up from the cold dirt, double-checked the nearest mounted patrols, and moved in. The captors had turned her friends left, so they would be in the keep to her right.

Staying low and darting from cover to cover, belly-crawling through one damned open patch, Des reached the keep. She stood flat against the wall as a lantern passed above. The archer's eyes were out, not down. Des had a thirty-count before he came back.

Her hands searched the dark stones until she found the irregular seam. Twenty-count. She could not recall which brick popped the door. She pushed each on the left side, bottom to top. Fifteen-count. The sixth one up gave. The seam widened. Des shoved her fingers in, planted a foot, and pulled. She slipped through an opening just wide enough to accommodate her and pulled the door closed by the inside handle. Five-count.

The fear she'd been ignoring was alleviated when she found this hallway empty. She held her breath and listened for footsteps.

She kept her breathing shallow and through her nose, her ears cocked, and her steps light through the narrow corridors.

First, she made for the seizure room. The keep was quiet at this hour, but now and then, a scuff or cough would echo down the maze of corridors. When that happened, Des found the nearest cover and counted to ten in her head. A dozing guard had his keys stolen, used, and replaced without incident. Des returned to the secret door with bundles of her companions' possessions wrapped in heavy cloaks.

She had nearly reached the dungeon stairs when two sets of footsteps approached the intersection. She faded into a cubby space that was empty but smelled of cat. Two guards, one loosing sharp, barking laughs at the mumbled joke of the other, passed within arm's reach and descended the stairs. Des spotted a ring of keys on the loud one's belt—not attached, merely shoved into the band. Mail clinked as they walked.

A minute passed. Then, the guards returned, prodding a starved vagrant before them. "Yeah, well, round here you earn what you eat, filth," the quieter guard said.

Des became aware of a grey cat sitting directly across the hall from the cubby, staring at her. *Don't you dare,* she thought, holding her breath.

The cat gave a loud meow.

"Tell him, girl," the key-bearer said, glancing at the cat and releasing that shrill laugh.

Des's hand reached out of the darkness and pulled the ring right up and out. Her fingers closed on the loose keys as she retracted, and their brief jingle was covered by bouncing mail, heavy boots, and a human hyena.

The guards passed on, rounding a corner to head deeper into the keep. Des slipped out of the cubby. The cat darted in and stared at her.

Stepping over the shallow pools in sunken flagstones, Des scanned side to side until she spotted Varja. She allowed an instant of lover's relief to pierce her practiced calm. Then, she was at the cell door.

Varja stood against the side wall with her eyes closed. They popped open when the lock clicked. She opened her mouth to speak, but Des put a finger to her lips and Varja bit the words back.

"Wait," Des mouthed. It was all she could do to not rush into the cell; this was the second time now that Varja had been ironed. But Des was on a carry.

She continued down the corridor and located Azran and Francesca. She again motioned for silence and unlocked the door. This time, she waved them along. The hinges creaked loud enough that a quick screeching was preferable to a slow, lower groaning. The pair was not as quiet as Des but would be quiet enough. They were nearly to Varja's cell.

"Right then, which of you pickpockets took my keys?" The soldier descending the stairs froze as he saw the three figures in the hallway.

Des reached inside her vest for a knife. In the slowed moment, she sensed Azran and Francesca tense and coil to charge. At the same time, the soldier's hand gripped his sword hilt, and he started to call.

"Dal—"

"Paran." Varja cut him off, stepping from her cell. "Now that I can see your face. I thought it was you—I'd recognize that laugh anywhere."

The hyena noise was more subdued than before. His grin was a nervous one. "Stormblood," he said. "How bout that."

Varja took a step forward. Paran stepped back, still ready to draw.

Des could hear the vicious smile as Varja growled, "Care for a rematch?"

A short chuckle—a yip, really—escaped Paran. "I think your band quite proved yourselves in Secose." His hand left his sword.

Varja pointed to the cell she had stepped out of.

"And take off your belt," Azran said.

Paran flashed him a dangerous look, but he complied. "Dalen will be down soon enough."

Azran slid the sheath off the belt and handed the sword to Des. She slipped it through the bars of another cell. Meanwhile, Azran expertly knotted the belt around Paran's hands. "Honey," he prompted.

Francesca ripped off her left sleeve, twisted it up, and gagged the soldier. "Too bad we don't have some rope," she said.

Azran pushed Paran into the cell. As Des locked it, he said, "Don't you be trying anything now. And if you get thirsty, just bend forward and drink."

"Enough now," Des said. "At the top of the stairs, go straight, left, straight, right, left. Watch my signals."

She crept up the stairs and listened. She heard muffled steps, to the right of the intersection and receding. She waved the others forward. They passed the cat's cubby, conscious of the slitted eyes on them. At the last turn, Des signaled a halt and pressed them against the wall. A pair of chatting soldiers walked by their hall. Des watched their torch-cast shadows. When they were far enough gone, she waved her charges across the corridor, to the storage room that housed the secret gate. She pointed to the wrapped bundles. Varja and Francesca affixed their blades to themselves while Azran gathered purses and pouches. Des picked up the heavy cloaks and handed them to the vampires.

"It's a long crawl," she whispered.

Their eyes widened in understanding. Azran shrank from the door, but Francesca took him about the shoulders and squeezed. He took a deep breath and nodded.

Des held up a hand and opened the secret door enough to peek out. She saw the archer's light coming their way. When he started back down his route, she whispered, "Stay low. Follow me exactly. Stop when I stop."

They moved in a crouch to the first patch of cover, then fell flat beneath the bushes as Des's thirty-count approached zero. She spotted the lights of a patrol trotting across the open field ahead, so they waited. The riders entered the gate, and six fresh ones followed the same path out into the darkness.

Des checked the sky—the moon had set. The east was faintly bluer than the black west.

They belly-crawled across the field and reached the raised copse from which Des had scouted the fort.

A shout rang out across the open ground. A patrol, maybe a quarter-mile off, turned in their direction, walking and wary of the terrain.

The others shifted at this, but Des hissed at them. "Not a muscle."

The riders drew closer, fanning out. The leader held his flameless lantern behind him and peered into the darkness. His eyes passed directly over Des's but continued on.

"Never mind," the rider said. "Night's playing tricks on me."

"Aye, this shift is too long. How long we gotta play border guard?"

"Till the law passes and folk can do it themselves. C'mon, men, we're almost over." The leader rubbed his eyes.

They turned their horses back out into the countryside.

Des felt the air in their hiding place grow lighter. She waited until the patrol was only a distant glow, then motioned the others on again.

Cover to cover, back the way she came. The eastern sky grew lighter.

"Almost there," she said to Azran and Francesca. "But we'll have to ride a bit till it's safe. Luc found a place to camp."

"How long a ride?" Francesca asked.

"Minutes, if we push hard."

"I won't die in the sun," Azran said. It was an oath, not a statement of fact.

Des looked back and saw more points of light exit the gates. "Faster," she said. They were far enough out to risk it. It was a race now, as the patrols spread and searched for the escapees.

At last, they reached Luc and the horses. The priest unhitched the reins from trees as they all mounted. "Lot of activity back there," he said, stepping into the saddle.

"I know," Des replied. "Ride."

They kept to the road, electing speed over stealth, tearing northeast across the paved stones. Heading that way, they had a good view of the lightening east. Azran and Francesca held their hoods low, just open enough to see the ground ahead.

The sun mounted the horizon. It seemed one moment, the riders traversed a dull grey landscape; the next, bright beams colored the ground. Azran and Francesca winced as though they were open flames. They bowed their heads, trusting their horses to follow the others. Francesca tried to cover her bare arm with the cloak, but it kept flapping open.

"Almost there," Luc called, leaning over his galloping steed's neck. "Right!"

The horses whinnied as reins pulled them in a sharp turn onto a narrow game trail.

Francesca clung to the saddle horn, barely keeping her seat. Azran wobbled to the side and retched.

Low bushes gave way to tall, thick trunks and foliage, and finally to a sheltered clearing with the heavy tents already set up.

Luc, Des, and Varja pulled their horses to a stop, and the remaining two halted out of instinct. Azran and Francesca let themselves hit the ground, both coughing and bleary-eyed. Luc and Varja dismounted and half-carried them to their tent. Francesca's left arm hung limp, fingers clutching at nothing. Across both vampires, burn marks snaked along their veins.

"Not in the sun, not like this," Azran muttered over and over in a parched voice.

Once inside the tent, he and Francesca sucked in lungfuls of air like half-drowned sailors.

"We'll be okay now," Francesca said between gasps.

Azran snatched a waterskin and took long gulps.

After taking this all in, Des walked up beside Varja and wrapped her arms around her. Varja returned the embrace.

Luc gathered up the horses and two bedrolls and headed back to the highway. On the chance Paran was with the outriders, Des stayed behind.

"If they ask," Luc said, "I'll tell them you're relieving yourself."

Des smirked. "We'll make a liar and a scoundrel out of you yet."

Luc returned the grin and left.

"Is this what it's going to be all the way to Aure?" Varja asked.

"No," Des said. "The border's always the heaviest. Lot of roads between here and Aure, and they don't have the numbers to stop everyone everywhere. And between me and the others, we should have a way into the city. Then, it's just a matter of reading the streets." She glanced up to see Varja staring at her. "What?"

"You're amazing," she said.

Des's cheeks grew warm, and she looked away.

"How did you learn to do all this?"

"It comes with the carries—the jobs," Des replied.

"You said you did security work. Like a bodyguard?"

"Of sorts, yes. Locks, they call us. More like sentries. For smugglers." Des trailed off. She'd experienced a lot of feelings about her Kraken days, but shame was new.

"Smugglers?" Varja echoed. "Well, I suppose they can't be worse than the lawmen in this empire."

"Oh, they can," Des said, lying back against a tree. "I did my best to avoid those that were." She paused. "How do you feel about your girlfriend being a criminal?"

Varja lay on her back, resting her head in Des's lap. The position reminded Des of her and Ari under their favorite willow back in Salles.

"I'm sure you had good reason," Varja said.

"I really didn't. I just sort of fell into it. It seemed like the thing to do, back when I was young."

"So, you were like me."

Des supposed she had been. "Those days are behind us now," she said, more to herself than to Varja.

• • •

In the darkness of the tent, Francesca watched the web of seared skin fade into her usual complexion. Her stomach still churned and her head still pounded, but it was manageable now, like a bad hangover.

She thought of that moment in the cell, when she had sympathized with Amadore. Looking at her veins, her fear of the sun should have seemed justified. But now that they were safe and the fear was distant, she realized it wasn't so simple. The naked sun would kill a vampire's body, but the naked darkness could kill one's mind. Amadore lived in the darkness, and he was lost. Every time she was alone at night, he was there. *Either extreme can—no, either* will *kill you.*

"Hey, Cesca?" Azran asked. He was on his back with one forearm over his eyes. "Was this a mistake?"

"We were seeing the sun either way," she replied.

"No." He propped himself up on his elbows. "I mean going home like this."

"He's not going to stop."

"I had a thought, though. If we got word to him, he might just arrange safe passage. No assassins, no angels, no soldiers."

Francesca flopped onto her bedroll and gazed at the ceiling. "I have to do this on my own terms. That's how it has to be."

She heard Azran shift back down. She considered the words bouncing around her head, then gave them voice. "And he wants you dead."

Azran shot back up. "What? Why?"

"I don't know. But I know he does. That angel tried to kill you like—like you were an obstacle. Whatever my brother plans, it doesn't involve you."

"Fucking hades it doesn't. I'm still going to be by your side."

She smiled and gripped his hand. "I know." The smile faded. "I'm worried I won't be able to protect you."

"That's why we brought friends. I'm not so bad at looking after myself, either. Look at all we've survived in the past few weeks."

"That's true." Francesca turned to look at him. "Let's agree— no more doubts."

"I can't promise that, and neither can you," Azran said. "But I can agree." He leaned in and kissed her.

She pulled back, giggling and grimacing at the same time. "Ugh, tastes like your old breakfast. I'm sorry, dear, but drink something. Whiskey breath would be better."

"My apologies, sweet lady. I only survived direct sunlight this morning."

"So did I."

"But sick breath, that's your breaking point?"

"Apparently."

Azran lay back down. "Your brother doesn't stand a chance."

33

The nights through Cortellum were as Des said—fewer patrols, no overt harassment. The border guards had not even reached Luc that day, either because of constraining orders or because they relied more on threat than doggedness. Still, despite a desire for haste, the five riders avoided the direct routes through larger cities after Lassaer. Circumventing was slower, but they had risked enough already.

From passing travelers, those on day watch garnered word that the chaos was confined mostly to Aure, and even that wasn't so turbulent anymore. An entire district had been claimed by Filvié Noctirin, its borders entrenched. A siege was occurring inside the walls of a city that hadn't experienced war in a millennium.

When Aure was only three days away, something started to prickle the hair on the back of Des's neck. Eerie shadows seemed to keep pace behind them, visible only on the rare straight mile.

"I think we're being tailed," she said to the others.

They looked back, around, ahead.

"I don't see anything," Varja said.

"They're good," Des said. "It's just creeping at the edges, but I'm sure we're not alone." She dismounted and handed her reins to Varja. "I'm going to scout."

"Do you want backup?" Azran asked.

She shook her head. "Keep at a walk. I'll see what I can find and catch up." They were on a dirt road running parallel to a stream. She knew the path continued on until it reached a ford, then doubled back along the far bank. She could find a nearer foot crossing. At worst, she'd swim.

"Be careful," Varja said.

"Always am." Des left the road and vanished into the night.

"Well, that's a lie," she heard Luc grumble. Regardless, the group continued east.

Des decided her best chance to spot any pursuers was to wait. She found a spreading maple and climbed.

Perhaps a quarter-hour passed before four riders materialized out of the gloom. They were dressed in dark cloths and leathers. Two had crossbows lying across their saddles. A third peered forward with eyes that glowed—magic, perhaps to not lose the band ahead. The fourth had red eyes—a vampire.

Still far from Des, just within earshot, one of the crossbowmen asked, "Cutoff's close?"

"Yes," the vampire said. "We should hurry, but just enough to close in. We want the others to give them feathers."

Cant—this was looking bad.

The woman with glowing eyes spoke next. "And when we get there, what's this vamp going to do, Theod?"

Theod—from Cruxia. Serile's night keep. What in hades is this?

346

"She's going to do what she does best," Theod said— definitely his voice. "She's motherfucking Lockiron. Or have you forgot?"

Des's stomach sank like a stone. *No. No, no, no. How?*

Lockiron was a legend in the Kraken. "Bounty hunter" did her a disservice—she was an artist in the realm of finding people. She had supposedly retired over two decades ago. Vanished off the map. But evidently, she was a vampire. This was looking very bad.

"Do you want your jingle?" Lockiron asked. Her voice was hard-edged, ragged. "Then fucking carry. Let's move."

The riders passed below Des's hiding place. She was on the edge of panic. She had to get back. Once the riders trotted into uniformity with the darkness, Des climbed down and hopped deadfall and rocks across the stream. Then, she ran.

Fuck, she ran. She scrambled up the opposite bank. She burst through vegetation, shielding her face from whipping branches. Breaking out onto the packed dirt road, she paused. With a quick estimation of time, distance, and pace, she turned right and dashed after—she prayed—her companions. And the whole time her feet raced, so did her mind. The Kraken. Vampires. Lockiron. And all these threats were at least one step ahead of them. Maybe more than that.

An image flashed through her head. In it, she was too late. Snipers in the trees loosed silent bolts. Varja was shot and fell from her horse. They were after Francesca; a char on the others would be level.

Oh gods, it's happening again.

● ● ●

Francesca kept her eyes peeled as they rode. She had some experience with this, both being tailed and being the tail. But she could find no sign of watch or pursuit. Perhaps they had seen Des and backed off.

Still, she trusted Des's instincts far more than her own. She stayed close to Azran. Luc took point, hand on hilt. Varja rode in the rear, leading Des's horse and watching behind.

They splashed through a shallow, pebbly ford and followed the road as it doubled back. This was likely the roughest terrain in gentle Cortellum. Streams and rivers fed by sea storms blowing inland flowed either back to the big water, or north to the basin of Palutel. The land here was marred by nothing as dynamic as a canyon, but ridges and exposed layers of sediment were common. The road wound and rose and fell; only the paved highways cut straight lines and flat planes from city to city.

Lush vegetation and blinding hills meant cover. And so, when they rounded a jut of sheer stone, they were surprised to find five riders in black clothes and half-masks. Bits of dulled steel armor protruded around joints. Swords were sheathed on their belts, hands never far from the grips. They sat calm, but their steeds fidgeted as if they'd been waiting.

Luc pulled up short, the others following suit. "You'd be better served finding easier prey, bandits," the priest said. Steel slid on steel as he pulled his blade an inch from the clasp.

Something told Francesca these weren't ordinary highwaymen, but she kept quiet. She appraised the terrain around them—hills dotted with low, thick trees. She caught movement up and to their left that did not match the leaves in the breeze. More behind the masked riders.

348

"Do you hear me?" Luc asked when they did not respond. "You risk the wrath of a Blade of Atora. Be gone!" He unsheathed his weapon, brandishing it above his head.

Varja and the masked riders reacted in kind. Francesca put a hand on her rapier but did not draw.

"Luc," she said softly. "We're surrounded."

"Crossbows, I'd wager," Varja said. "This is the perfect spot for an ambush."

"Smart," one of the riders said. "Here's how this works. The vampire lass steps down and walks over to us. You all let her do that, and in turn, don't get shot full by more snipers than you can see." Her voice was strangely familiar, though muffled by her mask. A hidden smile was audible as she said, "Agreed?"

"Where in hades is Des?" Varja whispered, eyes darting.

Francesca heard leather creak as Luc's glove tightened on his sword, then relaxed. She looked at Azran, whose eyes were surprisingly steely. He was about to do something stupid.

"It's dark tonight," he said to her. "But I can see you just fine."

She nodded, understanding. To the masked rider, she said, "Agreed." To her friends, she whispered, "Cover Azran."

Francesca dismounted and put her hands high and wide, in plain view. She walked toward the riders, perhaps twenty paces ahead of Luc. Her heart pounded in her ears, the loudest noise in the hushed atmosphere. She watched straight ahead, at the rider who had spoken.

The woman was alert but had relaxed a bit, confident in her allies and in Francesca's compliance. The rider to her left sheathed his sword and pulled a set of manacles from his belt. After a tip of the leader's head, Francesca angled toward the other one.

When she was ten paces away, activity exploded behind her. Horses whinnied and hooves beat. Luc charged to Francesca's right. Feathered shafts whipped past him, bouncing and burying themselves in the ground. Two of the masked riders met him. Luc ducked one swing and parried the other. He turned his horse in the midst of the fray, using his foes as cover against the snipers.

At the same time, Azran galloped past Francesca's left. She was ready, and when his hand clasped her outstretched forearm, she clasped back and leapt forward. Her free hand grabbed the back of the saddle, and she got one leg to either side. She held Azran's waist as he went wide of the now-unarmed rider on the left.

Francesca stole a glance back. Varja was on foot, circling around a tree as bolts thudded into it. She was going for the crossbowmen.

A stray quarrel struck Des's horse in the flank. It let out a pained cry, reared, and bolted back the way they had come.

Just as Francesca turned her attention forward again, Azran's horse lurched, bucked, and fell. She flew from the saddle, landing squarely on her back. Azran fell sideways, one foot in a stirrup. He disentangled himself and scrambled clear of the kicking, wounded animal trying to regain its feet.

Francesca, too, tried to stand, but the wind had been knocked out of her. She only succeeded in rolling onto her side. Then, a masked man was on the ground next to her, pulling her arms back. She kicked, but her boot met a solid greave. A band of metal locked around her left wrist.

She saw only Azran's foot as it planted in front of her face and launched him over her. He slammed into the masked man and tackled him backward.

Francesca coughed and pushed herself up. Azran jammed his knife into the man's armpit, just before a heavy gauntlet slugged him in the face.

"Enough!" A new voice rent the air. "I know you don't want to lose any men on this, Sayel."

All eyes went to the south ridge. There stood a forliri man in dark leathers. A long knife was pressed to his throat, and behind him, holding the blade, was Des.

"Stop!" the lead rider ordered. Her fighters backed off. Luc watched his two opponents like a wild dog. There was some rustling from the north ridge as the snipers there had a staredown with Varja. Azran's foe pulled out a cloth and held it to his bleeding wound.

"Is that—Gax?" Azran asked, looking at Des's hostage. He glanced at the lead rider—Sayel—who had pulled her mask down. "What in Tyreg's bloody castle is going on?"

"Sorry, music man," Gax said. "Business is business."

"Well, if it isn't the butcher of Inks," Sayel said, addressing Des. "You're right on that count. Let's see if we can stamp another seal."

"No," Des said. "Me and mine are leaving now. Varja, Az, Cesca, saddle up." She walked Gax down the incline, keeping the blade tight. "Now, people. They have Lockiron coming."

"Who?" Varja asked, backing down to the road, still on guard.

"Someone we're not going to tangle with," Des replied. "Sayel, are you aware your reinforcements are Kraken agents?"

Sayel smiled. "Sure. We have our differences, but we're not negs. Especially not when such a legend offers a cut for an easy drag. Well, ostensibly easy." She sneered at Des. "You'll let my man go?"

"When we're well on our way and out of bowshot."

Francesca mounted her horse, Azran behind her. Varja walked her own up to Des. Des locked her free arm around Gax's shoulder and her legs around his waist. With a grunt, Varja boosted them into the saddle. Gax and Des sat facing backward.

Hoofbeats sounded around the jut, growing closer and closer.

Varja climbed into the saddle as Des said, "Go, go, let's go."

Four new riders rounded the bend. Two held crossbows, leveled and ready. A third brightened the night with a spell. The fourth was no stranger.

"Wait," Francesca said.

"Ria?" Azran asked.

It was her, alright. More haggard than usual, wearing armor, with a dangerous look in her eyes, but Ria.

"Lower the knife," she said in a harsh, ragged voice devoid of the playfulness Francesca knew. "This won't get you anywhere."

"Won't it?" Des asked. "I will slit his fucking throat."

"I believe you." Ria raised a crossbow slung over her shoulder and levered it back. "And I'll thank you for the clearer shot."

"Now, hold on," Sayel started.

"Shut up, collar. I warned you before this carry." Ria loaded a bolt.

"Ria, what the fuck are you doing?" Francesca asked in a low, calm tone.

"The last job I'll ever have to—bringing you to Amadore."

"That's where we're going already. No one has to die for this."

"That'd be easier," Ria said. "But I've gathered the whole story. He wants to see you and you alone. I'm granting you a mercy by not killing Azran like he wants. I'll say he got away. Now, Francesca, come with me. Please. Your friends won't get hurt."

"Oh, one's dying for sure," one of the new riders said through clenched teeth. "And it'll be that little Kraken cunt right there."

"My word trumps yours, Theod," Ria said. "This is my carry."

"Fuck that, I didn't come for jingle." His face contorted behind the iron sight of his crossbow. "Serile's dead because of you."

"No she's not," Des said. "She's dead because of the same freak who hired Lockiron. *He* sent the thing that slaughtered the Broken Arrow."

Francesca felt Azran tense even tighter. "Money, Ria?" he said. "Is that all it took for you to betray your friends?"

Ria shook her head slowly. "No, Az, I'm not getting paid for this."

Understanding dawned in Francesca. "What did he say? What happens if you don't do this?"

Ria hesitated. "My past catches up with me. My life—my existence—ends. We can't change what we are, Ces."

Francesca wasn't sure, but she thought those steady hands were starting to tremble. *Look what he's done,* she thought. *Does he even realize how low he's sunk?* She wanted to scream. She had gotten them all into this mess. There had to be a way out.

"Listen, Ria," Azran said. "We're going to have some words with him anyway."

"That's right," Francesca said, following his lead. "And when we're done, I promise any threats he made to you will no longer stand. So, let us go, spend a few more days searching, and we'll get in touch when it's done."

Ria was shaking her head before she was done talking. "You can't promise that. You know him."

"Yes, I do. Better than you."

"He's mad."

"And growing madder by the day. But so am I." Francesca held Azran's hand and glanced at her new friends. "So are we." She focused back on her old friend. "This has been a long time coming. Don't deny me the chance to face him on my terms."

Ria's hands were definitely shaking. A tear formed in one eye. She looked so exhausted, so torn, like she'd passed her breaking point days ago.

Amadore would pay for this—this and everything else. Francesca began to realize there wouldn't be many words at all. She let the feeling show in her eyes, locked on Ria's.

In response, Ria closed hers, turned her face away, and lowered her crossbow.

"What are we doing here, Lockiron?" Sayel asked.

"Let them go," Ria said. "You still get jingle when Francesca reaches Aure, as stamped."

The crossbowman to her left lowered his weapon, but the other—Theod—did not.

"No, fuck that," he growled. He pulled the trigger.

Des fell from Varja's horse. The bolt whistled past where her head had been an instant before. As she hit the dirt feet-first in a low crouch, she flicked a smaller blade from her sleeve and threw it at Theod. It stuck in his leather armor. He kicked his horse forward, drawing a sword.

In one fluid, precise motion, Ria's bow came back up, clicked, and sent a bolt through Theod's ear. He lurched sideways and slipped from the saddle.

For a moment, it seemed like the fighting would begin anew. Then, Sayel let out a short, tensionless laugh.

"I think that about does it," she said. "Are we done here, then?"

"Yeah," Ria said, staring at Theod's corpse. Her voice was gentler now. "We're done."

"Excellent. Don't just dawdle, Galex—go fetch your crossbow."

The forliri man dismounted and climbed the ridge without a word.

Sayel and her riders cleared the road east. "Go on, then. And thanks for holding level on that forerunner stamp."

Des retrieved her thrown knife and mounted behind Varja. Luc still watched the riders but followed the others onward.

"Ces, Az," Ria said.

They stopped and looked at her.

She met their gazes only briefly. "I'm sorry. Audas's luck forward."

Azran let out a deep breath. Francesca just nodded. She got the distinct feeling that no matter how this all ended, they would never see Ria again.

• • •

The ride was quiet. After a couple hours, they crested a rise and, though still miles out, the Golden City of Aure glowed like a little patch of day.

"It's so big," Varja said, eyes wide in awe. "I've never seen a city like that."

"No," Francesca said. "I'm sure by this point, none of us have."

"How are we even going to get in?" Azran asked.

"Same way we got out," Des said. "I paid attention in the tunnels. With their boss and a bunch of guildsmen gone, we should be able to slip past what's left of those ex-Kraken."

Luc grumbled something unintelligible, then said, "I'm sick of sneaking."

"Don't worry," Francesca said. "We'll need your blade soon enough, I imagine. I know where my brother will be, and he won't be alone. Let's go."

They started down into the flatter, open ground around the city.

The silence now broken, Varja said to Des, "I was worried about you."

"I assure you, not as worried as I was," Des replied.

"Were you really going to kill that man in cold blood?"

"They can tell if you don't mean it. Does it bother you?"

Varja hesitated. "I don't know anymore."

"It should," Des said. "Once this is over, maybe—maybe we should part ways."

Varja's chest constricted. "What? Why?"

"Because Lockiron—Ria was right. We can't change who we are. Ari was killed by a Kraken-hired sniper in a tree. Same as almost happened to you. It's not safe to be close to me."

Varja pulled her horse to a stop, searching for the best way to tell Des how wrong she was. "They were there because of Francesca, not you. And you likely saved us. How is this your fault?"

"Theod knew me. That's how Ria tracked our path through Cruxia, I wager. I'm the reason the Kraken got involved in this. Chains, the other two probably had a cousin I killed in Inks. I'm haunted. Not just by Arilysa. I'm not a good person, Varja. I'm trouble." Des slipped out of the saddle and walked a few paces away, staring into the trees.

"I don't care," Varja said, following her in kind. "I've made plenty of my own enemies. I make new ones every week."

"It's about quality, not quantity."

Varja put the puzzle together. "You're being selfish."

"How?"

"You don't really blame yourself for tonight—that's you grasping at rationalization. You just think it would be worse if I died than if you did."

"Again, how is that selfish?"

"Because you don't think how I would hurt if you died. You push me away because you think you know loss better than I do, and that I'll just accept that. But you don't, Des. Quit acting like you're the only one with scars." Tears—angry tears, pained tears—welled in Varja's eyes. "You want to know what really hurts? *That* hurts. Like everybody else, you think you can pull one over on me. But you told me exactly who you are that night on the bluffs. If you run away from me, there'll be another ghost at your back. You want that?"

"No," Des chocked out. "I just—no." She arrested her breathing and wiped her eyes. "No, you're right. I'm sorry. I'm so sorry. I'm just—"

Varja put a hand on Des's cheek. "Before you call yourself a bad person again, I want you to hear another bit of my philosophy. I don't think anyone is as good as they could be. All we can do is keep trying to get better. And I've learned recently—you and the others have taught me—there's no straight path to that."

She placed a soft kiss on Des's lips.

"How do you know all this?" Des asked in a small voice.

"Because I'm not a good person, either. I'm just trying to get better."

Des held her close, then climbed back into the saddle. "Alright."

Varja mounted behind her. "Eyes forward."

"I'll try."

"I know you will. That's why I'm not leaving." Varja kicked the horse into a trot to catch up with the others.

Des kept one hand around Varja's strong forearm and watched the road ahead.

34

"I can't."

"What do you mean? You're not even going to try?"

"It's too complex. I can't even read it, let alone disable it." Daia stood up, her eyes narrowed at the hole beside an overturned flagstone. Inscribed within was an arcane rune—or many runes, with so many layers it was as indecipherable as a child's scribbling.

"That's disconcerting, then," Seneskar said. He had returned to his long-haired, blue-eyed human guise—his familiar, internally normalized one. "This close to the palace, there should only be wards."

"I assure you, this is not the work of an imperial arcanist," Daia said.

"It is charged with soul energy," Exus said, still kneeling. "Otherwise, I doubt I could have found it."

Daia nodded. "Hints of anti-detection, I can at least glean. And a trigger. A command receptor."

Seneskar walked over. "So, someone holds a key."

Exus remained silent, inscrutable. Finally, he stood. "Cover it. Mark this spot in your minds."

Seneskar hefted and replaced the flagstone. "When are the informants returning?"

"Nello and Elyra should report sometime in the next few hours," Daia said, throwing up her hood.

"We'll await them at the inn," Exus declared, starting off.

Seneskar gave one lingering look at the hidden rune, then a glance up to the lit space above the palace. This mystery reeked of his first target. He hoped the twin informants had a fruitful night.

• • •

Seneskar and Exus sat alone in the common room. Daia had retired to study her sketch of the rune alongside her personal notes. The informants—a listener and a cloak, they were titled, implying some subtle difference—had yet to arrive. Each member of this little band had their specialty, and a corresponding outlook, Seneskar had discovered. On the journey to Aure, he had poked and prodded these secretive Godshadows with open-ended questions. He found that discussing philosophy was an effective way to get a measure of someone. Daia hunted arcanists because she believed people were ruled by temptation, and there was no greater cause of suffering than a caster with delusions of godhood. The twins, meanwhile, owed their methods to a desire to guide others toward societal contribution—most people were inherently selfish, they said, implying good-natured egotism.

Exus, of course, had proven the most difficult to puzzle out. Seneskar got the impression that the Godshadow hunter had once been more open, before some altering, perhaps harrowing experience. When Seneskar had tried engaging him, Exus had simply replied, "I am not a philosopher."

"Most people aren't," Seneskar had said. "And yet, everyone has a philosophy. It's inescapable for a conscious mind. Even if you believe nothing has meaning beyond what it physically is, that is a philosophy."

Exus had gone quiet after that, but Seneskar could not tell if the silence was thoughtful or denying.

Now, in the late-night seclusion of an Aure inn, the dragon decided to try his luck again. He took a sip of his whiskey and said, "Interesting thing, the distinction between mortal and immortal. Don't you think?"

The elf turned from the window to stare at him. "It's pretty straightforward, is it not?"

Seneskar held his drink aloft and pointed one finger from the glass. "I would argue not. It's more than mere lifespan. They are alien in outlook, as well, and possess magical power beyond us. Serma and its sister tongues are unique in that they refer to these beings in temporal terms. For instance, in Zixarsi, the word is *thraer,* which is closer to 'god' or 'spirit.' And then take the cases of interbreeding. Audas and Tenebra were both said to be half-immortal before ascending. A strange term, if the two are so cut and dry."

"I suppose."

"Your role in the Godshadows is to hunt immortals, yes?"

"It was."

Seneskar gestured toward the window. "What are we doing, if not that?"

361

"We are hunting, but not for the Godshadows. Not me. This is more personal."

"Revenge?"

Exus shook his head. "Making up for a mistake. Earning a second chance I've been given."

Seneskar cared not for the mistake—the heart of the matter was not the action, but the belief. "And do you think you will earn it?"

"If I don't, I'll be no worse off."

Fascinating, Seneskar thought. *A man who needs not succeed, and yet tries.*

"But you were speaking of immortals," Exus said, his gaze drifting back to the street.

"Indeed I was." Seneskar took another sip while he gathered his thoughts. *Yes, let us prod that sore spot.*

"The mortal experience is not totally constrained, either," he started. "They say dragons and Aurasi were born of Caelix, not grown from the earth as others were. What does their divine blood mean in terms of this dichotomy? And on the subject of dragons, what of the Urathix, the dragon-gods of Charir?"

Exus's eyes snapped from the window to Seneskar.

"Faithful say the Urathix hold sway over the souls of their dead. Is that not an immortal power?"

Exus put his elbows on the table and interlaced his fingers. "It is an abominable overstepping of bounds."

"In what way?"

"Only the gods should wield such power, and immortals only at their behest."

"And yet, there are times when that is not the case. Regardless of morality or ethics, there is significance in the existence of such exceptions. If there is a line, it is crossed relatively often."

"And what is your opinion on that?" Exus asked.

"That binaries are limitations on perception and understanding. The world is as it is, and few things fit neatly in any particular box."

"An unsurprising view for a shapeshifter."

Seneskar agreed with a nod. "It does affect one's perspective. But you hold to dichotomies." He watched Exus's face closely for any twitch or sign of objection. "You are a mortal, not immortal. You are alive, not dead. You are here, not there. Awake, not asleep."

Exus did not reply, and Seneskar knew why. At the binary of life, the elf exhibited a slight, yet out-of-rhythm intake of breath— not a protest, but close.

"Am I mistaken?" Seneskar pressed.

"I believe in the right and wrong of things. I concede only that sometimes, the line can appear blurred if you lack the information to recognize your situation."

"Are you undead?"

For a moment, such anger flared in Exus's eyes that Seneskar feared he would leap over the table and strike him. "Are you a dragon?"

"Yes," Seneskar replied. There was no hesitation, but Exus's frozen face seemed to have expected one. "What are you?"

"Not undead. I haven't—"

"Recognized your situation yet," Seneskar finished. "There, now we've answered the question we each had at the outset of this venture. What is your real name? And why do you wear 'Exus' as though it's a mask?"

"I died in service to Mortis, bringing down a shadeseer that had been swayed by the rogue angel we're hunting. It would seem the Severance was not finished with me. I was called Syrus Azavel, but that name carries weight I don't need. No one else but Daia knows."

Seneskar toasted. "I understand completely, Exus." He downed the last of the whiskey.

He understood enough to be satisfied, at least.

• • •

The priest stood near the outskirts of the Golden Palace. He was far too close for a vampire to be permitted, given recent events, but that was only a problem if someone sensed him. Tenebra's cloak offered an intangible aegis while he worked.

A many-layered rune was carved into the underside of a broad flagstone. The priest only knew of it because he knew where—and how—to look. One of its multitude components was a powerful anti-detection spell. The priest crouched over it, bent almost double, hands held palm-down. Under his breath—a whisper for only the Goddess to hear—he chanted ancient litanies. He imagined he could see the soul energy pouring from his hands into the rune. It was pure, not just black but anti-light, its mere presence darkening the nearby air. It was invisible to his waking eyes but no less real. The rune—designed by the arcanist among the clan's Noblest, a creature older than any living elf—was a receptacle. The physical energy of arcana was far different from that of a soul. Mingling the two was a feat of genius seldom achieved and a secret never shared.

At last, the priest exhausted his reserves. His back and neck cracked as he straightened.

"So, you have elected to rejoin our efforts," said the soft voice of Zerexis behind him.

The priest turned to face the angel. "Yes. How many are left?"

"Six." Zerexis walked a tightening circle around the priest, appraising him like a slaver. "You can do no more tonight."

The priest turned his head to follow the angel.

"Did you retrieve your sister?"

He clenched his gnarled fist. "You know I have not."

"A pity. You sacrificed so much for that chance."

Zerexis kicked his lame leg, and he fell to one knee. He calmed the brewing storm within. He was too spent to play this game, and Zerexis knew it.

The priest stood once more. "What is it you seek, Angel of Shade?"

Zerexis seemed to consider the question. "I merely offer a reminder. Your sister is not needed. Less than ever, for the Valentreid scion is now in Aure—the valiant General Catia, daughter of Emperor Arcaeus. She has the loyalty of the military and recognition among the nobility and commoners. Chari forces slew her mother during the Rising Fire. She wants a war. She has come to discuss the state of the border with her father and will remain until the time comes."

The priest sneered beneath his cowl. *The scion—an impure living. Even awakened as a vampire, she would not compare to dear Francesca.*

"We must cooperate now," said Zerexis. "Final preparations need be made, and we have neither time nor energy for you to waste."

"I understand."

In no time at all, Zerexis was towering over the priest. "Is that true?"

The priest banished the contempt from his face. "Yes. I have delegated my search to an inconsequential commoner. We—I shall be ready for the Goddess."

Zerexis held his gaze, but he did not waver. The black eyes did not blink, but they twitched such that the priest perceived acceptance.

The angel handed him a sealed leather pouch. "Physical remnants of all Invicti in the palace. Ensure you have this in hand when you release the runes. It will tie the energy to the guards, and then—"

"Death," finished the priest. He hid the pouch somewhere beneath his robes. "What of the Dragonblades?" asked he, thinking of the seven formidable warriors supplementing the imperial guards.

"They are too well warded for this," said Zerexis. "They must be handled in person. But they protect only the emperor."

"Perhaps a distraction," said the priest. "Have the mercenaries go for Arcaeus first. Without Invictis, we and a few commoners can deal with the scion."

Zerexis smiled—an alien thing. "If only you applied yourself so more often. Yes, the mercenaries are expendable in this."

"Once the Goddess has taken the vessel, even the Dragonblades will be no threat."

"Indeed." The uncanny satisfaction faded from the angel's face. "Am I to take this as your acceptance of the new vessel?"

The priest lowered his head. "I bow always to Tenebra's desire. If this be it, I accept."

"At last. Good. Rest, then continue the work. I will inform the Noblest of the altered plan."

Zerexis vanished, appeased by the priest's half-truth. He did bow to Tenebra's wishes but knew he understood them better. The Angels of Shade had come to serve Tenebra; the priest had been tied to her since his blessed birth.

35

"It's around here somewhere," Des said, dismounting to locate the smuggling tunnel's exit.

They were a half-mile from the western wall of Aure. Except for Varja, the last time any of them had seen the city, a cloud of smoke hovered over it, fed by semi-organized arson. That was gone, but the sheer amount of light still hid many stars.

"No," Luc said. "It was farther north. In an outcrop, hidden by illusory arcana."

"We're not going through the stables," Des said. "That would bring us right into them. Last time we were here, I made sure to find another route, just in case of something like this."

"What of the horses, then?"

"Let them run. Someone around here will find them."

Luc grunted. "They were a gift, Des."

"We don't have many options right now," Francesca said. "Take off the gear, though. It might be a few days before they're found."

"Is this it?" Azran asked, a few paces off.

Des went to him and saw the old, wooden trapdoor, just large enough for a person with a bulky pack of contraband. The shifting season had warped it tight into place. She nodded, then went back to Varja's horse and helped unload. One saddlebag nearly pulled Des to the ground once she unbuckled it. She stood straighter and felt its lumpy, solid contents. "What in hades is in here?"

"Oh, that's my armor," Varja said.

"You have armor?"

Varja nodded like it was obvious.

"Why haven't you been wearing it?" Francesca asked.

"It's for when I expect a fight," Varja said. She took the bag and slung it across her shoulder. "It's not comfortable attire."

"Well, you'll likely need it before this is over," Des said. She looked at Luc. "Do you have armor?"

"Speed and faith," he replied.

Des would have laughed if not for that image of him staggering toward her after killing thirteen Kraken locks, eager to fight a fourteenth. She knew his ridiculous answer held at least some truth. "Let's get the door open," she said.

It took some work—prying with a dagger, then pulling with strong fingers and stronger legs. But within minutes and with night left to spare, they descended a creaking ladder to a steep, stepped passage. Sevex's house was their destination. Des remembered most of the way, and the smugglers' signs would help lead them through Aure's aged maze of tunnels.

It was dark, but they dared not risk a light. Azran and Francesca could see a bit, though even for vampires, it was quite dim. They described the slopes, turns, and intersections while Des steered them this way or that.

After about a half-hour, Azran halted the group with a whisper. "I think there's something moving up ahead."

"Figures," Francesca confirmed.

Before Des or anyone else could suggest a course of action, the tunnel flooded with light. All five of them shielded their dilated pupils from the glare.

The light became dimmer, but in that second of blindness, three unarmored figures had approached within twenty feet. Two held leveled crossbows, and one a knife in each hand. A fourth stayed back, holding a directional lantern. As Des's eyes adjusted, she recognized Sayel's second-in-command, the knife man.

"Why are you here?" he asked after an appraisal.

Des remembered this man had a talent for seeing through deception. She wouldn't try. "Striding again. Heading up."

"Where is Sayel?"

"Safe and free. Seal's been re-stamped. Yours will still get jingle, but we're on a keyed wing."

The knife man looked at them each up and down again. One of his hands started to idly spin its blade. He nodded. "I believe you, Desalie Vate. Respect, lock to lock. Stride on, no fee."

His comrades lowered their bows and stood aside.

Before they passed, Des asked, "How are the tunnels? Cant for stows."

"This side of the city is clear," the knife man said. "West, south, and central. The rest, under Rosaer Hills, are being used by the vampires. Not thick, but neither empty."

Des nodded thanks and continued on.

Luc lit a torch, and they made the rest of the subterranean trek in relative confidence.

They reached the passage below Sevex's neighborhood and heard no nobles taking refuge this time. Azran spent a solid fifteen minutes pounding on Sevex's cellar door and calling his name before the engineer opened an eye slit. The slit closed again, and there was a muffled exclamation. Lock bars clicked and grated, and then the heavy door opened.

"My friends, you've returned." Sevex looked equal parts joyful and anxious. He kept glancing behind him.

"Good to see you, Sev," Azran said. "We need a place to bed for the day. We won't be in your hair long."

"No, no, come in. As before, as ever, my home is yours." Sevex stepped to the side and swept a welcoming hand into his basement.

"Is everything alright?" Des asked.

"Oh yes. Given the circumstances, I could scarcely ask for more. There are quarters of Aure I can no longer attend, but it is all temporary, yes? I hope." He led them upstairs as he spoke. The curtains were drawn already. "I'm just about to leave for work, I'm afraid. Even in the midst of chaos, the gears and wheels of imperial machinery continue to turn. A testament to our structure, is it not?"

Varja shared a confused look with Des, who shook her head.

"It's a testament to something," Azran said.

"Oh, and you see?" Sevex continued, entering the sitting room and foyer. "All the detritus and debris removed, courtesy of my employers. Stay, rest, eat, drink. And you, Luc, I will have the necessary materials upon my return. You will not be disappointed. But I must go." Halfway through the front door, he stopped and pulled back in. "I nearly forgot—don't go outside. Not through the front, at any rate. The guards are doubled and have orders to capture or slay vampires on sight."

With that, Sevex left.

Azran gestured after him. "What did I say? Runs in the fucking family."

"Right, then," Francesca said. "Rest now, everybody. We stay the day. Tonight, we hunt."

"We should get the lay of things first," Des said. "We're coming in almost blind."

"We don't have time. Whatever is happening is happening tonight. I can feel it."

"It's a new moon," Azran added.

Des pondered how much stock they had been placing in Francesca's newfound "feelings" since Cruxia. But those instincts had not yet been wrong, which was more than Des could say of her own. And the first night Francesca had such premonitions was the same Des had sustained soul magic on Luc's blade. Who was she to say they were false?

"Very well," she said. "I hope you're right and we're not rushing for nothing. But either way, we're with you."

36

Francesca found her way to a guest room and collapsed on top of the bedding. She hoped she was right, too. It felt like she was—like for the first time in years, she had a sense of her brother. His mind wasn't so alien anymore. Ever since the angel. Perhaps that was it—by reaching so far, he had brought them closer.

Tonight made sense. The new moon—he wanted something to do with that, with his sister. They were all linked, though she could not articulate how or why. She felt only Amadore's desire, his presence suffusing the city around her. He was here, and he was waiting.

She closed her eyes and the shadows—*his* shadow closed in around her. If she opened them, he would be standing in the room. He was waiting, and it frightened her. Now that it came to

it, she wanted to run, just as she had run from their home in
Ostitel.

Their parents—what would they think if she hurt him?
Amadore had already hurt Francesca, and those around her. But
that was necessary, they would say. One did not justify the other.
They believed—not as hard as their son, but still harder than their
daughter. They had never accepted Francesca's "base desires"
taking priority over things like lineage or purpose.

They were a family of vampires born of vampires, after all. A
thing unheard of, that suggested—so everyone in on the secret
whispered—blood ties to Tenebra the Eclipse herself.

Francesca felt the feather mattress depress next to her and
Azran's hand take her own.

"I'm scared," she said.

"I'm here."

His presence eased her nerves, stilled her trembling hands, and
slowed her racing heart. That and sheer exhaustion from the
journey allowed her to slide into a fitful sleep, full of images and
dream-knowledge of family, old and new; of blood, where it
should be and where it should not be; and of shadows in places
expected and impossible.

• • •

Before she made her own way to sleep, Varja wandered the
strange house, looking for Des. At last, she found her in the
private wardrobe of the master bedroom. She stood in front of a
clear silver mirror, cutting her already shortish hair even shorter.

"I told you I'd be right along."

Varja walked up and tousled loose trimmings from the top of
Des's head. "I kind of liked it longer."

"It was getting shaggy. Besides, a new chapter starts tonight. This seemed like the thing to do." She made a few more snips and turned her head this way and that. "I was never keen on long hair. Not for myself, at least."

"Can't argue with all that," Varja said. She planted a kiss on Des's cropped scalp.

Des leaned against her, looking at their framed reflection. "We might die tonight. I try not to think about that before a piece of action, but for the first time in a long time, I have something to lose." She put a hand on Varja's forearm, itself around Des's middle.

"I can't argue with that, either. If we fight, I'll fight harder, then."

"We'll fight. I can see it in Francesca's eyes."

"Hey."

Des looked up at Varja.

"If we might die tonight, let's act like it." She swept Des up and kissed her like that first day in Quarrytown.

When they broke contact, Des was grinning ear to ear. "We should rest some."

"We will. We'll keep it gentle."

● ● ●

Luc was woken by a persistent rapping on his shoulder. He sprang up on the couch, reaching for his arming sword.

"No, no, it's me," Sevex said, backing off.

Luc rubbed his eyes and took in the room. The sun had not yet set, and Sevex was the only other person present.

"Sorry to wake you," Sevex said, smoothing his robes. "But I have a thing for you—a solution to my first solution to your hand problem." He held up his left hand and waggled his fingers.

"A solution?" Luc said back, still coming to consciousness.

"Quite. The mark two is ready, so to speak. Although, I suppose it would technically be the fifth iteration."

"What time is it?"

"Nearly four o'clock. I could not take the excitement, so I returned a bit prematurely. Shall we?"

"Shall we what?"

"Attach the new hand, of course." A grin of childlike eagerness came over Sevex's face. "It is more articulate and precise—much more. A clockwork marvel. I even ensured it was pre-threaded. The arcana is all there, no practitioner needed. Shall we?"

Luc blinked again. He had been quite asleep just a couple minutes ago. "Sure."

Sevex's grin somehow spread wider. "To my workshop. Come."

He led Luc to a room that resembled a study or private library, but with more table space and scrap metal. Sevex beckoned him to sit at a wide desk. The only items on this one were a wooden box and a set of fine clockworker's tools lain out on a cloth.

Sevex placed a stool to Luc's left and sat. He opened the box and used both hands to remove a bronze contraption, holding it like a holy relic. It was the hand. Segmented plates covered it, but the skeleton of gears and joints was visible through small gaps as its limp form shifted. Leather covered the palm and underside of the fingers. Fine lines of compressed, translucent, white gem dust ran from the fingertips to the wrist. There, dozens of needle-like protrusions made Luc's skin start to crawl.

376

"Is there pain?" he asked, bracing himself.

"Oh, yes," Sevex said. He lowered the new hand to the table. "Removing the one you have will not hurt. It hardly confers any sensation, as I'm sure you know. However, attaching this wonder will hurt. It is more sensitive and comes with pain."

"Why give it pain?"

"As we've learned at the bureau, pain is vital to sensation and bodily control. The mind, it seems, uses it in many ways. Treat this as you would a real hand, albeit a durable one. Now."

Sevex undid the straps of Luc's heavy prosthetic and picked up a tool that resembled a rigid pair of tweezers. He pulled the hand and twisted expertly, exposing the small rod that pierced Luc's stump. The priest could break a neck with a slug from that hand, but he could not have loosened it as Sevex did.

The engineer pinned the hand to the table and said, "Don't twitch." With the tool, he grasped the rod, turned it an eighth, let go, and repeated. Slowly, the attachment came farther and farther out. Strangely, there was no pain; Luc felt only a dull crawling. He clenched his flesh hand and his toes. It was like a tickle, but worse.

Then, it was over. The old hand was on the table.

"That rod, quite by design, did not touch any living nerves," Sevex said. "Those in your wrist are dead, so it had to reach for your mind's commands." He tapped the top of the bronze contraption. "This one does the same, but far more efficiently and by many more points of contact. You'll feel it."

Luc nodded and grabbed his Atoran medallion. "Do it."

Sevex picked up the stump and examined it, mumbling to himself. Then, he adjusted the needles of the new hand. Just as Luc started to relax again, Sevex grabbed his wrist, the new hand, and shoved them together.

The lines on the bronze hand flared as Luc's nerves fired, sending white-hot pain from his wrist to his spine to his brain. He staggered away from the table, biting his good hand to keep from screaming.

Within seconds, the pain subsided to a dull ache, then nothing. And then something—temperature, pressure. He closed the new hand and felt it close. He waggled the fingers and felt them brush each other. He shut his eyes and knew where they were.

"Your mind remembers a hand that could move like that," Sevex said. "It needed only a vessel to respond to its desire."

He tossed a small hammer at Luc. The priest caught it with the new hand and twirled it, feeling the weight and motion. Tears wet the corners of his eyes as he realized he could fight with this hand—truly fight, as he once had.

"There are no words to thank you for this," he said.

"The pleasure is mine," Sevex replied. "What purpose has invention without application? Such wonders we have planned." He walked over to a thick, locked tome and caressed its cover— Luc recognized it as the same one he'd carried on their flight south. "Ah. You can thank me by not dying on whatever misadventures you lot are engaging tonight. And do not let the others die. Consider that hand my contribution to your efforts."

Luc placed the hammer on the table. It was such a simple action. Yet, he was at once amazed by how gently he accomplished it and by how familiar it felt—a phantom limb given substance.

"I swear to you as a Blade of Atora, I will fight as never before."

• • •

Azran woke up again. Neither he nor Francesca seemed able to get comfortable. He had dreamt of the attack on Sevex's house all those weeks ago. It was the first time since they slept in the smugglers' stables.

He rolled over to find Francesca gone. He opened his eyes. The door was ajar, and light leaked through the hall from downstairs.

"It's time, then," he said to the empty room. He stood, stretched, and paused on his way out the door. A small nick remained on its inner surface, right at head level. Azran recalled slamming the door into his pursuer's face. *A tooth mark, probably.*

He looked back into the room he had almost died in. One of many, now, he supposed. "What a strange life we lead."

He went into the hallway and down to the living room, where Francesca, Luc, and Sevex waited. Sevex sat, pounding back wine. The other two shifted from foot to foot.

Azran nodded a greeting to Sevex, then wrapped his arms around Francesca. "Des and Varja?" he asked.

"Gearing up," Luc said.

"Armor, right," Azran muttered. "You should have some, Cesca."

"I do." She pointed at a pair of bracers, gauntlets, and a single pauldron on a table.

"Just a few bits I scrounged up from abandoned projects," Sevex said.

"Thanks," Azran said. "You should lie low tonight, Sev."

"Oh, I intend to." He took another swallow of wine. "You people are insane, have I ever told you that?"

● ● ●

Varja stood before the foot the bed, looking at her armor laid out on the unfixed sheets. She already wore her arming coat and other underlayers. A long mail hauberk rested beside a studded brigandine. Steel pauldrons, vambraces, and greaves sat above and below. Mail-backed gauntlets waited to grasp the hilt of her longsword, itself leaning nearby.

The gear was unpolished, but oiled and looked after. A patch of darker, replaced links on the hauberk reminded Varja of the spear that pierced the armor, then her flesh on a sun-drenched beach west of Liore. She picked up one vambrace, tracing her fingers over the many scratches and fine grooves. She tossed it back on the bed. Since she landed in Lunatel, she hadn't worn this armor. There were times in Procumes that she trained in it, to remember its weight and capabilities. But otherwise, this was war gear, and Varja hadn't gone to war in a long time.

The Second Flame. Breaking the Siege of Novos. The single-squad trek up the River Muntherzix. That was a different Varja Kepeskeižir who had fought those battles. Her life had changed so much in so short a time.

She looked at Des, who held the drapes aside to peer out at lamp-lit streets. Des was ready. She wore bracers, greaves, and lamed pauldrons in addition to her usual vest. Her fighting knife was sheathed openly on her back and a dagger on each hip. There were more blades yet hidden.

Varja took a deep breath. Enough reminiscing. It was time.

"Can you help get my armor on, love?" she asked.

Des turned, eyeing the arrangement on the bed. "It's not really my area, but sure."

"I'll walk you through." Varja picked up the hauberk and slipped it over her head. The weight fell mainly on her shoulders. The hems of its split skirt reached the top of her knees. "Those straps on the back—tighten those." Varja did the same around her waist, then the ties where the sleeves ended at her elbows. The heaviness became more distributed.

Next came the brigandine to guard her torso. It was also tightened to fit. In turn, Varja held each pauldron in place while Des tied it beneath her arm. She pulled on gauntlets and strapped vambraces over while Des attached the greaves.

When it was all done, Varja tested her range of motion and the security of each piece. She would be slower in this, but not as slow as her opponents often thought. She stood from checking the greaves to see Des beaming at her.

"Now there's the warrior I saw in the ring," Des said.

Varja almost blushed but grabbed her sword instead. She fastened the baldric in place and said, "You haven't yet seen the warrior." She headed for the door, missing a step as Des slapped her ass and quickstepped past.

"I'm sure I will."

37

Francesca belted on her rapier as she heard Varja's weighted footsteps descend the stairs; she didn't hear Des's, but the smaller woman entered the room first.

"No time to waste," Francesca said. "We're going to the Ciusa estate in the Rosaer Hills, not far from the palace. Clan vampires will be everywhere. Stay close to me and Azran."

"What about before that?" Des asked.

Francesca took her meaning. "He and I wear our hoods and stay in the middle of you four. If we see Solari, we take the nearest exit."

"And when we get there?" Varja asked.

"We find Amadore. You let me worry about what happens next." Azran gave her a concerned look, but she put it out of mind. She knew he'd be there if she needed him. For what, she didn't know. Her reply was intended to stall. "Let's go."

She headed for the back door, via the kitchen.

"Goodbye, Sev," Azran said, following.

"Good luck, all of you."

"You have a nice home," Varja said.

"Thank you, unknown war-maiden."

An alley ran behind the house, beyond a small, neat lawn. The group made for it, Azran and Des on point. They followed the back lane to an open street and signaled that the coast was clear for now.

On the street, they formed up as Francesca had suggested. Guard patrols were thick here, as Sevex had said, but seemed lax due to their distance from the barricades. Nighttime traffic progressed much as it always had. Here, in the wealthier districts, carriages were common—albeit with more armed guards than usual. Likely, that contributed to Francesca and the others blending in.

As they transitioned into the eastern estate neighborhoods, where the real money of Aure was, the streets emptied of civilians. There was no cutoff point, but the gradual dispersal continued until Francesca gave a thorough look and saw only caped city guards and tabard-clad urban legionaries. The gazes upon the little band became more alert, more severe, more suspicious. And under that scrutiny, Francesca began to feel vulnerable.

"How much farther?" Azran asked. He could feel it, too.

"We're getting close," she replied. "Turn right at the next street."

As they rounded the corner, the barricades came into view. The urban landscape sloped up to the Rosaer Hills, the high ground of Aure's old families. Halfway up the rise and bisecting the lane, overturned wagons and stacked crates and barrels marked the line of siege. Portions of the makeshift wall were charred.

Arrows protruded like thorns, and spears formed a palisade in the middle. On the far side, the lamps were broken and dark; on the near, braziers and torches had been added.

The buildings on the living side had been fortified into barracks—windows boarded but for arrow slits, piled bricks used for rooftop battlements. Guards and soldiers watched the east, none closer than two blocks from the line. Some turned to observe the newcomers.

"Stay calm," Francesca said, as much to herself as to the others.

"And be ready to run," Des added.

There were still several blocks to the barricade, and the guards seemed to accept their passage for the time being.

Goosebumps spread across Francesca's skin. She forced her breathing to steady. It was all so quiet. Guards ceased their conversations as the group passed. Braziers crackled, Varja's armor clinked, and their boots tapped the stone, but nothing more.

Another block went by. Three to go.

"You in the street! Halt and be recognized!"

"Run," Des hissed.

They ran. Heavy footfalls took up pursuit, and shouts sounded from three sides.

"Stop them!"

"Vampires!"

"Shoot them!"

"No, men, capture!"

"Sir!"

Even armored, Varja kept pace with the others. Francesca knew Azran could go faster, but he stayed close.

A pair of guards burst from an alley. One swung the butt of a halberd. Azran dropped low, slid underneath, and sprinted onward. The other guard grabbed for Des. Varja juked around him and planted a heavy slug in his side as she passed. He buckled, and Des and Varja ran on.

Almost there. Francesca spared a glance back—at least a dozen guards were on their heels.

Azran practically ran up the barricade, at a low point to the side of the spears. At the peak, he turned to help the others up.

Francesca leapt, planted a foot on the underside of a tipped wagon, and caught his hand. Beside her, Des hit the top and pulled Luc up. Varja jumped, caught the lip, and Luc and Des grabbed her arms as her feet climbed.

The guards reached them. One snatched Varja's leg and pulled. She kicked his face with her other boot. Another guard hooked her shoulder with the curved backspike of his polearm and pulled.

Something whistled past Francesca. The guard with the polearm collapsed, a bolt buried in his eye socket.

"Cover!" one of the other pursuers shouted, and the guards all fell prone or fell back.

Varja made the top. All five of them descended the dark side and hit the nearest alley. After a minute of quiet, Francesca edged back toward the street.

"What are you doing?" Azran whispered.

"Put your hood down," she said. She reached into a belt pouch and pulled forth a chained token, a small, black disk her brother had given her years ago. She held it in plain view and stepped into the street. "Praise Tenebra," she announced to the darkness.

There was no response. She replaced the token in the pouch and beckoned the others.

"Azran and I lead now. We're almost there." She pointed to the tall spire of the estate, a dark shape in the dark sky.

The city was damaged here. They passed two manors burned
to rubble. Some houses were bright inside or sported broken
windows, with some overlap. Whether the lit ones housed
vampires or living now trapped on this side of the barricades,
Francesca did not know. She saw obscure silhouettes here or
there, on the streets or rooftops. But overall, the quiet had
resumed. The seized turf of Filvié Noctirin was waiting, taking a
deep, collective breath.

At the Ciusa grounds, Francesca led the others to a discreet
servants' entrance—a small gate through the wrought iron fence,
across a bluish, overgrown lawn, and to the door of the kitchens.
No one, vampire or otherwise, guarded the place. That only
further confirmed Francesca's suspicion. Amadore craved solitude,
and like Luc, claimed faith as his armor.

The kitchen door was locked, but she remembered the false
brick that hid the key. She turned the lock, and it clicked.

As she hesitated to enter, Azran put a hand on her shoulder.
"We're with you."

Francesca heard blades unsheathe. She drew her rapier, turned
the latch, and gave the door a gentle push before going on guard.

The kitchens were dark and cold. They smelled of old blood.

• • •

Francesca took the first step in, and the others followed, weapons
ready—Des with one of her hip daggers, Azran with his, Luc with
a sword in each hand, the shorter blade defensively horizontal.
Varja took rearguard, longsword in half-grip. She scanned the dim
interior, pivoting right and left, focusing on every flicker of
movement and listening for sounds beyond their light footfalls.

They crossed a dining room, a bit brighter from the starlight and distant, ambient city light streaming through broad and tall gallery windows. The chairs of the long table were pulled out. An ash-filled hearth on the interior wall still radiated a little warmth.

Varja turned to watch behind them, wary of the new flank they presented. Past the dining room was a wide hallway with doors ajar to lavish sitting rooms. She peered into each one as they continued.

At an intersecting hallway, Francesca turned them right. Varja looked ahead of them and saw, through open double doors, a grand, sweeping staircase like one would find in a great entry hall.

A creak and woody groan snapped her back on watch, to the pitch black far end of the corridor. She paused, listening, but heard nothing further and resumed her backward stepping.

They entered the welcome hall. Varja took stock of the many points of entry—the closed doors to the foyer, the stairs to a balcony with many more doors, the way they came, and the mirrored hallway on the opposite side.

"Where now?" Luc asked, hushed.

"My gut tells me upstairs," Francesca whispered back.

Varja looked at the landing again. Then, a flash of movement jerked her gaze back to the floor. She shouted a warning just as the form met Francesca. She seemed to have caught it, too—steel rang on steel as she parried with her rapier.

Another flash, this one made of light, momentarily blinded them all. Varja blinked through it and started toward the fight.

Francesca parried again, but the cloaked figure slipped around her riposte, locked a free arm around her shoulder, and brought its sword to her neck. It was almost too fast to follow.

"Stop!" a familiar voice shouted from the hall across the room.

Varja's eyes adjusted to the light. She saw a silver-haired elf ready to cut down Francesca. Azran froze mid-charge. Luc circled wide, scanning for threats. Des was almost at the elf's back, dagger ready, but also stopped. Varja followed her gaze to the speaker, and her eyes went wide at the sight of Seneskar's old human guise.

"Exus, let her go."

"She's a vampire," the elf stated. "Her soul reeks of the same malaise that fills this manor."

"These aren't our enemies. I know them," Seneskar said, looking at Varja.

"Very well." The elf released Francesca, spinning and dashing out of reach of any retaliation. "Lower the light."

The room dimmed to a sourceless, candle-like glow. Varja shoved aside her mixed feelings about Seneskar and joined her friends in facing off against the unexpected party.

The elf stood straight, blade lowered. Seneskar stepped into the room, followed by two hooded women and a man. Two held rapiers, while the third was unarmed and, in Varja's experience, likely more dangerous.

"The fuck are you doing here?" Varja asked.

"I could ask you the same," Seneskar replied. "Not still on your little mission, are you, Varja?"

"No."

"Well, I'm still on mine."

"Then what is your purpose here?" the elf asked.

"Personal." Francesca spat on the floor.

Seneskar stepped between both parties, keeping his hands out wide. He addressed Varja. "We are looking for the new master of this house."

Francesca's blade lowered a couple inches.

"You know him?" Seneskar asked her.

"Who are your friends?" Varja asked him.

Seneskar gave them a glance. "Godshadows."

"We haven't the time for this," the elf said. He strode up next to Seneskar. "Amadore Darani. Where is he?"

"Here. He should be," Francesca replied. "What's your business with him?"

The elf's sword twitched. Varja took a step closer to Francesca.

"To stop him," the elf said.

"Then we have a common purpose," Des said. "No need for blood between us."

The elf gave them all an inscrutable, perhaps evaluating look.

Seneskar chuckled. "Strange how such things work out. Let us lower our blades, then. Help is appreciated."

Both sides relaxed somewhat. Varja debated telling the Godshadows they had allied with a Faithful dragon. But what would be the point? War made strange allies, and she had not forgotten Seneskar's role in her personal awakening. The world was more complicated than she had once thought, and now he did not seem so much the villain she had once believed him.

Her thoughts must have shown on her face because Seneskar gave her a pleading look. After a moment, she responded with a slight nod and lowered her guard. At that, her friends followed suit, though they still watched like hawks.

"You say he should be here," the elf said to Francesca. "But he is not. We have swept the house, the tower, and we are the only ones present."

Francesca's shoulders slumped. "Then I don't—I was sure he was."

The unarmed Godshadow spoke. "A few hours ago, you'd have been correct."

"So, we missed him?" Azran asked.

The elf nodded. "He's already moved on, and so we must move."

"Where?" Seneskar asked.

"The palace."

He nodded. "Those runes."

The elf sheathed his sword. "Let's go." As he walked toward the foyer, he called back, "Stay here, civilians. This is our matter to—"

"Amadore is my brother."

He stopped and whirled on Francesca. "That would explain much," he muttered. "Would he answer to you?"

"I'll make him."

"Then come. All of you. More blades, at the very least."

The other Godshadows followed, then Francesca, Azran, and Luc. Seneskar lingered. Varja glared at him. Des stepped up beside her and did the same.

"Don't make me regret this," Varja said finally.

Des sheathed her dagger but did not take her hand from it. "Don't make her regret this."

Seneskar gave a halting smile. "Noted." He headed for the doors, and the women followed.

• • •

The priest stood on the desolate thoroughfare, facing the tall gates of the Golden Palace. The plaza formed the space between, empty, lit by lamps and the reflective, gold-tiled roofs of the ancient structure. It was so bright down here, unlike the pristine blackness above.

The priest perched on the edge of an eclipse, and so did not fear the light.

He limped toward the dragonsteel gates. Armored figures of Invictis guards watched him from the parapet, curious.

He could feel the lines of connection encircling the palace, brimming with stored power. He reached into his shroud-like robes and retrieved the pouch Zerexis had given him.

The guards watched, heedless. Their ignorance was delicious.

The priest's withered leg stepped on the line. He held the pouch aloft and intoned.

"Daesïn animavi-echïnir maetrïzi ïn Iarxess echsotak!"

Far to either side of the priest, and along each side of the rectangular palace wall, the hidden runes flared, melting the stones that covered them. Arcs of white energy bent and forked like lightning into the grounds from all sides. Lightning without thunder—no sound but the thuds of corpses and ringing of steel on stone.

The gate sentries, like every member of the imperial bodyguard order in the vicinity, fell dead without a gasp.

Then came the shattering of glass. It was a secondary effect of the runes—a show, but one the priest appreciated as every lamp in the plaza and thoroughfare burst. Only the lights of the palace grounds and the city beyond remained.

The eclipse had begun.

The priest glided with ease through Tenebra's shadow, approaching the gates. Other vampires, trusted and loyal, followed him. They heard the expected clatter of grappling hooks hitting stone—the Jade Scorpions scaling other walls. The mercenaries would soon open the gates. And then, for the first time since vengeful rebels murdered Emperor Vylosis centuries ago, Valentreid blood would stain the Golden Palace.

The priest waited. As he did, he reached out with his angel-granted power.

Dear Francesca—she was in the city, as his dreams had portended. She was coming closer.

38

From their vantage point, Seneskar saw the other high ground of Aure—the city center, home to the palace, mausoleum, and Academy. The palace darkened from the violent flash moments before. He made out figures cresting the wall and moving unmolested. There were many, and Seneskar began to wonder if they would complete the other half of his mission for him. If not, there would be plenty of chaos in which to operate.

He would have to be cautious, though. The Godshadows seemed to trust him—it was a guarded, professional trust, but nonetheless. Varja and her friends were a different matter. The priest eyed him with particular suspicion. The woman with the knives even more so—likely Varja's lover, given her attachment to Varja's side. She was dangerous. She had killed more than once.

So, Seneskar kept close to his clearer allies. And useful allies they were—the barricades proved no obstacle. Word was spreading through the city of strange happenings at the palace—whispers of coups and the recent arrival of an ambitious general. Exus and his people flashed seals of their order, and the guards let them pass, wishing them the gods' protection.

The group hustled onward, catching more frequent and more precise snippets of rumor. Mercenaries, the Jade Scorpions. Plaza lights darkened. The palace gates opening wide for more assailants, these ones unidentified. A blinding flash of soundless lightning. Guard captains marshaled, waiting for orders that would not come.

They approached from the east, Exus leading them past one of the runes they had found. There was only a pit of blackened, melted, and re-hardened stone. The spot still radiated heat.

An explosion rent the air above the palace, smoke lingering in the still air.

"Black powder," Nello, the listener twin, said.

"What for?" his sister asked.

Exus looked at the group, formulating. "Daia, Nello, Elyra, take the east wall. Seneskar, come with me over the north."

"What of us?" Azran asked.

"I don't care. The gates, if it please you. They look unguarded."

"Excuse me, but fuck you. Are we bait while you flank?"

Francesca put a hand on Azran's shoulder. "It's fine. My brother will be front and center anyway."

Varja unsheathed her longsword. "Not my first time charging up the middle. At least there are no fire dragons this time."

Luc drew and twirled his swords, limning them with a faint glow. "Let us be quick, then. Atora guide our blades."

"And Mortis guard our souls," Exus said. He drew steel and took off north.

Seneskar gave Varja a salute and followed, pondering what shapes would suit this situation—the time for discretion was over.

• • •

The gates were indeed open and unguarded. Sentries lay dead, flat on the ground or slumped awkwardly against the walls and gatehouse. No wounds showed, nor even damage to their polished breastplates. It was as if they had simply ceased living. There was no pattern or order to the destruction. The only sign anyone had entered was the trail of snuffed lights leading across the grounds to the grand doors of the palace.

Azran, Francesca, Luc, Des, and Varja made their way along marble paths, past a long pool with many statuary fountains, through gloomy gardens of dying seasonal flowers. To either side stood the curving, colonnaded wings of the palace quarters and galleries. From here, they looked like massive jaws about to close on the foolish prey walking straight in. Some lights were on, other windows were dark. A thump and crack echoed across the open space. Their vision jerked to the source—a figure slumping down a glass pane, leaving a bloody smear.

Ahead, past the skywalk connecting the wings, the open dining area before the throne room was marred by a few proper, bloody corpses—staff and servants that had been in the way. Beyond that, the gilded doors stood ajar.

The throne room bustled with masses of armed individuals. Shouts, screaming, clangs, and thuds told of a subsiding fight.

Francesca gave one last look to the others and led the way in, rapier-first.

•••

Zerexis stepped back from the dead orc, the scion's final bodyguard. The angel turned to the priest and nodded.

The priest approached the scion, General Catia Valentrae. Though dressed only in a silk nightgown, she stood straight and tall, her jaw set, her whole form ready to face a dignified death worthy of her name. She did not know their purpose here—that Zerexis had chosen her as Tenebra's vessel, Her path back into the Mortal Realm.

The vampires and mercenaries had done well, herding Catia here to the throne room while holing up her father, Emperor Arcaeus, in the royal quarters. Now, many of those warriors formed a circle around the priest and the angel and the scion. Others lingered in the shadows of the great columns edging the wide hall. A rare magnuri vampire, massive and tusked, perched on and dwarfed the bejeweled marble throne.

The center of the circle lay beneath the hole blasted in the high, shallow-domed ceiling. The unlight of Tenebra's new moon filled that space, giving the Goddess a path to Her new body.

The priest loomed over Catia. Zerexis stood opposite, wings spread, ready to begin the ritual. He placed his unmarred hand on her shoulder, but her eyes went to the twisted one that now glowed with a purple-black light. He plunged the clawlike appendage into her chest, clutched her heart, and pulled it free in a spray of blood.

He examined the organ, then looked up at Zerexis. The angel's face wore their version of puzzled indignation. The priest dropped the heart onto the scion's corpse.

"Fool," spat Zerexis. "What have you done?"

"We need her not," said the priest. He turned to the doors. His sister, his dear Francesca, entered, followed by the deluded Azran and their living pets.

At the priest's willful projection, the circle broke to clear Francesca's path.

• • •

Francesca took in the scene as best she could. Dead guards, dead vampires, and a woman with her heart lying beside the bloody hole in her shift. More bodies her brother left in his wake.

And Amadore stood there, his mangled hand dripping red, an angel—this one corporeal—behind him, and a deranged grin on his face.

Azran was next to her, her friends just behind.

"Welcome, dear sister, to the fulfillment of your purpose!" Amadore extended his unbloodied, still-human hand. "Come, stand in Tenebra's gaze."

Francesca held her blade before her and charged. All thought fled her mind but for the pain he had caused her and those around her. The fuel had been built higher and higher, and now she allowed it to spark and flame.

She thrust for Amadore's chest. Somehow, even with his calm stance, he shifted sideways. Her blade struck only a grazing blow, tearing robes and drawing a thin line of blood. Azran, rushing in after, had similar luck stabbing at his back.

Before the others reached the fray, the angel vanished and reappeared in front of them. It swept one hand in an arc that trailed smoke, and Des, Luc, and Varja were thrown back several paces.

Francesca cut and thrust at Amadore, who continued to shift just out of reach.

"Kill the others," he said. "They are not needed."

The circle broke, vampires and living charging past Francesca and driving the trio of experienced fighters back.

"So angry, dear Francesca. This is a time for joy."

"Why won't you leave me alone!" She growled each word between strikes.

Her brother laughed. "You are the one who has come to me—come to embrace your birthright."

Azran grabbed Amadore's robes with his free hand, knife poised to strike. The angel latched onto Azran's wrist, ripped him loose, and threw him back. He managed to land in a roll.

Amadore caught Francesca's rapier with his twisted hand and held it. She kicked at his leg, but her foot hit something that felt like a tree trunk.

"Enough of this," he said, the mirth gone. He grabbed hold of her with his normal hand and rotated around to her back. He held her pinned to his front. The mangled hand tore the rapier from her grasp and glowed with the darkness of his soul.

"I have sacrificed so much for you, dear Francesca. But if that is the toll it took to see you ascend, it was worth every agony. It is time, Zerexis."

"Very well, then. So it shall be."

The gnarled fingers entered the side of Francesca's neck, opening an artery and slicing across the front. Blood poured from her and blackness closed in fast.

• • •

Varja backstepped and parried left and right as the crowd came on. The vampires wielded swords, knives, and an assortment of other weapons. The mercenaries wore short blades affixed to the top of each forearm—the signature of the famous Jade Scorpions.

She countered when she could, cleaving one Scorpion's arm open, slicing a vampire's chest while circling to use him as an obstacle. The few blows that met her were dampened by her armor, but there were many more to come.

Luc adopted a defensive posture of his own. He held his longer sword reversed by the ricasso, using it as a vertical shield. His short blade, in his main hand, darted out, landing hits between its own parries.

Des darted and dodged, striking the most blows of the three— using Varja and Luc as shields and distractions, stabbing and slicing the foes they threw off balance.

But there were too many, Varja knew. They all had to get on the offensive, and soon.

She got in a strong bind with one vampire, levered his sword wide, and bashed his face with her false edge. He fell back, and a Scorpion took his place, stabbing high and low. Varja slid into a half-grip and deflected the high, counting on her armor for the low. Her mail did turn the blade, but the blunt force would leave a bruise. Varja gripped her blade with both hands and came down with a murder-stroke. The mercenary crossed his blades above his head, but the heavy pommel drove through and brained him.

Another vampire got behind Varja during the exchange. Her hand pulled back Varja's face as a blade came for her throat.

Des interposed her own hand while stabbing a dagger past Varja's cheek and into the vampire's eye. She caught Varja's look and dropped prone. The crude axe meant for her back fell short of

Varja's front. Varja slashed across, opening the axe-wielder's throat.

Des rolled to her feet, grabbing the woodcutter's tool and going back to back with Varja as enemies closed in around them.

On the far side of the crowd, Luc circled wide of clusters, felling foe after foe in second-long duels.

From the other direction, they heard Azran's anguished cry.

• • •

Time slowed for Azran—no, he was slow. He ran toward Francesca, but it was like running underwater, or in a nightmare.

Someone grabbed him from behind, pinning one arm to his back. He arched his spine in pain.

"Let it happen," the vampire responsible hissed.

Wincing, his teeth clenched, his heart ready to burst from his chest, Azran watched.

Amadore, Francesca's brother, pulled her head back, exposing her bleeding throat to the black circle in the ceiling. The angel appeared next to her, slit its own wrist, and let the blood fall onto her wound. The angel's blood was not black, as Azran had expected, but red as his wife's pooling on the floor.

The immortal and the priest began chanting an old tongue, calling to Tenebra. As they litanied, Amadore's eyes glowed purple, and purplish-black energy entered Francesca from where he held her.

Azran did not understand what was happening, but he saw a mirror in this event. His wife's weak, limp form, the blood leaving her—it was so like his suicide attempt. And that gave him hope— he could save her, as she had saved him.

He ignored the pain in his shoulder—what was that to slitting one's own wrists?—and yanked the joint out of its socket. He swallowed the nausea, took the knife in his other hand. He rotated, plunged the blade into his captor's neck, spun again, and went to his dying Francesca.

• • •

The melee separated them again. Varja sidestepped a vampire's thrust, already countering with a chop from her high left that met shoulder and cut through the vampire's collarbone.

Another whipped a chain to wrap around Varja's sword. Before she could wind it free, yet another vampire rushed her with a shield. Varja put her left bracer up to block, but the force still bashed her face and knocked her to the ground. Dazed, she rolled, then realized she was no longer holding her sword.

The shieldbearer pursued, swiping an axe at her an inch above the floor. Varja slowed it by catching the haft, but it still bashed against her side. The shield went up to chop down, but a thrown knife stuck into the vampire's chest. As he staggered back a step, Varja reached, searching. Her hand closed on a familiar grip. She stood and thrust, impaling the vampire's abdomen.

A fresh surge of adrenalin lent her speed. She parried and countered a Scorpion, then went fully on the offensive. The bloodlust that had carried her through the campaigns of the west surged forth.

Void. Slash. Thrust. Half-sword parry, bind, blunt strike. Void. Strike. Strike faster than they can. Cut off lines of attack through ferocity, instinct. Strike in the moment. Leave them broken and bloody as you advance. Face the storm, become the storm.

403

Varja cleaved through her enemies, her sword slicing their flesh and even armor as it never had. Her blade was lightning, their bodies drought-dried timber.

• • •

Azran reached the pooling blood—Francesca's blood—and fell to the floor. He sucked and lapped, cupping some in his hands and licking it off.

Amadore and the angel continued chanting, heedless of his crazed efforts.

Francesca experienced all this, but distantly. She was drifting into the dark, like Azran had described the moments before death. Sounds grew fuzzy and louder, not quieter. The only thing she felt with any clarity was the beating of her heart. It pumped still, sending her blood out as something else replaced it. It felt like blood, and yet there was some foreign presence to it. It felt alive, awake.

Her fading consciousness brushed something, then. She imagined herself floating through a void, a starless night sky. With excruciating effort, she turned to see what she had touched.

She saw nothing—not with her eyes. The darkness before her was vast, cold, conscious. It watched her, reached out with an unseen appendage and caressed her. Its touch was corruption, leaving a sensation of energy but not temperature, peeling away mortal flesh, leaving her exposed to the enormity of this presence.

Her soul began to bleed, and the thing, the touch, seeped into the wounds.

• • •

When he had drunk all he could gather, Azran dragged his dagger across one wrist. Fire ran up his arm, but again he paid the pain no heed. He sliced the top of Amadore's unmarred hand. The priest ceased chanting and hissed, letting go. Azran pressed his bleeding wrist onto Francesca's open wound.

"Deluded fool!" Amadore shouted in his face. "She is already gone. You cannot bring her back—not with your unblessed blood."

Azran ignored him. He was beyond fear of failure.

The angel wrapped one large hand around Azran's neck and pulled him off. "We are nearly done," the creature said. "Let us finish in a more secluded locale." It threw Azran to the ground. It placed one hand on Francesca, one on her brother, and closed its pitch eyes.

Azran lunged across the floor and wrapped his arms around one of the angel's towering legs, and the world lurched sideways.

39

D es, one arm locked around a mercenary's shoulder from behind, opened his throat with her fighting knife. She shoved his shocked form forward.

A vampire sprang at her, swinging a meat cleaver. Des ducked, backstepped a second swing, and dove under a third, past her assailant. She grabbed a spiked billy club, rolled back to her feet, and drove long nails into the vampire's skull. Without slowing, she snatched the cleaver and dropped below a mercenary's thrust. The blade sliced through boot leather and bisected a foot.

Des launched forward, grabbed a fallen crossbow, and rolled onto her back as the crippled man pursued. She fired point-blank into his empty eye socket.

She leapt back into a crouch and surveyed the room. Bodies lay all across a floor slick with blood. Of their enemies, only three remained—the ogre on the throne and two mercenaries next to him on the dais.

Luc caught his breath against a pillar, bleeding from scrapes and cuts beneath his torn, red-stained clothes. Soft prayers fell from his lips.

Varja, too, was exhausted. She had taken a knee, wiping blood from a gash across her cheek while her other hand held that strange longsword she had acquired over her shoulder. The blade still sparked faintly, but the lightning that had limned it was gone.

Azran, Francesca, and the two monsters were gone.

Des's own fatigue hit her then, as did her dozen bruises and the shallow cut in the crook of her right elbow. She tore off a piece of shirt and wrapped it as she approached Varja. "Remind me never to piss you off," she said. "That was incredible."

Varja looked up at her as though startled.

"Are you okay?"

Varja stood. "Yeah, fine." She brought the sword down and stared at it, as if for the first time. "Where did this come from?"

"You picked it up," Des said.

"I could have sworn I grabbed my own blade."

"That is one of the Dragonblades," Luc said, coming over. "I never thought I'd see one outside an illustration."

"I thought the Dragonblades were the emperor's guards," Des said.

"Yes, named for the swords they carry. This is Tae'ezis, the Stormblade."

Varja continued to gaze at the weapon. Its blade was like polished silver, its crossguard sculpted like jagged storm clouds. The pommel was a dragon's eye. "It feels...alive."

Luc nodded. "Perhaps that is why you thought it yours—the soul within answered to the call of your ancestry."

Varja hefted and tilted it, testing its balance. It was longer than hers, but not by much.

Des searched the floor for familiar forms, keeping a wary eye on the ogre and mercs—none of whom seemed eager.

"Where are they?" she asked. She could spot no trace of Azran or Francesca, or the two freaks they had been fighting.

"Gone, if you mean who I think," one of the mercenaries said.

Des took a threatening step forward. "What do you know of it? What is all this?"

"Ah, damned if I know anything. We was just brought for some kinda coup. All this magic?" The man shrugged.

"Where would they have gone?" Luc asked as he and Varja joined Des.

"I just toldja what I know."

"Up." The answer came from the hall behind the throne. Exus and Seneskar entered, both bloodied. Seneskar was still human in shape, but his exposed skin was covered in silver scales. He was taller and broader in bone structure and muscle. Bits of bone spiked out from his knuckles and forearms. Those protrusions were coated in too much red for it to all be his.

"I sensed them move," Exus said. "They're at the top of Solris's Tower. But this one insisted we gather you first."

"Without Daia or the twins, we need help," Seneskar said.

"Let's go." Des looked at the mercenary who had spoken. "Unless you're going to stop us."

"Ah...." He laughed nervously. "Hey, big guy, make yourself useful, why don'tcha?"

"Aye," the other merc said. "We're gonna...regroup?"

"Right."

They slinked off to the side of the room, heading for the main doors.

"Fine," the ogre said with a rumbling voice. He opened his eyes, red like blood. "It was a fine seat."

The big vampire stood, towering at least eight feet tall and half as wide. He picked up a brutal, flanged mace from next to the throne.

Luc looked at Des and Varja. "You two go."

"Crazy bastard," Des mumbled. "No."

The ogre charged down the steps of the dais and swung the mace in a wide arc. The trio dodged. Luc interposed himself between his companions and the brute.

"Go, now. Save our friends. I have this."

"We're not leaving you alone," Des insisted.

The ogre turned and locked eyes with the priest, sizing him up. The vampire bellowed a wordless war cry and charged again. Luc circled to keep between him and the passage to the tower.

"Go!" His blades flared, and the white entered his eyes. He grinned like the face on his medallion. "I am not alone. I have Atora at my back!"

With a laugh, he ran at the ogre, slid under his mace, and nicked his leg.

"He's mad," Des said. "It's best we go."

Varja nodded, and the pair ran into the tunnel, leaving another friend to take the hit.

What had Des done to surround herself with such people?

● ● ●

More guard corpses littered the halls behind the throne room, along with scattered servants, mercenaries, and vampires. The guards, again, displayed no signs of violent death. The dead

410

assailants, however, were burned and hacked. Varja's intuition told her they died by Tae'ezis's siblings.

At a T-shaped intersection, a continuing struggle echoed from the left passage.

"Right," Exus ordered.

Seneskar caught the elf's shoulder. "That's the private studies. The tower is past the royal quarters."

Exus flashed him a curious look but nodded. Varja also wondered how her kinsman knew that.

They went left, past luxurious, carved doors that had been bashed open. Ahead, the sounds of conflict subsided.

Then, rounding a corner, they met a half-dozen vampires and Scorpions. They seemed to be catching their breath, regaining their feet as Varja and the others came into view.

Varja and Seneskar took the front. She narrowed her profile to void and counter-thrust from the hip, burying the sparking blade in a vampire's guts. The power of the sword charred clothes and flesh.

Seneskar put his forearms up like shields against a Scorpion's strikes. His punch snapped the mercenary's head back.

Des fired her salvaged crossbow past Varja's falling opponent, at the Scorpion hesitating behind. The bolt stuck in the mercenary's neck, and Varja finished him with a high downward cut.

Exus slid under Seneskar's wide reach and punched a forearm blade of his own into the soft flesh behind a surprised vampire's jawline. With his sword, he parried left and right, high and low against a Scorpion until he seized an opening and slashed a leg, then an armpit. The mercenary fell, bleeding out fast.

One vampire remained. A gnoll in plate armor emerged from a side passage and plunged a half-gripped longsword into her back.

A dull, bone white aura surrounded the blade. The vampire, instead of stiffening, went limp and slid from the weapon.

The gnoll went on middle guard, wary. He called in a voice like a snarling wolf, "They killed the attackers!"

Varja noticed the crescent moon crossguard and dragon-eye pommel of the gnoll's weapon. An elf woman in matching armor and wielding a bright blade also entered the hallway.

"Dragonblades," Exus said. "I am the Third Hunter of the Sunrise Chapter. We make for the Tower of Solris. The orchestrator of this madness is at the top."

The gnoll stepped aside. "We guard the emperor. Go, Godshadow."

As they passed, Varja looked down the side passage. It was obscured by a piled wall of corpses, but she saw other figures and blades beyond. Seneskar, too, peered with interest, then shied from the Dragonblades' watchful eyes.

"Wait," the elf guard said. "You carry Storm's blade."

"Where is he?" the gnoll snarled.

"Fallen," Varja replied.

"Return the sword, then."

"No, Moon, look," the gnoll's companion said. "It answers her." She fixed Varja with a stern gaze. "Wield it well. It will tell you when it wishes to return to its siblings."

Varja nodded in return and continued on.

Hustling, they reached a spiraling staircase in the center of a circular room. Urged on by the closeness to their goal, Varja and the others took the steps two at a time, ascending the Tower of Solris.

• • •

Luc ducked out behind a pillar, gaining momentary cover. Fatigue and wounds from the previous fight were catching up with him, prayers be damned. He had scored a handful of hits on the magnuri, but his swords were like knives to the beastly vampire. Inversely, one solid blow from his opponent would shatter Luc's bones.

The ogre rounded the pillar, swinging that mace. Luc ducked low and propelled himself backward. He entered the open space once more, feet moving him in his circular stance.

The ogre came on, heavy steps cracking the bones of many corpses. As he came within reach and swung the mace, Luc dashed inside and past. But the ogre had seen this move already. An arm like a catapult's caught Luc and flung him ten feet back.

Luc tripped over a body as he landed, and his foe was there to strike. He let go of his arming sword and pushed himself to the side. The mace sent up a splatter of gore from the corpse on the floor.

As the ogre pulled back, Luc hooked his foe's arm and rode it up. The brute tried to throw him off, but Luc switched his short sword to his main hand and held the ogre's hair with his metal one. His eyes flared anew, and so did the blade. He plunged the charged weapon into the back of the ogre's skull. It sank to the hilt, and the behemoth toppled forward, stiff.

Luc was thrown onto his back. The sword remained embedded, likely there to stay. He stood slowly and retrieved his arming sword.

Pain hit him then, deep in his chest, from the ogre's throw.

Trampling noise. Luc looked up from his fallen enemy to see more mercenaries—many more—swarm into the room. *So, the regrouping wasn't a bluff after all.*

"That's one of em," the mercenary from earlier said. His comrades went into fighting crouches.

As they closed in, Luc spat a gout of bloody saliva and smiled. In his core, deeper than the pain of broken ribs, he felt his god urging him on with every beat of his heart. His eyes flashed white again.

"No hero stands alone," he recited internally, *"when he has Atora at his back."*

A mercenary sprang forward and thrust. Luc parried with his remaining sword. His metal hand shot out and clutched the Scorpion's windpipe. He squeezed, crushing it.

The attacker fell. The others hesitated, and in the span, Luc laughed and charged.

40

Azran was cold. It was darker now, and he knew they were closer to the new moon.

The angel kicked him aside, and a low wall stopped him from falling off the tower. Straining, he reached a sitting position and pressed down on his bleeding wrist. Through bleary eyes, he watched the angel and Amadore loom over Francesca's prone form.

"He mingled his blood in hers," the angel said.

"It matters not. His common blood cannot corrupt the transference."

They began chanting once more.

Azran despaired. This was beyond him—beyond anything they had imagined would happen.

The chanting ceased. Amadore turned to him and said, "Weep not. You should rejoice in the presence of your rightful goddess.

And that it was dear Francesca—is there anything more beautiful?"

"Priest," the angel said. Its wings twitched with agitation.

"Yes, yes." Amadore laid a hand on Francesca's throat. Power flared, and the wounds closed. To Azran's relief, her chest began to rise and fall with shallow breaths. Then, her brother's unhinged smile grew wider, and trepidation replaced Azran's hope.

"It is done," the angel said. "Now we need only wait for her to wake."

"Her second awakening. Though, born as we were, we never truly had a first."

The angel locked eyes with Amadore. "Remember, priest, she is no longer your sister. She is our Lady of the Eclipse."

"Of course," Amadore said. "That is the beauty."

Azran heard distant thumping, growing louder. It came from below. Neither of the others seemed to notice. The angel faced the dark moon, eyes closed. Amadore stared at Francesca, hypnotized by some religious ecstasy.

A trapdoor burst open. Out of it sprang Varja, Des, Seneskar, and Exus.

The angel whirled and dodged as Varja and Exus pounced at it. Amadore's eyes turned black and he shifted like a ghost to avoid Des and Seneskar.

The angel sidestepped a thrust from Exus and slashed Varja's shoulder with a taloned hand, slicing through steel and flesh. She took the hit and, with a throaty growl, cut up. Her sparking blade sheared through the angel's wing, severing it near the joint. At the same time, Exus plunged his own glowing sword into its side.

Seneskar swung his scaled, spined forearm like a club. It met Amadore's warped, glowing limb, and the two matched strength.

Des took the opportunity to drive a dagger into the priest's back. He twisted off the blade and ghost-stepped behind Des.

Then, the angel loosed a piercing shriek beyond the ability of mortal vocal cords and went into a frenzy of strikes.

Des dodged a swipe of Amadore's glowing, clawlike hand and saw it happen—the angel lashed out with one hand at Varja's chest. A pulse of purplish-black light sent her flying over the lip of the tower, far into the empty space before she fell.

Seneskar coiled and leapt after her.

That rage welled up in Des again. She saw red more than she saw the angel she ran at.

The thing raked a claw across Exus's chest and face. He fell back.

Des's knife scraped harmlessly off its leg. It spun, slamming her with its remaining wing, which felt more like iron than feathers and bone. Des landed on her feet, poised to go back in.

Amadore shifted in front of her and swiped with his gnarled arm. Des rolled out of the way.

You first, then.

Azran forced himself to stand. He had to do something. It was too late for Francesca, but not for the others that had followed them to this horror. He tried to remain out of sight, waiting for an opening. Then, he remembered he had dropped his dagger.

The angel pulled Exus's sword from its side and tossed it over its shoulder. It stalked toward the fallen elf. Azran lunged and caught the sword.

Bleeding from lacerations in his chest, jaw, and cheek, Exus stared up at the angel. "Zerexis," he said. "At last. You are the corruptor of my order." He released a spring-loaded blade from his forearm and muttered a spell.

Azran crept up behind the angel, gripping the sword with both hands to compensate for his dislocated shoulder.

"And you are the pawn of an Interloper," the angel said to Exus. It reached down, then froze and turned its head. Black eyes met Azran's red.

Exus dove forward and drove his blade into the angel's ankle. It shrieked again. Instinct brought its eyes back to the Godshadow. Azran closed the remaining gap and drove Exus's sword deep into its back. He was weak from blood loss and heartache, but anger and desperation lent him strength.

The angel fell to its knees, then its side. Its back arched and its form writhed, spitting blood from its mouth and the hole in its back.

• • •

Varja fell, but her hand never dropped Tae'ezis. She'd always imagined dying with a sword in her hand.

The ground rose to meet her. She had no time to reflect or formulate last thoughts.

The air rushed from her lungs as force compressed her chest. The ground kept moving, but horizontally now. She saw strange, half-hand and half-scaled-foreclaw appendages holding her. She looked up at Seneskar, still shifting, but with wings enough to glide. Soon, he was fully a dragon and flying back up to the tower.

Varja regretted ever treating him like a betrayer.

• • •

Her eyes opened to a black sky dotted with faint stars. Sensation reached her—sounds of conflict and vibrations on the stone

418

beneath her. She felt at once broken and whole but knew that would pass. She held what she sensed was a hand before her face and examined the thing. She felt alien.

She slammed her gnarled hand into the pathetic living trying to kill her. No, that was not her doing—it was the servant, the priest. The one responsible for this moment. She felt him, just as she felt the dying angel.

She stood. Her legs were numb but responded to her command. That, too, would pass.

She approached the priest. He loomed over the prone living. The woman bleeding from her nose started to rise but stopped when she saw what was behind him.

The priest sensed it, too, and turned. His mortal leg wobbled, and he kneeled before his goddess. He wished to prostrate himself, but could not bring himself to look away from the face that was his sister's, now his deity's.

"My Lady Tenebra, Bringer of the Eclipse." His voice was filled with awe and religious terror.

She reached down and, with new strength, clutched his robes and hoisted him to eye level.

He saw her.

She took a step forward, then another, walking him backward. His lower back hit the lip of the low wall. She continued stepping. His body slid farther and farther out over nothing.

He saw her, then—truly saw her. He saw his sister and the distant, numbed pain in her crimson eyes. He had hurt her, they both knew, and that would not pass.

Francesca dropped Amadore off the tower.

• • •

"Cesca?" Azran asked. He was spent but would not collapse yet. "Francesca?"

She turned from watching her brother fall. Her neck and the front of her shirt were coated in blood. A ragged, fresh scar ran across her neck. But he saw recognition in the subtle, sad arch of her eyebrows.

Francesca walked toward him, and he staggered forward to fall in her arms. His weight pulled her down beside him.

"He said it wouldn't work—that my blood couldn't bring you back."

Francesca was quiet, as though she had to register what he was saying. Then, she brushed his cheek with the back of her hand. "Most people couldn't have. But I fed you my blood. Its power is in you, too."

Azran shook his head. "Did he not know that?"

"There were many things he did not know. I never wanted him to have anything to do with you. I knew no good would come of it."

Tears streamed down her face. They were not sadness, not anger, not even pain. They were tears of finality, those shed at the completion of a harrowing trial. Azran felt it, too, and he wept.

Des backed away from the tower's edge as a storm dragon alighted with a gust of trailing air. The dragon released Varja from its foreclaws.

They met in the middle, Varja sweeping Des up in a hug with her left arm. Her right hung low, gripping her sword. Her pauldron was cloven, mail split, and shoulder bleeding.

When their lips parted, Varja put Des back down and took a knee. Des knelt beside her, looked at Seneskar, and said, "Thank you."

The dragon nodded and spoke a word in his own tongue, his deep, guttural voice rumbling through the air. He walked with surprising nimbleness along the edge to Exus and helped the elf to stand.

"Is everyone alright?" Varja asked.

Exus wiped a smear of blood from his cheek. "I've had worse." He looked at Azran, then back to Varja. "We need a healer, though."

Seneskar caught Varja's attention and spoke. She translated, "He says he must go. He has another task to accomplish before the night is over."

Exus patted a huge foot. "My thanks. I hope we meet again someday."

Seneskar said something, but Varja did not translate. Then, the dragon leapt into the air, circling high and away.

41

Francesca helped support Azran while Varja did the same with Exus. Des led the way down the stairs. They proceeded back toward the throne room. The Dragonblades had disappeared from their grisly fortification, but several fresh mercenary bodies had been left in their place.

The main chamber was not as they had left it, either. The Dragonblades—the five of seven yet alive—stood around an old man in embroidered robes. They had retrieved the two bodies and unclaimed blade of their comrades. The old man knelt over the woman who had her heart ripped out.

A score of city guards and soldiers stood around the room, speaking and surveying. The ogre vampire was dead, a hilt protruding from his thick hair.

Luc was there, too. He knelt, one hand on the side of the throne and the other gripping his sword. He looked down, blood-matted hair obscuring his face. A circle of dead mercenaries surrounded him.

As the bloody and beaten group staggered in, the city guards advanced toward them, steel drawn.

"Wait," the gnoll Dragonblade barked. "They are allies."

"Two are vampires!" a guardsman shouted.

"On our side," Varja said.

"This would not be over if not for them," Exus added. His breath had grown ragged. "Is there a healer?"

Des looked over at Luc again. She yearned to go to him but dared not leave Varja yet.

"Tell me." The man amid the Dragonblades stood and turned. Des had seen his face on coins—Emperor Arcaeus Valentrae. His eyes were red from weeping. "Who is responsible for this?" He gestured at the dead woman.

"A dead vampire," Francesca said.

"Your doing?"

She took a breath. "Yes."

The emperor nodded. "See to them."

"Yes, Majesty." A soldier with white robes and cloak over his mail came forward, clutching a medallion. "Sit," he told the wounded.

Now Des hurried over to Luc. She knelt before him. Uncounted new wounds covered him from after they had parted. His medallion hung free, tarnished. She brushed his hair aside, already knowing what it hid.

Luc stared without seeing, a smile on his still face.

"You fucking howler," Des said, her voice choking. She wiped the blood from her lip. "This was all you ever wanted, wasn't it?"

Varja came and knelt, too, putting her good arm around Des's shoulders. Des leaned on her, weeping silently. Another set of feet approached.

It was the elf woman with a sword like the sun. "If not for him, we would have had many more to fight. I've never envied a Blade of Atora's life, but he is not the first I've been grateful for."

"I wish I'd been more grateful," Des said. "He was a real asshole sometimes, but he was often what I needed." She rose and kissed the top of Luc's head, careful not to disturb him.

Varja also stood and turned to the Dragonblade. "Thank for your words, um—"

"Call me Sun. Surisza is the blade I carry, and so who I am."

"Varja Kepeskeižir." She held Tae'ezis upright and examined it, trying to keep her mind off loss and pain. "These are wondrous."

Sun smiled and nodded. She gave Varja a twice-over. "Many of those in this room fell by your hand, didn't they." It was not a question. "It is soon for the others yet, but I've been at this long enough to recognize when we need a replacement. And Tae'ezis has chosen you. What say you?"

Varja glanced at the weapon, then back to Sun. "Will the blade tell me the answer to that, too?"

"No, child. Your heart will."

Varja looked at Des, who was going about the pointless task of searching for her lost knives. She felt Sun's hand on her shoulder.

"A fair choice," the Dragonblade said. "But as I said, keep the sword. Wield it well."

"I will," Varja said.

Sun returned to her post. The white-robed soldier came over next.

"Sit down, I said." He placed a glowing hand on Varja's torn shoulder, repairing flesh even as he pushed her to the floor.

• • •

Azran felt warmer now, and less bruised. His shoulder was sore from being reset. The healer had directed him to get some blood in him. As long as it wasn't that bone-powder-and-cow-blood concoction, Azran was fine with that.

He cast a worried look at Francesca. She stared at her hands. Without asking, he knew the struggle occurring inside her. He didn't want to tell her she had done the right thing. He believed that. Had he done the right thing? It was just a flash of an image, but he remembered stabbing his captor in the neck. Only now did he have the space and presence of mind to question it. He had acted without thought, out of an instinct to remove the obstacle between him and his dying wife. It was fast, it was justified, so why should he dwell on it?

In the Silver Sun, he had refused to kill a Godshadow. But the man had died, and Azran had killed. The result was the same, so had his choice even mattered in the end?

"This situation was different," Francesca said.

Had Azran been thinking out loud?

"You can't compare them."

"I'm not," he replied. "Only my emotions towards them. When we met Des and Luc, I called them killers. I thought we were better than these people. I was better. But we're all just doing what we have to, aren't we? Moment by moment, we're all just trying to survive. Living with guilt is still living."

"I want to go home."

"It burned down."

"I know, not there." For a moment, Azran feared she meant Ostitel. But then, she said, "I mean, I want a home to go to."

"We'll find one. We'll make one."

Francesca nodded. "We can't stay here. The Noblest will want us for what we've done."

"I think we can risk a day. I doubt they even know what happened here or who did it."

She nodded again.

Azran stood, less woozy. "Let's go back to Sev's for now."

She took his offered hand. Varja and Des rejoined them. They shared a quiet moment, grateful to have not gone through this alone.

"Let's go," Francesca said.

"Hold," the emperor said. "I would have you stay. You have been allies in a night of terrible enemies."

"And we must learn the details of what happened," an officer with a plumed helm said.

"I can tell you that," Exus said. His chest and face were bandaged, and he breathed easier. "I'm with the Godshadows. It would be my duty to report, sire."

The emperor nodded. "Very well. Then at least allow an armed escort."

Azran and the others shared a look, and then Francesca said, "We'll make our own way if you please, majesty."

"Then go. I will see to it you are properly thanked when peace returns."

"We need to take Luc," Des said. "We need to bury him."

Exus put a hand on her shoulder. "Allow me to prepare that. Mortis and I have a close relationship. I promise to treat the body well, and I'll contact you for a wake. Go and rest," he said, addressing them all. "This sort of night is not for you."

Des acquiesced wordlessly. She and the others started making their way out, each paying quiet respect to Luc as they passed.

A pair of guards did escort them to the palace gates, where more watchmen and soldiers arrived with each passing minute. Azran and Francesca paid little heed to the vitriolic stares leveled their way. Varja kept her new sword in open view—those that did not recognize it were soon informed by their companions.

Beyond the plaza, streets were filling with those too curious to heed their spouses' or parents' warnings. Without speaking, the wounded and weary foursome took a more circuitous route through quieter avenues.

"You there, hold!"

In their fugue-like state, even Des had lapsed in her watchfulness. They stopped and turned toward the party now approaching.

Eight figures, all bearing lanterns and garbed in the white and yellow robes of Sola clergy, blocked the street. Four also wore blades at their belts.

"As I thought," one woman said. She looked vaguely familiar to Azran, but he could not place her. She was of the half with swords. "Vampires—two of them."

The other Solari fanned out to either side of her.

"It has been another bloody night," she said. "And again at the hands of your cursed kind."

"Look," Des said, rolling her eyes. "We're just going home. I, for one, am too tired for this bullshit. Come on, if that's what you're set on." She put each hand on a dagger. "But I won't be playing."

Several of the Solari shifted and traded glances, but the leader remained calm. Azran's memory jogged—she was with the mob outside Sevex's house when this began.

"We've no quarrel with you, only the nightstalkers in your midst."

A hands-on-hilts staredown ensued between the Solari and Des, Varja, and Azran. Francesca, though, looked into the dark expanse above them, searching the night for the words to articulate how she knew the lantern bearers were wrong.

She returned her gaze to them and stepped in front of her companions.

"We don't stalk the night," she said, red eyes encompassing the cultists. "We don't stalk the night, but walk the space between light and dark. We have endured both sun and shadow." She focused on the lead Solar. "You might say the same. I can see it in your face. So, you know I speak the truth."

The lead Solar glanced between the two vampires, then said, "Then go to your homes, cursed. But soon enough, no one will need any more cause to hunt you than what you are. We will be your greatest concerns, but far from the only."

With that, she turned and left. The others followed. Two paused to spit on the ground before Francesca's feet.

After they had gone, Azran said, "We may have endured both, but we've made enemies among both extremes, as well."

"Fine by me," Francesca said. Distant lamps reflected off something small and silver in her hand—the dove on a chain. After a moment's debate, she slipped back into in her pocket. She started walking again.

"Not saying I regret it," Azran said, following.

42

Arcaeus Valentrae was overcome. Grief for his daughter, on whom he had relied despite difference of visions. Fatigue from spending over an hour waiting for his death blow. Disgust at the blood and worse filling the space between a carpet of corpses. Horror at what the Godshadow had relayed, at the prospect of being the last emperor before a blasphemous regime plunged the nation his line had built into war with Charir.

He needed distance. He needed air. With a word to his valiant Dragonblades, he was escorted out to the side gardens, where no bodies lay. The protectors kept watch but widened their circle, giving him the space he requested.

A poet was he—Arcaeus the Poet. This was a crisis like he had never faced. There was so much to do to right the wrongs of this night—if righted they could be.

The Senate was near to outlawing vampires, revoking their citizenship. After the Night of Blood and Flame, the body had Arcaeus's full support. But in light of the complete story—the specificity of the perpetrators, and the exceptional pair that had opposed this madness—perhaps the law needed emendation. Only Filvié Noctirin should pay for these crimes. What would indiscriminate vengeance achieve but another night such as this? The emperor adjusted his robes with bloody hands—it was everywhere and coated everything. He looked up to the sky, searching for some guidance, hoping to pierce the Seal and implore the gods. He was no oracle, but he was a man of faith, and held faith that the good ones yet listened. The stars above Aure were few, but they still twinkled. He marked their positions, searching for a message.

One star seemed out of place. It was bright and silver and right above him. It appeared to grow, shining with steady light. An omen, certainly, but of what? The coming dawn? Hope for the time ahead? A vigil for those now dead, a single tear from Itera?

One of the Dragonblades cried out. Arcaeus saw Sun running toward him at the same time the strange star flared. The emperor's hair stood on end the instant before lightning struck him.

● ● ●

Seneskar pulled up and swooped away, rising again and winging west, his task complete.

Fire was change, burning away the old for the new to flourish.

43

In one of two guest beds in Sevex's house, Azran and Francesca lay together, eyes closed, but not yet asleep. They had shed their blood-soaked clothes, and Azran held Francesca's toned form as she warmed his anemic chill.

"I don't think we can stay in this city," she said.

"No. It's not safe."

"Not because of that. I know that every time I look at Aure's skyline, I'll see that tower. I don't want that."

"Neither do I. Eyes forward."

"Yeah. But I don't know where else to go."

"We could see what Des and Varja want to do," Azran said.

• • •

In the second guest room, Des removed Varja's armor. When that was done, Varja set about cleaning the blood from the steel. Her new sword, already cleansed, lay dormant on the dresser.

"Do you have to do all that now?" Des asked from the bed.

"It will rust otherwise," Varja said, scrubbing with an oiled cloth. She sat on the floor, the armor spread out before her. "Besides, I have always done this. It's a ritual now. I need it."

"Rituals," Des mumbled, rolling onto her back. "I can understand. I think there's one I've been putting off for far too long." She reached down to her vest on the floor and took the emerald ring from a pocket. "Did you know I haven't seen Ari's grave since the day we buried her?"

Varja looked up from her work. "No."

"I think that's why she's followed me. She's been telling me to do what I've been avoiding." She sat next to Varja and held up the ring. "It's yours."

"Are you sure?"

"I carried it all this time because I felt alone without it. Or I thought I did. But maybe clinging to it like a holy relic was the reason I felt so alone in the first place. As long as my eyes were on this ring, I couldn't see the beautiful things ahead of me. I don't want to be alone anymore, so I'm giving it to you."

Des pressed the ring into Varja's calloused palm. Varja closed her hand around it. She couldn't find words in any of the four languages she spoke, so she just nodded.

"I love you," Des said, brushing Varja's tangled and matted hair from her face.

"I love you too."

Des knelt there, eyes closed, arms wrapped over Varja's shoulders until the ritual was done.

• • •

Late the next day, when they had all made their way downstairs, they discussed the path ahead. Des wanted to travel to Salles in Equotel, but only as a pilgrimage. She had no intention of staying. Varja would go with, of course, but neither woman had a plan for after.

Cruxia was brought up more than once but dismissed each time. Despite bringing them together, the low points of their time in the city had left them with no real desire to return.

In the midst of this discussion, there was a knock at the door. It was Exus. He had done as promised.

Des recalled a hill outside the city that was special to Luc—the site of his first duel as an initiated Blade of Atora. When night fell, it hosted a torch-lit gathering. Luc had never spoken of family, so it fell to Des, Varja, Azran, Francesca, Sevex, and a local priest of Mortis to see him off.

The priest consecrated the ground while the others dug the hole. Then, he lit white candles and placed them at each corner of the grave. The diggers cleansed their hands and affixed an armband to each bicep—bone white on the left for Mortis, and red on the right for Luc's death in battle. Des wore his headband for her red.

She looked at Luc. Even under the shroud, she knew his smile remained. To either side of his body, on top of the cloth, were his swords. His short blade had been retrieved from its final kill.

Before the ritual proceeded further, the priest of Mortis asked if Luc had any particular requests.

"Yes," Des said. "He told me of his cult's rite—the Passing of the Blade." She went to the bier and picked up the two swords with reverence. "He always said a good blade should not go in the ground. He inherited these from one of his masters." She walked over to Francesca. "I think he'd find it fitting if they went to his last student."

Francesca took the swords and cradled them. She nodded.

"Don't lose these ones," Des said with a smirk.

Francesca wiped a stray tear. "I won't."

As the others lowered the bier into the grave and the priest prayed silently, Des took a shaking breath and performed the eulogy.

"Lucian—Luc—was a man who spoke more with action than words. When I needed him, he was there with little cause to be. He never abandoned me, though I gave him plenty of reason to. I'd be dead or worse if not for him." She paused and blinked as the dirt crunched and the bier settled. "Luc was a mad fucking howler, but sometimes, that's exactly who we need."

White asphodels and red amaranth fell onto the shroud. Varja held Des around the shoulders as those gathered sang the wordless death hymn. The priest played a lyre to accompany the dirge. Des could have sworn she heard a second lyre playing harmony, somewhere out in the darkness.

When the song was done, they filled the grave. This, the priest helped with. He also placed a marking stone upright in the dirt.

The small procession left the candles to burn out.

They had a meal and wine, just the five of them.

"You know," Sevex said at one point in the dinner. "I hear Astrellus is a good place for musicians to make a living."

"I've heard that, too," Azran said. "Didn't Miranda mention going east?"

"It's where she was from," Varja said. "I hope she made it."

"She did," Des said. "If they caught her, that would have been a swift and very public execution."

"I like Astrellus," Francesca said. "It's far from the politics and paranoia. Somewhere we might make brighter memories."

• • •

Another visitor came the next day, this one a messenger. Varja opened the letter and read it to the group:

"It's come to my attention that you know an old friend of mine in Cruxia. Lucina speaks fondly of you all, calling you a spot of youthful adventure she seldom sees these days. She knows much of what transpired here—she knows much in general, and damned if I understand it. She wanted to ensure you had a fighting chance.

"Things are going to become chaotic here soon, even more than they have been. The emperor promised you a reward. For reasons that will become clear, he can no longer fulfill that promise.

"I can offer something, though. You will find horses and a sum of gold at the I.M.S. stables by the east gate of the city. It is paltry compared to what His Majesty would have given, but it will take you far.

"I offer my thanks again, and my word that not all here are victims of hysteria and fear mongering.

"Gods be with you,

"Sun."

When Varja finished, Des asked, "What did we do to find these people?"

"Something right," Azran replied. "We must have."

Right? Francesca thought. *Is that what we did?*

• • •

Two weeks' ride east of Aure, Des stood before a grave.

Arilysa Talbre
1319–1348
She Was Home

The stone stood beneath a willow by a pond, where they used to lay, and within sight of one of the many vineyards of Salles, where they used to walk.

A cool breeze billowed Des's cloak. Winter was nearly here.

"You've been following me. You've been nagging me, and for the life of me, I couldn't figure out why. But that's it, isn't it? The life of me. My life. All this time, I thought memories of you were dragging me down, but it was my guilt. My inability to move on. I couldn't protect you. That's true. You can't always protect those you love. That's also true. And you can't let that stop you—that truth's a matter of perspective. Lucky for me, my perspective's changing."

She glanced back to the road, where Varja waited with the horses. She traced the chiseled letters. "I'm going to do what you wanted, Ari." Des smiled. "I'm going to let myself be happy."

Without wiping her tears away, she walked back to Varja.

44

Francesca sipped coffee early one winter evening. The nocturnal tavern did not open for a while yet, but she'd had dreams again. She wasn't going to get any more sleep. It had been more than two months since the night she killed her brother. She no longer saw his looming specter. Now, her solitude was haunted by that cold void that had nearly subsumed her. She had felt the soul of a god—Tenebra's touch had left a scar deeper than the one across her throat.

She found solace in being free from Amadore. If only she could be free from the rest. In her shirt pocket, her fingers caressed the silver dove, tangled in its chain.

She looked out the tinted front windows to the parched grass and wilted bushes of the southern season. She tried to remember the last time she'd seen snow. Years ago. Not since she left Ostitel.

She waved to the general merchant across the street as he locked his shop and headed home. Her smile was mostly genuine. There were few emotions she now felt as completely as before.

This was a friendly town. It wasn't perfect—which was why they paid Des and Varja—but it was good. The local authorities had rejected the Senate's open season on vampires and promised to protect *all* their citizens. And it was close enough to Aeribe that Francesca and Azran could take the occasional day or two off to see it, while the other couple held down the fort.

Francesca turned back to the Howling Blade's common room. She and Azran owned a bar—again the surreal thought hit her. They were in a good place. That's what kept her going—that the nightmares remained just that.

She walked over to the freshly kindled hearth. Retrieving the silver dove, she stared as it hung by its chain, slightly tarnished by her old blood. She had challenged herself to keep it, to prove she was stronger than the memories. She then looked up at Luc's swords, cross-mounted above the fireplace, and thought about what memories she wanted to keep. What strength meant— whether it was something from within or something that was given and taken by the world.

Francesca let go, dropping the silver dove into the building flames. She put her cup of coffee on the mantle and took down the arming sword. Its weight was familiar in her hands—she still carried it when she went out.

She went on a middle guard and made some circles around the room. She imagined an opponent moving in his own circle and remembered the hits and bruises of her time training with Luc. She pictured him across the circle, moved in left, and launched a thrust.

"Did you get em?" Azran asked, right behind her.

Francesca started and spun around. "Love, I am not awake enough for that shit."

He gave her an apologetic kiss on the forehead. "Any coffee left?"

"A bit."

As Azran strained some into a cup, there was a knock on the main door. "Come back in an hour!" he called.

"Oh, come on," a muffled voice said. "I've spent enough time trying to get to you guys."

Francesca, curious, checked through a window. When she saw who it was, she hustled to unlock the door. "You're not going to believe this."

"What?" Azran asked.

She opened the door, and Miranda stepped in. The musician flashed one of her knowing smirks and said, "Wasn't easy, you know."

Azran ran up and hugged her, along with Francesca. "We were going to look for you," he said.

"Uh-huh, I'm sure you were." Miranda deposited her pack, which still contained her wrapped oud, on a nearby table.

"Really," Francesca said. "Des had some old contacts looking into it."

"So, where are those two? I heard there's a tall Procumi woman and some crop-haired scrapper defending this establishment."

"Out about town," Azran said. "They'll be back soon. Can we get you a drink?"

Miranda pointed at him. "Before we get to that—and we will—I have something for you. Word's been going around my circles that the Silver Sun in Aure is closed for good, and the owner had a parting gift for her old player.

Azran shook his head, bewildered.

Miranda stepped back outside and called, "Bring it in!"

A wagon pulled up in front of the bar. The driver and a pair of assistants opened the back and carried out a familiar harpsichord.

Azran spun in a circle, hands on his head.

Miranda smiled wider. "Ria sends her best, and her deepest apologies for how things ended."

Francesca pulled some tables away from the wall opposite the hearth and directed the men carrying the instrument.

Azran walked over and ran his fingers gently across the keys and glossy pine casing. Francesca did the same, and he hugged her tight out of sheer joy.

"Thank you." He turned back to Miranda. "I'm a bit out of practice—"

"Fuck it," she said. "Let's see if you can keep up. Remember what I said about arpeggios?"

Azran grinned. "Guess we'll see."

● ● ●

When Varja and Des returned from an evening breakfast, they entered to find Azran and Miranda trading melodies, Francesca sitting on a nearby table, and a bottle of good wine open and waiting.

The Howling Blade didn't open that night.

A Song, Love

M iranda was somewhere south of Libred when she came upon the Rogue's Rose. The single-story tavern stood alone on the roadside, weathered by the winds of the plains. Faded letters above the door read: *Wanderers, find your rest. Warriors, look elsewhere.*

The traveler wondered what had possessed the owner to open business so far out from the city. Still, the place seemed to be just what she needed—somewhere she could get a drink and be left alone.

She stepped inside and smoothed her windblown, dark hair. Her blue-green eyes and the slight points of her ears hinted at her mixed elven and human heritage. She sat down at a table opposite the bar, placing her pack and blanket-wrapped oud underneath while taking a quick appraisal of the common room.

It was clean and quiet. A few embers glowed in the hearth. Soft light diffused the room but didn't quite seem to fit the angle of the afternoon sun. A surprising number of patrons were present, given the tavern's remoteness. Some chatted quietly, but most drank in silence. The whole place had an air of abnormality Miranda couldn't pinpoint. It felt like she was in a foreign land.

Seeing no servers, Miranda stood and approached the bar. The keep arranged and rearranged bottles and flasks on the shelves with meticulous precision. He didn't turn around to look at the new customer. Miranda tapped the bar with her knuckles.

"What do you want?" the barkeep asked, his task remaining uninterrupted. His voice was like midnight silk.

"Ale," Miranda said. "How much for a pitcher?"

He rotated deftly and produced a full pitcher and empty glass from under the bar. He handed them to Miranda, but his face was too obscured by shadows for her to make out any details. As soon as she took the drink and glass, he was back to the shelves.

"Don't worry about it," he said.

Miranda hesitated, confused by this generosity. She shrugged, returned to her table, filled the glass, and took a long, deep drink. Yes, she needed this—a quiet night in a quiet bar. Nobody was demanding a song. No bureaucratic puppets were fining her for playing an Aurasi drinking tune instead of an ode to the nation. Gods, they were the worst. If the Bureau of Culture wanted a list of approved music, they could at least write something with a bit of energy.

She shook her head and took another drink.

As Miranda finished her second glass, a man was sitting on the other side of the table. She startled and almost choked on the ale—the stranger had appeared in a literal blink.

"Good day," the man said. He was thin, with a hawk-like face, tousled black locks, and steely grey eyes. His dull-hued clothes seemed to fall somewhere between a traveler's garb and a priest's vestments.

"Your name is…Miranda?" the man went on.

She nodded. "Who are you, then? We haven't met." Beneath the table, her hand inched toward the knife in her sleeve.

"I thought it was you." The man smiled. "And you're right, although we do have many mutual acquaintances. My name is Mortis." He extended his hand.

Miranda calmed at his pleasant tone, leaving the knife and accepting the greeting. Then she paused, turning her head and eyeing him sideways. "What did you say it was?"

"Mortis. Some of you call me the Severance. In Charir, they used to call me the Fate Warden. Both just fancy titles for the god of death."

"Right. I'm—I'll be going now."

"Please don't," the man calling himself Mortis said. "It's seldom I get to talk with a living mortal, especially these days."

"Look, it's just that—"

"You don't believe me? Understandable. Does this convince you?"

"Does what—" Miranda bit off her question as a shock ran through her chest.

The tavern fell away, leaving her in a void. She was neither standing nor sitting. She sensed nothing but a chill in her core and the smell of rain. Then, Mortis stepped out of the enveloping darkness. For one fleeting moment, Miranda saw eternity in his eyes, the lives and deaths of billions and billions of souls mirrored in those grey irises. He reached out. She felt a hand on her shoulder, and then a lurch like she was being pulled back from the edge of a cliff.

Miranda was in the tavern again. She felt a trickle of blood from her nose and wiped it with her sleeve. Mortis still sat across from her, calm as ever.

"That's the unpleasant part," he said. "Don't worry—it never lasts more than a moment, no matter how busy I am. Time is a relative thing."

Miranda topped off her glass and took a drink. She expected her hands to shake but was surprised at her own composure. "So, what's the Severance doing in a place like this?"

Mortis pulled a clay cup from a deep pocket and poured himself some ale. "I could ask you the same. You're the odd one here. As a mortal, I mean."

Miranda looked around the room. Every patron seemed just as ordinary as when she had entered. But then, that sense of foreignness still lingered. Not alarm, not even discomfort. It just itched at the back of her mind.

Mortis followed her gaze from patron to patron. "Immortals, one and all. The Keeper covered them, so as not to scare away your business."

"Have a lot of stock to get rid of," the barkeep said, still rearranging.

"And he always covers himself," the god went on. He leaned across the table and spoke in an undertone. "He scares even us. Far too many eyes." He settled back into his chair.

"What is this place?" Miranda asked.

"Not the Mortal Realm, that's for sure. Not exactly the Immortal Realms either, though. It's a place for us to get a break from the war. Or our duties, in my case." He downed his drink.

Silence stretched across the table for a long while. Miranda was still processing her circumstances when Mortis spoke again.

"Really?" he asked. "Nothing you would ask of the arbiter of death? Usually by now, I've been begged to release a loved one, or spare one who's dying."

Miranda pondered. "I can tell from your tone that you're unlikely to do either of those. And honestly, right now, I just want a quiet drink."

Mortis laughed. "I laud your honesty. And you are correct about death—such is the way of things. I am a guide, not a murderer. To be honest myself, though, I have been persuaded to intervene from time to time. I propose we converse as equals, then. We patrons are all equals here."

The god raised his cup, and Miranda answered his toast. For the first time since leaving Libred, she smiled.

They talked for several hours, the mortal and the god. Miranda told Mortis of her frustration living in a wayside town in Astrellus, watching people come and go along the highway and wanting nothing more than to follow them.

When she was twelve, her aunt gave her an old lute and taught her to play. Miranda was young when she left home, selling her services as a minstrel on a caravan bound for Oretel. She traded the lute for her oud after encountering a clumsy Aurasi thief during her first visit to Libred. He snatched the lute but tripped and cracked the body on the stone road. The Aurasi's family showed Miranda fine hospitality and gave her the oud as recompense.

She unwrapped it from the enveloping blanket and held it up for Mortis to see.

"It's lovely," he said. "I myself prefer the lyre." He reached into the folds of his cloak and produced a small, ten-stringed instrument made of dark wood.

"What's that one's tale?" Miranda asked.

Mortis sighed. "A sad story. Not good drinking conversation, I'm afraid."

She nodded, looking at the rays of the setting sun refracting through the empty ale pitcher. "So where do you come from, then? They call your kin the Interlopers. Whence did you lope?"

Mortis chuckled. "They do call us that. I find it amusing, since the First came here also." The god's voice deepened and his cadence became dramatic as he quoted scripture. "'Genesa came upon the world and found it a barren rock.'" He took a drink and returned to his amiable tone. "Think of it like this."

He held out his right hand, palm upturned, and flicked his wrist. A transparent, green globe the size of an apple appeared, floating in place about an inch above his palm. "This is your world in the Mortal Realm," he said.

Mortis flicked his wrist three more times, changing the globe to blue, to red, to white. "The Immortal Realms, the other planes, contain different versions of this world. Unique layers of reality. Same place, but with different beings and forces acting on it. Follow?"

Miranda nodded, brow furrowed.

He brushed his free hand over the globe, sending it to a corner of the room. In its original place was a purple sphere, half again as large. "We 'Interlopers' come from a different world entirely, one very far away." He closed his right hand, and both globes vanished.

"I see," Miranda said. "Why?"

Mortis shrugged. "I don't remember, precisely. It was a very long time ago. But I like to imagine our reason was similar to yours—we weren't content with where we were." He finished his ale. "Speaking of home and planes, you should get back to your realm."

"Couldn't I stay here?" Miranda asked, looking to the Keeper.

"No," the shadowed being said in his silky voice.

"I can pay—"

"Not the issue. Don't need money. Not safe for a mortal to sleep here. I run a tight bar, but not perfect."

"He's right," Mortis said. "Especially since I need to leave also. Duties to attend—more souls with every moment I spend here."

"Right." Miranda held out her hand. "Nice meeting you, Mortis."

He shook her hand. "A true pleasure, Miranda. May it be a long time before we meet again."

Miranda shook her head at the absurdity of all this. She stood, shouldered her pack, and walked out of the Rogue's Rose. The sense of foreignness remained behind in the tavern, replaced by a slight chill and the wind of the plains. She turned around, but now saw only a ruined foundation where the building had stood. She reached out but touched only air. With a sigh, she started south along the trail.

After some time peering into the twilight, Miranda spotted a dell sheltered by a rough outcropping. Large shrubs, or perhaps small trees, grew within. She found it empty but for an old fire pit.

"Luch parotak," she said, pointing next to the pit. A white glow emanated from the spot, dim and shimmering slightly. Miranda had picked up a few spells in her travels but wasn't much of a caster. Her threads between this world and the primal energies that fueled arcana were weak. Still, the fading light was enough for her to build a small fire from some deadwood. She laid out her bedroll nearby, quenched her spell, and thought about her curious day as the gloom gathered.

"Play me a song, love."

Miranda bolted upright, one hand closing over her knife. She saw no one, but was sure she had heard—

"Just one song, please." The voice was equal parts lilting and supplicant.

She stood as a vague figure emerged from the shadows of the tall shrubs. "Stop," she said, drawing the knife. "Who are you?"

The figure did not halt. "Saw you in the tavern," it replied. "Felt you. You felt good." The voice shuddered. "You feel good."

In the dim light of the campfire, Miranda recognized the sculpted face and crimson hair of the woman as one of the patrons.

"Stop," she repeated, brandishing her meager weapon.

"Do it," the other woman said. She continued to approach. "Stab me," she whispered.

Miranda backed off a step.

"Stab me!"

The stranger lunged at her, snatching her free arm. Miranda obliged, driving her knife into her attacker's abdomen.

The red-haired woman did not let go. She leaned close, releasing a pleasurable sigh. "Feels good," she murmured into Miranda's ear.

Miranda shoved herself away, but the knife stuck firmly in the stranger's diaphragm. The mortal trembled, her breathing rapid. The tavern had felt only a bit alien, and Mortis had seemed natural. But this woman felt wrong.

"What are you?" Miranda managed to ask.

The crimson-haired woman moaned as she pulled the knife out. No blood coated the blade, and no wound was left behind. She stared at Miranda, unblinking. "A saead," she said. "Emotion. Passion. Subject of Sensius. I could show you. Take this face off. But you would feel too much. Snap like a monk left out in the moonlight." She laughed hysterically.

Miranda started to back off again, slowly. But then the saead was behind her.

"Play me a song, love." The supplication was gone, replaced by demand. A warm hand, throbbing with hot blood, caressed Miranda's cheek. "I know you can. Play for me, or I will take this face off. Jump your heart right out of your pretty skull, love. Just one song."

Miranda nodded. She tried to speak, but her throat was too dry at the moment. She cleared it and echoed, "Just one song." She unwrapped her oud and set about tuning it, trying to keep her hands steady. Discordant notes filled the dell as she adjusted the courses.

The saead, now sitting cross-legged across the fire, seemed transfixed by the process. She stared at the oud, leaning left and right with the sharps and flats.

When it was finally tuned, Miranda took up her eagle-quill plectrum and paused. What should she play that would satisfy this bizarre immortal? She looked up at the stars, mentally tearing through her repertoire.

"Play!" the saead shrieked.

Miranda played. The song in her mind at that last instant, a somber Aurasi tune, emanated from her oud. She moved quickly between the strings, but the ringing of the minor scales produced a broad swell of melancholy tones. She drifted through the progression, eyes closed, losing herself in the song. She didn't want to remember why she was playing; she only wanted the music. On the refrain, Miranda added her voice to the performance with the smooth, long sounds of the Aurasi tongue.

She gazes up
As the night looks down.
Thirsting, but barred
By a broken wing that won't knit.

455

She sighs and cries,
But the eagles are long-gone.
She can't even recall the dream
Of riding those winds.
The night looks down,
And she looks away.
Watch the sky and see—
The moon still rises.

Miranda held the last, harmonized note with her instrument and voice for as long as she could. When she dared open her eyes, the saead was hugging herself and rocking in place. Tears streamed down the immortal's cheeks.

"Thank you, love. Play me another."

"You said one," Miranda said.

"Another!" The saead lurched forward, kicking the burning deadwood from the fire pit. Her voice lowered, growing sultry. "It feels good."

"It's sad when an immortal's word carries no promise."

Miranda and the saead looked toward the shrubbery to see Mortis step forward, holding a globe of light in his hand.

"She already played," he said. "And you are not supposed to be here anyway. If Sensius had his usual faculties, addled as they may be, he'd be quite displeased."

The saead sneered. "But he doesn't. Master's as lost as a compass on the sun." She disappeared from the dell, her laughter lingering a moment.

"Well, that is unfortunate," Mortis said. He turned to Miranda. "For what it's worth, I thought that was a lovely performance. I was tempted to join in."

"Thanks," she said quietly, looking where the saead had been.

Mortis stamped out the remaining cinders with his boot. "Gather your things. We need to discuss how you're going to handle this, and we cannot do it here."

Miranda raised an eyebrow. "What *I'm* going to do? You saying this is my fault?"

"Strictly speaking, yes. The saead latched onto the aura of your soul and rode it back to the Mortal Realm. And as I said, she doesn't belong here. Now, come."

Miranda obeyed, collecting her gear. "Where are we going?"

Mortis put a hand on her shoulder. The next moment, they were back in the Rogue's Rose. The common room was vacant now, but the Keeper continued his meticulous bottle reorganizing.

"I called in a favor for a temporary haven," Mortis said. "Absurd as it may seem to you right now, this is the safest place for a mortal in your position."

"And what is my position, exactly? What happens next?"

He took a long pause. "You must banish the saead back to Aeros, its original plane."

"All I wanted was a fucking quiet drink," Miranda said. She began pacing across the empty floor. After a minute, she paused and locked eyes with the god. "Why do I have to do it? You'd have a much easier time, I'm sure."

"Old laws. You're the one that most directly aided the saead in getting to your world."

Miranda opened her mouth to protest, but Mortis stopped her with a raised hand. "I know you didn't mean to. But such are the laws. Blame my brother-in-law."

Miranda crossed her arms and looked away. "And if I don't do this? Or can't?"

"You will be arrested and tried for breaching the barrier between realms by agents of Legex, or perhaps even the old man

457

himself." Mortis approached Miranda and took hold of her chin, forcing her gaze back to him. "You do not want that. Tartarus is no place for a mortal."

He released her, and she took a step back. Her shoulders slumped in weary assent. "How do I send her back?"

"I can teach you a spell."

Miranda gave a helpless chuckle. "I'm really not much of a mage. Never had the focus for that."

"I disagree," Mortis said, walking to the bar and settled onto a stool. "You managed to play an Aurasi ballad flawlessly after an immortal threatened to rip out your heart."

"That's a different kind of focus."

"Yes, it is. Tell me, do you know why mortals can wield arcana? Not how, but why?"

Miranda shrugged. "Because Praecar made it work?"

"Exactly. He rewove reality so that certain sounds or runes can direct the energy a caster channels. Mortal arcana is a construct, do you see?"

"I suppose. So what?"

"So, spellcasting as you know it is but one method of directing this energy. My kinsman Musymph has another that he used to teach his mortal servants." Mortis produced his lyre. "Get your oud and tune it to open A. I'm going to teach you a song."

• • •

A horseman rode south. His tattered cloak billowed from the speed of his passage. Dust clouded his wake, kicked up from the relentless pounding of his mount's hooves on the Oreteli plain. The elven rider had veered off the highway more than a dozen miles back. He needed no road to guide his pursuit.

He eased his horse to a stop. The animal, a hybrid of Equoteli power and steppe stamina, breathed calmly despite the long journey.

"As lokes in imortinav skidorak," the rider said, closing his eyes to let the spell guide his deeper senses. He felt his quarry following a slow, meandering path. He allowed himself a smile. His prey was close.

Syrus Azavel was an agent of the Godshadows, the Third Hunter of the Sunrise Chapter. His responsibility was to track dangerous monsters, whether arcane experiments or rampaging extraplanar beasts, and slay them. Three days ago, the shadeseer of his chapter had told Syrus of a grave threat in Oretel. This was no mere Cannean wolf or other lesser creature, but a true immortal. The war must not be allowed to reach the Mortal Realm, the shadeseer had said.

Syrus, however, saw this as an opportunity. The conflict was no explanation for the century-long silence of the gods that formerly spoke to him. An immortal could demystify this riddle and give Syrus the answers he so desperately sought.

• • •

Miranda hustled northward, making all the speed she could manage on the third day of her pursuit. She clutched the small device strung about her neck and held it parallel to the ground. It was a small compass made of translucent crystal. Unlike a normal compass, however, the needle did not bob in any suspending fluid but floated inside its outer ring. It pointed perfectly ahead.

Mortis had given her the mechanism before she set out from the Rogue's Rose. According to him, these compasses were common among planar travelers seeking gates. The instruments unfailingly indicated the nearest points of dimensional disturbances—in this case, the stray saead.

The god had also assured Miranda that she could overtake the creature. Most immortals were overwhelmed by the alien—to them—environment of the Mortal Realm until they acclimated. And saeads were mad for sensation to begin with. According to Mortis, this one would be "sauntering like she smoked some of Allusec's finest."

Still, Miranda did not relax her pace. She was unsure how far ahead the saead had…"teleported" was the word Mortis used to describe the vanishing act. Some kind of instantaneous travel mortals had yet to master.

She did pause, though, when she double-checked the crystal compass. Holding still, she noticed the slight change in the needle's bearing.

Northwest.

Miranda sighed in relief. Despite Mortis's guarantees, after three days of going north, she had begun to think he had given her an ordinary compass. A part of her wished that were so, that some aspect of this adventure remained grounded in her previous reality.

The greater part of Miranda was pleased, though. A noticeable change in direction meant she was drawing closer to the saead, and closer to finishing this. She let the compass hang once more, stepped off the road, and quickened her stride.

● ● ●

Syrus crept through a cluster of flatland shrubs, having left his obedient mount a half-mile out. He knew his quarry was very close, near enough for him to feel its exotic presence. Finally, peering around one dense plant, he spotted the immortal. He stayed behind cover as he observed the being and gripped the hilt of his sword. Its blade bore arcane runes that allowed it to pierce the flesh of such creatures.

The immortal bore the appearance of a red-haired human woman in plain clothes, but Syrus suspected the form was a ruse. Its aura was far too excited for such normalcy. The "woman" seemed mesmerized by a small, thorny bush, inhaling the aroma of the tiny, purple flowers and caressing the broad leaves. The immortal's hand grasped a stem, forcing the thorns deep into its palm. Rather than cry out in pain and recoil, it moaned in pleasure and tightened its grip.

Syrus determined it was a saead, a being that needed to feel like he needed to breathe. This was an excellent turn of events. A saead would not be immediately hostile and could be conversed with. But how to approach one?

"You've returned, love."

The saead's words shook Syrus from his planning. He was surprised to hear it speak, but even more so to discover the intended listener it now turned to face.

A young woman, at least half-human by her features, stepped into view from the far side of the shrubs. The newcomer's clothes were unkempt, and she looked exhausted. But Syrus could see a terrible determination in her blue-green eyes, some resolve that defied her breathlessness.

• • •

"Come to play another song for me?" the saead asked. It approached the stranger with a swaying stride, as though drunk.

"Yes, actually," Miranda responded. "Just one more song."

She had to fight to steady herself. Her legs threatened to give out at any moment from a combination of fatigue and fear. She recalled the effect her knife had on the saead. If this plan failed, the immortal would kill her. Miranda was fine spending more time with Mortis—just not like this.

She took a deep breath, clearing the mess of thoughts, and reviewed the melody Mortis had taught her. She dropped her pack and unwrapped her oud, checking its tune as she had at every opportunity on her journey. It remained in perfect open A.

Miranda glanced up at the saead, which returned with a hungry gaze. She sat to better play the difficult progression—basking for just a moment after relieving her legs—and strummed the first chord.

Just as before, Miranda buried herself in the music. The song began gently but grew in intensity. She felt something pulling at her mind, the same tug she had sensed when rehearsing each night. She had left it alone those times, having no need for the power it promised. But now, just as she struck a full chord, Miranda latched onto the mysterious pull. It was a thread, stronger than she had ever achieved with arcana. Energy coursed through her. Whether it fueled the song or the song was the fuel, she did not know nor have time to question. Both magic and music escalated in strength and speed, building.

The saead must have realized what Miranda was doing. The being's enraptured smile warped into a grimace, and for once, she cried out in pain rather than pleasure. Her fair complexion peeled away to expose crimson skin. She clawed at herself with blackened nails before lunging at Miranda, reaching for the mortal's throat.

• • •

Syrus was at a loss. An immortal stood not ten yards away. Some trail-stained woman was playing music to the creature, and the two seemed to know each other. Syrus hoped he was wrong about that suspicion. He hated dragging people to the listeners.

Something else was off, though—something to do with the music.

Magic. Syrus could feel the charge in the air as power gathered around the oud player. It matched the tempo and intensity of the song. A pattern took shape, one that matched a spell of banishment.

No—Syrus needed to question the saead. He needed to know why the gods had abandoned their faithful. Drawing his dull-glowing sword, he strode into the open.

The saead cried out, revealing its true, red-skinned form. It launched itself at the mortal woman.

"Damn you all," Syrus muttered. So much for interrogation.

He rushed forward and thrust. The blade plunged deep into the saead, charring the edges of the wound. The immortal shrieked as it stopped short and arched its back.

• • •

Miranda reached the climax of the spell-song, a rapid pattern of high chromatic notes. The power, rising and electrifying the around her like a coming storm, unleashed its torrent upon the suddenly halted saead.

Blue flames erupted at random across the immortal's flesh, coalescing and swallowing her. The conflagration vanished without so much as a wisp of smoke, taking the saead with it.

An elf stood just behind where the immortal had been. His worn cloak and silver hair settled, having been blown back by the directed force of Miranda's spell. Both mortals stared at each other as their minds reconciled what had just happened.

The elf moved first, relaxing his stance and sheathing his blade. He took a deep breath and half-turned as if to go, then whirled back on Miranda. "Do you have any idea what you've done?"

"For once, I do," Miranda said, staring hard. "And I'm rather tired of being asked that."

The elf let out a wordless yell and pressed his hands to his face. "I was so close. So close to my answers."

"Answers to what? I can't imagine what you thought you could get out of that deranged thing."

The elf put his back to her and waited a long moment before responding. "Why are the gods silent?"

"What do you mean?" Mortis asked, stepping out of empty space. "I'm as verbose as ever."

Miranda stood, ignoring the protests of her limbs, and the moody elf spun about.

"Hello, Syrus," the god said. "I didn't even have to scour my memories of the dead—I would recognize your soul anywhere. It's been a while."

"A century," Syrus said, crossing his arms. "You used to visit my dreams, and so did the rest."

Mortis nodded and shrugged. "We've been a tad busy of late."

"A tad busy? Do you even know what's happened in your absence? False gods and unholy abominations murder your followers daily, destroying any memory of you! And still your faithful pray for your aid, as they die, as you squabble among yourselves and neglect your duties!"

The world grew dark, as though a veil had been placed over the sun. The scrub grass and bushes wilted. A wave of enervation passed over Miranda. Syrus averted his eyes and put a hand to his temple.

"I do not neglect my duties," Mortis said with a voice as still and cold as death. "Nor do those who yet have the capacity to carry on. Presume not to censure the divine, mortal."

Miranda put a tentative hand on the god's tense shoulder. Mortis glanced at her and eased his posture. Light and life returned to the plains.

"Apologies," Mortis said. "But I have grown so weary from other troubles that I have no patience for tactless Godshadows."

"I...am sorry as well, my Lord Severance." Syrus dropped to a knee.

"Good. Still, though, I think you deserve some resolution. Ask your shadeseer. He knows more than he should, anyway."

Syrus nodded and asked, "Is this a quest, my Lord?"

Mortis smiled. "Yes, my servant. Go and perform your own duties."

The elf bowed, then rose and stalked away through the shrubs.

"You enjoy being so cryptic, don't you?" Miranda asked when he was gone.

"It amuses me."

She collapsed onto the rough grass and closed her eyes, utterly spent.

"Excellent performance." Mortis sat down next to her. "You added a bit of your own to it, I noticed."

"Tell me something, without the half-answers. Did you know I'd succeed?"

"I expected so, though I was uncertain."

"Some Fate Warden you are."

"The future is never certain," Mortis said. "Randomness occurs on a level your mind cannot even comprehend."

"But still." Miranda sat up and looked at the god. "You gambled. With me."

He sighed. "Whatever the saead could have done to you pales compared to the dungeons of Tartarus. I regret the danger this ordeal put you in, but now it's over."

"To make way for what?" Miranda asked, fiddling with the crystal compass.

"Well," Mortis said as he stood. "I think you've earned a respite. There is a place I'd like to show you, other than a tavern full of misfortune. After that, I may have another task for you. Or not. Future and all that."

He held out a hand and helped Miranda to her feet.

"What about that whole Seal business?" she asked.

"A mad immortal running amok is one thing. You will be my guest. I have enough pull with Legex for this—I'm probably the only god he respects at this point, and that includes his mother."

Miranda laughed and picked up her gear. She paused in thought. "Does this count as dying?"

"Oh, no. I'm sure you'll feel quite alive."

Mortis offered his hand again. When Miranda clasped it this time, he pulled her up beyond the Mortal Realm, stepping through the membranes of the planes.

Seeing Only Shades

S yrus entered the Sunrise Chapterhouse, an imposing structure whose architecture combined elements of a leering cathedral and a fortified keep. He navigated the dimly lit corridors and spiral staircases into its depths, paying no heed to the agents he passed.

Mortis had visited Syrus the night before, as he had in the elf's youth. The vision was enigmatic, but he knew the Severance was not pleased with the Sunrise Shadeseer.

As always, the shadeseer's chamber was dark. Blind men needed no light, and the head of the chapter focused his psychic sight elsewhere.

"I'd like a word," Syrus said to the encroaching gloom.

"You deign to speak on behalf of a god, do you not?" The shadeseer's frail, aged voice did not emanate from any clear point, but filled the lightless room. From his many visits to the chamber, Syrus had concluded it must be vaulted to produce echoes. Like the darkness, this enhanced the mystery of shadeseers—placed them beyond the reach of lower Godshadow agents. "Then let us speak, hunter. If I am to understand your purpose here, a mere hunter presumes to censure a shadeseer in matters of holiness. Is that right?"

"I do not so presume," Syrus said. "I speak for the gods themselves."

The shadeseer let out a cracked cackle, reinforcing Syrus's mental image of him. He remembered him from before he entered the darkness—an aging human, bald and bent, already wasting away from Syrus's elven perspective. That was thirty years ago. The old man must have been a withering husk by now.

"A god visited you in a dream, yes?" the shadeseer asked. "My predecessor mentioned you had such dreams before the Seal. He thought you ought to have become a tracker, did you know? He desired to groom you to lead this chapter with your sight. But you chose a more violent path. Alas."

"We all share in the violence."

"This is true. My point, though, is that had you walked the way of the diviner, you would know the difference between visions of reality and dreams of fantasy. The planes are sealed, and the gods are silent. It falls to the ordained to interpret their will."

Syrus tapped a finger on the pommel of his sword. "Then what reality do you make of the saead incident? What did I witness?"

"There was no divine event," the shadeseer said.

He was lying. Syrus could hear it in the rhetorical setup and vague response. So, then, the shadeseer knew of Syrus's dream meeting with Mortis, but perhaps not his waking conversation with the god out on the plains.

The hunter maintained a composed tone. "That does not answer my question."

Again the shadeseer paused. "My sight shows me that you need not be concerned. Remember that angels deceive as often as aid. This irregular audience is ended. Make your report to the first listener and be on your way, hunter."

It took all of Syrus's willpower not to snap at the condescension. No one had denied his visions in a long time—not since the first time he mentioned them to the local priests, over a century ago. Those priests had also been wrong.

Without another word, he turned on his heel and stalked out of the chamber. Meandering the corridors of the chapterhouse, he pondered the exchange and again ran through the god's cryptic words.

"The history of shades shall repeat. Laws both primal and mortal are transgressed. Deep runs the sin."

If this is how the divine speak, I understand why so many oracles sound mad.

Syrus did not recall the shadeseer ever lying so blatantly. He must have hit close to the mark. He had always trusted the leaders of the order. Mortis had planted a seed of doubt, and the shadeseer allowed it to sprout. Perhaps they deceived Syrus often, but he had never thought to question them.

When he paused to check his surroundings, he found himself outside the archives. The ironbound oak door was open, revealing the flickering glow of candlelight. Syrus stepped inside. The records were as good a place to start as any.

The room was long, dusty, and suffused with the scent of old paper. A few desks and chairs lined one wall, but otherwise, high shelves and racks of books and scrolls dominated the space.

A short woman with frizzy, black hair pulled back from her face sat at one of the desks, poring over a stack of parchment. Syrus knew Daia as his only friend among the trackers—most didn't concern themselves the field agents. He made sure to scuff the stone floor to avoid startling her.

Daia looked up from her work and stretched. "Hey there, mighty hunter. Arran said he saw you storming through the halls earlier."

"I had to speak with the shadeseer."

"You don't sound pleased about it."

"Nothing to worry about." Syrus unbuckled his sword and leaned it against the wall. He began searching the shelves. "I just have some research to do, is all."

Daia shadowed his path. "Have you washed from the road? You don't smell like it."

Without taking his eyes from the books, Syrus said, "I'm sorry, what rank are you again?"

"Different caste means I don't have to lick your filthy boots. I hope you're not thinking of touching any of this without at least washing your hands."

"They're covered in dust anyway." He reached for a tome, but Daia slapped his wrist. Syrus sighed and pulled a cloth from one of his belt pouches. He wiped the road dust from his hands and held them up before the tracker. "Clean. Happy?"

She rolled her eyes but nodded. "I was actually about to get a late dinner. Want me to bring you some?"

In his haste and focus, Syrus had not noticed how hungry he was. "Please," he said, carefully retrieving a massive book with a deteriorating spine.

He sat at a vacant desk within reach of his blade and began skimming the tome. It was a dry account of the history of the Godshadows, up to 1308. He slowed to read any mention of the shadeseers, but so far, found nothing new. The seers had learned their skills from the Angels of Shade, immortals that often served the goddess Tenebra. The shadeseers used their sight to locate threats and follow the field agents.

"The first Shadeseers of each Chapter were as follows: Falre of the Crescent Chapter; Lesan of the Crown Chapter...."

Syrus's eyes roamed over the passage three times, but he stopped reading after the first. He wondered if he could trust Daia. Trackers, by the nature of their role, worked more closely with shadeseers than other agents. Having seen more than a few Shadows destroyed by paranoia, he shook the thought from his head. He knew that she could be trusted just as instinctively as he knew the shadeseer could not.

He returned to the dull book, flipping through several chapters before something caught his attention:

"Shadeseer Evelyn delivered the news of the inferai's presence, which in turn had been delivered to her, so she claimed, by the Angel of Shade called Kyoxitel. This method of delivery shocked the other leaders more than the news itself, for no immortal had yet deigned to contact a mortal through the Seal, nor had any Shadeseer used such unusual soul magic, to this chronicler's knowledge."

The author failed to elaborate further on the angel and soul magic. However, Syrus spotted a small symbol next to the passage. It was crisscrossed with filigree but looked vaguely like a stylized eye.

He rushed back to the shelves, searching up and down the aisles. At last, he found the symbol again, etched in silver on the thick spine of a black book. Syrus had done little research since his initial training but remembered that Valentreid scholars often used such symbols to link texts together. He returned to his desk and opened the new tome on top of the first.

"Godsdammit," he muttered.

The book was written in Umbriri script, the sacred language of the Umbrid mystics in Sylgatum. The tongue was close enough to Gnoll that Syrus could understand the gist, but this lettering was

473

unique and incomprehensible to him. Except for A, and…was that a T? Yes, T.

"Godsdammit," he said again, louder.

"Damn what?" Daia asked as she reentered the room, carrying a tray of chicken, bread, and water.

"Languages in general. Can you read Umbriri?"

Daia placed the tray on a stool and leaned over the black book.

"I can," she said. "But I'm not translating this whole beast for you."

"No, no. But could you look for any mention of an angel called Kyoxitel?"

"Switch with me."

Syrus stood and reached for a chunk of bread while Daia took his former position at the desk.

She snapped her fingers. "Before I forget, a couple of the higher-up cloaks were looking for you—Ivre and Nellus, I think they were. Wouldn't say what for, though."

Syrus replaced his uneaten bread on the tray, picked up his sheathed sword, and moved closer to the door.

"Something up?" Daia asked.

"It's fine," he replied. Then he sighed, remembering his decision about trust. "No, it's not. I suspect some of the order may have been compromised."

"Compromised by what?"

"I'll let you know when I do. All I'm sure of are the words of Mortis."

"What?"

"Please," Syrus said. "Just find what you can on Kyoxitel. I promise I'll explain everything when we have time. Right now, I'm afraid the cloaks may not have gentle intentions for me. But I'm asking you to trust me. Do you?"

Daia studied him for a long moment. "I trust you."

He nodded and returned his attention to the door. "Hey, Daia—you didn't tell the cloaks where I was, did you?"

"Well, yes, I did—and I'm just now realizing why that was a bad idea. Sorry."

"You didn't know. Just tell me what you find."

The time passed in silence. Eventually, Syrus could deny his hunger no longer and began eating again. He took only a mouthful at a time, trying to maintain his vigilance.

"Alright," Daia finally said. "It seems Kyoxitel had two siblings—Archael and Zerexis. Legex himself sentenced them to the Tarterian dungeons for, get this, 'violating their contract and teaching forbidden techniques of soul magic to shadeseers.'"

Syrus turned to her. "What contract?"

"There's a rumor among my caste that shadeseers are not just instructed by their predecessors, but that they still commune with angels to learn the sight. I suppose this book is pretty strong evidence for that."

"What constituted this forbidden magic?"

Daia scanned the page, running a finger across the lines of text. Without looking up, she said, "The use of other people's souls by the caster."

Cold anger rose in Syrus. "Are they still imprisoned?"

"Archael and Kyoxitel were to be held for five hundred years, but Zerexis received mercy on the technicality that—not important." She turned a page, then continued. "Zerexis only received a century, and this trial occurred in 1244, by our calendar."

"So, he's been free for five years? And if he's communed with any shadeseers...."

"Now will you tell me what is going on?" Daia asked.

As Syrus opened his mouth to answer, he heard footsteps in echoing from the corridor. "Later," he said. "Stay here."

He stepped into the torch-lit hallway to face the cloaks. They were indeed the ones Daia had thought—Syrus knew them by both appearance and reputation.

Ivre was tall and strong, known for kicking in doors and tossing fugitives across the room. A small crossbow and a chain weighted at one end hung from her broad belt.

Nellus, an antileri, was smaller and wiry. His elven ancestry had granted him many decades to practice with the basket-hilt rapier at his waist. More than once, he had been reprimanded for killing his quarry without sufficient cause.

"How can I be of service to my fellow agents?" Syrus asked, presenting a pleasant façade. He still held his blade in its scabbard.

Nellus placed a hand on the grip of his own weapon. "We're here to apprehend you. The shadeseer suspects you of practicing outlawed magic."

Syrus laughed heartily. "He has quite a sense of irony, I must say." His mirth vanished. "I'm afraid I cannot obey."

He took quick stock of his surroundings. He had to keep the fight out here, lest the cloaks use Daia as a bargaining chip. He certainly wouldn't put that past Nellus. And though the duo could walk abreast in the corridor, it was too narrow for them to fight side by side or surround him. Nellus would likely come first, while Ivre used that crossbow. Nellus was good, but Syrus had been swinging a sword longer than the half-breed had been alive.

Syrus unsheathed his blade and tossed the scabbard behind him, settling into a ready crouch.

Nellus reacted immediately, drawing his rapier and thrusting. Syrus quick-stepped to the side and parried forcefully, trying to use his heavier sword to knock the rapier out wide. Nellus rotated his wrist, retracted, and thrust again.

Syrus just barely picked off the second strike. On the edge of his focus, he saw Ivre take a knee and raise her crossbow. She appeared to be waiting for an opening.

Again and again Nellus struck, but never drew blood. Syrus soon caught on to the cloak's patterns. They seemed more the product of endless drills than combat against experienced opponents.

Nellus stepped closer and swept his blade high. The sharpened edge near the tip cut a crimson line across Syrus's cheek.

That was the plan.

Syrus stepped back, seeming to fall deeper into defense. Spurred by the successful cut and apparent retreat, Nellus pursued recklessly. Syrus came forward, leaning past the rapier thrust. He launched a sudden kick into Nellus's abdomen.

The blow staggered Nellus. Syrus kept moving, as though trying to get at the cloak's back.

Ivre tracked him. Just as she started squeezing the trigger, Syrus stopped short and yanked the disoriented Nellus in front of him. Ivre managed to dip the bow reflexively, but the quarrel still caught Nellus in the left calf.

He yelled and fell as the leg gave way. Syrus swung the pommel of his sword down onto the cloak's head for good measure. Nellus hit the floor in a heap.

Syrus came back on guard, facing his remaining opponent. Ivre dropped the crossbow and took up the weighted chain, which was perhaps five feet long. She set it swinging vertically, keeping enough slack to avoid the floor and ceiling.

The weighted end shot out, straight at Syrus's face. He ducked, but it was too close a call for his comfort. As Ivre retracted the chain, Syrus lunged ahead.

She redirected the weight's momentum and swept the chain around, taking a half-step back. Her weapon wrapped around Syrus's, and she continued her movement backward. Tension and sheer strength pulled the sword from Syrus's grasp.

He kept coming anyway. Ivre released the entangled weapons. She spun back in, launching a haymaker, but Syrus ducked low once again. His left hand caught a mechanism on the inside of his right bracer. He punched straight up, inside Ivre's reach, as a spring-loaded stiletto blade extended over the top of his fist.

The thin dagger pierced her neck. She fell back while Syrus dragged the blade sideways. An enormous gash opened, gushing blood.

"Mortis guide your soul," Syrus said, eyes closed. "Oräk saniŋ mortinak in morsïn foriz."

The spell caused Ivre's blood to run off his skin and clothes, forming a viscous pool at his feet. He considered taking a blade to Nellus as well, who lay unconscious from Syrus's pommel bash and, knowing cloaks, some knockout drug from Ivre's bolt.

Syrus shook his head. Prick or no, one was enough.

Daia emerged from the archives room. "Oh, gods. You killed them—other Shadows."

He reset his stiletto blade. The mechanism clicked as he locked it back. "Just Ivre."

"Allow me to rephrase—you killed her, a fellow Shadow."

"She went for the kill. So did I." Syrus prodded Nellus with a boot. "So did he—tried very hard to stab me in the chest."

"Why?" Daia was not angry, though she trembled from agitation. She steadied herself against the wall. "What is happening? Why is it happening?"

Syrus hesitated. "Give me a moment." He closed his eyes and interlocked his hands so that only his index and little fingers pointed outward.

"Mor skidak av lokes ïn animavi makus us oräk orenz. Mor skidak avi animavi makus kineskanav ïn av shadeseer."

Though Syrus's eyes remained shut, he saw a glow emanating from above him—the aura of soul magic. His spell also indicated the source—the shadeseer in his dark chamber. But this was not enough. Soul magic in itself was practiced by every priest. It was what separated them from acolytes.

"Mor skidak oräk makus oni animavi parotävo."

The glow remained, but now Syrus could see each soul being used to fuel the shadeseer's magic—there were five, all in that room. Syrus severed his thread, ending the spell.

He took a deep breath. "The shadeseer is using other people's souls. No doubt that angel is teaching its techniques again. Immortals just can't fight their natures."

He paused, but Daia said nothing. She just stared at him, probably using her own magic to tell if he was lying. Daia had never before turned her powers on Syrus, as far as he knew.

"It does sound mad," he said. "Here's something madder—Mortis is the one who told me to investigate some corruption in our order."

"It's true," Daia said quietly. She averted her gaze and slid onto the floor. "Or, at least, you believe it is."

Syrus chuckled. "He told me that's all that matters to an individual—what they believe. It was a long time ago when he said that."

Daia looked at him again. He moved to sit directly across the corridor from her.

"This wasn't the first time Mortis has spoken to me. Have I ever told you about my family?"

She shook her head. "You never wanted to."

Syrus smiled weakly at his own reserve, which grew more pointless by the moment. "I was young when they died. Lunatic gnoll on a rampage. From one of the bad Umbrid cults. I wasn't there when my parents were killed, but I was present a couple weeks later when my brother fell to his despair and took a knife to his wrists. We lived too far out of town for anybody to help, and I was too young to know what to do. I watched him bleed out, and then I saw the Severance.

"He wore a wide, black hat and a cloak with tassels—like the ones that were in style back then. Walked right past me. He glanced down for just a second, but he knew I saw him. He touched my brother on the shoulder and disappeared."

Syrus wiped his eyes, but then realized the moisture he felt was just part of the memory. "Had dreams after that. Visions where Mortis and I...discussed things. He likes to converse. The reason I tell you this is partly to convince you that my task is true."

"Why else?"

"Mortis made it so I was no longer afraid of death—others' or my own. I needed to remind myself of that, I think."

"I'm sorry I said you smelled bad earlier."

Syrus laughed softly and nodded.

"What are you going to do now?" Daia asked.

"I've been trying to figure that out." He stood and retrieved his sword. "And I can't see any way past it now. I'm going to go kill that blind son of a bitch."

Daia stood as well. "I think that's a very bad idea. You should go to Sacre with this."

"If Mortis wanted command to handle it, he would have told them." Syrus gestured at the cloaks. "Think what could happen in the weeks it'd take them to get here." He took a breath to calm himself. "I'm ending this perversion of mortality now. I recommend you leave."

He strode in the direction the cloaks had come from. He did not look back at Daia. He did not want to.

The route was clear. It was getting late, and most of the agents would be settling into their bunks. Syrus suspected the shadeseer wanted to keep this affair discreet, as well.

He hesitated just a moment outside the chamber. "Luch parotak," he said. A luminous globe appeared near the ceiling as he entered.

The shadeseer sat cross-legged on a cushion in the center of the space, looking younger than when Syrus last had seen him in the light. His eyes were milky white, as expected, but his skin was taut and full. Black cloth draped him, flowing onto the slate floor.

The fabric led Syrus's gaze to the four emaciated bodies sprawled about the shadeseer. Their chests rose and fell, but barely. Eyes stared at the ceiling, seeing nothing, dried from unblinking. Runes for directing energy were scarred into pale, shrunken flesh.

Syrus suppressed a gag, reminding himself of the far more revolting things he'd seen over his career as a hunter.

"You are the one who brought light in this place," the shadeseer said, laughing at Syrus's disgust. Though the man looked young, his voice remained parched with age.

Syrus tightened his grip on his sword and rushed forward.

The shadeseer held up a hand. "Halt."

Syrus stopped not seven feet from him, as though his feet were suddenly glued to the floor.

"I command five souls—did you imagine you would simply approach and behead me?"

In response, Syrus drew a small knife from his belt and threw it. The blade stuck into the shadeseer's neck.

The man barely winced. He pulled the knife out, and the wound closed before he lost more than a trickle of blood. "I now wonder why I sent Ivre and Nellus if you had already planned to be this foolish."

Syrus grinned. "I guess you aren't much of a seer, then, are you?"

"I need not omniscience when I have such power as this."

Syrus heard footsteps behind him. Twisting around, he saw Ivre enter the chamber. The gash on her throat was sealed, but the spark of consciousness was missing from her eyes.

"I wield souls as no priest can," the shadeseer said. "Raising the dead is a trifling matter."

Ivre walked around Syrus to stand before him. He swung his sword but could put forth little power without moving his feet. She caught his arm with one hand and slammed her other fist into his gut.

Syrus coughed. *Godsdamn, she is strong.*

She pulled the sword from his weakened grasp and tossed it aside. She then grabbed him by the throat and thigh, lifted him over her head, and hurled him across the room.

Syrus rolled to a stop on the hard stone. He tried to rise and ignore the pain in his shoulder.

Ivre clenched both hands around his neck and pinned him to the wall. He struggled to get words past his closed throat.

"Now do you see, hunter?" the shadeseer asked.

Ivre's grip slackened.

Syrus sucked in air, despite the ache in his chest. "Is that even her anymore?" he managed to ask.

"More so than most undead, from a more enlightened perspective. Rather than construct a replica soul, I returned hers where it belongs. She only lost a portion to fuel the process."

Ivre stepped back, releasing Syrus. He leaned over, one hand on his knee and the other on his neck. He spotted a single tear running down her face.

"And you don't see why Mortis might have a problem with that?"

As Syrus spoke, he focused on a thread. He only needed a little energy as a catalyst. He knew a few obscure spells himself. However, his were forbidden only by the laws of mortals.

"It is as I said before," the shadeseer replied. "The gods no longer hold sway."

"Oh, just fuck off. Mor kovonak az ator."

An explosion of light and heat filled the chamber, emanating from Syrus. The shockwave blew back Ivre, the shadeseer, and the bodies before incinerating them. Flames rushed through the doorway as the air combusted. The whole Sunrise Chapterhouse shook from the blast.

When it passed, nothing remained of the chamber but scorched stone. The globe of light vanished in the instant of its creator's death.

The blinding light faded, stranding Syrus in a void. The pain in his chest was gone, leaving only a penetrating chill. He could see nothing, hear nothing, but smelled rain. An eternity passed in a moment.

Mortis stepped out of the endless darkness. He still wore the grey garb from their prior meeting, but now Syrus could see infinity in the god's eyes. The lives and deaths of billions and billions of souls danced across the ash-colored orbs.

The Severance placed a hand on Syrus's shoulder.

"That was one way to do things, I suppose. Not the most intelligent, but a method nonetheless."

Syrus and Mortis sat across from one another in an otherwise barren stone room. The elf was once again aware of the passage of time as he remained silent.

"Nothing to say?" Mortis asked. "You had so much before." The depth was gone from his eyes—or at least, reduced to a manageable level.

"I did what you tasked me to do," Syrus said.

Mortis sighed. "I had hoped you wouldn't kill yourself in the process. Your shadeseer was not the only one in your order committing magic on foreign souls. The other transgressors yet live."

"You could have told me that, instead of the cryptic warnings of corruption."

"Fair point. I say I'm mysterious because it amuses me, but sometimes I truly do forget how mortal minds work. My usual medium of communion—dreams—addles my words further, from your perspectives. I apologize. I shall simply have to contact others. Few will be as cooperative as you, I fear. Unless…. Hm. Possible." His gaze trailed away in thought.

"How many died?" Syrus felt he should ask.

Mortis counted in the air. "Ten. Nine, if you don't include poor Ivre, though you did kill her in the first place."

Syrus nodded, unsure how to react.

"Daia's fine," Mortis added.

That brought a slight smile.

"So, what now?" Syrus asked.

"Now comes the tale of your life. I make a point to learn every dead mortal's history. Someone has to."

"I think we're already well acquainted."

"Yes, but I want to know everything."

Two glasses of red wine materialized on the table.

"I remember you like Oratas," Mortis said. "Have a drink and start at the beginning. Oh, and welcome to the next stage of your existence."

The god raised his glass. The elf toasted, sipped the earthy vintage, and began speaking.

Breakwall

Des had never intended to return to Forente. And yet, here she was, standing in the salty breeze at some rooftop bar overlooking the West Docks. Downing, she once called that district. She leaned on the railing to distance herself from the clamor of the crowd. She heard the accents and jargon of people she thought she'd left behind, a blend of dropped syllables and innuendo to obscure their clandestine business.

But Des understood, eavesdropping despite her desire to ignore the conversations—an old habit from that life before. A woman was dealing silverleaf extract smuggled in from the jungles. Two men were discussing hands—unregistered slaves—from Procumes. Des hated this city, this cesspool of 400,000 rats scrambling to feed their greed and their vices while staying a step ahead of the authorities.

She had to come back, though, for Ari. Her killer had only one traceable effect, a contract stamped by a leader of the Kraken. Des did not recognize the personal mark, but each overwatcher had their own. Except for the old guard at the top, bosses came and went. The stamp could easily belong to a new face.

Luc returned from the bar, bearing a pair of mugs. He drew stares from the crowd, particularly toward the pair of swords—one long, one short—on his belt. A red bandana held his shaggy hair in check, and a medallion embossed with the grinning battle god, Atora, hung from his neck. He was the first and oldest friend Des and Ari had made in Equotel and was nearly as wrapped up in this bloody business.

The priest handed one mug to Des. She took a drink, surprised to find rum.

"You can't be using up all our coin," she said.

"I'm not. It was just a few aerni."

"No way the keep paid tariff on this." Des looked back out over the harbor, fixating on the rocky breakwall. "That's where she and I met. We got sent out to watch for a smuggler coming in from Aeribe and signal our dock team when he arrived."

The sun was setting as they gazed southward over the district, painting the sky a spectrum from orange to deep violet. Long shadows cast from the docks and platforms loomed over the water like enormous, gangly spiders.

No, not spiders, Des thought. *A web. One wrong step and you're caught. Try to escape, and that's when the spiders come.*

"So, what's the plan?" Luc asked. "Get in touch with your old contacts?"

Des grunted and shook her head. "I could try, but Ari and I cut every tie we could when we left. No one owes me a favor anymore."

"There has to be someone."

Des closed her eyes, running through a long list of crossed-out names. "Tiber, maybe. A big maybe. Last I heard, he was gaping. By now, he's either gone cape or got falced."

Luc looked at her, head cocked. "You got a Serma version of that?"

"Sorry. Slipped back into Cant there. He informed for the guard, so by now either he joined them, or someone killed him. Maybe both."

"How do we find him, if he's the only contact?"

"Only Kraken contact," Des corrected, pointing at Luc. "I'd be genuinely shocked if his sister has moved off Shant—that stilted neighborhood down there."

Des finished her drink, then continued staring at the breakwall.

"Do you want to go out there?" Luc asked.

"We shouldn't. We don't know who we might run into."

Luc nodded, locking eyes with her. "Sure."

Des had never fully understood why priests were so mistrusted in Forente until she spent some time with Luc. After a while, their gazes seemed to burn through any deceit, see every sin of those on the receiving end. Whether they spoke for Legex or Rixa—or Atora—Des was always aware she had done something wrong in the priests' eyes.

Now, she was certain Luc saw her real fear. Ari's ghost was already inside Des, screaming for vengeance. The presence was caged in a corner of her heart, and she heard the call with every beat. If Des walked the breakwall, returned to that place she held so sacred before she had completed this task, the ghost would escape. She needed to focus.

"We'll head to Shant tomorrow," she said, forcing her thoughts back to the job.

As they pushed their way through the bar crowd, people once again stared after Luc.

"You should really hide the swords," Des said when they had descended to the streets.

"You're the one who kept saying everybody carries weapons here."

"It's true." She leaned in, whispering. "But the trick is to pretend you're not." Des tapped her ankles together, indicating two of her concealed blades. She also had a small stiletto with its sheath sewn to the inside of her leather vest, and a fighting knife strapped to her back, under her shirt. "Just saying, you might make people a bit jumpy."

They stayed at a nondescript hostel, hoping to pass as simple drifters instead of reserving several nights at an inn.

Shant was less destitute than the beggar-strewn Copper District, but only just. The wooden neighborhood seemed to be waiting for a fire to send it tumbling into the harbor. Even on the open platforms, Des always swore she could feel the entire mass sway and tilt like a ship's deck.

She wore a brimmed hat, pulled forward to shield her face from the sun and any old acquaintances on the streets. The only one she wanted to meet was Selira, Tiber's sister and a woman who made a point of avoiding Kraken business.

At Des's insistence, Luc had wrapped his swords in a cloth bundle across his back. She wondered if it was worth the argument, glaring as the "deception" was.

Despite her worries, the pair received no harassment before reaching a two-story shack. The walkway led to a loose door on the upper level, while the rest sat below the platforms. Next to it, the shattered and charred remains of a smaller building stood open to the sky. Des paused, remembering where Selira's husband plied his trade.

"What the shit happened there?" she muttered, knocking at the intact place.

A cracking voice emanated from a shaded window. "Ma! Someone's here!"

Another voice, incoherent, yelled from somewhere deeper.

"Yeah, yeah," the first said.

The door opened, revealing a messy-haired boy dressed in nothing but loose trousers.

"Booze ain't ready yet," he said. "Come back in two days."

He started to close the door, but Des caught it and leaned in the frame.

"Which one are you? Reni?"

The boy narrowed his eyes.

"Tell your ma to get up here. An old friend's come back."

She stepped out of the way, and Reni retreated.

"How well do you know her?" Luc asked.

"Well, but Selira kept her boys pretty shielded from my ilk. Speaking of, don't ask her anything about the Kraken. She's neutral."

The door opened again. Selira was in her middle years, wrinkled but not yet grey, and scarcely taller than her young son. Her jaw dropped for an instant before a wide smile took hold.

"Desalie, my gods, I thought you were serious." She wrapped Des in a solid embrace. The smell of distilling grain saturated her clothes, but not her breath.

"I was," Des said, returning the hug. "Wouldn't have come back if I could sleep easy elsewhere."

Selira pulled back.

"This is Luc—no one to worry about. We were hoping we could talk to Tiber."

"Where's Arilysa?"

Des swallowed and glanced down.

"Oh no. Come in, please."

The interior was sparsely furnished and cleaner than Des remembered. The kitchen and living area comprised one room, while a curtain cordoned off the "bedroom." Crates of bottles, some empty and some not, sat next to the stairs.

"Make yourselves home," Selira said. "Reni, run get your uncle Tiber. He's probably sleeping, but tell him there's a bottle of Midsummer in it for him."

Reni sighed, strapping on a pair of shoddy sandals and eyeing the strangers on his way out.

Des and Luc sat down at the unbalanced table. Selira brought three clay cups and poured some clear, fruity liquid.

"A bit early, isn't it?" Luc asked.

Selira sat down, smirking. "For you, maybe. I was up before sun. Come on, it's just some thin white." She looked to Des, growing serious once more. "Is she really—"

"She's dead. About a month now. We were up in Equotel, but I guess three hundred miles wasn't enough for someone."

Selira shook her head. "She didn't deserve that. Neither of you did."

"That's why I'm here," Des said. "To make sure they—whoever they are—know that."

The three clutched their cups in silence. Then, Selira lifted hers.

"To Arilysa."

"To Ari," the guests echoed.

Des needed to keep moving forward. "So, what exactly happened over there?" she asked, jerking her head toward the blasted husk next door.

Selira shrugged. "The only end El would ever find with his work. My husband blew his lab and himself to Hades bout a year after you left."

"Sorry to hear that," Luc said.

"I'm not." Selira looked out the front window, absently tracing a long, faint scar on her forearm. "Damned fool thought he could make black powder better than them in Aure, then got it he could make something new and stronger. Only good things he ever gave me were my boys and the spare gear he kept downstairs—enough for me to start brewing for a few bars down this way."

"Glad things are better," Des said.

They held hands from across the table. Selira was more serene than Des had ever seen her. For all her drive, all her grief and rage, Des was reminded that this world, this city, was not all calling for blood. Not all death demanded death. There was still room for balance. She didn't want to lose herself in Ari's ghost but wondered whether she had a choice.

Within an hour, Reni returned, followed by a sturdy, bald man in plain clothes and heavy boots. Tiber glanced at the guests and stopped short. Before he could speak, Selira stood and handed him a bottle bound in twine.

"Here's the Midsummer. I'll be downstairs while you discuss."

Reni stepped up. "Can I stay—"

"No. Come give me a hand."

Tiber, still in some state of shock, watched his sister descend, dragging Reni by the ear. He turned back to the kitchen. "Chains, Des—you're alive?"

"Shouldn't I be?"

He sat down. "Only reason I'm here is I got the guard watching my back. Lots wanted me dead for leaving."

Des rolled her eyes. "Yeah, cause you spied and fucking defected. Don't take anything with, and the Kraken's fine letting you walk."

Luc stared at Tiber. "Do you know anyone who feels they've been robbed?"

Tiber leaned back in his creaky chair, matching the look and setting the Midsummer on the table. "Who's this?" He spotted the medallion. "You running with a fucking priest?"

Luc gave a slight nod, still not blinking. "A Blade of Atora."

"Shit, thought you madmen'd be gone by now, picking one with every fighter you meet."

"We're fighters, too. You imply otherwise?"

Des put a firm hand on Luc's arm.

"Look," Tiber said. "I seen men hang up their swords and learn the prayers. Never seen a priest who actually knows the blade."

Luc shrugged off Des's hand. "You have now. Want to dance, watchman?"

"What, in the street?"

Luc nodded.

Tiber broke out laughing. "Chains of Crusix, Des. Where'd you find this howler?"

"Equotel. Listen, Tiber, I know wearing the cape makes you want to wave your dick around, but we're here on business."

The mirth vanished from the guard's face. He sniffed and glared at the table. Des reached into her pocket and pulled out a worn envelope—the killer's instructions. The broken seal depicted an eye with a coiled serpent for a pupil. She slid it into Tiber's view.

He looked up at her, putting a hand out. "Hey, I'm in the guard now. I'm not getting into any Kraken plot, and don't owe you any debt."

"What about Ari?" Des asked. "I'm thinking you still owe her for the lotus incident."

496

Tiber covered his face. "She said we were square. Besides, a month after you left, the monks turned up. In a fog damp, but still. I covered her ass for that botch with the spice runner. If Ari wants to blackmail me, tell her to come herself—"

"Tiber, will you shut the fuck up for one godsdamn minute? Ari's dead."

"Bullshit."

Des picked up the envelope and held it out to Tiber. "This ain't Kraken business. This is personal. I need to know who stamped the seal."

Tiber seemed to deflate, his broad shoulders bowing. He seized the envelope slowly but firmly. Ignoring the seal, he took out the folded paper inside and began reading. Des watched his face. She had the neat script memorized, and could tell where Tiber was by the movements of his eyes and tiny twitches in his expression.

A middle dog with collar vizzed me your run. I have a carry miss to Avex's base. Curtain. Three dry ago, Arilysa Talbre winged Capital to Vines with Desalie Vate. I can viz if artery, but middle dog says you are a glassblow hound.

Arilysa nipped on her wing. Falc her. Desalie is a roll—char level. Parch me for jingle.

Tiber slammed his fists onto the table. The note drifted onto the floor. He cleared his throat but retained a rough edge. "What'd she take?"

"Nothing," Des said. "We left clean, which is why I'm bogged right now."

Tiber retrieved the envelope. "Water's rough. I already made peace with you two being dead. When I saw you—it's just, I always thought you'd come and go together."

"Me too."

The guard finally examined the insignia. "The seventh overwatcher. No shock you're bogged. He ain't been that high for long, and he only spent a year or two as a watcher in the docks."

"What's his name?" Des asked.

Tiber shook his head. "My patrol's the Bronze District. All else I can say is remind you how fucking rot-brained you'd be to go after an overwatcher." He stood, exchanging the envelope for his drink. He shouted down the stairwell, "Getting weary of you bribing me over, Sel!"

"Then come of your own accord, once a moon!" Selira called back.

Tiber grunted and started for the door.

"Wait—where's he den?" Des asked.

"Either Rose or Inks. He goes between them, I hear." He turned and glared. "Don't follow her, Des."

Tiber left the crooked door banging on its frame.

Des and Luc didn't stay long. They refused Selira's offer of a third round but promised to stop by again before leaving Forente. Des knew that even if she killed this overwatcher and got away, the whole Kraken would be sweeping the city for them. But still, she promised. Selira had been her and Ari's sole regret about leaving.

The pair walked the seaside edge of the district. Following her old haunts brought Des a strange mix of nostalgia and paranoia. She had long ago mastered masking agitation. She strode casually, hat forward, hands in view, and met no one's eyes. Luc tried his best as he followed.

Inks was a series of warehouses and offices, ostensibly serving merchants who needed to transfer goods between ships. The cellars, however, stored a vast quantity of poisons, mostly from Pluvitelles, either sold or used in certain Kraken dealings.

Des kept moving past, worried to pause and watch for familiar faces. Besides, she knew the interior layout intimately. They turned at the pier and had started to circle back along a different street when Des slowed. The end of the lane had an excellent view of the breakwall, as did the last office on the Inks row.

Luc nudged her from behind, and she quickened her pace.

They passed by Rose, a well-built but plain house that coordinated Kraken turf patrols. Des dared not approach too closely—she just wanted Luc to see where it was.

They spent the night at a different hostel, sharing a cot-filled common space with a half-dozen strangers. Des retired early, obsessed with drawing connections in her mind. Even without the overwatcher's name, she couldn't shake a certain sense of familiarity. It was his dens. Perhaps a third of the jobs she ran lock on had ended at Inks. Did she ever run with him?

Des didn't have the funds to start asking real informants— their prices at least tripled for those outside the Kraken. She didn't want to go in blind, but that was beginning to seem like the only option.

Thoughts still racing, she dozed.

Ari slouches against a thick willow trunk, with Des lying across her lap. They watch songbirds rustle through black mulberries and pond reeds. Des looks up into Ari's dark eyes, then pushes herself up with one arm and kisses her. Des settles against the tree, now leaning on Ari's shoulder.

"You're going back to Forente?" Ari asks. "Why?"

"I have to find someone, but I don't know who."

"They must be somebody important. Somebody we know."

Des doesn't respond. A gentle breeze rises from the south. Ari puts one arm around Des's waist and reaches into a pocket with her free hand. She uncurls her fingers, revealing a silver ring. The band is engraved with a vine pattern. A small emerald sparkles when it catches the sun between the willow branches.

"I want to get married," Ari says. "I hear the priests of Liba would do it."

Des wears a confused expression. She pulls the same ring out of her own pocket. "You already gave me this."

Ari laughs. "I guess I did." She replaces her ring and stands, looking out over the rippling water.

Des rises next to her. "Where did you get it?"

"Well, emeralds don't come from Equotel."

They interlock fingers and kiss again, holding it as the breeze ceases.

Des tastes blood. She opens her eyes and breaks off. Ari stares, her face growing pale and blank, trickles of red running from the corners of her mouth.

A man swathed in midnight blue, hooded and masked, looms behind her. He holds a short blade, driving it deeper into Ari's back. He retracts. Ari falls.

Without a word or cry, Des lunges at him. She drives his blade arm out wide, wraps around it, and pulls the weapon from his weakened grip, just as Luc taught her. The killer tries to flee, but Des seizes his shirt and flings him to the ground with solipsistic strength. She pins him down with one hand and runs him through the gut.

"Who did this?" Her voice is a shriek.

The killer pulls down his scarf, exposing a manic grin.

Des pulls the blade out and stabs again, higher. "Who did this?"

Over and over she stabs him. Blood soaks both of them as she tears his garb to shreds with her frenzied strikes, grinds his organs to pulp. Finally, she plunges the blade through his throat.

"Who did this?"

The killer keeps smiling as scarlet seeps from his eyes. Despite his lack of a trachea, he speaks. "All the way back."

Des sinks to her knees, arching her back and gazing into the blood-spattered blue sky. She crawls to Ari's cold form and collapses over her. She reaches into Ari's pocket and holds the emerald ring.

At last, Des managed to open her eyes. She wanted to wake up much sooner.

It was dark still, but for a low-burning lamp. Luc sat on the edge of his adjacent cot, watching her. "You were thrashing."

"Just a dream."

Des was unsure whether the nightmare was worse than the real memory. It had been nighttime, not midday. She and Ari were out walking the vineyards near Salles, the Equoteli town they had moved to, getting some space from the lights and music of its founding festival. A bolt struck Ari in the back. It must have been poisoned—it missed her heart, but she died with hardly a gasp. Des saw no attacker in her panicked glances before she dropped to the dirt and held Ari.

Luc, some distance behind, heard Des cry out and spotted someone dropping from a tree. The killer, watching over his shoulder, did not notice Luc moving to intercept. He bumped into the priest, then frantically performed his final act of pulling a knife and thrusting.

Des rolled off her cot and padded over to the lamp-lit table by the door. She held the ring in her palm. Luc followed.

"She was going to ask me to marry her that night," Des said quietly. "This was in her pocket. I saw it in her drawer the day before. We never got each other jewelry, so I knew. That's why I brought her out to the vineyard—so she could ask me in private."

Luc put an arm around her shoulders. "It wasn't your fault."

"I know—just not all of me." She paused, narrowing her eyes and staring at the ring rolling between her fingers. "All the way back."

The breakwall—that first job. There had been a third person, a man, on watch with them. After the cargo transfer, he and Ari had a loud, "private" conversation back onshore. Des hadn't made out what was said, but at one point, she glanced over and saw Ari throw something. He flailed but caught whatever it was as Ari stormed in Des's direction.

"Don't suppose you want to grab a hard drink?" Ari had asked her.

Des had seen the man once in a while after that, but never while Ari was with. He was always mannered, but more polite than kind, like he was disguising his resentment. And he wore an emerald ring.

This ring.

Fuck, what was his name? Des ran through every chance meeting she could recall until she heard some past voice call out "Ecar!" In that foggy scene, the man turned to respond.

"His name is Ecar," Des said, looking up at Luc.

"You know him?"

She shook her head. "Not really, but his name's enough."

Des returned to her belongings, strapping blades into place and donning her night cloak. "I'll be back."

Luc caught her on the arm. "From where?"

"I need to confirm a few things and get some supplies. Wait here."

"What? No." Luc grabbed his weapons belt. "I'll come with."

"Wait. Here. I've tried to explain, and hoped by now you'd realize this isn't your world. I mean, you tried to pick a fight with fucking Tiber. I let you come because I know you loved her too, but keep to your own strengths."

Luc's nostrils flared. "Let me come? That's not—"

"Will you shut it?" a soft voice demanded from somewhere in the dark room.

Des made a sweeping gesture in the direction of the harsh whisper. The anonymous guest echoed her sentiment, if not her diction. Shadows swallowed her as she left the hostel.

When Des returned, Luc was leaning next to the doorway, shaded from the rising sun. His eyes tried to burn holes in her, but she stood by her decision. Luc wouldn't have done what was necessary.

"There's blood on your arm," he said.

Des examined her wrists—sure enough, she had missed a spot. She rubbed out the stain. "Well, I know he's at Inks now. And I can get us in."

"Us?"

She nodded. "You have to follow my lead, though, if you want to get through this."

Luc glanced away. "Depends where you lead. I've no problem killing in battle, but backstabbing is another matter."

Des removed her cloak and threw it over her shoulder. "Then you came to the wrong fucking city. Here, honor's rooted in respect, and respect in practicality. Nobody but me gives a damn about you. I'm going in to sleep a while." She recalled an old street poem and quoted, "'Death comes with the dark.'"

Before drifting off, Des removed her prize from a belt pouch—an electrum coin molded with a kraken. She turned it over between her fingers, revealing the D for Downing. She was on a carry. It had taken a few days, but Des was finally back in Forente, body and mind.

Des and Luc emerged from the alleyways into the lit street leading up to Inks. Only half of the oil-fueled lamps shone. Luc wore his swords openly, while Des kept her weapons concealed. Almost immediately, a blank-faced elf with a cutlass intercepted them. Des recognized Laryn, the watcher for fencing and dealing in this section. She kept her eyes hidden under her hood.

"Business?" Laryn asked, lighting a pipe with a spark from his fingertips.

Des held up the envelope containing the kill order, letting the elf see the insignia. "Return on a seal for Ecar." She flashed the coin as well.

Laryn nodded, puffing smoke. "And who's this?"

"Glassblow stow," Des replied. "It's all on the parch—for him."

"Alright, lass, no breakers. He's in the main." Laryn stepped aside, letting them pass.

Once they were out of earshot, Luc asked, "Which one's main?"

Des nodded at the end of the row, the two-story warehouse and attached office facing the breakwall. Luc continued in that direction, but Des herded him into a gap between buildings.

"Front door's sealed at night."

A small walkway behind the warehouses led down to the contiguous stone cellars. Scattered waves sloshed against the rocky outcropping that formed the neighborhood's foundation. A single lantern hung above a back door, illuminating a pair of lightly armored sentries.

Des held up a hand for Luc to wait a few paces back as she approached. Again, she showed the letter and coin. "For Ecar."

The first lock nodded and started a discordant pattern of knocks on the ironbound door. The second hissed at him, then quickly gathered herself and asked Des, "What color's the banner?"

"Blue." It was a wild guess.

The sentry raised her eyebrows and nearly called out—in a blink, Des snapped out her stiletto and drove it into the guard's throat.

The door opened. The other lock reached out to slam it shut. Des let go of her blade and tackled him away, shouting, "In!"

Luc rushed past, grappling with someone inside. Meanwhile, Des held the sentry pinned, face in the dirt, arm twisted across his back. She pulled a dagger from her right boot and slit his throat. *Security's declined since we left.*

A crash and scuffle sounded from inside. Removing her cloak and entering, Des saw the doorman going limp in Luc's sleeper hold.

"Just kill him," she said, retrieving her stiletto from the dying woman. She turned back to see Luc give a disgusted expression. He set the unconscious man down.

"He saw us," Des said.

"He's not a threat. And you didn't have to go straight for the kill out there."

"Yes, I did. We don't have time or resources for a nice, neat slith."

Luc sighed. "Didn't even have their weapons out."

"Have you listened to anything I've said?"

"They aren't who we're after! You want to cut Ecar's throat, fine—that'd be justice. But at least give these ones the chance to fight or flee."

I should not have brought him.

Des knelt down to the doorman and finished him. She stood and locked eyes with Luc, speaking slowly. "There's no honor here. Not for you, not for me. Not for them. We didn't come to fight. We came to hunt."

"We could fight."

"Against a few, sure." Des started down the entry corridor, pausing at an intersection of stairwells, one up and one down. "But we can't hack our way through this whole building."

Luc drew his swords. A faint shimmer flared in his eyes and around the blades, the signature of his priestly magic. "I'm a Blade of Atora. Watch me."

He started up in the direction of the offices. Des clenched a fist, then took a slow, deep breath. This was a carry. Luc was a howler, prone to sending carries into the deep. She needed to believe this if she were to have any chance of success. She would do this her way, the way she knew Ari would.

A shout echoed through the halls, followed by clashing steel. Good—Luc was a distraction.

Des started in the opposite direction, down the stairs. The main storeroom for the various toxins lay behind another secure door. Des held a dagger in a reversed grip, hiding it between her arm and body. With her free hand, she knocked.

A viewing slit opened. "The fuck's going on out there?" a gruff voice demanded.

Des shook her head, gasping as though out of breath. "Fucking howler with swords broke in. He's somewhere back up the passage. Please, let me in."

Silence, then another echoing cry.

"C'mon, dog, please! Howler killed Laryn outside!"

"Laryn? Fuckin hades. Fine, be quick."

Des heard the sound of a bar being lifted, and the door opened just enough for her to slip through. Before the guard even got the bar back down, Des plunged the dagger into his lower back.

"Gah, cunt!" He fell to a knee and reached for his belted knife with a shaky hand.

Des pulled it first, tossing it aside. She leaned in close, still holding her blade in his back.

"Ecar up on the office?" she whispered into his ear.

"Get fucked," he said through grit teeth.

Des twitched the blade. He groaned, the muscles of his torso contracting, but nodded slightly.

"What's the pass tonight?"

The guard just heaved ragged breaths.

Des laughed. "Come on, he's been an overwatcher less than a year. Is he really worth dying for?" She twisted the blade. The muscles contracted tighter than should have been possible.

"Crow!"

"Hm. Fitting." Des pulled out her dagger. The guard sagged forward, sucking air. He looked up.

"So—"

She ran him through the eye, then barred the door. Shelves of vials and flasks, of all sizes and colors, all labeled, filled the former wine cellar. Des hurried down the rows, sweeping the vessels with her gaze. She didn't need it, necessarily, but Ari's ghost thirsted for this particular brand of death.

"Right where it always was," Des muttered, taking a small, clear vial. Greyfang tears, according to the label—a powerful paralytic harvested from a sea snake on the jungle coast and refined with trace amounts of potent herbs to keep the victim still yet conscious. A needle-like blade dipped down from the underside of the stopper.

Des checked through the door slit—clear. She pulled the dead guard to the side and closed the portal behind her. Creeping back up the stone steps, she ran one hand along the inner wall, covering as much area as possible. Halfway up, she caught the tiny pressure plate. She had to lean into it, but finally, the stone sank into the wall and popped the hidden door.

She crouched low and extended her fighting knife into the secret passage. The blade pulled a tripwire, and several darts flew across, clattering against the opposite wall. She entered cautiously, but found no further traps defending the steep, curving staircase. The far door opened into a wood-paneled hallway better lit than the cellar.

Des glanced right, the way that led to the warehouses and main stairs. Clear. She started left, to the office.

A woman hustled in the opposite direction, holding a crossbow in one hand and bundle of bolts in the other. "Good thinking," she said, banking toward the passage. "We can get behind him. Holy shit, Des?"

Des drove her fighting knife into the underside of Cali's chin. She felt a slight twinge at killing an old comrade, but then remembered that Cali had once keelhauled three priests of Armis.

She heard a thump behind her. Luc leaned his shoulder against the wall, having just turned the final corner. His eyes and swords emitted a pearly luminescence, and he was covered in blood. The glow faded as he stiffly straightened and started forward with an obvious limp in his right leg.

"I didn't find him," Luc said. His stare was vacant. "Killed thirteen, but none were him."

Thirteen? Chains, Luc. Des loaded the crossbow. "I know where he is. How bad are you hurt?"

Luc blinked and glanced at his leg. "I'm not bleeding. I closed the wounds, but I'm no healer. I don't know how to fix the insides. You were right—I should have followed you."

"I know."

Luc smirked. "The line between valor and stupidity is a narrow one to balance. But damn my eyes, it was invigorating."

"That attitude will get you killed one day."

"I know."

Sense told Des to leave Luc behind, that he was a liability. He might buy her some time if more Kraken agents showed up. This was a carry to Des, the Desalie of cold skill and results. The Desalie who had been left behind in Forente, just as Ari had left her old self. She wasn't here for that Ari—it was the compassionate and resilient side she had fallen in love with. Sense told her to abandon emotion; Ari told her to embrace it. The ghost fueled the wrath of revenge. Emotion was the reason Des was here.

She put a hand on Luc's shoulder. "Come on. Let's get this motherfucker."

The ironbound door to the office was shut. Des knew the lock had a mechanical override on the inside, and it was likely barred, as well. She guided Luc to the side, tight into the corner, and put a finger to her lips. She faced away from the door, holding the crossbow in plain view. For once, she was grateful Cali shared her short, dark hair. Des knocked twice, once, and four times—a universal call that wouldn't have changed. She heard a slit open.

"What went to Slick?" a muffled voice asked.

509

"Crow," Des responded.

The slit opened further. Cocking her head and listening, she heard faintly, "It's Cali."

"Let her in."

A series of clicks and creaks emanated from the unsealing door. Des gave a slight nod to Luc. She whirled, bringing the crossbow into line.

Past the burly axe-wielder opening the door, standing next to a cluttered desk, Des saw him—Ecar.

She had a kill shot but lowered her aim. He didn't deserve a falc. Des pulled the trigger, firing a quarrel into Ecar's thigh. She dropped the bow and charged. The axeman reached for her with his free hand, but Luc intercepted, launching off his good leg and driving the bodyguard back.

Luc winced as he landed on his bad leg. He held his arming sword reversed in his left hand, gripping the ricasso and keeping the makeshift shield in line with his opponent. In his right hand, the shorter blade was poised to thrust.

Ecar lurched from the bolt, snapping a knife from his belt. Des went for a tackle, grabbing his weapon arm to keep it wide and planting her other forearm against his neck. They bounced off the sturdy glass of the large window.

The overwatcher wrapped his free arm around Des, flicking the knife into a reversed grip in that hand. He slashed across her back. The leather vest and Des's own knife sheath mitigated the strike, but she felt the burn and oozing blood. He tried to stab back down into her neck, but she shifted her shoulder and got off with another graze. Ecar pulled his main arm free, reversing and locking Des. He shoved her into the desk, bringing the blade to her throat.

The bodyguard held his axe in both hands. He tried to swing past Luc's vertical sword, but a slight shift from the priest was enough to block. The short sword darted in, piercing leather and sinking an inch into flesh. Luc's injury prevented him from pursuing.

The axeman growled and thrust the head of his weapon into the longer sword. Luc's blade caught against the headspike. The bodyguard pushed it out and swept his axe back across. Luc brought his short sword up to parry. As the weapons deflected, the bodyguard kicked Luc's wounded leg. He hit the ground, losing the long blade.

Ecar's knife closed in. Des got her free arm up, desperately holding it at bay, but he was overpowering her. Balancing her back on the edge of the desk, she thrashed with her legs. She found the protruding bolt and pushed it with her knee. Ecar continued pressing for a moment, then lost his focus in the pain. Des thrust the knife arm wide and slammed her forehead into his nose. She freed her other arm from the weakened hold and twisted the knife from Ecar's grip.

The axeman chopped down. Luc did all he could from his position, throwing up his left arm. The axe cleaved Luc's wrist, nearly severing his hand.

Luc screamed. The wrath of Atora rose in him. His eyes shone again with the light of soul magic. He let go of his remaining sword and drove his open hand upward, trailing wisps of silver. He sent his hand into the bodyguard's face, through his face, out the back of his skull.

Des held the knife up to Ecar's throat. Blood dripped from his nose. His eyes were wide and fixed on the blade. A soft red glow left his sharp, corvine face in half-shade.

Without looking away from her prey, Des asked, "Luc? You okay?"

The priest ignored her, praying with ragged breaths. "Atora, Laughing Blade, I serve you with faith. Seal my wounds that I may live to fight again."

Slowly, Ecar regained some composure and lifted his gaze.

"Desalie," he said. "I had no idea you were here. Clever, using this howler as cover."

A moment of silence passed, a surreal accompaniment to the fading adrenalin in the room.

"I take it this means she's dead?" Ecar asked.

"Yes."

"Are you going to kill me?"

"Absolutely," Des said. "But first, you're going to tell me why. You said Ari stole something. You had her killed over a fucking ring?"

Ecar swallowed. "The ring? The ring is just a symbol. I gave Ari my heart." He pushed forward, letting the knife prick his skin. "I gave her my soul, and she just ran off with it—with you. I loved her more than you ever did."

"That so? Funny she didn't talk about you more. She didn't even mention you that night after the breakwall carry. And you know, there was the part when we ran off together."

"Yes, that's my point! She threw it all away—our life together."

Des shook her head. "So, what, if you can't have her, nobody can? How old are you?"

"No, that wasn't it." Ecar closed his eyes and sighed. "I knew I needed to move on. I'm an overwatcher now, for Rixa's sake." He opened his eyes. "So, I moved on. Killing her killed the distraction, and since then, the heart's been pounding."

Des didn't know how to respond. She risked a glance out the window. The dark line of the breakwall loomed, silhouetted against the waves by moonlight and the lighthouse at the far end. Her gaze stopped on three red-tinted lanterns farther down the windowsill. *Shit.*

She hadn't consciously registered the crimson glow in the room. They sat here talking while the silent alarm called to every agent on the pier.

"Luc, shut the door," Des said. "Bar it."

He did so, letting his left arm hang at his side.

Des took out the vial of greyfang tears. She tossed the knife aside. Before Ecar could react, she popped the cap and stabbed the venom-coated needle blade into the base of his neck.

"Whas tha…."

The toxin worked fast with his quick pulse, strangling his speech first and then paralyzing his limbs as he lurched to escape. Ecar sprawled onto the floor, eyes wide open.

"What's wrong?" Des asked, noticing Luc's arm.

Luc turned and lifted the appendage. The hand was attached, but hung at his wrist, fingers drooping. He touched it with his right.

"Can't feel it," he said. "It won't answer me."

"We'll get it fixed, but we need to go," Des said. "Any moment now, this place will be crawling with Kraken. They'll blast the door with powder if they have to."

Luc stared at Ecar. "Then, is he dead?"

"Not yet." Des snuffed the lanterns, leaving only the ambient light from the pier. "Come on. There's an escape passage through the side wall."

Luc sheathed his blades one at a time. "What are you going to do to him?"

Des looked out at the breakwall again.

There, Ari's ghost said. *All the way back.*

"Take him to where it all started," Des said. "You don't want the details."

"Probably true. Let me help carry him, though."

Des found the switch to open the passage, similar in design to the other one. She pulled it closed behind them. A steep, narrow stair led below the street, to the opposite side from where they had entered. A rowboat was tied up, bobbing in the current. Des and Luc placed Ecar inside.

"We'll part here, then," Luc said. "Sorry I fucked this up."

"You didn't—well, yeah, would've gone better if we stayed quiet, but it's done. Sorry for what I said before. I'd have been a mess after she died—more of a mess—without you. I am glad you came, and Ari would be, too."

She clasped Luc's good arm.

"Follow this path until you hit sand, then take the ladder into an alley. I'll be back before dawn."

Luc nodded.

"Oh, and you might want to wash the blood off if you find the chance." Des untied the boat and climbed in, rowing out to the breakwall as straight as the current would allow.

Halfway across, she said, "Let's have a little talk, Ecar. I know you can still hear me. At first, I couldn't understand your reasoning. I think I get it, though. To you, Ari was an acquisition. What you two exchanged was just that—an exchange. I get it. Spend enough time in this city, and everything's a carry. Everyone asking for stamps and lends. That's why we left, you know. We wanted more people being people.

"I also wondered why Ari bothered to take the ring. But you said it—it's a symbol. I'm sure you two had a good thing at some point, because why else would she have used that symbol to propose to me? I figure she wanted to give it new meaning."

Des's voice dropped to an icy depth. "Oh, yeah—she wanted to marry me. We had decades ahead of us. For stealing that, I'm going to salt your wounds. Ever hear of that one? Cali told me about it. You think that bolt hurts?"

She guided the boat to the landing spot on the breakwall, a series of flat rocks that, from a distance, seemed like nothing more than the lay of the stones. She tied the boat to a rotting wood piling and managed to heave Ecar onto the landing. She reopened the scabbing cut on her back but didn't care. She dragged him up a weathered stair, over the brick center, and down to a similar spot on the far side. Ecar veritably tumbled down the steps—a bonus, in her mind.

Des stripped off his armor and cut open his shirt, then tied a bowline around his torso and secured him to the landing. She stared at her knife, then at Ecar. Maybe she should just run the blade through his heart.

No. Ari's ghost demanded more.

Des cut Ecar, leaving shallow wounds about his torso and limbs, purposely avoiding arteries and other vulnerable areas. Lines of red covered him, each barely bleeding. She tested the short rope.

"Here comes the painful part. This is from Ari, you prick."

She rolled him into the sea. The waves on this side were larger, but it was a calm night. Secured by the rope, Ecar's paralyzed form bobbed at the surface. His lolling head stayed mostly above the water.

"If you're lucky, a shark will smell you and come by to speed things up. But then, if you were lucky, you wouldn't be here at all."

Des walked back to the top of the wall, collapsing into a half-sitting, half-laying position. She scanned the structure. No ghosts, not even roosting gulls—only the brick center, the piled rocks to either side, and the soothing repetition of breaking swells.

"I expected you to be here, Ari," Des said. "I was afraid to come earlier because I hadn't found him yet. How could I set foot here, when every wasted moment was a failure to you?"

She pulled out the emerald ring, rolling it in her fingers. "I know that's stupid. This is what I had to do, though. Not just for you, but for me. Lots of preachy types would tell me revenge doesn't solve anything. But now, knowing Ecar's dying in pain, I breathe easier. Is that wrong? If I honestly feel satisfied, is that evil?"

Des shook her head and slipped on the ring. "Fuck. If I'm getting this philosophical, I'm going to need a drink."

The sky was still an early-morning grey when Des knocked on Selira's crooked door. Luc stood next to her on the step, using his sheathed arming sword as a makeshift cane. A face peeked between the window drapes. The door opened.

"Morning, Selira," Des said, grinning. "I've got some thoughts on life and morality that I'm too sober to pursue."

Selira smiled back. "Of course. And you did promise."

"That I did."

"Come in. I've got one bottle of Midsummer left."

Appendix I: Pronunciation Guide

A quick reminder before we get into this. All these names are fictional. They're made up. They exist only in the author and readers' imaginations. You should feel free to skip this entirely. The characters will not jump out of the book and correct you on the pronunciation of their names.

Many of us are no strangers to debates regarding certain dark elves or dastardly barons of desert planets. This is simply intended to mitigate those squabbles.

VOWELS: Serma, the common languages of the Valentreid Empire, generally follows Romance linguistic norms.

A (ä) as in **ca**ll

I (î) as in **rea**l

O (ō) as in **o**ver

U ($\overline{oo}$) as in **boo**t

Certain vowel sounds are formed by combinations of letters.

AE (ā) as in **fa**ce

AI as in **ri**de

AU (aʊ) as in **ow**l.

When followed by a different vowel, U acts like an English W: UE (wā) as in **way**, etc.

E (ɛ or ā) is usually relaxed, as in **re**d, but if before another vowel or at the end of a word takes on a higher inflection, as the in **fa**ce. Thus, Septrion is pronounced *sep-tree-on* (sɛp-trî-än), while Aure is pronounced *ow-ray* (aʊ-rā).

A more archaic pronunciation of I exists in some geographical names. In the suffix –id, I (î) is pronounced as in **ki**t. The suffix marks the place as belonging to the name that precedes it. For example, the Valentreid Empire is the empire of the Valentrae family.

All other combinations of vowels in Serma names are pronounced as independent syllables. Valentreid is four syllables: väl-ɛn-trā-ïd.

CONSONANTS

C—In Serma, C is always hard, as in **c**ar, he**c**ti**c**. However, the dialect of Ostitel follows the same rule as Italian when C is followed by E or I. In these cases, it is pronounced like the English CH, as in **ch**air. For example, Francesca's name is pronounced as Fran-ches-ca.

CH: This is a foreign sound to Serma. When it appears in Arcana, Chari, Draci, or Zixarsi, it is pronounced like Scottish lo**ch** or native Mé**x**ico—a voiceless velar fricative, for the phonetically minded. To make this distinction clearer, these languages replace the normal hard C with a K.

J—The English J does not exist in the Serma alphabet. Some regional dialects do use the soft G. In those cases, the consonant is followed by E or I, similar to Italian *gente* or *ragione*. When a J appears in a different language, such as Zixarsi, it sounds like the consonant use of Y in English. Thus, Varja is pronounced Var-ya.

Q—Unlike in English, Q in Serma it can be followed by any vowel. In cases such as Antiqir, the Q makes a sound like a hard C, but farther back in the throat.

Ž—This one is a sort of hybrid of Z and SH, like a smoother soft G. An example of this sound in English is the G in mirage— held longer than J-like instances such as genius or allege.

Double Consonants: With pairs of consonants between vowels, such as the LL in Cortellum, the sound is held longer or enunciated more strongly. This is common in Italian, such as *capello* (hair) vs. *cappello* (hat).

Glottal Stops: These are common in Chari and related languages (see Glossary) and denoted by an apostrophe between syllables: *austras'akunsak*. It is pronounced by restricting airflow. The most common example in American English is in the middle of *uh-oh*. It can also be heard in other dialects where the T at the end of a word is dropped (ex. *tha'* instead of *that*).

Appendix II: Cant Guide

This dialect, half-slang and half-code, originated among the old smuggling guilds of Forente. Though somewhat formalized for convenience, it remains very flexible and is used to pass along messages and instructions all along Imperir Mare without being caught by authorities. Details of operations and cargo are usually omitted or understood through context. Any turncoats that threaten to expose Cant to the law soon come down with a case of death.

Abbreviations:
  n.: noun
  v.: verb
  adj.: adjective
  adv.: adverb

Writing Conventions
First, Second, Third…: indicates paragraph in a message
A, B, C…: indicates sentence in a message
Capitalization: indicates a specific noun. For example, that Cape from last night, rather than any old guard.

Speech Conventions
We: indicates one is speaking on behalf of an organization

Vocabulary
Artery (adj.): necessary
Base (n.): rule or policy
Bog (v.): lose or get rid of someone or something
Bronze (adj.): old

Cant (v.): speak

Cape (n.): city guard

Capital (n.): Forente

    Downing: West Docks District

    Hawk's Nest: Market District

    Hearth: Imperial District

    Slicks: Gold District

    Tools: Bronze District

    Upping: East Docks District

    Waft: Copper District

Carry (n.): job or assignment

Caz (n. or v.): smuggler, or to smuggle something

Chant (n. or adj.): magic or magical

Char (n.): collateral damage

Cloudy (n.): Aeribe

Cracked (adj.): of inferior quality

Curtain (v.): keep this quiet

Cutoff (n. or v.): point of intercept, or to intercept another party

Cutter (n.): common pickpocket or thief

Damp (n. or adj.): cellar or basement, or something underground

Den (n.): base of operations

Dog (n.): friend

    Collared dog: ally to be cautious around

Down (n. or adj.): west

Drag (v.): capture

Dredge (v.): search

Drowner (n.): bar, tavern, or similar establishment

Dry (n.): year

Eclipse (n.): the opposite or reversal of something

"Take the eclipse": take the opposite meaning from a message

Falc (v.): kill quickly and cleanly

Fisher (n.): setup

Firelight (n.): campsite

Fireside (n.): prostitute

Flint (v.): burn, usually literally

Fog (n.): any drug meant to be smoked

Forerunner (n.): horse

Freedman (n.): former city guard

Gape (n. or v.): a narc, or to narc

"Gape to Cape": defect to the city guard

Gild (n.): Aure

Give [he/she/them/it] feathers (v.): ambush

Give the key (v.): trust

Glance (v. or n.): to suspect, or a suspicion

Glassblower (n.): expert or skilled person for a particular task

Hand (n.): slave not registered with the government

Haul (v.): kill painfully

Heart's beating: business is steady

Heart's pounding: business is going well

Beats are slow: business goes poorly

Ink (n. or v.): poison, or to poison someone

Iron (v.): arrest someone under the law

Jingle (n.): money

Keep [he/she/it/them] in the light (v.): they intend to betray or kill you

Keeper (n.): lock, as for a door or container

Lend (n. or v.): a favor, or to do a favor

Level (adj.): acceptable, usually used regarding a deal

Liberty (n.): Liore

Listen (v.): interrogate

Lock (n.): an illicit security worker, both sentry and bodyguard

Mark (v.): cheat or con

Med (n.): drug

Miss (adj. or n.): contradictory, or a contradiction

Nail (v.): torture

Neg (n.): open enemy

Nip (v.): steal

Parch (v.): write to someone

Plat (adj.): of high quality

Prow (adv.): upfront, at the beginning

Roll (n.): something up to chance

Run (n.): business or skillset—what an agent is known for

Salt (n.): the sea

Salt (v.): also a specific form of slow, painful execution involving saltwater and many long, shallow cuts in the victim's skin

Seaside (n. or adj.): south

Sent (n.): person

Slip (n.): a state of quiet

Sliply (adv.): to do something quietly

Slippish (adj.): a quiet person or thing

Slith (v.): infiltrate through deception, as opposed to sneaking in

Sitter (n.): cargo

Spring (adj.): new or fresh, pertaining to a person or product

Stamp (v.): make an accord to deal

Stow (n.): someone not in the Kraken who is involved in Kraken business

Stride (v.): pass through

The Green (n.): Pluvitelles

Theater (n.): Cruxia

Up (n. or adj.): east

Vein (n.): river

Vines (n.): Equotel

Viz (v.): inform or show

Watcher (n.): a boss, usually an official position in the Kraken

Overwatcher (n.): one of the Kraken's ten leaders in Forente

Wide (n. or adj.): north

Wing (v.): to leave

Wink (n. or v.): bribe

Appendix III: Glossary of Terms

Everything necessary to follow the story is exposited or alluded to in the main text. This appendix is for those readers looking for more information on the setting.

COINAGE

Aerna (plural aerni): A copper Valentreid coin

Arga (plural argi): A silver

Aurla (plural aurli): A gold

FACTIONS

The Bureaucracy: A catch-all for the departmentalized governmental reforms in the Valentreid Empire. The distinct bureaus were intended to create efficiency and enhance central authority in the outlying provinces. However, in many cases, the extra levels of management and approval needed to commence government actions have only slowed things down. Many citizens are frustrated with the sluggishness and increase in fines, bribes, and myriad other new ways for "crats" (as officials are often called) to bleed them of money.

The Faith of Fire: A religious empire situated west of Maceria. The Vigna clan of fire dragons already ruled a vast swath of northern Charir when contact with the Immortal Realms was severed (see Gods and Religion). Since then, the dragons have demanded true worship and spread this veneration through proselytization and warfare. Leaders of the Faith preach that the Pantheistic gods are gone forever, warring to their own mutual destruction.

According to the basic tenants of the Faith, fire is life. Thus, fire dragons are the rightful inheritors of the domain of life, the

Mortal Realm. From this foundation, the religion diversifies in interpretation to fit local cultures.

Less-willing nations and tribes faced conquest. The series of conflicts known as the Rising Fire began in 1294 by the Valentreid calendar and ended with the Faith's retreat from the western Valentreid Empire in 1320. Another attempted invasion of the empire, the Second Flame, occurred between 1338 and 1342.

The hierarchy of the Faith of Fire is as follows:

- Urathix: The three gods, the eldest Vigna dragons. They have adopted the Chari philosophy of sovereignty, which states that good rulers are equal parts nobility, wisdom, and vengefulness. The male elder, Haraska, represents nobility; two females called Othakira and Arytarka represent wisdom and vengeance, respectively. Adherence to these aspects has legitimized their rule in many Chari cultures.

- Athirix: The angels of the Faith. These include all other dragons of the Vigna clan. The Athir hierarchy is based on age and power, and each dragon bears a title relating to a virtue or vice it represents.

- Elementals: Any other dragons, fire or otherwise. Elementals are considered worthy of respect, but not worship.

- Prophets: Marexuri or non-dragon Indegeri (see Species) with draconic blood. Such people are considered sacred based on their lineage, especially if it includes fire dragons. Most are groomed for leadership roles within the religion.

- Sunathach: Priests of the Faith. These are ordinary mortal leaders who possess no draconic blood.

- Faithful: Worshippers with no religious authority.

- Faithless: Those outside the religion, whether they have not yet converted or refuse to.

Filvié Noctirin: Children of the Night. This open cabal was founded by Tenebra's decree to provide vampires with shelter and animal sustenance. In recent years, it has become more involved in politics, providing funding, consultation, and other means for its members to have a say in how the Valentreid government treats vampires.

Filvié Noctirin possesses a hierarchical structure overseen by three leaders called the Noblest. Only those in other leadership positions can vote a Noblest into office. They serve until retirement, death, or impeachment by a three-quarter majority of voting members.

Godshadows: A state-sponsored Valentreid organization tasked with hunting dangerous arcanists, planar creatures, cultists, and other such threats. Though headquartered in Sacre, a number of chapterhouses are found across the empire. Each chapter is run by a shadeseer, so called because the first of them were taught powerful clairvoyance and divination by Angels of Shade (see Gods and Religion). Other agents are highly trained and specialized, falling into one of five roles:

- Bane: Specializes in eliminating dangerous arcanists and priests.

- Cloak: Sent to infiltrate dangerous cults and orders, obtain information, and retrieve sensitive targets.

- Hunter: Trained to slay immortals, rogue experimental creatures, and other supernatural monstrosities.

- Listener: Informant and interrogator.

- Tracker: Priest skilled in locating threats through soul magic that assists the shadeseer.

Kepeskeižir: The storm dragon clan of Procumes. Older members have a reputation for pride in their ancient lineage, often lording themselves over their splinter clan in Occas Divisum. Ardent worshippers of Caelix (see Gods and Religion), the Kepeskeižir took exception to the Vigna declaring themselves gods. During the Rising Fire, many of the clan's fiercer members joined the fight against the Faith of Fire. However, seeing the costs of the war and little chance of dislodging the Vigna grip on the land, the storm dragons remained neutral in subsequent conflicts.

The Kraken: An extensive smuggling guild headquartered in Forente. Legislation in 1300 brought the Valentreid Empire's hammer down on illicit trade in the city and the heads of previous guilds to justice. The ensuing power vacuum was soon filled by their lieutenants, ten of whom united under the symbol of a kraken. Operating out of two hidden headquarters and eight other safe houses, they conquered all competition. Through the use of a coded language called Cant and dedication to keeping leaders out of the law's reach, the Kraken thrives. Its arms reach all along the Imperir, dominating black market trade from Pluvitelles, Procumes, and the southern empire.

Requiem: A close guild of assassins. It was founded by five killers hired by Emperor Vylosis to slaughter the ruling families of Socions in 1094, allowing the empire to conquer modern Ocarma and Pastoratel. The guild continued operating for the government until greed and backstabbing nearly ended centuries of cooperation. By 1333, only one master assassin remained. Eliel Avex wrote a code that included an approval system for accepting contracts—no more hits on other members. Any dissenters were purged. The imperial government would prefer to be the exclusive client but remains content so long as Requiem does not kill imperial officials.

The Valentreid Empire: The greatest nation of Marexuri in terms of size and military power. It was founded when Saela Valentrae, Queen of Equotel, conquered the elven kingdom of Antiqir. She declared herself emperor (a gender-neutral title) and claimed Aure as her new capital. The common calendar is dated from the conquest, now 1,349 years ago. The Valentreid Dynasty has ruled ever since, gradually expanding their territory. A series of rapid conquests occurred during the Warring Period (990-1117), when many powerful states of the region vied for dominance. The Valentreid Empire came out on top and at its current size—fifteen provinces, stretching 1,500 miles across at its greatest extent. A senate was instituted in 1150 to help maintain unity. Each province chooses three representatives according to its own methods.

After centuries of consolidating power, expanding infrastructure, and founding trade colonies, the empire has adopted an isolationist policy. Bloody conflict with the Faith of Fire pressured the imperial government to redirect funding away from the colonies and push for cultural hegemony. Citizens in the outlying provinces don't care for this campaign of glorifying the heartland. Local traditions and arts are restricted, histories revised, and current events spun into propaganda. The increasing bureaucracy in government has also frustrated many citizens, regardless of geography.

GEOGRAPHY
Given the diverse species and ethnicities of the Valentreid Empire, geographic origins are often more important to citizens

than racial divisions. In many cases, the borders of provinces far predate annexation. This section also includes neighboring lands mentioned in the book. The Serma demonym for each province or region is given in parentheses, where applicable.

Allusec (Allusi): The south-central province. Its capital is Transote, though Forente is the largest city in the whole empire. The name Allusec means "the Landing," as this is believed to be where the Marexuri arrived on this continent (see Species). The bulk of its economy is based in the sea—fishing, shipbuilding, and trade. Crops that thrive in the humid air are grown inland. Once a client kingdom of the Antiqiri, Allusec was annexed by the Valentrae not long after its sovereign.

Astrellus (Astrelli): The southeastern province. Its capital is Aeribe, an ancient city originally built by alturi (see Species) and a hub of high art. Aeribe fell to an amphibious assault by Emperor Ilias in 1020, and the rest of the province soon surrendered. The old nobility of Astrellus has a reputation for clean hands and dirty feet, smiling and bowing while profiting off vast feudal estates and exotic trade from Pluvitelles. Still, its senators have earned the respect of the people by standing against the empire's more restrictive cultural legislation.

Charir (Chari): The Red Earth. To the locals, this name refers only to the large, arid plateau just west of Maceria. Most Valentreid citizens use it as a catch-all, thinking of the entire region as a desert. However, beyond this lie ore-rich mountains, rainy coasts, fertile rift valleys, and vast floodplains. The Faith of Fire has come to dominate these lands, with only remote fringes left to their own devices.

Cortellum (Cortelli): The Heartland. Over a millennium ago, this urbane and developed land was the domain of the Antiqiri Kingdom. Its greatest city, Aure, has remained the capital under the succeeding dynasty. The imperial calendar is dated from the year Saela Valentrae led her army through the gates. Cortellum is also the seat of military and religious authority—new legionaries train in Praesid, and the grand Temple of the Pantheon stands in Sacre.

Darachzartha: The Dragons' Hearth. This volcanic ridge is the ancient territory of the Vigna, the clan of fire dragons that created the Faith of Fire. As such, it is the holiest land of that religion, where the new gods dwell and souls reach the end of their journey.

Equotel (Equoteli): The Land of Horses. Rolling hills, fertile fields, and the great floodplain of the Magnir characterize this province. Horse breeding and winemaking are long and successful traditions. The capital, Equesor, began as a small and threatened city-state that grew to crush its rival, conquer its neighbors, and give birth to the Valentreid Dynasty. Since the founding of the empire and relocation of the throne, Equesor has fallen far behind Aure in influence. However, the province remains wealthy and vibrant as a whole.

Glacire Mare: The Icy Sea. Despite the name, this vast expanse is actually a freshwater lake. Beyond lies Boreatel, thousands of miles of uncharted wilderness inhabited by strange, isolated populations. Even in the height of summer, the Glacire Mare remains cold. Its seasonal gales are treacherous. The mountains of the northern empire protect the lowlands from such weather. Around a century ago, government-sponsored expeditions established colonies on the northern shore, but funding cuts and increasing isolationism have left these ports largely independent.

Imperir Mare: A partially enclosed sea to the south. Trade ships sail along the Valentreid coast or cross to Procumes and Pluvitelles in pursuit of more exotic goods. Fog banks and storms from the Imperir keep the southern provinces fertile for farming, but chains of mountainous islands help break up more powerful weather from the ocean beyond.

Infinitir: The Endless Steppe. This dry grassland stretches for thousands of miles east from the empire. Humans, Aurasi, and daci (sometimes called halflings) comprise competing tribes with strong traditions in herding and horsemanship. The more aggressive tribes raid the eastern provinces. Yet, there are lands even beyond this expanse. Some goods from these mysterious nations make their way through staggered trade into the hands of Valentreid merchants.

Liore (Liori): Once known as the Free Coast, Liore is the smallest and westernmost province of the empire. It was also one of the last to be conquered, falling to Emperor Ialid in 1107. Its capital, Novos, has always been a formidable port. Since the Rising Fire nearly claimed all of Liore before the invaders were repelled, the entire land has been fortified. Crossing Maceria with an army is daunting, so both sides expect this rocky, sparse frontier to play a major role in future conflicts, as well.

Lunatel (Lunateli): The province that edges the eastern Imperir Mare. Like Allusec, Lunatel is dominated by the fishing and shipping industries. It was conquered over a millennium ago by Mirena, the fourth Valentreid emperor. Since then, it has remained relatively peaceful. Its soil was spared from the bloodshed of the Chari invasions, and many Macerian and Zixarsi refugees have come to Lunatel in search of this peace. In turn, city guards are eager to protect it from real or perceived threats among these newcomers.

Maceria (Macerian): Known colloquially as the Wall. This massive chain of mountains marks the physical and, by extension, cultural divide between west and east. In the ancient past, Maceria was home to alturi kingdoms (see Species). In their wake, the newly arrived dwarves built their first cities. Maceria is dotted with passes, and trade occurs, but the difficulty of marching an army across the ridge makes this a historic buffer zone. However, the Faith of Fire recently proved that the barrier is not impregnable—its forces conquered, converted, and, in some cases, razed dwarven cities before descending into the western Valentreid Empire.

Muntherzix (Zixarsi): Literally "the Humans' Water." The powerful currents of this river begin as small tributaries in the highlands of eastern Charir. Over thousands of years, it has carved wide, striated canyons between the mountains of Ternezorak and Maceria. The surrounding land is home to most humans who live west of Liore, an old ethnic group called the Muntherziach in Chari, or Zixarsi in their own tongue (see Languages, Species). Several of their clans converted to the Faith of Fire by choice or by the sword; those who did not were forced from their ancestral homes into foreign lands.

Ocarma (Ocarmani): The Western Shield. The rugged mountains and hills in the west slope inexorably down into the basin of Palutel. This land has known little peace over its history, changing hands from the warlords of old, to the militaristic kings of Armaton, to succession limbo and eventual Valentreid conquest. Most recently, imperial legions in Ocarma staved off two Chari invasions aimed at the empire's heartland. Lines of fortification stand ready for the inevitable third.

Oretel (Oreteli): The arid, easternmost province. The fertile flats in the west give way to the dry grasslands of Infinitir. The Free States of Oretel were once a loose collection of cities that united only for common defense. The greatest of these, Libred, was conquered in 1060 by Darotes Valentrae in the midst of the Warring Period. Oretel has always relied on trade for much of its economy and saw a boom when the Valentreid government sponsored caravans to the distant nations across the steppe. However, as the empire turns ever inward, this vibrant exchange has slackened. In the same vein, the push for cultural hegemony has created unrest in cities with significant Aurasi populations (see Species).

Ostitel (Ostiteli): The Unyielding Country. Protected by a ring of mountains, this aged and stubborn nation was the last to fall to Valentreid forces—and not for lack of trying. Despite many attempts by many kingdoms over the centuries, Ostitel has only been conquered once. Even now, its old royalty serves as its representatives in the Senate. The common people of Ostitel mine the mountains and herd livestock in the valleys, overseen by longstanding noble houses. Upward mobility is scarce.

Palutel (Paluteli): The great basin at the geographic center of the empire. Countless rivers drain into these lowlands, where marshy wilderness is interrupted by wooden cities of stilusi, a reptilian species of Indegeri. They and a smattering of other citizens hunt, fish, and grow medicinal herbs and wet crops. The wide lake Vadum is known as the Shallows, as no point reaches more than a couple hundred feet in depth.

Pastoratel (Pastori): A land of rugged highlands in the northwest corner of the empire. After central Septrion fell to Valentreid conquest, Pastoratel united with Ocarma to form Socions, holding out for a few more decades before succumbing to the hungry empire. It is the homeland of the magnuri (see Species), most of whom still herd livestock in scattered villages. Lumber from Silventim, mining in Septent Iugum, and textile work are also common trades.

Pluvitelles (Pluvitelli): The Lands of Rain. This region is dominated by thick jungles and wide, sluggish rivers. Mountains to the north trap moisture and storms from the sea. The intelligent and enigmatic asath, a species of Indegeri often compared to snakes, rule from hidden cities and act through enslaved alturi. Some official trade manages to flow even between the asath and the increasingly isolationist Valentreid Empire, but unregistered slaves and illegal substances are the most lucrative exports of Pluvitelles.

Procumes (Procumi): The Storm Cliffs. This chain of large, mountainous islands is home mainly to dwarves. Some settled here during the original Marexuri migrations (see Species), while others fled south during the Rising Fire. The Kepeskeižir clan of storm dragons gives the region its name. Only they and the native dwarves regularly brave the treacherous winds and currents between islands.

Scissum (Scissuri): The Torn Land. Even more than Ocarma, Scissum's history is replete with rising and falling warlords. It was the first conquest of the Warring Period, which began when Emperor Myracin's sudden invasion became a seven-year test of endurance. It's said that war is in the blood of the Scissuri. Today, the province serves as the military coordinator and defense headquarters for the western empire.

Septrion (Septri): The great northern province. Septrion's terrain is diverse, dominated by high mountains in the north and wetlands to the south, along the border of Palutel. Its mining, quarrying, and metalworking industries are unrivaled in the empire. Before the conquest, Septrion compared to the Valentreid Empire in both size and power. At its height, Pastoratel, Sylgatum, and Palutel bowed to the kings in the north. However, the Septri heartland fell to Valentreid forces only decades after this peak, bringing an end to a millennium-long succession of dynasties in Fodina.

Sylgatum (Sylgati): A province of forests and mountains. This rough country is home to the largest gnoll population in the empire (see Species). Whitewater rivers descend to floodplains that are sheltered from the cold winds of Glacire Mare. Through a tumultuous history of territorial disputes and regime changes, one constant for the people of Sylgatum has been their respect for natural magic. The dark paths and ancient, crooked trees of Umbrid lend themselves to supernatural folktales. In turn, these gave rise to a mystical tradition among the hermits brooding in the forest's depths (see Umbrid mysticism under Gods and Religion).

Ternezorak: The Silver Stone. This chain of low, coastal mountains in southern Charir hosts rich veins of its namesake metal. The alturi and charoch that dwell here parcel it out to traders and occasionally repel greedier invaders. So far, they have avoided the full conversion force of the Faith of Fire and still worship regional aspects of Pantheistic gods.

GODS AND RELIGION

The entities that comprise the Divine Pantheon are very real beings. They bear different names and customs of worship in disparate regions but have left indisputable marks upon the world. Most people in the Valentreid Empire still worship them earnestly, but recent events have caused others to question continued faith in them. Other than Airis, all gods mentioned below are members of this polytheistic belief system. It is not an exhaustive list—only a compilation of those mentioned in the text.

Immortal Realms: Reality is composed of many planes of existence. The Immortal Realms are numerous and varied, each with their own features and physical rules. They are the domains of gods and their servants—angels, inferai, satyrs, and many other creatures that do not age and die like denizens of the Mortal Realm. These worlds are beyond the reach of most mortals, but not all. Powerful arcana and soul magic can open metaphysical paths or even literal portals to other planes.

Or rather, they once could. About a century ago, all mortal lines of contact with the Immortal Realms were severed—gates were closed, rituals of psychic contact ceased functioning, and immortals could no longer be summoned to the Mortal Realm. Before the gods went silent, they delivered a message to their highest mortal servants—war was spreading across the worlds, and the Seal would protect the Mortal Realm from a divine conflict that would otherwise level mountains and sunder the earth.

Airis: Soon after the realms were sealed, four mortal prophets across the known world simultaneously claimed to have received a new revelation. Airis, a vague and genderless entity, was the One True Deity, the Light that birthed all mortal and divine life. Each prophet gained knowledge of one aspect of this being—Light, the Sun and the Body of Airis; Truth, the Seeing-Eye of Airis; Nobility, the Heart; and Justice, the Hand. Followers of the Divine Pantheon and the Faith of Fire agree on little, but both religions consider Airinism a cult of madmen.

Amalus: The Binder, god of marriage. Amalus is one of the Interlopers. He represents a traditional view of marriage, stressing faithfulness and procreation. The rings Amalus carries bind two souls together eternally. This is why rings are exchanged as part of Pantheistic matrimonial rites.

Atora: The Laughing Blade, god of battle. Atora is a First God and concerns himself with duels and conflicts between small bands of warriors. His wife, Bela, reigns over mass warfare. His blood is said to inspire those who seek the thrill of combat. Atora is commonly depicted as a tall and rugged fighter dueling monsters and warriors with an irrepressible grin. His followers say the greatest act of courage is to smile or laugh even in the face of certain death.

- *Blades of Atora:* A mystery cult devoted to the Laughing Blade. Its initiates receive extensive training in swordplay and using soul magic to enhance their weapons and combat abilities. Full-fledged Blades travel the world in search of worthy opponents to prove themselves to Atora, and to prove Atora's power to others. According to a common mantra of these fighters, "No warrior stands alone when they have Atora at their back."

Audas: The Bold, the god of daring. This Risen God is the son of an angel and an antileri (see Species). His love for Armis, goddess of mercy, drove him to perform legendary feats of athleticism and fearlessness in efforts to impress her. Armis is faithfully married to the god of healing, but she eventually rewarded Audas's perseverance and skill by granting him divine power. Mortals invoke his name to gain a bit of his legendary luck.

Caelix: The Dragon God, ruler of the skies. He is an Interloper. While usually depicted in his scaled and winged form, Caelix is also fond of human shape. He holds influence over the weather and is the progenitor of both dragons and Aurasi (see Species).

Crusix: The Chained, the god of pain and discord. He the most controversial of the First Gods, said to be responsible for mortals' ability to feel pain. What's more, in ancient times, Crusix was stripped of his possessions and bound naked to a great stone pillar in the Immortal Realm of Tartarus. The most common explanation involves him attempting to usurp Genesa's rule. Few openly worship Crusix, instead calling on him to assist in dark pursuits like torture, bloody revolution, and painful vengeance. To most people in the Valentreid Empire, he is simply the source of a casual curse—"chains of Crusix."

Faith of Fire: See Factions.

First Gods: The Divine Pantheon is divided among three groups. The First Gods shaped the world and filled it with life. Their blood runs through living things, infusing them with different passions and predilections. All First Gods are the children of Genesa.

Genesa: The First Goddess, the ruler of the act of creation. The most ancient myths tell of Genesa coming upon the Mortal Realm in her chariot and finding it nothing more than a barren rock. She gave birth to the other First Gods so they could help her fill the emptiness. To this day, Genesa is the most revered member of the Pantheon; even if most people don't call on her in the course of a typical day, they respect her sovereignty and give thanks on holy days.

Hades: The Immortal Realm of Death. Unless another deity claims a soul for service, Mortis and his angels guide all dead mortals to this plane. Accounts dating from before the Seal describe it as looking much like the Mortal Realm, but infinite in size and home to countless, ghostly figures going about the next stage of their existence. The actions and motivations of the dead in these accounts are difficult for the living to decipher.

Immortals: The denizens and namesake of the Immortal Realms. They don't age, and many resist or are immune to ordinary weapons, requiring specialized arcana or magic to slay. There are dozens of kinds; the two that appear in the text are presented here:

- *Angels:* The most well-known immortals. Every angel belongs to a particular thematic order and is sworn to serve a single god. For instance, the Angels of Shade answer to Tenebra, while Angels of Souls obey Mortis. Each resides in the realm of their order's patron. While the details of their appearances vary by order, all angles are tall, statuesque, winged, and genderless humanoid beings. Like many immortals, they can teleport short distances on a whim. Beyond this, each order possesses unique talents and powers.

- *Saeads:* Fickle beings native to Aeros, the Plane of Mists. Saeads possess greater senses than mortals but are prisoners to their own need for stimulation. They constantly seek out new pain and pleasure, becoming irritable or dangerous when deprived of intense physical or emotional sensation. Out of familiarity more than anything, Saeads have come to serve Sensius, god of passion. Their natural appearance features bright red skin and matching hair that waves and shifts according to their mood. However, they are also shapeshifters, and in many stories, take on mortal form in search of carnal pleasure.

Interlopers: The second family of gods in the Divine Pantheon. They are said to have arrived in the domain of the First Gods from distant realms beyond mortal reach. While the two groups fought at first, resulting in deaths on both sides, they eventually reached a truce that has lasted ever since. All the Interlopers are shapeshifters, though each has a favored form.

Legex: The Codifier, god of laws and the hearth. He is a First God whose blood drives the need for structure and rules of behavior in mortals. Legex developed the earliest laws of both mortals and immortals, many of which still hold sway. As part of the truce between First Gods and Interlopers, he married Sailae, fickle goddess of trade. Myths do not speak well of their union, or his relationship with their daughter, Rixa. The clergy of Legex is one of the most powerful in the Valentreid Empire, operating the courts and deciding whether new legislation conflicts with the Codes of Legex.

Liba: The Liberator, goddess of freedom and love. Liba is a Risen deity, born as a stilusa slave during the Septri occupation of Palutel. After escaping from her taskmasters at a quarry in Septrion, she led thousands of her people to freedom. For her dedication and personal sacrifice, the Interloper Passus granted her divinity. Her clerics are often considered political radicals for their desire to end slavery altogether. Servants of Amalus take issue with them performing marriage rites for same-sex, Marexuri-Indegeri, or polyamorous unions.

Mortis: The Severance, god of death. Mortis is the most powerful of the Interlopers, often said to be nearly omniscient in his ability to predict the fates of mortals and judge their histories. He is usually depicted in vestments adorned with bones and plucking a lyre, though some images show an unassuming traveler with the same instrument. Mortis and his angelic servants seek out the souls of the dead and guide them safely to Hades. His mortal clerics perform funeral and burial rites.

Musymph: The River Singer, god of music and waterways. He is an Interloper and credited with inventing song. According to myth, the oldest music in the world is the sound of rushing water. He is a popular deity invoked by both minstrels and those who ply their trade on rivers and lakes.

Nabura: Lust, goddess of fertility, sex, and wild instinct. She is a First God, and her blood inspires carnal attraction in all living things, whether the union is procreative or not. In myth, Nabura shies away from cities, keeping to the untamed woodlands. Mortals invoke her for success in romantic endeavors.

545

Praecar: The Divine Archmage, god of arcana. Praecar is a First God, and invented arcane languages and runes (see Languages). He wove threads into the fabric of reality that allowed mortals to utilize these words to cast spells. Myths describe him as immensely clever and something of a trickster. He is often depicted with a shield that reflects spells, emphasizing his dominance over his creation. Many arcanists pray fervently to him, especially before performing a risky experiment or engaging in battle. All owe him a debt of gratitude for allowing their powers to exist.

Risen: The third class of gods in the Divine Pantheon. Several Risen share close blood ties to older deities, but the only commonality among them all is that they attained or were granted godly power. Each Risen has their own origin myth. As the youngest gods, the Risen are significantly weaker than the First or Interlopers. However, their mortal followers are often more zealous in their devotion—many Risen exist in recorded history and represent reachable achievement.

Rixa: Anarchy, the goddess of impulse, drunken fights, and thievery. She is the daughter of Sailae, Interloper goddess of merchants and trade, and Legex, First God of law and just retribution. Neither cares for Rixa's rash antics. Her blood inspires mortals to take what they want and damn the consequences. Mortals call on her for protection, skill, and ferocity when society's rules go out the window. A common phrase for such situations is "a Rixian night."

Sailae: Merchant's Luck, the capricious goddess of trade. Sailae is an Interloper. As part of the truce with the First Gods, she was made to marry Legex, god of law. Neither is happy with this arrangement. Their union bore a daughter, Rixa, who complicates both of her parents' agendas. Sailae considers her husband rigid and blunt, herself favoring shrewdness and long, patient schemes.

Merchants and business owners pray to Sailae for success and protection from the symptoms of her displeasure—disasters and disruptions to trade.

Sensius: the Passion, the god of emotion. He is a Risen who, as a mortal, attracted the attention of Decra, Risen Goddess of art. But Labes, god of disease, craved Decra's love as well and poisoned Sensius's very soul. Decra gave a portion of her to save him. Ecstasy, despair, and everything in between fall under the domain of the Passion. His devoted followers often chase their god through mind-altering means, seeking the greatest heights and depths of emotion.

The Seal: A metaphysical barrier between the Mortal and Immortal Realms. Mortal understanding of the Seal is limited. Mainstream scholars believe every god contributed to its creation. Breaching it is beyond the ability of most arcanists or priests, and attempting to do so is forbidden by both religious and secular law.

Sien: The Seeker, god of knowledge. Sien is a First God said to inhabit a library atop the highest mountain in the realms. Many of Sien's followers emulate his hermitage, but most serve in cities as librarians, lore-keepers, philosophical advisors, and other sages.

Sola: The Light, goddess of the sun and the horizon. She may be the first Risen, with oral myths reaching back before the Marexuri crossed the sea thousands of years ago (see Species). According to these stories, Sola was a wandering mystic who traversed every land and sea in the Mortal Realm, growing in power, wisdom, and followers. The twin goddesses of travel, Itera and Orvia, lifted her to divine status. She is invoked by mortals seeking the sun's warmth and light, and for courage in the face of darkness. Sola's animosity toward Tenebra is centuries-old and so great that she cursed vampires to never walk under the sun.

547

- *Solar (plural Solari):* A mystery cultist of Sola. Initiates are trained to harness the power of the sun in their soul magic. Many of them use any excuse they can to hunt and slay vampires, believing them to be unholy, corrupt souls.

Soul magic: The inborn talent of some mortals to affect the world through focus and willpower. Soul magic is not hereditary, believed to be a gift from the gods. Most people with this ability become priests in an effort to understand and master the power. Faith helps them focus the magic, and most scholars believe it can only be used at the behest of a god, whether the practitioner invokes a name or not. (Individuals who serve in temples but cannot use soul magic are known as acolytes, and far outnumber priests.) Depending on the god and practitioner, soul magic can take many forms and influence reality in different ways. It can be used to heal, hurt, control objects or minds, conjure elemental power, enhance one's muscles or reflexes, and generate myriad other effects.

Tartarus: The Plane of Law and Imprisonment. The earth of this Immortal Realm has been carved into extensive dungeons and catacombs. Immortals—and a rare few mortals—that have transgressed the laws of the gods are tried and sentenced in Legex's court on the surface. Those found guilty are usually punished with long incarcerations in the dungeons. One exception is Crusix, who is chained to the top of a seven-mile pillar.

Tenebra: The Eclipse, the goddess of darkness. Tenebra is a Risen, born the daughter of a mortal man and Itera, goddess of the stars. She became a legendary assassin in the Mortal Realm, and her reputation attracted the attention of an ancient vampire lord who sought a powerful thrall. Tenebra's divine blood allowed her to retain her free will, and she slew her would-be master. The mixture of vampirism and divinity caused her to develop ever-greater powers, and she eventually ascended to godhood. She became the patron of vampires, and her ambition and guidance led to the creation of Filvié Noctirin (see Factions). Tenebra's bitter rival is Sola, for shadow and sun have ever been in conflict.

Umbrid mysticism: A system of beliefs native to the Umbrid Forest in Sylgatum. A history of ghost stories and strange phenomena has long attracted radical spiritual leaders to seek revelations under the thick canopy. Over time, a set of traditions emerged for communing with fundamental energies and forces of reality. According to Umbrir mystics, these forces flow deeper in the fabric of the multiverse than the powers of gods do, underlying the earth, the sky, and all planes. Practitioners achieve this communion through meditation, chanting, native herbs, and primal soul magic. On occasion, a mystic will attempt to break new boundaries through blood and sacrifice. While citizens of Sylgatum know these are lone radicals, Umbrir mysticism is misunderstood and often feared in the empire at large. Most rituals are now done in secret.

HISTORICAL FIGURES

Antiqir: The ancient dynasty that ruled Cortellum before the Valentreid Empire. This elf-led nation is the starting point for most official imperial histories. The Antiqiri Dynasty built Aure and much of the original infrastructure across Cortellum and the Imperir coast. It attempted to conquer the growing kingdom of Equotel for five years before being driven back. Shortly after this Golden War—named for the sheen of Antiqiri shields—a young Saela Valentrae ascended the throne of Equotel, conquered Aure, and founded the Valentreid Empire. Many surviving Antiqiri officials convinced their new ruler to keep them in the court, and the tradition of elven advisors continues to this day.

Mirena Valentrae: The fourth Valentreid Emperor, titled as the Cavalier. She was born in the year 98 and ruled for forty-four years before dying of natural causes in 171. Mirena is remembered as a fierce warrior and the conqueror of Lunatel. Her personal diaries, kept well out of public reach, detail the atrocities and slaughters she ordered during the Crescent War and the ensuing guilt that plagued the rest of her life. Mirena also married into survivors of the Antiqiri Dynasty, uniting the two houses for several generations to come.

Solris Valentrae: The ninth Valentreid Emperor, titled as the Arcane. Solris was the last of the Antileri Emperors that resulted from union with the Antiqiri line. He was born in 453 and died of natural causes in 621, after ruling for eighty-three years. He founded the Academy in Aure and made many personal contributions to arcane research. He took no wife and fathered no legitimate children, naming a cousin as his heir. His successor, Sceyusa, commissioned a library tower to be added to the Golden Palace in Aure and named in honor of Solris. It stands as the highest structure in the city.

LANGUAGES

Arcane Language: Used for casting spells using arcane threads. There are several variants throughout the world that Praecar selected to serve this function (see Gods and Religion). In everyday speech, these languages are dead. What survive are formulaic components strung together by arcanists to guide energy toward specific purposes. The Arcane Language of Valentreid lands bears some resemblance to Old Antiqiri or Old Serma, but with several foreign phonemes and inflections. Because a caster needs a target before releasing the energy, the syntax of Arcana is object-verb-subject. This helps prevent casters from harming themselves by releasing energy that has nowhere to go.

- *Arcanist:* A practitioner of arcana. Anyone can develop the discipline and focus to hold onto at least a weak thread of energy, but most people either don't try to learn, don't believe they are capable, or simply don't have access to this sort of education. New applications of arcana are researched like any other science; it is considered distinct from soul magic or superstition.

- *Rune:* A spell stored on a physical surface. An arcanist can carve or write a spell formula using an arcane language a special alphabet. A thread can then be tethered to provide energy for the spell. When the conditions specified in the formula are met, the energy is released in a manner according to the spell. This can be a sudden burst similar to a landmine, or sustained, like a streetlamp.

- *Thread:* A direct line to a cosmic power source. An arcanist can connect their mind to vast sources of energy, usually stars. The more experienced, disciplined, and willful the caster, the more energy that can be harnessed and converted into different forms—kinetic force, temperature differentials (heat, cold), transference of information, and so on. If a mage overreaches, the thread usually disintegrates before the energy reaches the caster. However, rarely, an arcanist manages to call an obscene amount of energy to their person, and then loses control. This requires as much stubbornness as it does skill. Professors use famous cases of arcanists turning themselves to ash in order to encourage caution in their students.

Chari: The common language of Charir and nearby lands. Many dialects are spoken in different regions and by different nomadic tribes. The mother tongue is descended from Draci and now-dead althoch and charoch languages (see Species). Nouns are pluralized with –ch (see the Pronunciation Guide) in the case of people, and –x in all other cases. Glottal stops are used to separate components of conjugated verbs. For example, in describing a flock of birds you saw earlier in the day, you would take *austraz* (to fly), add a glottal stop to the end, then tack on *akros* (the past-tense suffix) and *och* (the plural suffix): *austraz'akrosoch* (they flew).

Draci: The language of dragons. It's almost a misnomer to refer to Draci as a single language, so diverse are its dialects. Each version is used by a different clan in a different region, and most adult dragons can tell which one a speaker hails from in a matter of moments. It is a harsh, guttural language that Marexuri and Indegeri (see Species) often have trouble speaking due to differences in vocal chords.

Serma: Imperial Speech. This is the official and common language of the Valentreid Empire, descended from Old Equosori blending with Antiqiri after Saela Valentrae's conquest. Serma has smooth, flowing consonants and open vowels. In more distant provinces, it has mingled with local tongues into regional dialects. However, "proper" Serma is taught in schools and expected of anyone seeking a government position.

Zixarsi: The language of the Muntherziach. Zixarsi is an offshoot of Chari that shares many cognates with its parent. Many Valentreid citizens cannot pinpoint the differences between the two, but they are glaring to speakers of one or the other.

MUSIC

Astrelli jaunt: An upbeat style developed in Astrellus. Jaunt features fast, simple percussion, repetitive woodwind melodies, and strummed chord phrases separated by staccato. It has spread far and wide as popular dance music across the southern, central, and eastern Valentreid Empire.

Astrelli ode: An emotional style that takes rhythmic cues from its lyrical content. Poetic odes are focused around a single person, event, or object and were originally spoken as poetry. The music that developed around these lyrics reflects the subject but otherwise tends toward somber and longing tones. String and percussion instruments are the most common accompaniment, allowing the performer to sing and play. However, the music of older odes has become popular to perform without vocals.

Aurasi ballad: A traditional style of Aurasi nomads (see Species). String parts feature legato and ringing open notes. Those meant to be danced to often contain whimsical, rhyming lyrics, but more somber, narrative forms exist as well. Between verses, performers incorporate wordless vocals that capture the emotional tone of the piece. Most Aurasi ballads have slow tempos and 6/8 or 7/8 time signatures. The nomadic world in which this music developed makes it so that popular ballads often have no definitive version.

Riverfolk: Developed in the floodplains and wetlands of eastern Palutel. The style is built around lute, mandolin, and other necked instruments. Riverfolk musicians pluck strings with their fingers at a rapid pace. These progressions are complex—players often pluck a low string with their thumb to keep a beat while melodizing on higher strings with their other fingers.

Shallows ballad: A lyrical style native to Palutel. Unlike Aurasi ballads, Shallows ballads are rarely danced to. They feature slow chord progressions and woodwinds harmonizing with the singer. Lyrics have no set rhyming scheme, but alliteration is common throughout each line.

SPECIES AND ETHNICITIES

Mortals run the gamut in form, outlook, and history. Other intelligent species exist besides those that appear in the text, such as the reptilian stilusi of Palutel and asath of Pluvitelles. Relationships between these many races are defined in large part by their origins and migrations. Valentreid tradition places mortals into one of two categories: Indegeri and Marexuri.

Indegeri: The Native Peoples, species that have dwelled in these lands longer than any mortal memory. While some share traits with one another, not all Indegeri share unified ancestry like the Marexuri do.

- *Alturi/Althoch:* Known as giants in common vernacular, alturi in Serma, and althoch in western tongues such as Chari. Alturi are credited with the first true civilizations. Their early kingdoms were established before the arrival of the Marexuri. Today, alturi society exists in Occas Divisum and the fertile regions beyond Charir. Valentreid explorers tell of giants in Pluvitelles enslaved to the enigmatic and reptilian asath. Physically, adults tend to range between ten and fifteen feet in height. Like charoch, they have four digits on each and foot, as well as nasal slits.

- *Charoch:* Natives of Charir. Their societies range from nomadic tribes in the desert to agricultural city-states on the western coast. They were the first to join the Faith of Fire, and a blend of conscripts and zealous volunteers made up the bulk of invading forces during the Rising Fire and Second Flame (see Factions). Like alturi, they possess eight fingers, eight toes, and nasal slits. Their skin is red or reddish-orange like their arid homeland. Charoch have yellow eyes and little hair on their heads and bodies.

- *Dragons:* The mightiest and rarest species of mortals. The seven races of dragons are descended from the god Caelix and inherited his shapeshifting talents. They are known to use this ability to extend their lifespans and occasionally interbreed with other mortals. In their natural forms, all dragons have four legs with clawed feet, a pair of wings, long necks and tails, and—except for feathered ice dragons—scale-covered skin. Each variety is subdivided into regional clans, each with their own dialects of Draci.

  o *Fire Dragons:* Distinguished by red scales, short snouts, and long horns that protrude from behind their brows and sweep back over their necks. Their large wings catch rising thermals from deserts and volcanoes. The name of these dragons comes from their ability to spew fire from their mouths. The most famous fire dragon clan is Vigna, which lairs in Darachzartha. The three elders of the Vigna gave rise to the Faith of Fire (see Factions).

  o *Storm Dragons:* Possess aerodynamic, narrow faces and bodies. Adjustable, finlike protrusions on the sides of their heads give storm dragons extra maneuverability. They are regarded as the best flyers of all dragons and are sometimes spotted by sailors caught in gales. They can ionize their breath, generating plasmatic discharges similar to lightning.

- *Gnolls:* Known as caniri in proper Serma. Gnolls are tall, muscular, furred, bipedal canines, roughly humanoid in shape, but with wolf-like heads and faces. The fur ranges through drab tones, with brown and grey being the most common. Most reside in the northeast of the Valentreid Empire, especially Sylgatum. Tension between gnolls and Marexuri has often sparked violence. In the past, gnoll-led armies habitually plundered Equotel and Fundaer. Today, the government's push for unified culture has conflicted with mystic traditions of Umbrid that many gnolls hold as sacred as (or more than) pantheistic worship.

- *Magnuri:* Often called ogres or lesser giants. These Indegeri average between nine and ten feet in height, with long arms, broad shoulders, and thick torsos. A pair of tusks protrudes up from a magnuri's lower jaw, larger among males. Most reside in the northern Valentreid Empire, especially Pastoratel and Septrion. Despite their fearsome appearance, magnuri tend toward gentler cultures based around herding and farming the highlands. But when they do fight, whether as slave-soldiers for historical Septri dynasties or as the feared Crushing Legion of the modern Valentreid Army, ogres make and break battles.

Marexuri: "Those Who Crossed the Sea." In ancient times, before any but the alturi kept written records, a great migration took place. Diverse tribes from a legendary land called Vaetera crossed the open ocean. Most modern scholars believe this fleet landed in what is now Allusec, shepherded in their voyage by

Matrua, goddess of the sea. The descendants of these people came to dominate the lands east of Maceria and spread beyond even Glacire Mare. Racial divisions exist, but unlike the Indegeri, any Marexuri can produce children with any other. Imperial demographics include a large minority of mixed-race citizens.

- *Aurasi:* The People of the Winds. Aurasi have unique origins, being descended from several human tribes across Infinitir and the god Caelix. Their divine blood grants them lifespans comparable to elves and makes them preternaturally graceful and quick. Being only centuries old as a distinct people, some members of the second generation remain alive today. Most clans continue to wander the eastern steppe, but many have meandered into the Valentreid Empire. In many cases, the Bureaucracy's recent cultural reforms have disproportionately affected Aurasi communities, leading to conflict (see Factions).

- *Dwarves:* Monsiri, the Mountain People. They tend to be short, averaging around the four-foot mark. Dwarves are hardy, with dense bones and stocky frames. As the name implies, they settled mainly in mountainous regions, occupying a niche left by fallen alturi nations in Septent Iugum, Procul Montes, and Maceria. A significant portion took up seafaring among the craggy islands of Procumes. In Maceria, two broad cultures emerged. The Surface Kingdoms built their cities on open terraces and plateaus. The Deep Kingdoms followed natural and artificial tunnels deep into the earth. Many of both groups refused to join the Faith of Fire and were driven away from their ancestral homes.

- *Elves:* Antiri, the Long-Lived People. Similar to humans in stature, elves are distinguished by their pointed ears, slightly larger eyes, and often exotic natural eye and hair colors. Silver or gold irises are as common as brown or green, and children are born with silver, red, or blue locks as often as blond or black. The elven lifespan is vast—they age at about half the rate of most Marexuri until adulthood, and routinely see their fourth centuries. Elves settled mainly along the coast of Imperir Mare and what is now Cortellum. There, the Antiqiri Kingdom emerged, the grand nation that Saela Valentrae conquered to found the modern empire (see Factions and Historical Figures).

- *Humans:* Abiliri, the Adaptable People. The most widespread of the Marexuri, humans are as varied as the regions they call home. The Valentreid Dynasty rules the empire, and great numbers of humans are found in every province, as well as lands beyond.

  o *Muntherziach:* A human culture named for the canyon-carving river just west of Maceria. The people of these clans adopted traditions from nearby tribes of charoch and have developed alongside them for thousands of years. What unity the people of Muntherzix had was sundered by the Rising Fire—many clans joined the Faith, while many others fought or fled east into Liore and Lunatel (see Factions). Despite their reasons and the passage of years, these refugees have yet to earn the empire's trust.

- *Orcs:* Fordiri, the Strong People. Orcs stand tallest among the Marexuri, averaging above six feet in height and boasting powerful physiques. Their skin is dull, with a slight grey pall regardless of overall complexion. Large canines sometimes protrude from their lower lips to form small tusks. The largest orc populations are found among the central and eastern provinces, especially Cortellum, Fundaer, Equotel, and Sylgatum. Legends among the charoch tell of a ferocious offshoot population in a dark and hostile forest west of Procul Montes.

- *Mixed Races:* Like most creatures with language, the Marexuri found words to categorize everything, including mixed-race individuals. These terms generally apply only to the first generation, or when there is a close split in ancestry. The words themselves are combinations of their two roots. Some examples appearing in this book are antileri (elf-human), forliri (human-orc), and mordiri (dwarf-orc).

MISCELLANEOUS

Dragonsteel: An alloy of steel developed in Valentreid Septrion. Iron is smelted in crucibles along with other trace elements to filter out impurities. Once cast and cooled, it is treated with alchemical agents that protect it from rust and add strength without sacrificing flexibility or making it brittle. This is an expensive process, reserved for the weapons and armor of elite guards, the Valentreid family, and favored military officers. The largest pieces of dragonsteel ever produced plate the outer doors of the Golden Palace in Aure.

Drakes: A broad family of creatures so called for their resemblance to dragons. Drakes are mainly found west of Maceria. Large, wingless varieties are bred in place of oxen as beasts of burden in Charir. Smaller, winged drakes are trained to carry messages, manage pests, or perform as exotic pets. Larger ones with wings are rumored to live far north of Charir, ridden into battle by isolated tribes.

Acknowledgments

I could fill another book with the people who helped me get here and how. Many authors eventually do so, sprinkling it with stories of personal trial and triumph and calling it a memoir. In the interest of space, here's a curated list. Along the way, I've had great family, great friends, great teachers, and great writers of all media supporting me and inspiring me. If you don't see your name but think it should be here, you're probably right. So thank you, too.

First and foremost, to Mom, Dad, Dante, and all my numerous relations: Thank you for your unshakable belief in me, especially during those many times I had none in myself. I am fortunate to have experienced so much love and support. I love you.

To Lisa: I had spent much of my college career mentally prepping myself to work minimum wage—liberal arts degree and all that. You offered me not just a good job, but a chance to learn so much about writing and self-discipline. You have been a mentor and a confidante and provided the special kind of encouragement that a writer can only receive from another of their ilk. And, of course, you paved the way for me to get published. Thank you.

To Rosabel: Thank you for lending your talents to this project, and for your patience and willingness to work with my feedback. Your illustrations helped make this book what it is, and I couldn't have asked for better.

To Lauren: Both for your feedback on an early draft and for your diligent interior design, thank you. You're a wonderful colleague to have, and I look forward to working with you in the future, in whatever capacity may be.

To Claire: When you sent me those sample covers, I was at once giddy and awestruck. It was brought home to me that yes, this is real. A bit surreal, too. Thank you for your brilliant take on my rambling ideas.

To my writing professors: Thank you for continuing to challenge me as my ability grew, and for encouraging me to challenge myself. Special thanks to Dan Keane, Khaled Mattawa, Dan Gocella, Josh MacIvor-Andersen, Rachel May, and Jon Billman. You guided me through important revelations regarding this craft.

To my tabletop groups throughout the years: Whether I was a PC or GM, you provided a platform for me to experiment with my storytelling and get instant feedback. And more precious to me, you provided a weekly anchor when the rest of my life was spiraling.

To Thad: I'm forever grateful for the funding you provided so I could finally get this off the ground. Lost gods know when I would have saved up enough on my own.

To Amanda, my first colleague: Though it was many years and many stories ago, I'll never forget the hours we spent talking about what we were writing. You feel less mad when you're not the only one with mad ideas. Thank you for keeping me on this path.

To the Peter White Public Library in Marquette, building and staff alike: Thank you for giving me a second home while I wrote the first draft and, on occasion, while I revised.

To the unnamed man at Taiga Games who gave me a pencil when both of mine ran out in the middle of writing the border scene: Thank you. There were no office supplies for sale in the vicinity, and you helped me in a time of need.

To you, the reader, whether your name is in this section or not, whether you bought this book or borrowed it or acquired it through other means: Thank you for taking this journey with me and the people who live in my head. Now, they live in your head, too. No matter what, I will always write. I will always strive to create something new. But you're the reason I gave it all I had at every turn. Whether you enjoyed it or not, I hope this book made you feel something. As a storyteller, I couldn't ask for more.

About the Author

In many ways, Adrian is like the typical human—sometimes sleeping, but usually awake. Sometimes eating. Often drinking tea. They are corporeal, with a beating heart. Occasionally, they reveal red, viscous content that is probably blood. It is almost certainly blood.

Adrian can be spotted wandering the woods and paths near Lake Superior, perhaps talking to the cold water like an old lover.

Adrian has inhabited this vessel since 1992. They are told they were late coming into the world.

Without music, things would be much worse.

Their favorite color is black. They are aware that black is a shade, not a color, but they reject the constraints of your basic inquiry. No further questions.

LOST GODS BOOK I
SUN AND SHADOW

42464053R00357

Made in the USA
Lexington, KY
17 June 2019